Off

Emma Rae graduated from Plymouth University and joined the Foreign Commonwealth and Development Office in 2003, working in British Embassies across the globe. She writes both new adult romance and thriller novels. She now lives in Guildford with her husband and two children.

Also by Emma Rae

Love Game
I Knew You Were Trouble
Off Limits

OFF Limits

EMMA RAE

hera

First published in the United Kingdom in 2025 by

Hera Books, an imprint of
Canelo Digital Publishing Limited,
20 Vauxhall Bridge Road,
London SW1V 2SA
United Kingdom

A Penguin Random House Company
The authorised representative in the EEA is Dorling Kindersley Verlag GmbH. Arnulfstr. 124,
80636 Munich, Germany

Copyright © Emma Rae 2025

The moral right of Emma Rae to be identified as the creator of this work has been asserted in accordance with the Copyright, Designs and Patents Act, 1988.
All rights reserved. No part of this publication may be reproduced or transmitted in any form or by any means, electronic or mechanical, including photocopy, recording, or any information storage and retrieval system, without permission in writing from the publisher.
No part of this book may be used or reproduced in any manner for the purpose of training artificial intelligence technologies or systems. In accordance with Article 4(3) of the DSM Directive 2019/790, Canelo expressly reserves this work from the text and data mining exception.

A CIP catalogue record for this book is available from the British Library.

Print ISBN 978 1 83598 266 2
Ebook ISBN 978 1 83598 265 5

This book is a work of fiction. Names, characters, businesses, organizations, places and events are either the product of the author's imagination or are used fictitiously. Any resemblance to actual persons, living or dead, events or locales is entirely coincidental.

Printed and bound in Great Britain by Clays Ltd, Elcograf S.p.A.

Look for more great books at
www.herabooks.com | www.dk.com

To Paul, Izzy and Thomas:

my squad.

Chapter One

Serenity

My mother's chosen name for me is of Latin origin. It means peaceful.

Lately, it seems like my life is anything but.

'Ren! Ren! Where are you? You're up!'

The shrill voice cuts through to my consciousness. I'm lost in my own thoughts again. I look at my reflection in the mirror in the communal dressing room, my fingertip drawing invisible letters on the surface of the vanity: a C, followed by an M and finally, another C.

The Canyon Mutineers Cheerleaders. And as of today, I get to say I'm one of them. I'm an official cheerleader for the NFL.

Today was decision day. The day I made the squad.

I should be out celebrating with my new teammates. Only, I'm here, at Surly's Tavern, Canyon's finest strip club. Preparing to go back out onstage.

I study my heavy, smoky eye makeup, my gaze trailing lower to my sequinned corset, the cut way too revealing for most folk in this city. But I guess that's the point. That's my look. It's what the patrons of Surly's have come to expect. What makes them slip dollar bills into my matching panties and the rim of my high-heeled boots. I guess the disappointment in myself will always be there. I've just been here long enough to know that somehow, I gotta ignore it.

'Ren? Seriously. Now, sweetheart!'

'Coming!' I holler sweetly, getting to my feet.

Misty's coming off the stage and I'm due on as her replacement. She's older than me, with two young kids, but, boy, can that sister move. Her stage name is *Kitty Thighs*. The music kicks up a notch. She blows me a kiss as she finishes her routine. I give her a big smile, one that the patrons can't see.

'Good luck out there,' she hums in her southern drawl, coming down the stairs, giving me a high-five as she passes. 'Slow crowd tonight.'

Somewhere over by the bar, the bar's manager, Jaxon, introduces me in his gravelly tone over the mic. He changes the lights so there are more neon reds and pinks to match my wig for tonight.

Brandy Velvet is my stage name and has been for the last five years I've been dancing here. Not my choice, but some of the newer girls have worse, like *Montana Cream*, *Mimi Whips* and *Candy Chains*.

The whistles are a little louder than an hour ago. In the shadows, I snatch a breath, wait for the beat. Under the corset, my obliques are killing me: the result of twelve weeks of rigorous and gruelling auditions for the CMC. Last thing I need is to dance on stage, using only a chair for the second time tonight.

Kathleen Lafferty is the CMC head coach. Today, she gave all of us rookie cheerleaders a lecture about how to take proper care of our bodies.

Ice. Stretches. Hydration. A healthy diet. Plenty of rest.

Little did she know, there was a stripper on her team. So, I'll be doing double the work, whether my body likes it or not.

'Fellas, she's back for more...' Jax announces over the mic. 'From Dallas to Austin, Frisco to San Antone, y'all know she's Texas' finest. Show a little love for... Brandy Velvet!'

Cheers go up. Guys straight up hollerin' for me. I step up to the stage. The backdrop shimmers and glitters, the music strikes up. *Gimme More* by Britney Spears. It's my signature number, and the crowd knows it. There's a whole heap o' thrustin' involved. Not what my NFL cheerleader hips could do with right now either.

But as I head for the chair that's positioned at the front of the stage, my movements deliberately provocative, I shut down.

In my mind, I fly far, far away.

Because this is not what I planned for my life.

And I'm not here by choice.

—

Twenty minutes later, I'm with Jaxon in the back office, counting out my cash tips. One hundred and twenty bucks. We all have to do this. The other girls get a fifty per cent share of whatever they make.

All the girls, that is, except me.

'That all of it?' Jax says with a single eyebrow raised, looking down at the pile of dollar bills piled up in his outstretched palm.

I give him a look like a helpless kitten. 'Please, Jax? I gotta drive to my first official squad practice tomorrow. I need money for gas.'

Jax sighs a heavy sigh. He used to work in a club uptown until somebody planted illegal narcotics on him and he'd gotten fired. 'You know the rules, honey.'

I push out my bottom lip.

'How much you got left?'

I pull out a fifty from my corset and hold it out to him between my fingers. 'This is the last of it, I promise.'

His eyes flit over my shoulder to the closed door. 'Take it,' he mumbles, with a wave of his hand. 'I didn't see nothing.'

'Thank you,' I say with a grin, tucking the bill back inside my corset. 'You're an angel.'

'So… I hear congratulations are in order. You're really doing this cheerleading thing, huh?'

I roll forward onto the balls of my feet, stretching out the backs of my calves, proud of myself. 'Sure am. Got the news today. I'm a CMC now.'

'Well, that's just swell, Ren. What happens when they find out about this joint? Don't imagine the boss man is gonna let you quit this place.'

I feel my cheeks warm. 'Figure no one has to know. I'll head here straight from practice on work nights.'

Jax cocks his head to one side and gives me a half-smile. 'And when are you meant to sleep, Serenity Harper? That's three jobs you're working now.'

It's sweet that he cares. 'Come on, Jax. You know I've always dreamed of being a Mutineers cheerleader,' I say quietly. 'And this job, it's...'

He nods his head once. He knows my situation. That I'm not here for the fun of it.

There's a knock at the door. Hurley – one of our security guards – puts his head inside the office. He's tall and broad and there ain't a man in the whole of Canyon he can't handle.

'Serenity,' he says in a low tone. 'Customer's asking for a private dance.'

My chest starts to flutter. 'Can't somebody else do it?'

He sniffs. 'Asked for you personally,' he responds in a gruff tone.

I look at Jax, my eyes pleading again. 'Not tonight. Please?'

Jax has been busy putting the pile of cash I handed him into the safe. There's a ledger dedicated to my tips only, which he's supposed to fill out. I have the same at home, so I can keep track, and my records are precise, down to every last goddamn cent.

'I'm sorry, Serenity,' he says as he spins the dial. 'You know I think the world of you, but... not my problem.'

He turns, holds up his palms as if in surrender, looking guilty before he adjusts his cap. Given the boss is away tonight, I figured he might go easy on me.

I follow Hurley from the office, a weight in my stomach. Mila – aka *Candy Chains* – is back on stage. She's getting a lot of attention. There are four of us on rotation tonight. I keep my head down. It's dark in here, and despite me wearing a wig, I'm conscious that now I'm a cheerleader for the local NFL team, some of our regulars are bound to be hardcore Mutineers fans. I hadn't figured I'd have this feeling of panic in my chest.

Everybody knows the rules here: customers who want a topless lap dance must pay up front. Surly's has private rooms with double-door entry. Hurley, or one of the other security guards, remain outside the inner door throughout, and the club has a strict no-touching policy. There's a panic button for us girls if we need it. Lap dances last a total of seven minutes and it's not possible to pay for double time.

Inside, the customer is already seated on the large, rounded leather couch, as per club rules. He's not a regular, and I note that he's wearing a wedding band. He probably has kids waiting on him at home. He wears a cap and a baseball shirt over baggy denim shorts, and in this light, it looks like his hair is strawberry blond. A layer of stubble covers his face.

No matter how many times I do this, it's never easy. The first few minutes I face away from him, dancing, rolling and swinging my hips, stroking my thighs. I turn and lower myself into his lap around the three-minute mark. Usually they're aroused at this point, and this guy is no different. I can feel the length of him pressing up into my ass as I grind into his jeans.

I think about my good news today, to take my mind off what I'm doing. I always wanted to be a dancer, only I never pictured it would be like this. I was born and raised in Canyon, on the west side, and growing up, the CMC were like something in a dream. Elegant, poised and beautiful, I wanted to be like them, from the first time I saw them perform at a local fashion show. Even before I became a high school cheerleader, I knew I wanted to dance for the crowds in the real-life NFL. To have all that positive energy and use it for good, like they did. To represent my city and be a future role model for all the little girls like me, who didn't grow up all fancy with nice, shiny things.

The guy between my thighs lets out a low grunt, bringing me sharply back to reality. When I glance down, I think of his poor wife, and it makes me wanna puke.

'Oh yeah, baby,' I hear him growl as he leans back, into the grooves of the couch, pushing his groin against me. Unpleasant though it might be, the guy's not breaking any rules. His hands remain by his sides.

The last two minutes are my least favorite. Leaning back, I unclasp my corset and let it fall away from my breasts. The hair from my wig falls across my face as I shift my hips atop him. I feel his arousal strain against his pants, my nipples tantalizingly close to his face and lips as I grind in his lap. My expression is indifferent. I don't look at him. I can't.

At least dancing topless on stage, you don't feel like you're being violated.

'Ride me, baby,' he says huskily on an exhale. Underneath me, his dick pulses, but apparently, only his hands are part of the no-touching rule.

The music fades. Seven minutes are up. I slide off his lap, get to my feet, thankful it's over. I pick up my corset and stand facing the wall, as is policy. It's always at this moment that I blink back tears, because it reminds me how powerless I am, and how I'd leave Surly's tomorrow if I could.

'For the lady,' I hear the man say as he leaves the room. Hurley escorts the customer out, then comes back to pass me my tip. I glance down. It's a lousy ten bucks. Rolling my eyes before I wipe them, I fix my corset back in place and hope that his friends don't get any ideas. Private dances are expensive.

Yet I don't see a dime of that fee.

—

The neighborhood's deathly quiet when I roll up in my beat-up Ford C-Max, pulling up into the driveway. Temptation Heights is not exactly known for its deluxe vehicles. It's three a.m. and the outside porch light still flickers. I ease the screen door open, so it doesn't clatter or squeak – which it always does – and slide my key inside the lock. I can hear the TV on the inside.

In the living area, to the left, Dad's fast asleep, still on the couch, fully dressed, in the same clothes he was wearing when I left him this morning. I sigh and reach for the remote, switch off the commercials on TV and cover him with a blanket. I creep toward the kitchen. When I open the refrigerator, I expect to see it half-full of groceries, only all that's left is some cheese slices and an open can of soda. My second sigh is more pronounced. I straighten, check the freezer and retrieve the tub of Ben & Jerry's that I stashed right at the back.

I sit outside on the porch in a butterfly stretch, scooping ice cream straight from the tub. In her lecture, Kathleen warned us rookies to avoid dairy. I keep telling myself, just one more spoonful. I sit, heels pressed together. I feel the pull in my adductors as I listen to the cicadas. The neighbor's dog sleeps tethered to the fence, whining in his dreams. I gotta be up in five hours to get to the diner. Alongside working at Surly's, bussing tables is not exactly how I saw myself making a living.

You were supposed to order groceries today, Dad.

I remember the day, five years ago, when they came after him. They wanted their money, and for my father, Glenn Harper, to pay it back, when they knew darn well he wasn't good for it. He'd gambled it all away, every last dime. Momma stuck out the year 'til I was seventeen, but left when she couldn't take it no more. She encouraged me to leave too, saying that he wasn't worth it, that he was a drunk and a deadbeat and didn't the whole neighborhood know it.

I thought about leaving.

Then he got sick.

The men who came for him... all they saw was Dad's *pretty little girl* – so they said – with the long blonde hair and bright green eyes, and their minds were already racking up dollar signs. And just like that, the day I turned eighteen, I became a pawn in a no-good man's game.

The message to Dad was clear. Either pay the money back or suffer the consequences.

That's how I got started dancing. Five, sometimes six nights a week for the last five years. I don't get paid, and any tips that I make belong to Kale McCoy. Local crime lord in Canyon and owner of Surly's Tavern.

He owns me now. Until the debt is paid off.

I knew when I sent in my video audition for the CMC that there was a risk. That if I qualified, somebody might recognize me from dancing late at night.

It's why I'm gonna work damn hard to make sure that doesn't happen.

My two lives need to remain separate. In the daylight hours, I'm Serenity Harper, diner waitress and clean-cut Mutineers cheerleader. At night, I'm Brandy Velvet. Private dancer.

I look down at the ice cream tub and bite my lip. It's empty.

I look behind me at the house, knowing Dad is sleeping soundly inside.

They would have killed him if I hadn't agreed to the terms.

I blow out my cheeks. I need to get some shut eye.

Recently, there's been this question lingering in my mind. *Is it possible to do this, and not get found out?*

Because right now, it feels like I'm about to play with fire.

Chapter Two

Jake

I glance down at my phone. There's a picture of a brunette in a white bikini who's sent me a message, offering to show me the sights of Canyon.

Another one.

I swear I lose track of all these chicks coming at me. This one has a big smile and curves in all the right places. She reminds me of a girl I used to date in college. But something tells me I need to be careful.

'Hey, assface,' a voice says in the direction of the pool as my seventeen-year-old sister, River, throws a volleyball toward my head. 'Quit looking at your phone. Those girls who you think are sliding into your DMs are just bots tryna catfish you.'

The ball whooshes past my ear and bounces off the wall of the house. I glance down at my phone again. 'Nah, this one looks real enough.'

It's the first week in August and ninety-three degrees out. In the late afternoon sun, River rests her chin on her arms at the water's edge. Then she runs her tongue across her retainer. I've just gotten the keys to this place this morning and already the brat is treating it like her own personal palace. 'They prolly generated the picture using AI, idiot. But if it was real, like, would she pass the Mom test?'

I check out the picture one more time, then tuck my phone away in my pocket. It vibrates again. It's not quit doing that since I moved here for pre-season training from Pennsylvania a month ago. The girl is cute for sure, but looks like she's had a little work done, or maybe she's just wearing too much makeup. Meaning, no, she wouldn't pass Bridget Walsh's unreasonably strict standards on who can, and cannot, date her son.

'Prolly not,' I mumble.

'Because the answer is never yes!' River declares, throwing herself backward in the pool waters and kicking up her legs violently. 'No mortal is good enough for the King himself! Ugh!'

I rub my eyes, rolling out the tension in my shoulders. 'Can you quit it with that?'

River treads water, wiping her face. 'I'm so sorry, I failed to use your full title! Forgive me, oh mighty King Midas.'

I wince. I know she's just trying to be funny, but whenever she uses her brotherly nickname for me, her words twist in my gut. Because that's how my parents view me. That everything I touch turns to gold. In fact, the term 'golden-boy' gets thrown around a lot these days and I hate the implication, even if I did just sign a mega-bucks deal to star in the NFL.

As a kid, I was fast. Agile, too. Maybe that's why I became a running back. I played college football on a scholarship for Penn State. Of the twenty-four running backs in the NFL Draft, I was the first-round pick, fourth overall, aged twenty-three. My agent and I discussed all the options on the table, with Mom and Dad in the room. We knew from the outset that the Mutineers were prepared to pay top dollar for me, were prepared to trade for me, and they were on our list of teams I wanted to play for. So here I am: the Canyon Mutineers' newest running back, an offensive lineman. In a brand-new house, paid for wholly out of the money from my signing bonus.

But family matters to me. I wasn't going to leave them all behind. So, they've uprooted their lives for me, even though it means River transferring high schools just prior to her senior year.

'River!' Mom's voice cuts through the tranquil air of the back yard. 'Sweetie, get outta that water! School starts in a matter of days, honey. We gotta stock up on supplies. And groceries.'

'I can get groceries,' I offer up with a wave of my hand, because it's my new place and technically they're my long-term guests, living in an annex off the main house, but sharing my kitchen. And right now, I got a brand-new double-door refrigerator with precisely fuck all in it.

'Do you even know where the nearest store is?' she asks as River heaves herself out of the pool and into my mom's waiting towel. I didn't even know we had towels.

'I saw a few places on our way out here,' I say with a shrug. 'Shouldn't be that big of a deal.'

'Then buy something healthy. Not just bags of chips and peanut M&Ms. I know the way you like to shop, Jake Walsh. You wander aimlessly with a cart and pay no attention to what goes into it. I do not want to be eating Cheetos with cheese strings for dinner tonight.'

I give her a mock salute as River leaves wet footprints across the veranda. 'Ay, Captain,' I say, because she's the kind of woman you don't say no to, not if you can help it.

I go inside to get showered and changed. Ten minutes later, the doorbell sounds.

When I open it, two of my new teammates are standing there, side by side, wide grins on their faces, both wearing shorts and chequered shirts. One of them is the Mutineers' captain and our quarterback, Dalton Briar. The other is our wide receiver and Dalton's younger brother, Hudson Briar. I look up to these guys so much – even literally, Dalton is taller than me by a couple of inches, standing at six foot three. He's broad, clean shaven, and the shining example of a legend in the game. While Hudson has a layer of stubble, wears a backwards cap and chews on a piece of gum.

Honestly, I'm surprised to see them here. 'Hey, fellas,' I say and we bump fists.

'Hey, man,' Hud says with a grin. 'Do you not check your phone?'

I laugh, shaking my head. There's a team WhatsApp group with, like, more than fifty members in it. Seems like its main function is so everybody can trash talk everybody else. 'It was blowing up; I can't keep track.'

'That happens when you just signed for the best team in the NFL,' Dalton says and Hud cocks his head to one side.

'So, you're gonna have to get used to the popularity,' Hud adds.

'You guys wanna come in for a beer?' I ask.

Dalton holds up a plastic container. 'Can't. But thanks for the invite. We're doin' the rounds. Calling in on all the rookies. This is a housewarming gift from my wife, Ally. She baked you a cake.'

My eyes go wide. I take it from him. 'Wow. That's so nice of her. Please tell her I said thank you.'

River appears behind me in the doorway, her wet hair from the shower falling straight at her shoulders. Looking shy, she comes out onto the porch. I decide it's best to introduce her before she can embarrass the hell out of me. 'This is my sister, River,' I say. 'River, this is—'

'I know who they are, idiot,' she says, stepping forward and shaking their hands, the shy act not lasting very long. 'Hi.'

'You going to school here, River?' Dalton asks.

'Transferring in for my senior year,' she confirms, making a look as though she's gone loco.

'You like football?'

'Sure, I like football. Not always the jocks who play it. In high school, my brother was a total jock.'

I rub my forehead. The guys are laughing. She's good at embarrassing me.

'Yeah, my brother was a jock, too,' Hud laughs, smacking Dalton in the chest.

'Least I wasn't a complete jackass,' Dalton counters, then checks his watch as we're all still laughing.

'We gotta make a move,' Hud says. 'But we came to remind you of our pre-season celebration, tomorrow night. Checking you can make it. To welcome the rookies and to celebrate the guys making the roster. We all go for Mexican food, followed by drinks, and for those that are allowed... some of the guys head to a place call—' His eyes flit to River and he rearranges his hat. 'It's a, uh, late-night establishment on the west side of town.'

River screws up her face. 'Ew, I don't wanna know.'

'Sure,' I say. 'Yeah, some of the guys were talking about it at practice. I'd like that.'

This time, Hud slaps Dalton on the back. 'It's the one night of the year when the lovely Ally turns a blind eye so Cap here can join in all the fun.'

'Then I'm definitely in,' I say.

'Bring cash, man, and plenty of it,' Hud says with a wink.

Minutes later, they depart.

'I like your new teammates,' River says. 'But I cannot wait to try this cake.'

'You can't wait 'til I get back from the store?'

'Nuh-uh,' she says, and she's already taken the container inside.

Some of my college buddies told me I was insane to even consider a move to Texas, of all places. I'm not from the south – never even been here before I got drafted – and especially not *this* far south. A hundred and twenty miles out of San Antonio, close to the border with Mexico, Canyon is a coastal city. People told me it had a subtropical climate, like Houston. Hot, humid summers, and mild, temperate winters.

My friends also told me it would be Hicksville. But so far, I kinda like it out here. And honestly, I don't give a shit where I am, so long as I can play football for the NFL.

I get lost on the way to the store because, despite my in-car sat-nav in my brand-new Chevy pickup, I take a wrong turn in an unfamiliar area of town. I know I'm somewhere not too far from the Danube Stadium – home to the Mutineers – but the sun's dipping low on the horizon and I know I need to hurry the hell up. I've ended up inside some mini mart in a plaza off Main Street. Plus, my mom is right, I suck at grocery shopping. I thought about getting a cart but ended up with a basket instead, now I'm staring at a whole aisle full of nothing but potato chips and thinking I can't serve them up on a platter and call it dinner.

Getting out my brand-new pickup, a couple of people raised their eyes to me, then pointed. Canyon has a proud history of American football, so it makes sense I'd get noticed in some parts, but I pull my cap low all the same. When I think I've done a decent enough job of planning dinner, I head for the checkouts, thinking I'll probably just order takeout instead.

I don't pay a whole lot of attention as I load the contents of my basket onto the conveyor belt. What catches my eye initially is the look of dissatisfaction on the cashier's face. Her mouth is a tight line as her face contorts into annoyance, frowning at the woman ahead of me in the line as she searches blindly in her tote bag.

She looks flustered. Her cheeks redden as she pushes her long hair behind her ears so I can see her face.

Holy shit.

For a couple of seconds, I just stare at her. Usually, I go for brunettes, but she's got honey blonde hair that falls thick and straight. She's going through the bag, searching for something.

'It was in here somewhere...' she says hopelessly, digging through the contents of the leather tote before pushing her hair off her face for a second time. She's got the most luminous green eyes I've ever seen. She wears a plain black hoodie and yoga pants that cling to every curve of her thighs, with sneakers on her feet.

'Want me to try your card again, ma'am?' the cashier asks her, holding out her hand.

She swallows. Her voice sounds breathy. 'I'd like that, yes please.'

The cashier inserts the card into the reader and the woman enters her code. Moments later, the cashier clicks her tongue. 'Sorry, honey. Declined.'

She says it loud enough for the whole store to hear, and the woman's cheeks flush even pinker. I have no idea who this woman is, but I feel bad for her. Her bags have already been packed.

'I—' she begins, lost for words, and she's back into the tote bag, hauling stuff out of it. 'I know I have the cash in here somewhere.' She sneaks a look at me. 'I am so sorry. I don't mean to hold anybody up.'

I notice the cashier's eye roll. Maybe that's what does it for me; what has me reaching for my wallet, and my credit card. I can't watch any more of this unfold.

'Allow me, ma'am,' I say, beginning to reach over.

Seeing the card in my hand, the woman lets out a gasp. Turning to face me, I see her even clearer. Those eyes, they're… *striking*. But that doesn't even cover it. Her eyelashes are so long, coated in black mascara and lined with shadow. Okay, so I'm not sure she'd pass the Mom test, but fuck that, she passes *my* test, and then some.

'Oh no,' she stutters, 'I can't ask you to do that.'

'You didn't ask,' I say. 'I'm offering.'

She shakes her head, looking like she's desperately trying to compose herself. 'Really,' she says, in the sweetest way. 'It's a very kind offer, but I—'

She tails off. She's facing me, this beautiful, sweet girl with the most amazing hair and eyes, and I'm overpowered by the idea that right now, I might be able to help her.

'I insist,' I say and turn to the cashier.

'Thirty-four, eighty-five,' the cashier says sharply as I tap the reader.

The woman breaks out into a grin, shaking her head furiously in shock. 'I… I don't know what to say,' she says, her hands going to her mouth as the cashier starts ringing up my groceries. 'That was the kindest thing. Thank you so much.'

'Anytime,' I say.

'Seriously, I—' she begins, all flustered again. 'I'm so grateful.'

With that, she scoops up her tote bag, her paper bag of groceries and walks backward toward the store exit, giving me a slight wave as she goes. The only thing going through my mind is how desperate I am for the cashier to double the speed of her movements right now.

I stay cool as possible, but once I've paid, I'm out the door, my eyes darting left and right in the plaza parking lot. I can't see her. *Fuck*, I curse silently to myself. I should have asked for her name. Her number. Anything.

I wipe one hand against the back of my head in disappointment, until I look up and she's right there, smiling at me, clutching a handful of dollars between her fingers.

You can't leave this lot without asking for her number, Walsh.

'I had it!' she says with a grin. 'It was in my car all along. Please, let me pay you back.'

Her cherry red fingernails grasp the cash in front of me, but I hold up my own hand in response. 'Really, no, that's not necessary. I'm happy to pay. You keep the money.'

'No, I couldn't possibly!' she raises her voice, sweet but assertive. 'You don't need to be a hero. Take it. I can't not repay you.'

'How about this,' I suggest. 'How about you keep it, and instead you buy me coffee sometime? I mean, uh… if you're available.'

She seems to flush red again. 'Oh, I, uhm…' She smiles. 'I… you're sweet, thank you.'

She thinks *I'm* sweet. 'Is that a yes?' I prompt.

She's shy, and for a moment I wonder if I overstepped the mark and misread her completely. 'I don't know about that. I'd rather you took my money.' She takes a step closer, as do I.

'One drink. Please. Or at least tell me your name.'

'Serenity,' she says.

'I'm Jake,' I say tentatively, and I wonder if she recognizes me, but doesn't admit it out of good manners. Either way, I'm glad.

'Nice to meet you, Jake. Please, take my money. I'm so sorry, but I have to go, I'm late for practice.' She urges the cash toward me, but I ignore it. What I can't ignore is how close she is, and the way her hand briefly brushes against mine.

'Practice for what?'

She looks down at where our hands touched but doesn't hesitate against the movement. 'Oh, I mean, for class. It's a, uh... an evening class.'

'And the drink?'

'Oh, that.'

'Are you a teacher?'

'Actually, I'm a... waitress.'

Her voice hitches when she says it. I don't know why I'm a little surprised. I thought she was gonna say dance instructor or yoga teacher. No slight on waitresses, but I wonder how she's able to have such an athletic frame and time to maintain makeup if she's busy bussing tables every night. 'So maybe I could swing by where you work? Buy you a coffee on your break?'

'Maybe. But I don't wanna be indebted to you.'

'So... is it like a restaurant?'

'A diner, actually.' She looks embarrassed, smoothing down that glossy, shampoo-ad hair. She looks up at me through her dark lashes. 'It's over on seventh and Lexington.'

'So, can I take your number?'

She bites her lip, a smile edging on her mouth before she shakes her head. 'I really am gonna be late. Maybe swing by the diner sometime?' She raises her brow.

'When's your next shift?'

'I, uh... Friday. In the morning.' I notice her glance around the parking lot as she shares the information. I must be keeping her, and I start to feel guilty.

I give her a smile. 'I'll be there.'

In one swift move, she tosses the dollar bills into my paper bag and before I know it, she's backing away from me again.

'And you're buying,' she says, raising her voice.

I shake my head in disbelief, impressed by her quick moves.

'Thanks again for saving my ass!' she calls out.

I roll my eyes in jest. Can I still claim to be a hero if she paid me back already? 'You're welcome, Serenity.'

—

I'm still grinning when I walk through the door to three expectant faces.

'What's for dinner?' River blurts out, giving me a once over and noting the sole paper bag in my arms. It's dark outside.

'Uh, thought we could get takeout?' I mutter.

'Takeout?' Mom splutters. 'I knew it, you just bought chips!'

'And some guac. And salsa.' *And then I got distracted by a staggeringly hot woman.*

'Snack food does not a meal make,' my father chips in, wagging his finger in my mom's trademark style.

'You drove all that way, and you couldn't even buy dinner food?' River complains. 'How is it the Mutineers wanna pay you all this cash and you can't even run basic errands?'

I open the refrigerator and place the quart of milk I bought inside the door. 'I'm better at running plays.'

She shakes her head at me. 'I'm hungry. Pass the chips. Or should I say, the main course.'

My father's bringing up an app on his phone with a sigh. 'Come on, what y'all hungry for?'

Mom may look pissed at me right now, but I'm not hungry. All I can think about is the chance meeting at the store. I leave Dad to do the food order while I search on my online maps for a diner that's on seventh and Lexington. It looks to be called The

Bounty, and I'll be making damn sure I head that way Friday morning.

Because there is no way in hell that I'm not getting Serenity's number.

Chapter Three

Serenity

'And five, six, seven, eig— Serenity, you are late!'

My first thought is, *I'm throwing this away. I'm throwing this all away down the river.*

'I'm so sorry!' I shout, a pair of poms already grasped in my fists as I fall in line and match the moves of my squad members, plastering the biggest smile on my face as we go through the motions for our opening number. Underneath the floodlights illuminating the field and row upon row of empty seats, my smile doesn't break, even when I catch the look that our head coach Kathleen Lafferty gives Harmony Reese, a fifth-year veteran and captain of the Mutineers' cheer squad, a look that says *talk to your rookies about being on time*. Behind my glittering smile, and through my high kicks, my sense of panic begins to mount.

Sometimes, I swear my brain is not engaged. I must have imagined putting that cash for groceries in my purse, because it was on the back seat of my car all along. I wouldn't have had to stop for groceries after my shift if Dad had done as he'd promised he would. Times like these I think Momma was right. And never even mind the tall, cute guy with dark hair and solid build who came to my rescue. My mind was racing during the whole interaction, and I've tried to retrace the memory as best I can. *Jake*, was that his name? He seemed nice, almost too nice. But maybe I'm being too harsh. After working at Surly's for so long, I've gotten too used to sleazy guys who view me solely as an object. But I still couldn't understand why he wouldn't take the money. What the hell was he thinking? When it comes to money, I'm not a girl who fools around.

Do I mind him coming to the diner? He seems a little clean-cut for the Bounty's usual clientele. And that accent definitely wasn't from around here. A part of me hopes he doesn't follow through on his promise to come visit me Friday. I don't even know *why* I said Friday. I'm pretty much there every day. But Friday gives him a few days to forget all about me and reconsider the decision. Even if I was completely charmed by him.

My guess is that Mr Wholesome will be a no-show.

'I'm so sorry,' I say, coming up beside Harmony when rehearsal is over.

She's taller than me. She's got long, dark hair and her eyes are a stormy shade of dark blue. I know she qualified as a rookie cheerleader aged twenty, which would put her at twenty-five now, three years older than me. Everybody knows how supportive she is, but Kathleen expects her to lead us, and that means keeping us all in line.

'Don't worry,' she smiles at me. 'Just try to be on time in future.' She lowers her voice a notch. 'Kathleen's a stickler for punctuality.'

'I ran into traffic downtown.'

Because I had to pick up groceries and got held up talking to a cute guy at the store.

'Always leave an extra half hour earlier if you can. That way, when you're sat in traffic, you don't need to worry so much about being late. Plus, I use the extra time to apply my makeup. I take a mirror for when traffic's backed up.'

The truth is, I parked my beat-up Ford C-Max on the farthest edge of the lot at the Danube Stadium. I could see the other girls had all parked a lot closer, but my car is a heap of junk, and I can't afford a better one. So, I'd grabbed my tote bag from the trunk and headed toward the staff members' door of the stadium, the over-sized, dark navy 'M' for Mutineers emblazoned on one side of the sizeable venue, taking up the full height, together with the crossed swords: the emblem of Canyon's football team. Parking so far away added another five minutes to my journey.

I submitted my application to join the squad at the beginning of the year. I got invited to the first round of auditions in March. It's August now, and it feels like we've been rehearsing all this time, only week by week, some girls failed to make the cut. It was hard to say goodbye to them. Tonight was a dress rehearsal as the finalized squad for Thursday's opening game of the pre-season. I'm in my full kit: the shortest, snuggest pair of white hotpants a girl ever had to wear in her lifetime, a chunky belt with red stars, a long-sleeved top that leaves my midriff bare, the dark navy shape of the 'M' on the front in contrast with the clinging red-and-white fabric. It's made-to-measure. On my feet are white leather cowgirl boots with a heel. It's humid in the August heat; sweat and makeup are not the happiest of bedfellows.

'Forget about it,' Harmony continues and puts her arm around my shoulders. 'You should be celebrating, tonight you get to sign your contract!'

She's right. Tonight is a big deal for all of us, but especially us rookies. I never thought I'd be standing here, wearing the Mutineers cheerleaders' uniform.

A half hour later, and still in our uniforms, the squad is assembled once more, this time around a table in a windowless conference room, a paper copy of our contract placed in front of each one of us, alongside a Mutineers branded pen that they sell from kiosks on game days. I look around at these incredible women I've joined forces with, and I feel proud of myself. Proud for submitting my initial application and proud that I've made it this far.

That is, until I open up the paper and skim over the list of rules I'm expected to abide by during my tenure as an official member of the Canyon Mutineers' cheerleading squad, and my stomach bottoms out:

Candidates must demonstrate full commitment to the CMC squad. Attendance at all rehearsals is mandatory, not optional. Any cheerleader who feels they cannot give 100% commitment to the squad should reconsider their appointment.

It is essential all CMC be punctual for all rehearsals and on game days.

CMC members should not stray from within the boundary of their ideal body weight as designated by their BMI ratio (within three pounds in either direction). Full hair and makeup are required for <u>all</u> rehearsals and on game days.

Conduct (Pt. 1): It is forbidden for any member of CMC to bring into disrepute the upstanding reputation of the Canyon Mutineers football team, or their emblem of the crossed swords, by any means, through improper or unladylike behavior. This includes wearing of appropriate attire at all times.

Before I've even finished reading, I look up, because Angel, a second-year veteran, and the owner of the longest legs in Canyon, and Shawny, a third-year veteran, are both pointing at a clause in the contract and snickering.

'*Every* year,' Angel sighs under her breath, looking down the table. I follow her gaze. She's looking at Harmony, who, at the other end of the table, is quietly reading through her contract.

'If I was her, I would have quit last year,' Shawny hisses back, keeping her voice low and flicking her white-blonde hair over her shoulder.

Angel pulls a face. 'Didn't I hear somebody say she'd promised him she would? I mean, one more year feels like salt in the wound.'

Shawny pouts. 'For him, maybe.'

'What are y'all talking about?' Jewel – who is a rookie like me – with black, corkscrew curls and a whole heap of confidence, leans over and whispers in their direction.

Angel and Shawny look at one another, before checking nobody else is listening. I mean, it's not like I'm trying to overhear, but they're right next to me.

'You get to clause five yet?' Shawny asks us.

I glance down at my contract.

> Conduct (Pt. 2): It is strictly prohibited for members of CMC to fraternize with, or date, any NFL pro-player, but most pertinently, any member of the Canyon Mutineers football team, while under contract as a serving member of the CMC. This includes any phone contact or contact through social media platforms. Some professional, polite interaction is permitted where it is necessary for the benefit of the Mutineers team, but this shall be supervised. Players and cheerleaders are therefore forbidden to be sweethearts or enter into any kind of courtship with one another. Violation of any of these rules outlined above will result in immediate dismissal from the squad.

Jewel frowns. 'You mean I can't even talk to any guy on the team?'

Shawny's snickering again. 'You can't even breathe the same air. Not unless you wanna get fired and have the pointy end of Kathleen's Jimmy Choo stuck up your ass.'

Angel raises her eyebrows in Harmony's direction. 'Let's just say Cap has an admirer on the football team and has done since she was a rookie.'

Jewel's eyes light up. '*Who?*'

Angel raises an eyebrow. 'I'm not sure y'all are supposed to know.'

Shawny's lips twist. 'Oh, come on,' she whispers. 'Everybody knows it's Hudson Briar.'

Jewel's eyes go wide. My gaze travels between them both. 'Who is Hudson Briar?' I ask.

'Honey,' Angel says. 'I thought you was from Canyon?'

'I am,' I tell her. 'But I don't really have time to follow football.'

Shawny's frowning at me. 'What's keeping you so busy?'

'I have a job. Plus, I… I have to look after my dad. He's not well.'

'I'm sorry to hear that,' Angel says, with genuine sympathy.

'Hudson Briar is a Mutineers wide receiver,' Jewel informs me. 'And he is *all man*,' she adds in a low hum.

'I'll have to look him up,' I say with a smile.

'His brother Dalton is the captain of the Mutineers,' Shawny adds.

'So, what's the deal with Hudson and Harmony?' Jewel whispers.

'He met her at a Mutineers event,' Shawny says, still keeping her voice low and checking no one is listening. 'Five years ago. Asked her out and she turned him down, knowing it wasn't permitted. He's been asking her out ever since. I heard two years ago she was gonna quit the squad, only Kathleen offered her the captaincy, and Hud Briar lost his mind.'

'That's garbage,' Angel says. 'The man only wants what he can't have. He'll be getting some elsewhere. And I swear, they haven't even been on a date yet and he spends his time professing his undying devotion.'

'He's been waiting for her for five years, hasn't he?' Shawny argues.

'I think that's sweet,' I say. 'Romantic.'

Angel shakes her head. 'Until reality sets in and it turns out they're just hot for one another, and it all fizzles out like water on a scorchin' hot tin roof.'

Shawny looks between us. 'Y'all see the hot new recruit? The number fourteen?'

'Which one?' Jewel shoots back. 'You mean the running back, Ja—'

The door opens and Kathleen stalks into the room, followed by her assistant whose name I haven't learned yet. We all fall silent. I've only spoken to Kathleen on a handful of occasions, but each time she's made an impression. As a former cheerleader herself, she has high expectations. I know the one thing I cannot do is let her down. 'Okay, girls,' she says, raising her voice the length of the room. 'Does anybody have any questions before y'all sign your new contract?'

My eyes dart back down, because I haven't finished reading yet. I can't stop going back to clause four – the one about not bringing the Mutineers brand into disrepute. Which is exactly what I will do if anybody finds out what I do in the late-night hours.

I skim read the remainder of my contract. Some of the girls further down the table are already signing.

'You know there are the unwritten rules too, don't y'all, ladies?' Angel says to me and Jewel, picking up her pen.

'What unwritten rules?' I ask.

Shawny lowers her voice again. 'Y'all know… the ones that say you can't chew gum, you can't wear sweatpants when you go out in public, you can't drink, you can't smoke, you most definitely cannot party…'

You can't dance in a man's lap for money, I think to myself.

'At least there's the no touching rule,' Angel sighs as she signs her contract, and my stomach performs another somersault. For a split second, I thought I'd voiced my thoughts out loud. But it appears that, as CMC, members of the public can request a photograph, but they're not allowed to touch any of us.

I reach for my pen and sign my name carefully. I look around, my heart beating fast. All the women in the room are smiling and congratulating one another in their uniforms. I do the same, and I hope they can't see the fear in my eyes.

There is a ripple of applause. I fix my smile again. 'Thank you, girls!' Kathleen's voice rings out. 'Congratulations. Group photo time! Back out onto the field, please!'

We file out and Jewel grabs my arm. 'Can you believe it? We're official cheerleaders for the Mutineers!'

I squeal along with her, because why wouldn't I? Yet deep down, I'm afraid. I'm scared that it could all unravel, and that I'll get found out.

Outside on the field, we have group photographs taken. About halfway through, I see a woman emerge from the tunnel. Like Kathleen, she's wearing a sharp suit, purple in color. I recognize her from the news, and because, like me, even if you don't follow football, everybody in this city knows who owns the Mutineers: the Conway family. A ripple goes through the group as she comes closer into view. Samantha Conway is the chief brand officer for the Mutineers. It's hard to tell her exact age due to the number of procedures she's had, not that anybody would dare say that to her face.

Under the floodlights, when the photographs are over, she addresses us. Kathleen urges us to sit on the ground, and it feels a little like we're second graders taking a seat on a mat in front of an elementary school teacher.

'Girls,' she says with a smile that doesn't quite reach her eyes. I note her well-manicured nails and immaculate makeup. 'To the rookies, a warm welcome to the Mutineers family. To the veterans, we're so glad to have y'all back. You look *wonderful*, and it is my absolute pleasure to have y'all represent our exceptional brand out here on the field. I cannot wait for the fans to come and see you perform on this turf for the first time as a new squad on Thursday night. We're so very excited. Now, as some of y'all know, my son, Brody, is marrying his sweetheart Mary-Martha Adams at the Canyon Country Club a week from Saturday. As a way of thanking y'all for your hard work, we would be honored by your attendance.'

Another ripple goes through the group. Kathleen starts to applaud loudly. I note Harmony is swift to do the same, and so, kinda like little baby cubs, we all follow.

'The dress code,' Samantha continues, 'is *demure*. All dresses should fall below the knee, and absolutely no dress should be low cut. Now, I know y'all have worked hard today, so go change, go home, get your beauty sleep, and feel proud of yourselves for stepping into the Mutineers family.'

There is more applause, so I follow suit, and Kathleen and Samantha lapse into conversation while we get back on our feet.

'*Honored by your attendance*,' I hear Angel snort behind me under her breath. 'What does that even mean anyway?'

'It means, girl, you better haul ass to her son's wedding 'cause you ain't got no choice in the matter,' Shawny adds. 'Now you signed a contract, it's our job to *represent*, whether you like it or not.'

Angel gives a low laugh, and I pretend like I'm not listening. 'Prolly inviting us 'cause they couldn't get anyone else to go. Now we finally get to see the poor female who snagged Brody Conway for a husband.'

'How about his momma *pays* me a little more if she's goin' to make me attend her nepo-baby son's wedding?' Shawny muses, before I find Jewel is pulling me back toward our locker room.

'You see?' Jewel says after a moment, linking arms with me and walking me back across the field. She's still buzzing from signing our contract, just like I should be. 'Ain't this just fantastic? Welcome to your new, improved life, Ren.'

Chapter Four

Serenity

'You're a little late tonight, sugar,' Misty comments as I enter the dressing room at Surly's, having changed back into my ordinary clothes.

'I'm so sorry,' I say, out of breath, going straight over to the hanging rail and pulling off my jacket. 'I had to stay late to sign my contract and pose for group photos.'

'Oooh, a *contract*, that sounds mighty important.'

I go over to my mirror and kick off my shoes, tonight's outfit on a hanger looped over my fingers. I drop my shoulders. 'There's a clause that says I can't bring the Mutineers brand into disrepute.'

Misty raises her brow. Tonight, she's a blonde in black leather hot pants and long gloves. 'Good lord, it's just a football team. I'd argue half the players bring that brand into disrepute most nights of the week.'

'Guess they hold us ladies to a different standard.'

Now she's rolling her eyes. 'Ain't that always the way?'

Dancing on stage hits different tonight. The moves are the same, so is the crowd, but while normally I can ignore those eyes on me, I feel like, tonight, everybody knows. They know I'm the same girl, who on Thursday night, is gonna make her maiden performance as a law-abiding, rule-following, wholesome cheerleader on the sacred field at Danube Stadium for the opening game of the Mutineers pre-season. How did I possibly ever think I could get away with living this double life? Under the red lights, nerves cut through me, my palms sweaty against the pole as I cling to it.

After, I head straight to the office, wrenching ten and twenty-dollar bills from the rim of my boots.

'You doin' alright, Ren?' Jaxon asks me once the door is closed.

I give him a once over. He's wearing a suit tonight. The realization is a gut punch. 'Please don't tell me—'

Jaxon grits his teeth, offers me a shrug. 'Boss man's in town.'

He's referring to Kale McCoy, proprietor of Surly's. 'Just in town or heading this way?'

Jaxon looks at his watch. 'As in heading this way any moment.'

My heart hammering, I quickly count the last of my dollar bills and hand them over to Jaxon so I can make myself scarce.

Jaxon takes my money, walks it over to the desk. 'Got a tip off today, Ren. Heard we got a bunch of NFL players coming here tomorrow night to let loose for a pre-season party.'

This time, my eyes go wide. 'NFL?'

'Heard they all Mutineers players. Want me to switch your shift?'

I can't even form a response. All I can do is nod my head. 'Please,' I manage in a whisper, turning and heading for the door.

'Thought you might say that.'

My fingers go to the handle. I thrust it open, glancing back to acknowledge Jaxon before slamming straight into the hardest wall.

I don't even have to look up to know who I've just walked into.

'Woah, darlin',' a low tone echoes, and I'd know the voice anywhere, because it sends chills down my spine. Kale grabs one of my wrists and I flinch. 'What's the hurry?'

With his body, he eases me back inside the office and closes the door.

'Evening, Mr McCoy,' I hear Jaxon say, though Kale's gaze hasn't shifted away from mine. The more he leans forward, the further back I go. He's chewing gum and I can smell the remains of cigarettes on his breath.

'You staying on top of that logbook?' Kale asks Jaxon.

'You mean, for Serenity? Yes, sir.'

'Good,' Kale says, then looks me up and down. 'Ren's still my prettiest girl, wouldn't you agree?'

Jaxon doesn't answer straight away. 'Yes, sir. Absolutely.'

Kale reaches out and cups my chin. When I try to turn my head, he grips me harder, forcing me to face him. He's a heavy-set man, and his face is always moist with a layer of sweat. 'I got a job for you, sweetheart. And he expects the best, so I'm gonna give him the best I have to offer. So, when I say, you're to go give him some sugar. *Surly's rules.*'

I gulp. *Surly's rules* refers to a private dance for a client – usually one of Kale's associates – where there is no security or chaperone present, and the dancer must strip down, fully naked. What makes it more unbearable is that the no-touching rule becomes ancient history. I've done it once before, and it was enough to know that I never wanted to do it again.

'I don't want to,' I say, and I'm betrayed by the tremor in my voice, because he knows I'm afraid.

His mouth is set in a grim line. 'It's a gift, darlin'; it ain't up to you. Don't be shy now.'

I try to stand my ground. 'Then I want Hurley present throughout.'

Kale clicks his tongue. He bears down on me, forcing me back. 'You know better than to make demands of me, Serenity. I seem to remember I'm the one bailing you out here. So, pucker up. Get your pretty ass out there and show my buddy a good time.'

Inside, the lights are low. Lower than usual, a lot of neon blues and deep purples. In some way, I'm grateful, because my face won't be so visible. I'm wearing a wavy, dark brown wig, with bangs. Hurley is nowhere to be seen either. Apart from the client, I'm on my own.

'Remember,' Kale had hissed at me before he'd slapped me on the behind and shoved me inside the room, 'Surly's rules.'

My mouth has gone dry. Us girls call this the Throne Room, because it contains a high-backed chair covered in red velvet with a gold trim. The man I'm dancing for is already sat down. Even seated, he appears tall. He wears jeans and a fitted cotton polo, brown shoes and a dark baseball cap.

I walk over to the sound system. I try to send my thoughts to the usual mundane places, but I can feel his gaze on my back.

'What's your name, sweetheart?' he asks, and I'm struck by how deep his tone of voice is. He's local too, a Texan, possibly from Canyon.

I keep facing away from him. 'Brandy,' I say, using my stage name.

I hear him chuckle. 'Oh, it's like that now, is it? I mean your real name.'

'My name is Brandy Velvet.'

'Then turn around, Brandy Velvet, so I can look at you.'

I do as I'm asked.

'We don't need no music,' he says. 'Come closer.'

I take a tentative step forward. Does he want me to dance in silence?

'Raise your eyes to me, honey.'

It takes me a moment to look at him. I can still hear the music from outside in the main bar area thumping through the walls, one of the girls up on stage. The man's face is still in shadow underneath his cap. All I can see is the shape of his chin.

'How old are you?'

'Twenty-two.'

'How long you been a dancer?'

This feels strange to me. We never talk to the clients if we're performing for them. Not when we're up on stage, either. Only occasionally if we're serving drinks. 'Since I was eighteen.'

'Go on, then. Gimme a little twirl.'

It occurs to me that maybe he's shy. Or embarrassed. Though he sounds sure of himself. I turn all the way around slowly, and when I'm done, I think I hear him sigh.

'Kale was right about you, Brandy,' he says on an exhale.

'You want me to dance for you?' I ask with my heart thumping in my chest.

Another moment passes before he replies. 'How about we skip to the part when you undress for me?'

I stiffen. Okay, so he's definitely not shy.

'Nice and slow,' he instructs. 'Start with them boots.'

I'm not used to this. There's no music and ordinarily, my boots remain on for the duration. In my head, I try to figure out how I'm gonna keep things sexy, though a quieter voice asks why I even have to. Stepping forward, closer to him, I lift my leg and place my heel on the top of his thigh, bending my knee. I never need to remind myself that I'm doing this for the sole reason of paying off my father's debt.

'Help a girl out?' I say.

Taking his time, he lowers each zipper one at a time. Straightening, I swallow a lump in my throat and step out my boots. Sliding them out of the way, I reach around to my back and unclasp the corset, allowing it to fall away. As I do so, I hear him inhale through his nose. He adjusts his position on the throne, resting his ankle on his knee, leaning back a little.

I try to control my breathing. I don't know whether it's better or worse that I can't see his whole face.

'Keep goin',' he says.

Raising my hands, I grip the hemline of my panties.

'Slowly,' he reminds me.

Hooking my thumbs inside, I peel the material away, my heart in my throat. This is how I felt last time. Standing in front of a stranger, exposed and vulnerable and just wanting to run.

When the material reaches my thighs, I let it drop to my ankles. I step out of my panties and with my toe, glide them toward my boots.

His breathing is deeper. So loud he's like a bull and I can tell that the sight of me naked has got him excited.

'Come over here,' he says.

I take a single step forward.

'Closer,' he hums.

I take one more step, willing this moment to be over.

'You're beautiful. You got a guy waitin' on you at home?'

'No.'

'That just Brandy answerin', or the real you?'

'I don't have a boyfriend, no.'

'If I was your boyfriend, I'd never let you outside the house.'

I stay quiet, questioning what he wants my response to be.

'Turn around,' he says.

I do as I'm told. Tears prick my eyes. I want this to end.

I flinch as his hand grazes my hips. He tugs me backward, and within a moment I'm in his lap, facing away from him.

'Mmm,' he hums quietly as his palms snake from my hips up to my rib cage, and a moment later, cup my breasts, squeezing the nipples between his fingers. I feel his reaction under my thighs. I close my eyes as his fingers mould and squeeze my skin.

'No enhancement,' he comments in my ear. 'I would have sworn they would be. Makes you even more irresistible.'

His breath rasps against my ear, the sensation giving me chills. When his teeth nip my earlobe, it's enough to send a tear sliding down my cheek.

His hands are on the move again, sliding down the plains of my belly and coming to rest on the tops of my legs. I glance down. His fingers are long, his palms moist against my skin. Then he does something I don't expect, he pushes at the inside of my thighs, willing them to part.

The urge to run is almost overwhelming, but I've seen evidence of what happens to people who defy Kale McCoy. And so I let it happen.

My entire body tenses as the same long fingers trail a path along my flesh, inching toward my most intimate part. I squirm, then, because fear takes over me, my ass grinding into him. As I do, I feel him tense up, his nails digging into my thighs. Then he hunches over me as a low, guttural groan escapes his lips. I remain still for a moment and he's breathless, but his fingers have come to a halt.

In the next moment, he pushes me off his lap.

'Thank you, Brandy, you can go now,' he says in an even tone.

I get dressed faster than I've ever done in my entire life.

Chapter Five

Jake

Tuesday night, I got a belly full of beer, tequila and Mexican food, and I'm not even sure I can see straight.

There are fifty players on the roster for the Mutineers. We filled out the entire restaurant. I'm slowly getting to know my team, and they're all good guys. More than half of 'em are married with kids, or in steady relationships. Family men, guys who know that, if they get injured, their football career could be over in a heartbeat. For that reason, they're passionate about bringing their best performance to every game. They know as well as I do that this life is only temporary, but family is forever. So, they savour every minute of this opportunity.

There are two types of guys on the team. The ones who don't drink, who – like all professional athletes should – look after their bodies, keep healthy, work out, stay in peak physical condition. Those are the guys who still have at least five or six years left of their pro careers. Then there are the older guys – the ones edging closer to retirement. Tonight, it's those guys who seem to wanna let off steam and have a little fun.

Us rookies? We're just here for the ride.

From fifty, we're down to ten as our cars pull up outside a bar called Surly's Tavern. It's a red brick building with a big, red neon sign and its own parking lot. I got no idea where I am exactly, only that we're somewhere on the west side of Canyon. Hud Briar has us a couple of tables booked. Mostly, we're the single guys on the team, other than Dalton, who reportedly is allowed a very limited number of passes per year to go on wild nights out with his brother.

On entry, I look around. Inside, there are a lot of neon lights, a stage with a dancing pole planted in the middle, where a topless woman writhes around for some guys who look like truckers staying in town overnight. They're on bar stools facing the stage. More widely, there are other occupied tables.

I guess I'm wide-eyed at the sight of the girls, because Dalton Briar picks up on it as soon as we enter the VIP suite.

'First time in a joint like this, huh?' he laughs as we take our seats and order drinks.

I can't help but smile. 'Is it that obvious?'

'Lemme guess,' Dalton raises his voice toward me over the music. 'In college, you dated the captain of the cheer squad and went to church every Sunday.'

I wince. He's not so far off the mark. At Penn State, I did date the captain of the cheer squad, who I broke up with after she cheated on me with one of my teammates. I nursed a broken heart for weeks. After that, I hooked up with a social sciences major, who said she didn't wanna be an NFL WAG and decided not to follow me out to Texas when I got drafted. I was never single for long in college, and never long enough that my buddies could drag me out to anything close to resembling a club like this.

'Honestly? I hate these kinda joints,' Dalton lowers his voice when I don't reply. 'I'm only here to keep my brother happy.'

We both look over to Hudson Briar, who is talking animatedly to two of my fellow rookies. Outta all of us, he's the most wasted.

I lean forward. 'So how come Hud doesn't have a girl?'

Dalton tries not to smile. 'Oh, it's complicated.'

'How so?'

Dalton leans back in his chair. 'Truth is, Hud met the woman of his dreams a while back, but she's not, uh... let's just say she's not available.'

'Why? Married? Already taken?'

Dalton shakes his head. 'No, nothing like that. Her name is Harmony Reese. You ever heard of her?'

I stick out my bottom lip and shake my head. Her name doesn't sound familiar.

Dalton checks his brother is not listening, then leans across the table so I can hear him.

'Harmony Reese is captain of the Mutineers' cheer squad. The CMC. There's a clause in their contract the cheerleaders have to sign, prohibiting them from fraternizing with any pro-player. As in, they can't go anywhere near us, and we can't go anywhere near any of them. Those are the rules. This is Harmony's fifth year on the squad.'

My brows draw together. 'That sounds like a dumbass rule.'

Dalton pulls a face. 'It's by order of Sam Conway, chief brand officer for the Mutineers.'

Samantha Conway, as in daughter of Hank Conway, the owner of the Mutineers and the whole reason I'm sitting here with a big-money contract. 'Oh,' I say.

'I mean the players on the field might be the ones bringing home the loot, but it's the cheerleaders… they're the ones pulling in the big crowds. Sam Conway wants people to believe they're superior somehow. Beautiful, classy, feminine… so perfect to seem, like… unattainable. Like almost holy. Ally told me they have all these unwritten rules they gotta abide by, like always having perfect hair and makeup whenever they go out. There's even a no-touching rule. So, Hank Conway might own the Mutineers, but let me tell you, it's his daughter pullin' all the strings. She got him wrapped around her little finger. Her son, Brody, he's her deputy. She's positioning that asshole to take over the entire outfit one day when her dad meets the big adios.'

I tilt my head toward Hudson just as our drinks arrive. 'So, what's the deal? Hud plans to, like, wait for Harmony or something?'

Dalton checks his brother is not looking our way. 'Keeps saying he's not. But deep down, I know he is. If he has a girlfriend, she usually lasts less than a month.'

'What about Harmony? She feel the same way?'

'Well, she chose squad captain over him, so I'm not all that hopeful.'

'So how does he know she's the one?'

Dalton's lips curl into a smile. 'You've never been in love, have you, rookie?'

I shrug. 'I mean… I thought I had.'

'You got a girl right now?'

Without warning, the woman from the grocery store pops into my head. Serenity. These past few days, she keeps doing that. Sweet, kinda shy, seemingly no idea how smokin' hot she is. My perfect kinda girl. I'm excited for Thursday night's pre-season opener, but, man, Friday can't come soon enough. I keep wondering if I've turned her into something else in my mind, and that really, I'm just being delusional – dreaming about the idea of her, rather than who she actually is. But instinct tells me that she's somebody I need to get to know, and I'm already planning what I'm gonna say to persuade her to give me her number.

'No, nobody,' I say with a sniff.

Our captain is smirking right now. 'But I'll bet you're not short on offers though, right?'

I can feel my cheeks burn. *Why the hell am I like a little kid when it comes to this stuff?* 'I switched off my notifications. They were draining my battery.'

Dalton nods knowingly. Suddenly, some of the guys are being offered private dances. Zach Dorsey, one of my fellow rookies, from Baltimore and the Mutineers' newest kicker, is on his feet, rubbing his hands together, the widest grin on his face. Just the sight of his giddiness makes me laugh.

'Mon-tana Cream!' he croons, allowing her to lead the way, and it's pretty obvious he's admiring the shape of her ass, '*Mmm-mm.*'

'Montana Cr— that's her name?' I ask, wide-eyed. *Fuck, Walsh, quit acting all virginal.*

Dalton shakes his head, also grinning.

Hud raises his eyes to me. 'What about you, rookie?' he shouts over the pulse of the music. 'You gonna follow Dorsey's lead?'

'I'm good, maybe later,' I holler back, raising my bottle of beer to him. A little voice in the back of my head says I can't be this golden boy all the time, and that I should just let the guys sign me up for a lap dance. That I shouldn't be so damned chicken or worried about what other people think.

'Whatever my brother's sayin' to you, it's not true, by the way,' is Hud's slurred response, looking at Dalton warily. 'None of it.'

'Whatever you say,' I shout back, and Dalton is laughing again.

—

'Rise 'n' shine, your highness. It's game day.'

River's voice enters my dream. It's the opening game and I'm about to lose control of the ball. In my bedroom, I stir. We agreed that, when my family moved into the same property as me, we'd try and keep things separate. Compartmentalized, so I'm not that dude who still lives with his parents, aged twenty-three. Apparently, River didn't get the memo.

I groan, pull my pillow further down over my ears. I didn't sleep well, because –

goddammit – I'm nervous.

Tonight is the first time I'm gonna be on that field, as a Mutineer, playing for the NFL. The *actual* NFL. More than three months on from the draft and it still hasn't sunk in. That I'm here. But last night, I lay here, stared at the ceiling and asked myself, what if I screw it all up? What if I let my team down? Doesn't matter how much college football I played, this is the big leagues now, and it ain't for fucking snowflakes.

'Didn't we agree you wouldn't hang out on this side of the house?' I say to River, but it comes out more like a grunt.

'It's my first day of school, dipshit. I'm not gonna see you before the game tonight. Thought I'd come and wish you luck.'

I raise my head. 'Right. First day of school. I forgot.'

I haven't been able to focus on much else other than training. Except for when the girl from the grocery store pops into my head. No woman has ever occupied my thoughts like this. I must be down bad.

'How do I look?' River asks.

'Why you wearing so much makeup?'

'You think it's too much?' she counters.

'You don't normally wear so much is all.'

She goes over to a mirror I hung on the wall only yesterday. 'Does it look like I'm wearing too much?' she asks again.

I turn, push myself up on my elbows and glance back at her. She's wearing jeans and high-top sneakers with a black tank top. 'Good luck. Just be yourself. Everybody will love you.'

'I know what's gonna happen,' she sighs. 'All the girls are gonna ask if you're single, and all the guys are gonna ask if I can get 'em tickets to the game.'

'Then just tell 'em no, I'm not, and no, you can't. If they just wanna hang out with you just 'cause of me then they're not worth hanging with in the first place.'

She rolls her eyes in the mirror. 'Says he who literally never had to struggle with being popular.'

'I already told you... I was never... Mr Popularity.'

'That's what a popular kid would say.'

I let my head fall back into my pillow. 'Don't you have to go now?'

'I got like... five minutes. So, first game of the pre-season. How do you feel?'

'Like somebody went at my insides with a hacksaw. I got... I don't know. Butterflies.'

My sister snickers. 'You're gonna ace it. I know you are. That stadium is gonna be filled to the rafters, and when the game is over, all you're gonna hear is your name on every Mutineers fan's lips.'

'Not for the wrong reasons, I hope.'

When she's gone, I take a hot shower. Tonight, I'm the starting running back. A lotta guys have game day rituals: like, they'll wear the same pair of underwear or eat some weird purple food. I guess I'm yet to find my ritual. I spend time in my (half-empty) closet and pick out an outfit to wear to the stadium, then throw on a T-shirt and shorts to eat breakfast. Pre-game nerves mean I'm not even hungry.

—

In the locker room, the atmosphere is like nothing I've ever experienced before.

We're all dressed in dark navy and white, the crest of the crossed swords of the Mutineers on our jerseys. I'm number fourteen in the squad. The noise from the stadium crowd reverberates through everything. It's in the walls. My heart's not stopped pumping at an elevated rate since I left my house.

It's a Mutineers ritual that the captain applies eye black to each member of the starting line-up. Dalton Briar wipes his blackened, greasy thumbs across the tops of my cheeks.

I glance at my reflection in the mirror. Players wear eye black to supposedly reduce glare from the floodlights. I've always thought it looked like war paint.

'No rookies on the field,' he says to me, a reference to a speech Coach Holland made to the team earlier about every one of us having a right to be out there, no matter our level of experience. His way of saying 'we've got this'.

No matter what happens out there, I'll give it my all. Show the fans why I was a first-round draft pick. And no matter what happens, tomorrow morning I'm heading over to The Bounty to tell Serenity the following: I'm a football player, I'd like to get to know her, and would she like to go on a date with me. Nothing could be scarier than this moment, waiting to approach the field, so I can't chicken out on asking a girl for a drink.

'Players on your feet, get in line!' Coach Holland hollers, breaking me out of my daydream, thinking about Serenity's pretty eyes.

We snap to attention. I was warned this would happen. Another Mutineers ritual. The first game of the pre-season sees the Conways come and shake hands with all the players before we head out onto the field to have our names announced, our images beamed out on the jumbotron to the waiting crowd, running through the tunnel in a plume of dry ice that I can only assume is meant to build the hype.

We line up in order from defense to offense. Hank Conway has the door held open for him. I've shaken his hand before. Behind him is his daughter, Samantha Conway, who I've met briefly, and the two people behind her I assume are her kids: Brody, a taller guy with black hair, and Lemon, whose dress kinda oddly matches her own name. One by one, they work their way along the line, shaking our hands and wishing us luck.

Brody Conway looks bored, like he doesn't even wanna be here, but he follows his mother's lead. He has dark hair and freakishly long fingers. When Lemon gets her turn, she holds onto my hand for way longer than is necessary. I give thanks to the Lord that our gloves are already on.

'You're Jake, right?' she says, and her smile gives her dimples. Her white-blonde hair is tied back into a French braid, though she has dark roots showing. She seems to be about my age.

'Yes, ma'am,' I respond. 'That's me.'

'You know, my grandpappy lets me choose who to go after in the draft. You were my top pick this year, Jake Walsh.'

Her voice is all light and breathy. She's still gripping my hand and swinging her hips, biting her lip like she's about to ask me out on a date or something. I can hear the guys snickering, and I don't have the first clue what to say to this girl because I'm reeling right now. I'm questioning whether what she said is true, that her grandfather, Hank Conway, lets his grandchild choose his Mutineers draft picks and the only reason I'm here is because Lemon Conway had some desire to flirt with me.

'Thank you, gentlemen,' Hank Conway's voice echoes around the walls of the locker room and suddenly Lemon's looking to her feet. 'Do us proud out there.'

'Huddle up!' Dalton Briar roars and the team comes together. I think I hear Lemon squeal as she moves out the way, following her grandfather out the door and heading toward the Conways' VIP suite.

My heart is racing. I see the hunger in my teammates' eyes. This is what we were born for. This might only be the first game of the pre-season, but the desire to win is oozing out these guys' pores. And all I know is that I gotta prove myself a winner.

'Mutineers!' Dalton shouts loud and in this moment, we are his disciples. 'Tonight, we go out there, we dominate! We give one hundred per cent in every play! We take no prisoners! We make the most of every moment. Every opportunity! And we do it to win. 'Cause we're MUTINEERS!'

'MUTINEERS! Hooah!'

The sound is almost deafening. I feel hard slaps against my back. More cries of 'no rookies on the field.' Nobody gets treated like the new kid. We're a team.

When I finally pick up my helmet, I'm ready. I've never been more ready for anything. When we line up in the tunnel, the excitement from the crowd is palpable, the atmosphere electric.

This is it.

When I run out onto the field, holding my helmet in my gloved hand, my image broadcast onto the jumbotron, it feels like everything is moving in slow-mo. The roar from the crowd makes my blood pump in my ears. I'm aware of the cheerleaders to my left, of their synchronized movements to the strains of

Mötley Crüe's *Girls Girls Girls*, blaring over the speakers around the Danube Stadium, the signature tune of the CMC. I take in their faces. I wanna glimpse of their captain, Harmony Reese, so I can see for myself the girl who Hud Briar is so crazy about. Yet just when I think I spot her, I'm drawn to another face and without warning, my legs are lead weights.

It can't be.

She can't be here.

Because if she's here, sharing this field with me and she's holding two motherfucking pom poms, it means she's a…

She's a…

Serenity is a goddamned Mutineers cheerleader.

With those pretty eyes, she stares right back at me.

And by the looks of it, she's as surprised as I am.

Chapter Six

Jake

I can see her. I'm inside my pickup in the parking lot outside The Bounty diner in downtown central Canyon, early Friday morning, watching her through the windows. The building is on the crossroads, next to a gas station and opposite a used car showroom, underneath a giant billboard advertising a brand of dog food. It's ninety degrees out.

The radio is on. The breakfast show hosts are analysing last night's pre-season opener, won comfortably by the Mutineers. We took no prisoners. Commentators are describing my debut as 'solid'. I'd say my performance was decent, and that's what matters overall.

But that's not what I'm thinking about right now. Serenity looks different to last night, when she was inside the stadium. This morning, she's wearing a pale-colored dress, her hair pulled back into a simple ponytail. Last night, her hair was loose but styled like she'd come direct from the salon, with a whole lotta makeup and a beaming smile for the crowds. And her moves... it took everything I had to focus on our plays and not turn and watch her dance, and it took me until the end of the first quarter to manage anything close to concentration. Sure, all of the cheerleaders looked awesome out there. But it wasn't them I was wanting to look at.

Last night, I was nervous about the game. Yet my heart wasn't hammering like it is this morning, when the door to The Bounty creaks on its frame as I open it. Even my palms are sweaty. I'm wearing a cap pulled low, a plain white tee and jersey shorts, a brand-new pair of high-top sneakers. There's a bar to my left. I head for a table near the back, near to where she's serving a bunch of college kids, ordering their eggs over-easy.

'I'll be right with you, sir,' she says to me, without looking up.

Their order taken, she goes over to the counter and comes back with a menu.

I slide off my cap, fold it between my fingers. She slows as she sees me, and we lock eyes. Man, she's really something.

I greet her with a 'Mornin', Serenity.'

She stops at the edge of my table, places the menu under my nose. Her lips twist into a smile. 'Good morning,' she says. For a moment, she looks lost for words.

'So...' I continue, 'you didn't tell me you were a cheerleader.'

She puts one hand on her hip. 'And you didn't mention you were a football player.'

'Guess it never came up, huh?'

She's still smiling. It's the sweetest goddamned smile. Then she pushes her tongue into her cheek and rolls her eyes. 'Guess not. What can I get you?'

I pick up the menu, but I don't look at it, keeping my gaze trained on her face. 'A drink.'

'What kind of drink?'

'The just-you-and-me type-o-drink. I'm buyin', remember?'

She twists the end of her ponytail between her fingers, unaware of how endearing it makes her look. *Why can I not get enough of this girl?*

'Uh-uh,' she says with a grin. 'I signed a contract. There are rules about you and me being in close proximity.' She glances down at the menu. 'I'll be right back to take your order.'

I lean to my left and watch her walk away, back toward the bar. My eyes glide all the way down her body and linger for a moment on her ass. I can't help it. It does things to me. She doesn't look in my direction, not once, and the fact that she turned me down once already only strengthens my determination to leave here with her phone number.

She delivers a couple of plates to the college kids and comes back to my table, then reaches into her apron and flips to a new page on her notepad.

'You didn't think I'd come, did you?' I ask. 'Not after yesterday.'

'I didn't know that the guy who bought my groceries for me was the Mutineers' newest draft pick, Jake Walsh, no.'

I like the sound of my name on her lips. 'You follow football then?'

'Not at all. I only know your name 'cause I asked for it. And I did wonder if you'd show.'

'Well, here I am.'

Her eyes meet mine again and I feel it, right between my ribs. I don't care if she's a cheerleader, I have to know her better.

She straightens. 'What can I get you? Coffee?'

'Uh, I don't drink coffee.'

'Fresh juice?'

'Sure.'

'You want something to eat?'

'How about you come and eat something with me? Tomorrow night?'

She's grinning again. 'Did you filter out the part about me signing a contract?'

'I have selective hearing. Comes from being hit in the head too many times, I guess.'

She laughs. It's like music. 'Okay, so let me spell it out for you one more time. I signed a contract. Clause five in that contract states that it is forbidden for a Mutineers cheerleader to fraternize with, or date, *any* NFL pro-player. And *this*—' She indicates the space between us with her hand. 'I believe this already counts as fraternizing. So, I'm gonna go get your juice, and I'll be your server, but that's about all I can offer you right now.'

She backs away, still with that cute little innocent smile on her face. I should be crushed by the put down, but I'm not giving in because of some stupid rule. There's something about her that makes me wanna *not* back down. Maybe it's that she can give me the brush off and still have that beautiful smile on her face. Her heart is pure. I can tell.

A few minutes later, she's back with the other plates for the college kids.

'Uh, Miss, I'm ready to order now,' I say.

'I'll be right with you, sir,' she replies.

One of the college kids has turned his head. He seems to recognize me.

Serenity comes back with her notepad. I swear this girl never stops smiling.

'What can I get you?'

I'm at physical therapy all morning so may as well get a good breakfast. 'I'll take the half classic with two extra eggs, all poached.'

'You want four poached eggs?'

I tap my stomach. 'Need the protein.'

'Anything else?'

I cock my head to one side, trying not to come off all confident, 'cause something tells me she wouldn't like that. 'I'd really love your phone number.'

'I'm sure you would.'

'You think you might give it to me?'

'Not today, cowboy.'

'How about tomorrow? Think I found my new favorite breakfast spot.'

'Something tells me this place is really out your way.'

'So, I'll leave a little early. I like a little sunshine in the morning.'

She knows I'm referring to the sight of her.

'You did not just say that.' She raises an eyebrow before her eyes flit to the door. More customers coming in.

'I caught the end of your half time show,' I tell her.

'You did, huh?'

'Those were some pretty high kicks. I saw you celebrating the touchdown.'

She bites her lip, shakes her head, like she wants to compliment me. 'Would you like anything else, sir?' she asks.

I look to her pen hovering over her notepad. 'You could write it on my hand. That way I won't lose it.'

'One half-classic with four poached eggs and one fresh orange juice, coming right up. And that's all you'll be getting. Sir.'

Man, she's not gonna make this easy for me. 'Call me Jake. Please.'

She picks up the menu. 'I'm not in the habit of calling my customers by their first name,' she says before she's walking away.

I have to wait another ten minutes before she's back with my food. 'One fresh juice,' Serenity says, placing the glass in front of me. 'One half-classic with four poached eggs. Can I get you anything else?'

'How about I don't have to ask again?'

'Ask what again? I don't think I caught the question.'

'It's really a game-changer for you? That I'm on the team?'

'Yup,' is her reply and my shoulders droop just a little.

'How 'bout I quit the Mutineers?'

She laughs at that. 'Let's not be too hasty, now. You don't even know me.'

'Then let me *get* to know you.'

'You know there are a lotta pretty girls in Canyon who just *love* football. You tried all them dating apps?'

'Why would I wanna meet a girl on a dating app when I just met a girl in real life?'

'I have to go. Eat up, your food is getting cold.'

'Serenity—'

She turns and looks back. Grants me another sweet smile, and man, I am gone for this chick. But I'm pretty sure that's all I'm getting out of her today.

'Last chance to give me your number,' I say at the cash register on my way out.

She raises her eyes to me. 'How was your breakfast? Taste good?'

'Delicious. When's your next shift?'

'I'd need to check my schedule.'

'So… if I came back tomorrow for more eggs… would you be here?'

I hand over my cash payment and she rings me up. I think I see her blush.

'I should tell you, I'm persistent,' I state.

'You have a good day now, *sir*,' she says, and her emerald eyes sparkle when she says it.

'See you on the field?' I say, pocketing my wallet.

'See you on the field.'

I back away to the door, her sweet smile like a big hit of adrenaline that's gonna set me up for the day.

Nope. She is definitely *not* gonna make this easy for me.

—

I arrive home after a day's training to find River hunched over the kitchen table, surrounded by books.

'Homework already?' I ask, heading for the sink and switching on the faucet.

She leans back and lets out a groan. 'I swear, in Philly, I got half this amount. Monday, I got a Spanish test already. And everybody down here is really good at Spanish.'

I wash my hands. 'It's called a border with Mexico.'

'You left early this morning.'

'Had to get to practice.'

'It was the morning after your first game! Thought you said practice didn't start 'til later.'

I switch off the faucet, dry my hands and head for the fridge, which has been well-stocked by my mother. I survey the contents and help myself to some sandwich-making materials.

'Had to make a pitstop first. How was school today?'

River gives a shrug.

'You talk to anyone?'

She pulls a face and talks like she's a redneck. '*So, like, is your brother really Mutineers running back Jake Walsh?*'

'And did they believe you?'

'I don't care if they did or not. It was all they could ask me yesterday too.'

'So did you meet anybody nice?'

'The guys are all jocks and all the girls wanna talk about is makeup tutorials. So far, so high school.'

She's pulling more zombie faces. 'I should rephrase my question. Were you nice to anyone?'

'I'm not a *complete* idiot.'

'Just try to make friends, okay? Only gotta make it 'til you graduate.'

'Hey, dipshit, it's your fault that I'm the one having to change high schools for my senior year in the first place.'

'I know that. I just think you'd make your life easier if you could be a little more... maybe a little *less* controversial.'

'Alright, your royal highness... jeez. By the way, you have mail.'

She reaches across the table and passes me an envelope. The paper feels expensive. I open it up and read the contents.

'What is it?' River asks.

'Wedding invitation. Brody Conway.'

'Who's Brody Conway?'

'Son of Sam Conway? Grandson of Hank Conway? Owner of the Mutineers?'

'Why are you invited to his wedding?'

'Whole team is invited. I don't know. You wanna be my plus one?'

'You get a plus one?'

'Weird, right? Guess that's what rich people do. Invite everybody they ever met to their wedding. Wanna come?'

'When is it?'

'Week from tomorrow. Canyon Country Club. Free food and drink. All you have to do is wear a dress.'

River gives another shrug. 'You sure you wouldn't wanna take a date instead of me? One of those sexy girls on your Insta account?'

'Prolly a little weird, taking somebody I've never met to a wedding.'

Mid-bite outta my sandwich, I hear the front door, and the unmistakable sounds of Bridget Walsh floating through from the hallway.

'So far, we are loving it here. Everybody's so friendly! And Jake's had a great start on the team...'

My heart sinks because it's definitely not Dad that she's talking to.

'Oh god, who the fuck is that?' River hisses.

'No idea,' I say, still chewing.

'You got mayonnaise on your chin,' River says, and I wipe it away with the back of my hand.

'Oh look,' Mom announces as she enters the room. 'They are here! Jake, River, this is Olivia Francis. Olivia just graduated from Cornell, majoring in meteorology.'

This is what my mom likes to do. She likes to introduce women of my age to me and include their credentials, like she's tryna sell me a house. Like, *this is Lisa. Lisa is a veterinarian and owns her own apartment. This is Cindy. Cindy went to grad school and her father is an oncology specialist at Johns Hopkins Hospital.*

Olivia is tall and slender with a straight nose, light brown hair, wearing a green polka-dot dress and sneakers. What she's doing hanging out with my mother is beyond me.

Olivia smiles shyly in my direction. 'Hello,' she says.

'Hey,' I say in return.

'Hi,' River says at the table.

For a brief moment, the air turns thick and it's awkward. 'So... why don't we go in the back yard and sit by the pool with some iced tea?' Mom suggests.

They go out back together and River raises her eyebrows in my direction. 'King Midas, he need queen,' she says, putting on her best caveman voice.

'Quit it,' I sigh.

A few moments later, my mother is back in the kitchen. 'Jake, come drink iced tea with us.'

'Ma. I'm tired. I just got back from practice.'

She looks at me like she's already lost patience. 'Did you not hear me? *Cornell*. She's got an interview with WKRZ.'

'The local TV station? So?'

She points to her head. 'So, she's pretty but she's got smarts. Very solid potential. I think you'd like her.'

'How did you even find her?'

Mom opens the fridge. 'She's in my tennis class. At the gym. *And* she told me she's single. I think you should get to know her a little bit.'

'Yeah, Jakey,' River laughs at the table. 'She's good wife material. Go outside and talk to your future wifey.'

'Ma. I'll find my own girlfriend. Alright? I don't need your help.'

Mom pulls a jug of chilled iced tea from the fridge. 'Of course, sweetheart. I'm just trying to guide you in the right direction. You know, some of those girls on social media or TikTok or whatnot... well, they're just... well, they're not the right sort of girl. You know? And there *is* a right sort of a girl, Jake, before you ask. So, come. Say hi. And if you like her, maybe you could take her to dinner.'

She's already heading back outside. I look at River, who is grinning at me.

'Can't I at least just settle in first?' I say, abandoning the remainder of my sandwich.

'Apparently not. If I were you, I'd find a girlfriend, and fast. Or the weather girl out there is gonna be first in a very long line of candidates for the position of *Mrs* Jake Walsh.'

I watch the two women in the back yard. And all I can think is that the only woman I'd want for a girlfriend right now is apparently off limits and doesn't even wanna give me her number.

I'm just gonna have to double my efforts.

Chapter Seven

Serenity

'Persia Takeda, I hope you've got another dress to wear because you're not stepping onto the bus in that outfit.'

Still in my towel in the CMC locker room after early-morning practice, my hair wet, I look across at Harmony. Our captain's eyebrows are arched toward the third-year veteran, hands on her hips. Persia holds out both hands, glancing innocently down at her bodycon dress. It's short, off the shoulder, baby pink in color with a pretty lace overlay.

'Harm, this is an *Alaïa*,' Persia says.

'That might be, but I can practically see your pussy.'

Next to me, Jewel snorts. I bite my lip. Looking up from applying her makeup in the mirror, Shawny stifles a laugh. Persia pouts her lips in response, then tosses her long, straight black hair over her shoulder in defiance.

'You so cannot see my pussy.'

'Below the knee. That was the rule, remember? Ren got the memo, see?'

Harmony's pointing to my dress, hanging next to me on the edge of my locker door. It's sleeveless, green with a high neckline and long pencil skirt. It's the opposite of anything I'd ever wear at Surly's, yet while it looks brand-new, I bought it on an app for pre-loved clothes. And unlike Persia's dress, it's regrettably more *conservative*, and most definitely not designer.

Persia looks at my dress with well-disguised disdain, but I know dislike when I see it. 'Well, I don't have anything else,' she says.

'That's why I brought spares. You're what, a two? Same as me.'

'You brought spares? Harm, seriously?'

'Go take a look.'

'I'd rather not go.'

'We go as a team, remember?'

Persia glowers at our captain, lets out an impatient sigh then turns on her heel. She heads for Harmony's locker, almost bumping into Angel as she goes.

'What's up with her?' Angel asks.

'Inappropriate wedding attire,' Shawny confirms.

'You know, I didn't have any dresses falling below my knee,' Angel complains to Harmony. 'I had to buy something especially. Are they gonna refund us the costs of that?'

It's impossible to know what Harmony Reese is thinking because she always keeps such a poker face. 'Probably not,' our captain sighs.

Shawny's finished with her mascara. 'Who goes to a wedding by bus anyways?' she blurts. 'Seriously. We're like a tour group showing up to Brody Conway's wedding. Kathleen might as well be holding up one of those stuffed animals with a stick up its ass so we can all follow it around. We might as well wear matching visors.'

'You know, I heard the guys all got an invite in the mail *with a plus one*,' Jewel says, turning so I can zip her into her dress.

'Which guys?' Angel asks.

'Like, the whole football team. They're all invited too.'

'The football team is coming to the wedding?' I blurt without thinking, because this whole week Jake Walsh has been coming to the diner most mornings trying to get my phone number, and he didn't mention he would be there at the ceremony today. And my thoughts immediately turn to whether he'll be bringing a plus one.

'Why, you interested in a player, Ren?!' Angel laughs, until Harmony gives her a stern look in my defense.

Shawny is frowning. 'How come they all get a plus one? We don't get plus ones. I bet they don't gotta go by bus neither.'

'Are we allowed to talk to them at the wedding reception?' Jewel asks wistfully, looking to Harmony for the answer.

'Definitely not,' Angel clarifies, and I swear I see a look of sadness shimmer across Harmony's features.

'That's too bad,' Jewel continues, 'because I sure as hell would like to speak to Jake Walsh. Ask him if he'd like to take me to dinner one time.'

My stomach churns. 'Girls, hurry it up,' Harmony says, reminding us that we only have twenty more minutes before the bus is due to depart.

—

Kathleen ushers us all onto the bus, muttering 'good' and 'very nice,' as one by one she checks each of us is dressed appropriately. In front of me, Persia is now wearing a long, flowing peacock blue dress.

'Stunning, Persia,' Kathleen says as Persia grants her a perfect smile. 'Nice work.'

Jewel and I stand side by side as she looks us over. 'Just lovely, girls. On you go.'

We're the last of the squad to get on the bus and there aren't two seats together.

'I'll go back, you go front,' Jewel says as I retrace my steps. The only seat free is next to Harmony.

'You mind if I sit down?' I ask her.

She shifts over a fraction. 'Sure,' she says, and I sit.

Kathleen steps onto the bus and exchanges words with the driver. Then she's grasping the tops of the seats and addressing the squad as a group.

'Ladies,' she says as she raises her voice. 'Y'all look beautiful today. Now, I know this is a wedding, and weddings are a time to celebrate. No doubt there will be plenty to eat and drink. May I remind you that first and foremost, you are CMC. That means, you are still on representational duty. While there will be many guests there from the NFL, there will be many guests who are unfamiliar with who you are and what you do. Please be courteous and act respectably at all times. Any inappropriate behavior could result in your expulsion from this team. The entire Mutineers team will be present today with their partners. As per the terms of your contract, it is not permitted to speak to them, so please do not do so.'

From behind, I hear Shawny's voice. 'Kathleen, what happens if they talk to us?'

'Then you politely excuse yourself. They have been asked not to approach you.'

'What if it's one of their wives? Or girlfriends?'

'Well then, that's fine,' Kathleen says with a sigh.

I then hear Angel's voice. 'What happens if you're talking with one of their wives and the husband wants to join in the conversation?'

Kathleen rolls her eyes. 'Ladies, please just use your common sense. They have been reminded of the rules for our squad.'

The driver starts the engine and it stutters into action. As we begin our journey to the Country Club, on the far east of Canyon on the Texas coastline, I look across at Harmony, offering her a smile.

'I like your dress,' I say.

'Thank you,' is her response. 'I like yours too.'

I like Harmony. I guess I'm in awe of her. This is her second year as captain of the squad, and she has to walk a fine line between keeping everyone in check but also maintaining friendships. Everyone loves and respects her, but I sense she keeps her distance a little in order to remain impartial and just a teensy bit authoritarian.

'Thank you,' I say.

We sit in silence for a moment. 'Can I ask you something?' I ask, keeping my voice low. 'What if Persia had refused to change her dress?'

Harmony's lips twist. 'Then she'd be sitting on her own in the CMC locker room right about now.'

'Would that have bothered you?'

'Not as much as if it had been game night and she'd refused to go out on the field for any reason. It's only a wedding. I doubt anyone would miss her.'

'You do a real good job.'

She laughs, looking out the window. 'I don't know about that.'

'Can I ask you something else?'

She turns her head back around to face me. 'Ask away.'

'I was gonna ask about...' I swallow. I want to know how she manages to keep her cool, knowing that a hot NFL player is crazy for her and she's managed to resist his advances the entire time she's been on the squad. I want to know how she manages to put up fences around her heart. Because the more attention Jake Walsh pays me, the more I'm tempted to give him my phone number, violating the terms of my contract.

'Actually, don't worry. It's none of my business,' I say.

I feel my cheeks burn. I keep my eyes forward, looking out the window as the coach leaves Danube Stadium behind.

'To be in this squad, we have to make choices sometimes,' Harmony says after a moment. 'But we also have to back our own decisions, even if we doubt the validity of them, or if it makes us unpopular. Doin' the right thing by you might not be the right choice for somebody else. I think you have great potential, Ren. I think you could be captain of this squad one day.'

I blink at her. 'You do?'

'I really do. I know we don't know each other well. But I can see you're the kind of person who always wants to do the right thing. And that's an asset to be exulted. I believe we uphold values of common decency in this squad. And you're the embodiment of those good values. I can tell.'

I grant her a big smile, but on the inside I crumple.

She doesn't know about my double life.

None of these girls do.

And just the thought of it makes me sick to my stomach.

—

The Club House at the Canyon Country Club is an enormous white building with black-and-white tiled floors and pillars out front. On arrival, men in suits usher us through the building to a large patch of grass at the back, where rows of gold seats have been lined up in a half-moon shape, facing a pretty white pergola with fresh pink roses woven through its wooden frame. We're high up, and the view is stunning out across the gulf, the crashing waves audible in the distance.

The other guests are already seated. I feel all eyes on the squad as we enter. Kathleen stands at one end of a row, shepherding us all in one by one.

'Sit with me, sit with me,' Jewel hisses at me from behind, grabbing my hand. 'That's him over there, see?'

I glance to my right. On the other side of the central aisle, which is lined with a long carpet, is the Mutineers football team and their plus ones: glamorous wives and girlfriends and otherwise. It doesn't take me long to locate Jake Walsh. He's looking over his shoulder and smiling at me, the breeze ruffling his hair. He looks different in suit and tie. There's a woman in a purple satin dress sitting next to him.

Jewel squeezes my hand. 'Oh my god, don't look,' she breathes. 'He's looking this way.'

Kathleen makes eyes at me, and I move down the row, Jewel on my tail. We both sit down at the same time.

'What do you think?' Jewel asks me. 'Seriously cute, huh?'

'What's there to get so het up about?' I ask innocently. 'You do know you signed a contract, right?'

'I swear, if Jake Walsh asked me out on a date, I'd tear up my contract right there.'

'You're serious? All those auditions? Everything you dreamed of? You'd give all that up?'

Jewel gives me a withering look. 'I mean, I wouldn't do it for just *any* guy. Do you know how much he earns in a week?'

We collapse into giggles, and I don't even know the answer to her question.

I crane my neck. I can see the back of his head. The girl he's with leans close to his ear and I wonder if they're related. 'Who do you think the girl is?'

'I read he brought his whole family with him to Texas. She's gotta be his sister. They look like one another.'

I feel an odd sense of relief at her words, but his presence has got my stomach all twisting in knots, asking myself what I'll do if he tries to speak to me. 'Maybe he's got a girlfriend already.'

Jewel glares at me, eyebrows raised. 'Girl, do you not look at social media? He's as single as can be.'

'It's not like you can do anything here, right under Kathleen's nose,' I whisper.

'A girl can look,' she says with a smile. 'And admire from afar.'

We laugh again and before I know it, Kathleen and some of the other girls are shushing us. We watch as Sam Conway accompanies her son down the aisle, along with Hank Conway. Brody Conway is tall and slender, with black hair. Together, they greet various guests, before Sam and her father take their seats on the front row, Brody greeting his best man in front of the pergola. The breeze catches my hair.

It isn't long before we're invited to stand for the arrival of the bridal party. The bride wears a princess-style gown with a wide chiffon skirt, her hair cascading down her back underneath a long veil.

When we sit down again, the man who is officiating the wedding gives an address. There are microphones, so I can hear everything crystal clear.

The first time I hear Brody Conway's voice, it sounds oddly familiar.

Then it hits me.

As he reads aloud his wedding vows, I feel myself craning my neck again, to get a closer look at him. I need to see his hands.

And when I do, I panic inside. My breathing alters. My palms go sweaty. Jewel gives me a wide smile which I attempt to return, but the discomfort in my chest is spreading wildly to my limbs.

I've met Brody Conway before.

At Surly's.

There's no mistaking those weirdly long fingers, the ones that pressed into my thighs as I writhed naked in his lap.

I danced for Brody Conway, only a week ago. *Surly's rules.*

Now I'm watching him get married.

Chapter Eight

Jake

'Who are all those girls?'

Thankfully, the ceremony is over. It went on forever, made worse by the fact that Lemon Conway was a bridesmaid and kept looking over and smiling at me while the bride was reciting her vows. Even the guys have started to notice the extra attention she's been paying me. Doesn't help that I'm here with my sister, so everybody knows I don't have a girl. Even now, holding onto my drink, I can feel Lemon watching me with those hungry eyes of hers.

Serenity is inaccessible right now. I know she's here. All I wanna do is see her and talk to her and—

'Earth to Jake.'

'Sorry, what?'

River raises her eyebrows. 'I said, who are all those girls over there? The ones you're staring at.'

'CMC.'

Her mouth drops open. 'They're the cheerleaders?'

'Uh-huh.'

'No. Way.'

'I didn't know you cared.'

'*Duh*. Like, do you know how competitive it is to become CMC? Their audition process is notoriously ruthless. And there's the damage all that performing does to their bodies.'

'How do you know all this?'

I don't think I've ever seen River so animated. 'I watched an exposé on TikTok. Compared to you guys, they literally work for peanuts. And they get none of the perks you guys do either. Is that why they're all over there and not over here with everyone else? You know they have a clause in their contract? They can't go near the players.'

I stare at her, aghast. 'I did know that, yes.'

'I'll bet you don't have the same clause in *your* contract.'

'You're right,' I admit. 'I don't.'

River shakes her head in disgust. 'Yet again, always with the double standards.'

I don't have a reply for her because, once again, she's correct. 'Do you like one of them, or something?' I hear her ask.

I straighten my back. *Oh god, am I no better than Lemon?* 'Why'd you ask that?'

'I don't know. You keep looking over there like you're searching for something. Or somebody.'

I rub the back of my neck. Then I look at Hud Briar on the grass to my right, who's holding a beer in his hand. He's wearing sunglasses but I'd bet my last dollar he's staring in exactly the same direction I am.

'Can you give me a sec?' I ask my sister.

'Sure,' she shrugs, looking nonplussed as I move through the crowd to Hud, pressing one hand on his shoulder.

'Who's the gatekeeper?' I ask him and he snaps outta whatever thoughts he was sunk deep into. 'The redhead over there.'

'Kathleen Lafferty,' Hud says with a grimace. 'CMC squad coach. Professional cock blocker.'

'Right now, she looks like a goddamned cattle rancher.'

He laughs at that. 'It does look kinda ridiculous, right? I mean, what's the point of having them as guests if they're just gonna be rounded up and segregated?'

I lower my voice. 'I got an idea. You wanna talk to Harmony, right? I say we go over there, point out to Ms Lafferty that this is a wedding reception. Nobody's going to do anything to embarrass themselves if we mingle a little with some off-duty cheerleaders for an hour or so. No harm can come of it, right?'

Hud looks at me, inhales and puffs out his chest, as though psyching himself up. 'You're right,' he says.

'Want me to be your wing man?'

'You bet.'

I slap him on the back. 'Then let's go, man.'

Side by side, we walk across the lawn toward Kathleen Lafferty. A band with violins is still playing. As we edge closer, I can pick Serenity out of the crowd. She's in a long green dress, next to a woman with corkscrew curls tied back. For a brief second, her eyes meet mine, and it only makes me more determined to talk to her.

'Good afternoon, Kathleen,' Hud says as we stop in front of the fierce-looking fifty-something, elegant redhead, standing with her legs apart.

She looks down at his beer, gives his suit a visual appraisal. 'Good afternoon, Mr Briar. Who's your friend?'

Hud puts his arm around me and now I'm wondering if he's not a little lubricated. 'This is Jake Walsh. He's a rookie.'

'First-round draft pick. I saw. Congratulations, Mr Walsh, welcome to Canyon.'

I grin. *Man, she makes me nervous.* 'Thank you, ma'am. Good to meet you.'

We shake hands. 'What can I do for you gentlemen?'

'We, uh,' Briar begins, and behind Kathleen, Harmony appears. As she does so, Briar straightens. I wonder if Kathleen has heard the rumours about those two. 'We were thinking that perhaps, you could let the squad socialise a little with the rest of the guests. Seems a little unfair to keep them all cooped up over here, don't you think? I'm sure everyone would behave themselves.'

'It is a wedding, after all,' I add, and I feel all eyes on me and Hud.

Kathleen looks to Harmony, as though to confer. The girl with the corkscrew curls has come over and is holding her hands in a prayer position. Harmony gives a shrug, but her expression remains unreadable.

Kathleen clicks her tongue. After what seems like an eternity, she says, 'I'll allow it, but just this once.' She raises her eyes, looking over the crowd of guests. 'I'll talk to Sam,' she then mutters, more to herself. 'And only because this is a wedding.'

Hudson gives a nod. 'Thank you, Kathleen.'

'It's Ms Lafferty to you, Mr Briar.'

'Ms Lafferty,' Hud corrects himself, standing to one side, but a pleased smile is threatening to explode onto his lips.

'Girls, you can mingle if you want,' Harmony instructs and within a second the group breaks up, the girls all walking over to the main group. 'Please remember to exercise CMC decorum.'

I glance at Hud. His eyes are fixed on Harmony. For the first time, I think I see the whisper of a smile on her lips, but I can't hear their conversation as the girl with corkscrew curls is now standing squarely in my face.

'Hi, I'm Jewel,' she beams. 'And this is my friend, Ren.'

My heart starts to pound. I grip my glass. So I guess it's 'Ren' for short.

'Hey, Jewel,' I say, and she shakes me by the hand. 'Hi, Ren.'

Serenity holds out her hand. I swear, when I shake it, it sends little lightning bolts racing up my spine. But something's off, because she's not making eye contact, and it hits me that she's pretending not to know me. The disappointment hits me with the force of a high tackle. Before I know it, Serenity's excusing herself, leaving me alone with Jewel.

This was not in the plan.

'So, how you finding Canyon?' Jewel asks me. 'I'm new here myself.'

I turn my head. Serenity's walking back across the lawn away from me. 'Oh yeah? Um— where you from originally?'

'Missouri. St Louis. It's always been a dream of mine to qualify for the CMC.'

'Why's that?'

She gives a dramatic shrug, but she's still grinning at me. 'The prestige, I guess. CMC is the best cheer squad in the whole of the NFL.'

She's cute. Her hair is a mass of spring coils and the way they bounce around distracts me a bit. But she's still not who I wanna be talking to. I glance across at Hudson and Harmony. Hud's removed his sunglasses, and I swear – the way he looks at her – I've never seen a guy more ga-ga for a woman in my life. It makes me happy that we were able to engineer this.

Jewel is still talking when I find myself sneaking glances across the lawn to my left, trying to see what happened to Serenity. That's when I witness Sam Conway in her mother-of-the-bride outfit walking our way, the heels of her shoes sinking a fraction into the lawn with each step, and it's only after a moment that I realize she's making a beeline for me.

When she stops in front of us, Jewel hangs up whatever she was saying, mid-sentence. Her back goes straight but her grin remains fixed, and it's obvious she's kind of terrified.

'Hello to you both,' Samantha Conway breathes with an effortless smile that exudes inauthenticity. 'Young lady, I wondered if I could borrow Jake for a second?'

'Of course!' Jewel beams at her and grants me a little wave as she skips off across the lawn. I wish I could tap out of this conversation and follow her, because my spidey-sense tells me where Jewel goes, Serenity will be.

I've met Sam Conway before, when I had my official welcome to the Mutineers following the draft. I had to hold up a signed shirt and have some photographs with Sam and her father. A former player himself, Hank Conway is, by all accounts, a decent man.

'Thank you so much for coming,' Samantha says. She has a stain of lipstick on her teeth. Up close, it seems like she's indulged in a little Botox.

'You're welcome, ma'am, thank you for inviting me.'

'Did you bring a date?'

'Uh, I brought my sister. I kind of abandoned her a minute ago, I should probably try and find her.'

'I'm sure she'll be fine. I just wanted to have a quiet word.'

'About football?'

She purses her lips. 'About my daughter, Lemon.'

Oh god. Anything but Lemon.

'Uhh—'

'Look, I won't beat around the bush here, seeing as you don't seem to have a girlfriend. Jake, I would very much appreciate it if you could take my Lemon to dinner one night.'

I hold her gaze, swallowing hard. I don't want to give my true feelings away, not when this woman is technically my boss and I've only played two pre-season games for the Mutineers. But... What. The. Actual. Fuck?

I can feel my teammates' eyes on me. 'I, uh—'

'Look, hear me out. She can be a shy girl. But she's a heart of gold. Being my daughter, and given that her Daddy ain't around no more, I sometimes feel men are... well the fact that I'm her momma makes them nervous to ask her out.'

'Nervous?'

'Men are sometimes a little afraid of me, Jake.'

You don't say.

'All I'm asking for is one dinner,' she adds when I don't say anything – due to being lost for fucking words. 'Nothing too fancy, though my Lemon is known to have her mother's impeccable taste. The Country Club, right here, has an enchanting restaurant. Great steak.'

Her smile is fixed, like the Botox is stopping it from being any wider, and there isn't a single wrinkle in that forehead. How the hell did I end up in this situation?

'Hank adores his granddaughter. Did I mention that?'

Holy fuck. *Was that a threat? That if I don't be nice to his granddaughter, Hank Conway will have a word with Coach and have me dropped from the team?*

'Sure, I can take Lemon to dinner,' I say, and my throat sticks when the words come out. 'Should I— Do you wanna—'

'Why don't you ask Lemon for her number? Before you go home. That would be just fine. Thank you, Jake. And everybody is real pleased with your performance on the field so far. Keep it up.'

When I watch her walk across the lawn, I swear a little part of me dies on the inside. Hudson and Harmony are gone and I'm standing on a patch of grass all alone.

'Where'd you go?' River asks me when I eventually find her hanging out near the bar, at a table on her own. She doesn't look happy. I pull out a chair.

'I am so sorry. I was helping out a teammate before I got cornered by Samantha Conway.'

'Right. Can we go now?'

She glances over her shoulder, looking uncomfortable. 'What's up?' I ask.

'Two of the waiters are in my high school class.'

'They are? Did you talk to them?'

'No. They were pointing at me and laughing. I only agreed to come with you to be nice. I didn't expect to see anybody I knew here. Now my whole class is gonna think it's normal for me to hang out at places like the Country Club.'

'Do you know their names?'

'One of them. His name's Scottie Lincoln. He's a soccer player.' Her eyes well up and now I feel like shit for leaving her. 'Can we go now?' she asks again.

'There's the whole wedding breakfast to sit through. We can't leave yet.'

River groans, massaging her forehead.

I rub her arm. 'I'm sure those guys weren't laughing *at* you. They prolly didn't even recognize you.'

'Oh, they recognized me. And now everybody at school will know I was here.'

'So what? It's just a wedding.'

'I didn't wanna be singled out, Jake! I just wanted to blend in and be like everybody else. Do you know how hard it is to transfer schools before senior year?'

She looks like she's gonna cry. 'I get it. I'm sorry. This is all my fault. Look, we'll just stay for a little food then get an Uber home, okay? Is that alright?'

She nods stiffly, holding the tears on the inside. 'You wanna hear somethin' funny?' I say.

'What?' she asks.

'You know the bridesmaid I pointed out? Lemon? Samantha Conway wants me to take Lemon to dinner.'

River brightens, wipes her eyes. 'You are not serious. She looks like a crazed stalker.'

'A crazed stalker who I now have to ask out on a date.'

'Woah. Is she, like, gonna arrange it or something?'

'She wants me to ask Lemon to her face.'

'That's insane.'

'All true. Cheered you up, though, didn't it? And if you see anybody laughing at you again, tell me. They'll have me to deal with.'

I hold my smile, but in my mind, my sister is right. Something tells me Lemon Conway has more than a little crush on me, and that taking her out on one date is not gonna spell the end of this. She's the boss's granddaughter. She has power over me already, and I've barely said a word to the girl. Worse still is that I've been at this wedding for what seems like a decade, and I haven't even gotten to speak to Serenity yet. I look around, hoping to catch a glimpse.

Except she's nowhere to be seen.

Chapter Nine

Serenity

I'm standing in a corner at the back of the main house, at the French doors that open out onto a pretty veranda. The wedding breakfast is over. There's an open bar and for two hundred guests, this party is just getting started. The light outside is beginning to fade. In a separate part of the grounds at the Country Club, a grand festival tent over a dance floor is decorated with pretty, twinkling fairy lights. Behind it, palm trees surround a network of narrow paths leading to a golf course.

I check the time on my phone. I gotta be back at Surly's in three hours. I need to check in at home with my dad first, maybe grab him some dinner from some of the hors d'oeuvres that are still being circulated on platters, even though we all just ate a delicious three-course meal.

I've been keeping my head down. Some of the CMC are tearing it up on the dance floor, alongside some of the Mutineers players and their partners. Even Kathleen is busting some moves. Jewel tried to persuade me, but I don't have the heart right now.

I swallow. I feel like the worst kind of buzzkill.

I straighten when I see him. Brody Conway in deep conversation with another man. He stops on the veranda and Brody places one hand on the man's shoulder as the two shake hands. I sink further into the shadows, but the moment he's alone he raises his eyes to me.

I turn and bolt, crashing into a waiter carrying a tray of hors d'oeuvres.

'Oh! Oh my god, I'm so sorry!' I exclaim.

The waiter looks at me. He looks at *all* of me, his eyes burning a trail down my body, yet he can't be more than sixteen or seventeen.

'Don't worry about it,' he smirks.

'Get this cleaned up,' a voice commands from behind me, and for a moment, my eyes drift shut. It's the voice from Surly's. If I needed confirmation, that was it.

'Yes, sir,' the waiter says. He drops to his knees and begins picking up all the food.

I feel one hand curl around my bicep. I stiffen. My skin crawls. I can't look. I can't have him recognize me.

'Hello there,' the voice says behind me.

The lump is back in my throat. His other hand goes to the small of my back.

'Hurry it up,' Brody barks at the waiter, who doubles the speed of his movements, gets to his feet and scarpers.

'Well, this is a pleasant surprise... *Brandy*.'

I turn my head. Raise my eyes to his. No, he can't. It can't be that he knows me.

'I don't know what you're talking about,' I breathe.

'Oh, I'd know those eyes any place, sugar. Think I prefer you as a blonde.'

I yank my arm away, take a step back. He's younger than I thought. Not even thirty. Thick, dark brows with a pointed nose.

'You gonna tell me your real name now?'

'No.'

His eyes darken. 'Now that you're here... I believe it won't take me long to find out. You're one of the rookies, no? So come on now. You know who I am. It's only right that we share.'

'I got no interest sharing anything with you.'

Without warning, he grabs my arm again, yanking me into the next-door room. I stifle a squeal. Inside, it's a study with rows of bookshelves, though the lights are all off except for a small table lamp. Sweat breaks out on my upper lip. I can feel my heart thundering in my chest. He turns his head to one side.

'Brandy Velvet,' he says again, and there's a wickedness to his tone. 'You know, you were the final part of my bachelor party gift? Your boss is a very generous man. And he told me you were his best girl. Tell me... does he know Brandy's also a cheerleader for the Canyon Mutineers?'

The truth is that I asked Kale's permission to audition. He wouldn't care whether somebody recognized me or not, so long as I keep the dollar bills rolling in at the club. He's not letting me go anytime soon.

But Brody Conway is a different story. He *is* the Mutineers. He could turn around and tell his mother and Kathleen what I really do for a living. Men like him are supposed to go to the high-class strip joints over on the east side of town, not down-and-out venues like Surly's on the west side. Men like Brody Conway aren't supposed to know men like Kale McCoy.

'He knows,' I whisper, and Brody takes a step closer.

'Figure you've kept Kathleen in the dark?'

He can tell by the look on my face that I don't like this road he's going down.

'You don't wanna give me your real name, Brandy, why, that's fine. You wanna play games with me, you go right ahead. I don't have to tell Kathleen a damn thing. Or my momma. But I know where to find you, Brandy Velvet. And you know what? I can't get enough of these curves, that ass. So, I plan on getting me some of that sweet, sweet sugar again.'

He's so close I can smell the food on his breath, mixed with his cologne. His fingers stroke my side at my waist.

'You just got married,' I whisper.

'The new Mrs Conway... she's very understanding of my needs.'

I swallow.

'I like you… Brandy Velvet. I'll be thinking of you on my honeymoon when I'm with my wife. I'll be sure to pay you a visit soon as I get back.'

The hand at my waist slides down, cupping my ass. He pulls me closer, and I thrust him away. He laughs at that, then backs away before he ducks out the door. I stay still for some moments, trying to stem the flow of tears threatening to spill over onto my cheeks.

I gotta get outta here.

I head to the dance floor, raise my head to get Kathleen's attention. She sees me and moves to the side. There's a cocktail in her hand.

'I don't feel so good,' I tell her. 'You think it would be alright if I called an Uber and headed on home?'

'Oh, honey, you're sure you're alright?' Kathleen exclaims over the music and she's searching my face. Her eyes are glassy. 'Can we get you anything?'

'Maybe I just need to lie down.'

'Well, sure, honey. You'll be alright on your own? I'd like to hear that you made it home safe.'

'I can send you a message.'

'You do that.'

I wave to some of my squad mates, including Angel, Shawny and Persia. Harmony is nowhere to be found, and I can't see Jewel anywhere either. On my way out, I sneak past the buffet table, scooping up a few items for Dad, wrapping them in a paper napkin. I call an Uber and head out front to the parking lot, keeping close to the house where the light spills over the sidewalk, under the shade of some palm trees. I can hear the cicadas over the music floating up to the stars. Brody Conway's words stick in my mind and I'm close to tears again. I just need to get home, then get to Surly's for the start of my shift.

At the sound of footsteps, I turn.

'There you are,' a voice says. 'I've been looking all over for you.'

Jake Walsh stops about five paces in front of me, a wide grin on his face. But it fades when he sees me. 'Are you alright?'

I force a smile. I'm not sure I can deal with Mr Wholesome right now. 'I'm fine. Heading on home.'

He glances back at the club house, toward the dance floor and the open bar. 'Already?'

'I'm, uh— I'm real tired.'

He looks to the paper napkin in my hands, the food held inside threatening to spill out over the sidewalk. 'And hungry too, by the looks of it.'

I feel the base of my neck start to prickle. 'Oh, I, uh—'

'Oh, I didn't mean anything by it. I practically sleepwalk to the fridge every night.'

I keep my eyes down. I tried not to engage with him today. Not to hurt his feelings or nothing, but I know the question he wants to ask me, and I already know what my answer has to be. Plus, Jewel clearly has a crush on him. But standing here, looking all nervous… man, he's too cute. He does things to my insides, and other places too.

'That was real nice of you earlier. You and Hudson Briar, talking to Kathleen like that. Harmony looked so happy.'

'Well, it was my goal to talk to you, but that didn't exactly work out how I planned. You left me with your friend.'

'Jewel. She's a rookie, like me.'

'She's nice, but no offense, I don't want her phone number.'

'Jake—'

He shifts his position. 'It's alright. Guess I'm starting to get the message.'

'Look, I'm not a rulebreaker, alright. I'm not rebellious, or anything. I'm not even brave—'

'One date,' he says. 'Let me take you on one date. Outside of Canyon, we'll set it up so nobody can see us. Nobody has to know. Please, Ren. Can I call you Ren?'

I bite my lip. Mr Wholesome is making this so damn hard on me.

'You can call me Ren. Was that your sister you came here with? What's her name?'

'River. She's still in high school. So, what do you say? Can I take you out?'

'Outside of Canyon? Where?'

'I'll make a plan. Come by the diner and give you instructions. Just one date.'

I stifle a laugh. 'One date and you'll leave me alone?'

In the dim light, I think I see him blush. 'Well, I uh—' He falters, rubs the back of his neck. 'I was hoping if you had a good time, you might give me a second shot.'

'Guess you'd better really impress me, then.'

'I'll put my heart and soul into it, that's a promise.'

I laugh. 'I'm still not giving you my number, Jake Walsh.'

He holds up his palms, accepting my terms. 'No numbers. Got it. Yes ma'am.'

This guy's so sweet he could give me a cavity.

'So is that a yes?' he asks hopefully.

I don't know what possesses me to even consider this idea, because it's crazy. I'm crazy.

My Uber pulls up. 'I gotta go,' I tell him.

'Please don't leave me hangin'.'

'It's a yes,' I tell him, and he punches his fist in the air. 'Nobody, but *nobody*, can know. Not even your sister.'

He seals his lips with an invisible zipper. How can a guy who can tackle literally anyone on a football field be so dorky and adorable?

'Not even River,' he repeats. 'My lips are sealed.'

He takes a step and opens the car door for me. It's the only thing that separates us and I linger on the sidewalk.

'I'll wait for your visit, then,' I say. 'To the diner.'

'When's your next shift?'

'Monday morning. Early.'

'Monday, I have practice. What time do you get off?'

'I'm there most days. My shifts finish around four.'

He frowns at me. 'You work too hard. Okay, so I'll be there. Monday after practice. Save some eggs for me.'

I go to get in the car, but something stops me. 'Why do you wanna go out with me? Is it just because I'm CMC?'

'No,' he states. 'Absolutely not.'

'Then why?' I think about Brody Conway and his words come back to haunt me. 'Don't answer that. Curves and ass. Right?'

'I was gonna say your smile.'

Now I feel bad for not thinking more highly of him. He runs his fingers through his hair.

'You should be getting back to the party,' I tell him. 'Goodnight.'

'Goodnight, Ren,' he says and when I'm in the car, he closes the door behind me. The Uber driver doesn't give me a chance to wave him goodbye, so I turn around on the back seat and wave through the rear windshield. He waves me off and I almost feel excited that I don't have to wait long to see him again.

—

'Ren? That you?'

The screen door creaks as I open it. I finish sending a message to Kathleen to confirm my safe return home. Little does she know, I'm heading out again.

'It's me, Dad.'

'Where you been all day?'

'A fancy wedding. I told you, remember? I brought you some food.'

I go directly to the kitchen and fetch him a plate. I unwrap the paper napkin and empty the contents into the middle. Some of the food from the buffet table got crushed on my way home, and the ones that were warm are now cold. I put it all in the microwave and go to the fridge to pour him a glass of milk. Then I deliver everything to the couch. He's watching baseball again with his feet up.

'Thank you, sweet pea,' he murmurs as I crouch down next to him. 'You at Surly's tonight?'

'Uh-huh.'

'Again? When was the last time they gave you the night off?'

'We talked about this. Sooner I pay back the debt, sooner I can be done with it.'

He bows his head. 'I hate that you have to dance there 'cause of me. I hate goddamn Kale McCoy.'

I lean forward, kissing his forehead. We don't talk about the particulars. What I must do for tips to pay off his debt. 'Well, I couldn't bear the alternative.'

'I'm grateful to you, sweetheart. Promise you're still being careful out there…'

'I am, Daddy. I can handle myself. How's the breathing today?'

Around the same time Momma left, Dad started having trouble breathing. He was diagnosed with emphysema. It was just another reason I couldn't leave.

'It was okay, sugar pie. I should be the one taking care of you. Not the other way around.' He eats another one of the hors d'oeuvres, his gaze drifting back to the baseball. 'How fancy was the wedding?'

'Country Club fancy.'

'Who all was getting married?'

My stomach performs a somersault. 'Brody Conway. You know, as in the Mutineer Conways?'

He shakes his head. 'I know 'em. More money than sense.'

I need to get moving. 'Don't wait up for me, okay?'

Upstairs, while I change outta my dress, my phone pings. I unlock the screen to find an unknown number has sent me a message.

I open it up. It's a screenshot of my official photograph from the CMC, the one that's on the website. With a single message beneath.

> *When it comes to the Mutineers, I have the highest security clearance. Every employee. Everything I need to know is at my fingertips.*

My throat goes dry. It's him.
    And he's making a point.
    Brody Conway's not gonna leave me alone in a hurry.

Chapter Ten

Jake

Monday afternoon, I check my watch. It's three forty-five. Sweat dapples my brow. I've come straight from cone drills and traffic across town has been a bitch. I just pray I haven't missed her.

When I pull up in the parking lot at The Bounty, it's five minutes before four. I swing open the door to find the diner bursting at the seams with customers. I search the room. My gaze falls on Serenity and I breathe a sigh of relief. She's still here.

There are no free tables, so I take a seat at the bar. I look over at her. She's rushed off her feet. I pick up a menu, though instead of deciding what to order, I watch her out the corner of my eye. Even her fake smiles are cute.

River texted me and asked if I wanted to go see a movie with her after school, seeing as she didn't have any friends in Canyon. I felt guilty turning her down, when I didn't have an excuse that meant I could be truthful. I told her I was going to hang out with some of my teammates, except she asked me who and I fudged a response.

'Excuse me, can we get a selfie?'

I turn my head. There's a woman standing there with her teenage son, holding up her phone. The kid looks embarrassed. I panic, thinking I can't get tagged in a photo taken at Serenity's place of work.

'I, uhh... Not to sound rude, but I don't really say yes to selfies. Would you take an autograph?'

She looks a little annoyed at first. Her son takes off his Mutineers cap.

'Do you have a pen?' I ask.

The woman looks blank, like she's expecting me to carry one.

'Here,' a voice says to my right, and I find Serenity is behind the bar, holding out a black Sharpie.

I give her a wide grin. 'Thank you.'

I still find it weird, that strangers would want my name on their stuff. Still, the kid looks pleased and thanks me when I sign his cap. His mom puts her phone away.

'Seriously, what kind of major league athlete doesn't carry a marker around?' Serenity asks when they're gone and I hand her back the pen, though she's smiling when she says it.

'Not this one, clearly.'

'That the first time you got asked for your autograph?'

'No, I just… lesson learned. Always carry a pen. What about you? You ever get asked for an autograph?'

There's a woman at the other end of the bar trying to get her attention. The apples of Serenity's cheeks look pink and dewy, and it's hard not to focus on her lips and think about what it must be like to kiss them.

'We had to pay a visit to an old folks' home last week. I signed a T-shirt for a raffle, does that count?'

'Sure, it does.'

'Miss!'

The woman at the end of the bar looks irate.

'I'll be right there,' Serenity replies in the sweetest tone, though the look she gives me tells me she's exasperated.

'Your shift ends soon, right? Can we talk?'

'Can't be seen with you, Jake. You know the rules.'

She's already walking around the other side of the bar with a pay machine. As she passes me, I whisper, 'Then how do I give you the details for our date?'

She reaches into her apron, passes me back the Sharpie, then leans over me, grabs a paper napkin and places it in front of me on the bar. 'Write it down,' she says.

'But we didn't even agree on a day yet.'

The woman yells again. 'Miss! The check!'

'How about Friday night?' I suggest.

'It's Labor Day weekend. CMC is taking part in the Mayor's parade. How 'bout the Friday after?'

I hate that she's making me wait to spend time with her. 'I guess.'

'Would you settle for the Friday afternoon? Pick me up from here at four?'

'Done.'

'You won't be needing this, then,' she says. 'Now get out of here before somebody asks for another selfie.'

She takes her pen and doesn't give me another backward look. I watch the woman at the other end of the bar chew her out and I'm mad on Serenity's behalf. The girl has two fucking jobs, cheerleader and waitress, neither of which appear to be very well-paid.

So, despite my reluctance, I leave.

-

'Hey, son,' my dad calls from the living room where he's watching baseball. 'How was practice?'

I toss my bag down on the carpet. 'Hey. All good.'

Mom's voice floats through from the kitchen. 'Jake? Jakey, is that you, honey?'

'Hi, Ma,' I say, raising my voice.

'You didn't call what's-her-name,' Dad grunts at me, and his eyes don't stray from the TV.

'What?'

'Your mom saw her at tennis class. You know, the weather girl.'

'Oh. Right.'

Mom appears from the kitchen clutching what looks like pink lemonade. 'Hey, sweetie, how was practice? You want a drink?'

I take the glass and down the contents. 'Thanks, Ma.'

'Somebody's thirsty. We thought you'd be home earlier.'

I hand her back my empty glass. This is why I sometimes regret bringing my entire family with me to Canyon. 'You don't need to track my movements every minute of the day.'

'I saw Olivia at my tennis class today. She told me you never called her.'

'She was nice, Ma, but I didn't wanna ask her out on a date.'

'Why not? Why would you not wanna go out with a girl like that?'

Because you chose her for me, I think to myself. *Plus, I got somebody else in my sights.*

'I'm serious, honey,' Mom continues, and I see Dad roll his eyes. 'One, she's gorgeous. Two, she's *very* well-educated. Three, she got that job at the TV station she went for.'

'So now she'll actually *be* a weather girl?' Dad pipes up with a chuckle.

'Four—'

'There's a four?'

'I've seen the kind of girls these players like to date. You know, with their fillers and their Instagram pages and *all* dripping with jewellery…'

'What's wrong with any of that? Did you meet Dalton Briar's wife, Ally? She seems pretty down-to-earth to me.'

'I'm just trying to help you make good choices, sweetheart.'

'I don't need your help, Ma. Like I told you, I'll find my own girlfriend, alright? Where's Riv?'

'Upstairs. Sulking.'

'Why's she sulking?'

'Oh, you know. New school, lotta kids already know each other. Some of her classmates aren't going easy on her.'

I grimace. I suspect that's because of me. 'I'll go talk to her.'

I swipe up my bag, and head upstairs on River's side of the house. I can hear music emanating from behind her closed door.

I knock hard. 'Hey, can I come in?'

A moment later, the door opens. River pokes her head out. Behind her I can still see boxes piled up.

'You know when you move somewhere new,' I say, 'it's customary to unpack.'

She gives me a look like I can go to hell. 'Hey, jackass, you're back. Did you have fun with your teammates?'

'Sure. Getting to know 'em a bit.'

'Which ones?'

'Uhhh... Dorsey and Grayson.'

'You didn't spend very long hanging out.'

I shrug. 'We hit the gym, you know. Talked about guy stuff. How was school? Those kids still bothering you some?'

River rolls her eyes. 'I'm keeping a tally of the number of times I get asked for tickets to the game.'

'Which is how many?'

She disappears then comes back with her school textbook. There's about thirty tally marks in groups of five. 'Yikes. Maybe I can hook you up.'

'Uh-uh. No way. The only people I would take to a game are the ones who *don't* ask me for tickets.'

'Okay, well... you wanna catch that movie now?'

Her brow creeps up her forehead. 'You're serious? His majesty actually wants to hang out with me now?'

I give her a mock bow. 'He does.'

She gives a shrug. 'Fine. But you're buying the popcorn.'

—

On Thursday, for our game against the Las Vegas Raiders, I arrive at the Danube Stadium in my sweats, only to find I must do this weird pap walk past a bunch of guys with cameras.

'It's called your game day outfit!' Zach Dorsey cackles in the locker room when I complain about it.

'I play football, I'm not here for the fashion show.'

'Dude, soon you gonna get designers sending you shit to wear, instead of you showing up like you just rolled outta bed.'

I pull at my jersey – one that I've had since my first year of college football – and notice that Hud Briar just swaggered in wearing a bright blue matching two-piece with a huge designer logo on the front. Expensive headphones hang around his neck and his sunglasses are still on.

'Now that's what I'm talking about,' Dorsey tells me. 'You gotta know how to make an entrance.'

'Noted,' I say, and I hate the way my voice falters.

I'm excited for the game. I'm more excited that I get to see Serenity again. I haven't seen her since our last brief encounter at the diner. I got everything planned out for our big date.

'Walsh!' I hear from across the other side of the locker room, and I snap to attention.

'Yes, Coach?'

'Don't get changed yet. Head on upstairs. Ms Conway would like to see you in her office.'

The moment he says it, my body goes rigid, and all my teammates are hollering and whistling in my direction. I feel my cheeks flare hot. I still haven't asked Lemon out on a date, like I was supposed to.

I get a bunch of slaps on the back as I head for the door. Others ruffle my hair. I hate that I feel like the kid in my own workplace. The one who everybody laughs at. Hud Briar gives me a wolfish grin. He's chewing gum and still hasn't removed those damn glasses.

'Got any advice?' I ask him.

'Other than take Lemon Conway out on a date and show her a good time? Unless you wanna get benched for the rest of your season? Sorry, man, no. No advice.'

My feet are like lead weights as I climb the stairs to the main offices from the first floor. On route, several people I don't know wanna shake my hand. I can hear the crowds already.

River and my parents are somewhere out there in their seats, but we don't get free tickets for the game. Some of my teammates have a suite, but I'm nowhere near that level yet.

'I'll let Ms Conway know you're here,' a woman says to me when I arrive.

My stomach's a ball of nerves. It's been almost a week since Sam Conway dropped a colossal hint that I should ask her daughter out, and since that moment, all I've thought about is Serenity Harper. Lemon hasn't even entered my mind, not once.

'You can go on in,' the woman says.

I inhale, force my legs to move. I should be getting ready for the game with my teammates and resentment sits squarely in my gut. If I'd have known that my first-round draft pick was all down to a crush, I'd have gone with another team. Except now I've signed a contract.

'Jake,' Sam Conway says as I enter, and takes off her glasses. 'Thanks for taking the time to come up here. Have a seat.'

'Is there something I can help you with, ma'am?'

She produces a smile that I think is meant to put me at ease. I guess ticket sales are what paid for those straight, white teeth. I've only met this woman a few times, but I've heard the rumours. If she's nice to you it's because she wants something.

'Good luck out there today. We're so pleased to have you here. I just wanted to ask if you'd thought any more about our conversation at my son's wedding.'

A lump balloons in my throat and I swallow it down. 'You mean about Lemon?'

'It's just that you gave me the impression that you were gonna talk to her.'

I wanna tell her that I've met a girl already, a girl who I intend to make my girlfriend, except that, right now, when out the back of her office I can see the lines of people entering the stadium, I know I can't argue with her.

'I'm sorry, ma'am, I hadn't gotten around to it yet.'

'So, you will still ask her.'

That's a statement, not a question. 'If that's what you want me to do, ma'am.'

'Oh no, please, keep me out of it,' Sam Conway says with a wave of her hand. 'But I really would appreciate it.'

'I better go get ready for the game,' I tell her, getting back to my feet.

'Of course. Give 'em hell out there, champ. Thank you, Jake.'

I give her a nod and I'm out the door before I know it. I take a left and nearly crash into Lemon herself.

'Oh!' she exclaims, and almost drops the folders held in her arms.

'Sorry, sorry,' I say, before it hits me that this was the set-up all along. Apparently, this is my cue.

'It's Lemon, right?' I say.

She looks thrilled. Like, beside herself. Her blonde hair is scraped back into a high ponytail, held in place by a giant polka dot bow, her dark roots just visible underneath. 'You remembered me, Jake Walsh.' She grins at me, which reminds me simultaneously that she knows exactly who I am.

I'm a dead man if I don't do this. 'Sure, why wouldn't I remember?'

'Oh, aren't you sweet,' she says, elongating the sound of the double 'e' before she descends into giggling laughter.

'Say, can I take your phone number?' I ask as I rub the back of my neck and it feels like I'm reading from a script, like this is the way I get to keep my place on the Mutineers starting line-up.

She seems to feign shock, like for sure she didn't see that one coming. *Yeah, right.*

'Why, of course you can!' she squeals and takes out her phone. 'Why don't you give me yours and I'll call you right now.'

I watch her enter my name into her contacts. She holds out her handset. I catch the eager look in her eye as I type in my number. Once I've saved it, she calls me, and I feel my phone vibrate in my pocket.

'Maybe we could go for a drink sometime?' I say, and I feel like a robot going through the motions.

She stands too close to me and grins so hard that I can see both her upper and lower teeth. 'I would *love* that,' she says.

'So, I'll… uh, message you?'

'I'll await your message.'

She walks backward away from me and flirtatiously waggles her fingers in farewell. Her nails are peach-colored, and it matches her shade of lipstick.

'Bye, Jake,' she hums and makes a phone shape with her fingers. 'Call me. And good luck out there.'

—

Back downstairs in the locker room, Dalton's already giving his pep talk as I walk in. Coach makes eyes at me to hurry the fuck up, and within a few minutes, I've thrown on my compression shirt, padded shirt, number fourteen jersey, pants and white stockings. I tie my cleats then grab my helmet and gloves and join in the huddle.

'Doin' alright?' Dalton asks me after as he wipes eye black on my cheeks with his thumbs. 'You all set?'

'All set, Cap,' I say, because right now, I need to focus on the game.

Dalton lowers his voice. 'Was it what we thought?'

'Yup,' I say miserably.

'We'd fight your corner if you'd turned her down, you know,' Dalton says. 'Not the first time Lemon's been known to pull a stunt like this on her grandfather's watch. She's got him wrapped around her little finger.'

'Seriously?'

'Two years ago, she was down bad for Will over there. Told everyone who would listen.' He dips his head toward our bearded, towering left guard, Will Dent. Dent raises his head, like he knows we're talking about him. 'Only difference is, Will got engaged to his now-wife, so Lemon had to back off. Want my advice? Get yourself a girl and make it obvious you're into her. Send a message but try to let Lemon down gently. The Conways are not the kind of people you wanna piss off before the season's even started.'

A shout goes up. Coach Holland. We're hitting the field, our game versus the Raiders about to begin. This is it. Our final pre-season game. Dalton gives me a single nod and readies himself to lead us to the tunnel.

I can hear wild cheering over the thud of the music when my name is announced as part of the Mutineers' starting line-up, the excitement in the crowd. I picture my parents and River out there.

I wish I could say my focus had switched solely to football, but the moment I see her, I can't not look. The sight of her almost stops me in my tracks.

Serenity's right on the fifty-yard line. Her body writhes in effortlessly choreographed moves, along with her fellow cheerleaders. As she shakes her navy and white pom-poms, her hair cascades down her back.

And all I can think to myself is, one day I'm gonna ask her to dance for me like that. Because right now, I don't want her dancing for anybody else.

Just me.

And yet, watching her from the corner of my eye, she doesn't look my way. Not once.

Getting her to like me is gonna be harder than I thought.

Chapter Eleven

Serenity

I check my watch. It's two minutes after four. As I was getting changed in the bathrooms at The Bounty, my phone chimed with a message.

> Block me again, Serenity, and I'll show the whole of Canyon what you really are.

I wasn't afraid to block him. Not the first time. I thought blocking Brody Conway's number without sending a response would make my stance clear. That I wasn't going to play games with him. Almost a week of silence, and after the Labor Day weekend, today he comes back on a new number, and with these words.

He hasn't said that it's him, but I know that it is. He's been careful not to give anything away. There's been no mention of when he might return from his honeymoon, or when he might next appear at Surly's. None of that. But the idea makes me wanna vomit. His aim is to keep me on my toes. Every shift this week, I've been anxious that I'll walk through the door to find Brody Conway returned from his honeymoon and waiting for me to writhe around in his lap.

I straighten up as Jake Walsh pulls into the parking lot in his black Chevy pickup. I haven't seen him in a while. Behind the windshield, I can see that he's wearing a cap and shades, and if I'd convinced myself not to be worried about anything, then I was wrong. He's the guy everyone's talking about right now, the guy who scored two touchdowns in the last pre-season game. And I know once I get inside that truck beside him, I'm in trouble, because he's gonna be sweet, and charming, and probably handsome as hell. I check around me, hoist my bag onto my shoulder and head for the vehicle, reminding myself that no matter what, this is a one-shot deal. I'm wearing tight-fitting jeans, a sequinned top, tan leather jacket and cowgirl boots, because I don't have the first clue what we are doing for our date.

'Hey.' He beams at me as I slam the door behind me.

'Right on time,' I reply coolly, pushing my bag down between my legs into the footwell.

He takes off his sunglasses. Handsome, *check*.

'You look nice,' he says, glancing down at my outfit. 'Really nice.'

Charming? *Check*.

He's wearing a short-sleeved chequered shirt and standard blue workman's jeans. Wholesome, of course. The cotton material clings to his impressive biceps, but I can tell by the look in his eyes that he's nervous, like he's lost a degree of confidence since our last conversation.

Just one date. Don't get the hots for this guy. One date is all you agreed to, and one date is all Jake Walsh is gonna get. Cheerleaders can't date football players. End of story. You don't need any more complications in your life right now, Ren.

'Thanks,' I say, and run my fingers over the dash. 'Sweet ride.'

'It's, uh… well, it's brand new. I mean… I bought it when I moved to Canyon.'

'Looks expensive.'

'Uh… I guess. I mean, I guess… yeah, it was pretty expensive.'

'But that's like lunch money for you though, right?'

Oh god. What did I just do? I've rendered him speechless.

I squeeze my eyes shut. 'That was so rude. I'm sorry. I don't even know why I just said that.'

He laughs. I'm waiting on him to move the car. 'It's cool. We can talk about money on a first date.'

'We definitely cannot talk about money. So where are we going?'

He puts his sunglasses back on and turns his cap around. Checks the mirrors before moving off. 'So, I did some research. I found this lake.'

I raise my brow. 'Lake Thunder?'

He moves out into a busy lane. 'That's the one. You know it?'

'I used to go there as a kid. Everybody around here did. 'Til this guy nearly died from swimming in the water there and they discovered it was badly polluted. Everybody stopped going after that. They say now the only people who go there are junkies and prowlers. That, and the odd gator.'

He's silent for a moment. 'You're serious?' he then says, looking my way with one hand resting on the wheel.

I bite my lip. 'Did you have a back-up plan?'

I see his throat working as we take the road north out of Canyon. 'Uh-uh. Not exactly. No back-up plan. You got any ideas where else we could go?'

'We can go to the lake. It's alright. I'd like to see it after all these years. What were you planning on us doing?'

We stop at some lights, and he rubs the back of his neck, something I've noticed him do before. 'Well, I got us a picnic. Thought we could sit in the back and watch the sun go down. Get to know one another better.'

Sweet? *Double check.*

My heart sinks a little because there's something I gotta tell him. 'I, uh, is it okay to drop me back at the diner around eight?'

His look is one of surprise. 'You got another shift?'

'No, I… I just have other plans is all. Is that alright?'

Guilt washes through me. How do I even begin to be honest with this man about who I really am?

'Sure,' he says, but I can hear the waver in his tone, like he's disappointed. 'I can do that.'

'It's just that… I mean, I live with my dad and… he needs me to take care of him sometimes.'

This time he nods his head, maybe in relief. We're moving again. 'Your dad, does he work?'

'Not anymore. He has emphysema.'

'I'm sorry to hear that.'

'He smoked cigarettes all his life. He's given it all up now.'

'What about your mom?'

'She left when I turned seventeen. She's in Mexico right now. At least she was. I haven't seen her in a while. What about your parents?'

'They live in Canyon. They moved with me after I got drafted. But it's not like… you know… I wouldn't want you to see me as that guy who still lives with his parents.'

'Well, we're even, because I still live with mine.'

He laughs. 'That's true.'

We lapse into silence as he navigates traffic. I glance to my left, let my eyes drift down his body, but not in a way that's obvious. And it's truly something to behold. Jake Walsh is a protector-type, with broad shoulders and sculpted arms, a strong jawline. *A body made for footballing greatness*, is how Jewel described him.

I don't need a protector, or some white knight. I told myself during my shift at The Bounty that I would remain indifferent. That whatever happened on this so-called date, I'd roll with it and let him down easy at the end. It's not like we can ever be anything while I'm a CMC squad member.

Yet I don't remember the last time I got asked out on a proper date. If you don't count the regulars who sit beside the stage at Surly's who ask me to have a drink with them while they're slipping twenty bucks into the hemline of my panties, or the college kids at the diner who ask if I'm single. Jake Walsh is a decent guy, and talented no less. He's a guy you'd be proud to call your boyfriend. And I like the idea of having somebody in my life that I can trust. But every time I let my guard down, I'm reminded of the contract I've signed with the Mutineers that says this guy is off limits. Even sitting in his car right now is against the rules. If Kathleen saw me now, or Samantha Conway, they'd fire me faster than I could say 'guilty'.

I'm in dangerous territory. I can't fall for this guy. I can't show any interest. It's safer to keep my distance.

'Good game yesterday,' I say. 'That was a nice touchdown.'

'Yeah, we got the win, that was the main thing.'

'Don't underestimate yourself. Everybody was talking about you when it was all over.'

He looks over at me. It's a shy smile he gives me. 'I don't know about that. It was a team effort.'

I wanna say that I call bullshit. That he was one of the main reasons the Mutineers took the game. Everybody said so. But rather than heap praise on him like everybody else, I ask him a different question.

'How do you recover? After a game like that?'

'Uhm. Last night I went back to the training facility for an ice bath. I didn't sleep all that much. Still sore this morning too. Training room was packed full of guys. Heat therapy, stretches, deep massage, all that. What about you? Those high kicks must murder your glutes, huh?'

I bite back a laugh. 'Glutes, adductors… medial hamstrings, deltoids… I didn't think you'd be focused much on what the cheerleaders are doing.'

He beams. 'Oh, hell yeah. You guys steal the show. Really. Feels the whole stadium showed up to see what you guys can do. I mean, I'm blown away. It's the way you're all so in sync.'

The way he takes one hand off the wheel at a time and twists his wrists in some pretend dance moves has me giggling like I'm back in high school.

'Seriously,' he continues, maybe pleased that he's managed to make me laugh. 'That's good muscle knowledge. Where'd you learn to back flip like that?'

'Gym class, when I was ten.'

'And the dance moves?'

'Gymnastics from I-don't-remember-when. Modern dance classes in middle school. My mom was a keen dancer.'

'Was the CMC always the goal?'

'It's one of the best squads in the whole country. Last year I didn't make the cut. Made me a little more determined to make it this year.'

'Why'd you wanna be a cheerleader?'

I look out of the window. I can see the mountains in the distance, the sun already dipping low on the horizon. The traffic that was around us in the city center has petered out. 'I don't know. Growing up in Canyon… the Mutineers were… they were like this shining light. Something unattainable. I never went to any games. We couldn't afford it. But I saw the girls in a show once, and on TV, and I knew I could dance as well as they could. They were so glamorous. I wanted to be like them. To have all that positivity.'

'And now you are like them,' he says. Except I remember that he doesn't know me at all, because while I might be like my squad mates, there are things that none of them know about me. Those same things that I can't tell Jake Walsh about.

When we get to the lake, I find myself craning my neck, remembering how it used to be. The access road is the same dirt track that we used to go down when I was a kid, but years of abandonment have caused the ground to become overgrown. Tree branches scrape against the pickup's windows. The same, too, can be said for the lake. While there used to be a large clearing with sun loungers lined up in neat rows, and a food truck for refreshments, now there's just long grass, ragweed and old tire tracks.

Jake stops the car, leans over to the glove and opens it. He pulls out a small compass and checks it, before returning it and reversing the pickup into a small patch of rocky ground. When he kills the engine, the inside of the cab falls silent.

'Okay, this place looked a whole lot different in my mind's eye,' Jake declares after a moment.

I press my lips together and try not to laugh. I can just about hear the lapping of water at the lakeside.

'Are we safe here, do you think?' he continues.

'Maybe 'til the sun goes down. Then we prolly shouldn't stick around.'

'Okay, uh… are you hungry?'

'Sure, I could eat.'

'Then wait here for a minute.'

He scrambles out the vehicle. I hear the back of the truck being opened, and the sound of shoes on metal. There are some scuffling sounds, and minutes later, he comes and opens my side door for me.

'Okay, I'm all set,' he announces. 'You can come out now.'

I step down from the pickup and follow him as he walks backward to the rear of the vehicle. At the back, in the cargo bed, he's laid blankets and placed a couple of bottles of Budweiser beer in a bucket. There are snacks too: corn chips and guac, popcorn and dipped pretzels.

'I know it's not the height of sophistication,' he stutters, his hand once more running to the back of his neck. 'But given our situation… I can't take you to a restaurant and, well… well, the truth is, I can't cook for shit.'

'It's perfect,' I say as I climb up into the back and take a seat to one side.

He follows. 'Keep one eye out for prowlers. And hungry gators.'

I laugh. 'I'm pretty sure you could take 'em.'

'The prowlers or the gators? A guy comes rushing at me with no helmet or a player's jersey on, I'd prolly run the other way.'

'I don't know about that.'

He passes me a bottle of beer, once he's twisted off the cap, and does the same for himself. The sky is a pretty shade of coral pink, the clouds stretching out like fish scales.

'Can I ask you something? How come you... how come you don't have a boyfriend? I mean, a girl like you...' He pulls a face.

'A girl like me, what?'

For a moment, he looks awkward. 'A girl like you should have guys lining up around the corner just to date you.'

I shrug. 'Maybe they ask me, but I don't want to date them,' I tell him. *Because the kind of guys who ask me are not the kind of guys I wanna go out with.* 'I could say the same about you. Young, good-looking, NFL player...'

'You think I'm good-looking?'

'I was speaking in general terms.'

He laughs at that. 'That's cool. I know my place.'

'I'm serious. You could have any girl you wanted right now. You could take her out to a fancy restaurant—'

'And not bring her to a polluted lake...'

I love that he gets this twinkle in his eye when he laughs.

'I'm serious, Jake. If they found out about this, I figure you'd just get a rap on the knuckles. Me, I'd potentially lose my job.'

He sobers up. 'I'm not gonna let that happen. I promise you that. But it's not gonna stop me from asking you to go out with me.'

I feel like whatever invisible barriers I've built up, he just knocked another one down. I sip my beer. My shoulders tense involuntarily.

'Are you cold?' he says. 'Do you need another jacket?'

Before I can answer, he's hopped over the side of the truck. I can't help but admire his lithe movements, his well-built frame. I hear a door to the cab open, and he comes back with a jacket. He climbs back up to the cargo bed.

'Here, put this on.'

I put down my beer. I take it, hold it up for a moment. It's a varsity jacket from Penn State.

I thank him and slide my arms inside. The jacket's too big for me. 'I never dated a guy who went to college before.'

'You didn't? What kind of guys did you date? Am I allowed to ask?'

'My high school boyfriend fixed up cars. That was my most serious relationship. I did internet dating for a while when I was younger, but I never met anybody who stuck around. Did you have a girlfriend in college?'

'Uh. Two serious relationships. That's about it.' He blushes. 'So, I guess now you know my body count.'

'We're talking body counts on a first date?'

His cheeks grow redder. 'I didn't plan on that coming out. I mean... you don't have to tell me yours.'

I bite my lip and wrap his coat tighter around me. I feel at ease with him, but I've slept with more people than he has, and I didn't come out here to damage his ego.

'One day I will,' I say.

I draw my knees up to my chest. Long shadows stretch over the lake, the sky now a shade of burnt orange.

'Can I make a confession?' he then says.

'Sure.'

'Just between you and me. It's kind of a weird situation, but I don't wanna keep it from you, because it's kinda awkward.'

I search his face. 'What is it?'

He blows out his cheeks. Looks into the sunset. 'Samantha Conway asked me to take her daughter out on a date.'

I blink at him. 'She *what*?'

'You know Lemon Conway?'

'I know *of* her.'

'At that wedding. Sam Conway asked me if I could ask Lemon out. And I didn't do it, so yesterday, before the game, she hauls me into her office and asks me again.'

My brow crawls up my forehead. 'Did you wanna ask Lemon out on a date?'

He straightens. 'You think I'd be here with you if I did? I mean, nobody's said so, but it kind of feels like I'm being pressured into it. Somebody said that Lemon's down bad for me. But... what if that's the reason I'm here. That the reason the Mutineers drafted me is because Lemon persuaded her grandfather to go for me.'

'That's crazy. You're one of the most talented players out there. Everybody says so. That's why you got picked.'

'Then why do I get the feeling that if I don't take Lemon out, I might get benched?'

'No way. Did somebody tell you that?'

He sighs wearily. 'Maybe it's my mind playing tricks on me.'

We're silent for a moment.

'So, do what you've been asked,' I tell him. 'Take Lemon out on one date, show her a nice time, then let her down gently.'

It sounds ironic, because in my mind, until this moment, that's exactly what I planned to do to Jake. Except hearing him talk, he does things to my insides. He has me imagining all kinds of things I shouldn't be picturing right now.

'You think that's what I should do?'

'You keep everybody happy. I mean, don't show her a really good time or anything.'

The corner of his mouth curves upwards. 'I'm thinking fancy restaurant. No trips to the lake.'

I stifle a giggle. He watches me. He has my stomach doing somersaults.

'You haven't eaten anything,' he says after a moment, changing the subject.

I pick up a chip and nibble on it. 'I'm not real hungry.'

'River told me the rules about your shorts.'

I meet his stare. 'She did?'

'She watched some documentary. She was outraged.'

He's referring to the fact that the CMC are only issued with one size of made-to-measure hotpants for our uniform. We're not allowed to go up or down a size. It's part of the contract. Gain any weight and you're out.

'I like the sound of River.'

'I'd love for you to meet her one day.'

He's still watching me. My breath hitches in my throat. When I raise my eyes to his, an electric current shoots through me, then I panic and look away, back toward the sunset. He's been so truthful with me. Where do I even start to show him the same level of honesty he's shown me?

'You got any brothers or sisters?' he asks.

'Just me.'

We lapse into silence.

'Is there something wrong?' he asks quietly.

I push my hair behind my ears and put my bottle of beer back down. Swallow the lump in my throat. When I glance back at him, light from the sun illuminates his skin. He really is a golden boy: handsome, considerate, sweet-natured. My stomach churns. I can tell by the look in his eyes that he wants me. And it's not just my contract. If he knew who I really was, and what I do most nights of the week, would he still wanna date me?

'Jake, I can't do this,' I say, and there's a quiver in my tone. 'It's in my contract. I'm not supposed to be here. I'm not supposed to be near you.'

He looks down, his fingers peeling the label on his bottle of Bud.

'And... I can't be near you,' I add.

There's a muscle in his jaw that pulses. He keeps his eyes down, then wipes his hand over his head to remove his cap. 'In my head, I had this all figured out,' he says. 'I hoped you wouldn't be able to resist me, and we'd come up with some kind of... I don't know. There'd be some way we could see each other in secret. But, hey, guess I gotta accept that I'm not that irresistible.'

He's smiling, but it's a sad smile. Guilt washes over me.

'I hope you know I'd never try to get you into trouble. I know what being in the CMC means to you.'

'I know. And I'm grateful. If I wasn't a CMC, I'd say yes in a heartbeat.'

Except he wouldn't know the truth.

'You would?' He smiles and suddenly my cheeks feel warm. 'How 'bout I quit the NFL? What then?'

I laugh because the idea is too crazy. Now our situation just feels impossible.

'Maybe Lemon'll turn out to be a real nice girl,' I say.

He looks miserable. 'Lemon isn't who I want.'

The sun has dipped on the horizon. It's getting dark and the breeze rustles in the long grass.

'Take me back to the diner?' I ask lightly.

He nods. 'Sure.'

By the time we've packed up, darkness has fallen, and it feels like the right time to leave the lake. We complete the ride back to The Bounty mostly in silence. Jake parks the truck in the farthest corner of the parking lot so I can see inside the diner windows. It's a slow Friday night, one of the waitresses is leaning up against the bar studying her nails.

He kills the engine. I'm still wearing his varsity jacket, so I wriggle out of it. Even the tiniest sound is amplified inside the cab. It's hard to make out Jake's expression in the shadows.

'I'm sorry if I wasted your time,' I say after a moment.

He looks to me then shakes his head. 'You haven't wasted my time. I'm just happy that I got to spend some time alone with you. And I respect your choice. No matter how much I wish that clause in your contract didn't exist. If it didn't... I'd be asking you to be my girl right now.'

Something stirs in my chest. If that clause in my contract didn't exist, I'm pretty sure I'd be saying yes to his offer.

'I don't mean to pressure you or anything,' he continues. 'I just meant that... I think... I think you're really something, Serenity. And I can't get you out of my head.'

His fingers brush up against mine on the leather seat. The sensation causes me to catch my breath. I'm caught up in an overwhelming desire to kiss and be kissed by him.

In the shadows, he holds my gaze. It's so quiet inside the cab, I can hear us both breathing.

'Can I kiss you?' he murmurs.

I can't say yes. I don't want to say no. When he leans closer, I don't move. He lifts one hand, the backs of his fingers brushing my cheek in a feather-light touch.

The seats crunch underneath him as he moves closer still. My heart races. I know I should leave now, before things get complicated, but I'm anchored, caught by his gaze and the way he's bearing down on me.

I swallow. I want to tell him that this has to be a kiss goodbye, but I'm craving it, now that his mouth is inches from my own. I want his lips on mine.

'Serenity—' he whispers, and the ache in his tone obliterates the last of my resistance. I nod my head and lean into him, just as my lips part. His fingers slide into my hair at the nape of my neck and in that moment, I'm crying out on the inside for him to lay claim to my mouth. Finally, when he lowers his head, his lips touch mine and I realize the extent of my denial.

I've wanted this. I've *needed* this.

I've made out with guys before. In high school, I had jocks yank me into their laps then slam their mouths into mine and call it kissing. I've been on dates with guys who only want to get to third base, mostly bypassing the foreplay. So much that I think that, until this moment, I don't think I've ever really been *kissed*.

Jake's big hands are at my waist, easing me closer. The altered angle deepens our kiss. His tongue tastes mine, and it sets off a spark, underneath my skin bursting into flames.

Heat surges through me. He gathers me up, and his low moan into my mouth tells me he wants this as much as I do. In the silence, the noises our kissing makes are broadcast around the cab: every slick peak as we break apart, every trembled breath. His hands are on my thighs. My intimate muscles are taut, and I can feel myself getting wet for him.

The shrill whimper that emerges from the back of my throat brings me to my senses. It's the sound of unbridled desire. I don't remember the last time I made that sound. Without warning, I pull away from his grasp and go for the passenger door. I grab my things and step down from the pickup into the cool night air, forgetting to close the door behind me. I run directly over to my car, parked away from the light from the diner interior. I fumble for my key and my fingers tremble when I yank open the door.

I hit the gas as soon as I'm able. I practically fly out of there. I glimpse the passenger door of his pickup and it's still open.

Guilt rinses me for the second time tonight. I shouldn't have kissed him. I shouldn't have let him kiss me.

But dang if that wasn't the best kiss of my entire life.

—

'Where the hell you been, Ren?' Jaxon complains at me as he follows me backstage at Surly's. 'I've been leaving you messages all afternoon.'

I don't stop walking. 'I'm sorry,' I say, as in the dressing room, two of the other girls voice their objections and cover up at his presence. 'I'm early, aren't I?'

Jaxon lowers his voice. 'Boss is here. We needed extras.'

I pull off my jacket and frown at him. 'For what?'

'He's got guests. Out back.'

I stiffen. It means the games room is in use. Kale is likely hosting a few rounds of Texas Hold 'Em. 'What guests?'

'I don't know names, do I? But he told me to tell you to get your ass back there soon as you arrived. You're not performing out front tonight.'

I swallow. I remember Brody Conway's message to me earlier today. *I'll tell the whole of Canyon what you really are*, and I know it in my heart. He's back from honeymoon, and he's *here*.

'Oh, and Ren?' Jaxon says.

'What?'

'Boss says lose the hair tonight. *Au naturel*. Or whatever it is they say. No wig.'

My stomach performs a somersault. Jaxon leaves and I swiftly change into tonight's outfit: a red corset trimmed with black lace and matching high-waisted panties. I pull on my thigh-high patent leather boots and raise both zippers. I add to my makeup that I was already wearing for my date with Jake. Then I defy Kale's orders and pull on a long, straight, mahogany wig and fix it into place.

Behind me, I hear Misty suck air through her teeth. 'Somebody's playing with fire tonight,' she says.

'I'll fight my corner if I have to,' is my response.

'Sweetheart, why would you try and antagonize him on purpose? You know what he's like.'

'It's this cheerleader thing,' I sigh. 'Every time I go out there, I'm scared somebody's gonna recognize me.'

'You knew the risk, honey pie.'

She's not helping. 'I *like* being a cheerleader.'

'Should have thought about that before you sent in your application.'

I whirl around and fix my gaze on her tired eyes. 'I can't have dreams now? My life is over until I pay this debt, is that it? Should I have let my Daddy die?'

She raises her brows and goes back to fixing her makeup.

Minutes later, Jaxon opens the door to the back room. The lights are low, other than a dim light over the poker table. Four men surround it, smoke from their cigars swirling about their heads. One of them is Kale McCoy. He has his back to me. Mila – or *Candy Chains* – sits closely at his side. I step forward. The two men sitting to his left and right I don't recognize.

Talia – otherwise known as *Baby Bullets* – is in one of their laps, and Kaycee – dancer name, *Heaven Scent* – has her arms draped around the other's shoulders. She's wearing long pearl necklaces and is sucking on a lollipop. Only one man sits alone. I don't need to see his face to know who it is. I'd recognize those long fingers anywhere.

'Finally,' Kale's voice rings out as he looks back at me. 'There she is! Where you been Brandy? Come on over, have a seat.'

My heart pitter-patters. There's already a chair waiting for me at the table.

When Brody Conway's face comes into view, he meets my gaze.

'Evening, Brandy,' he says. 'We've been expecting you, come sit.'

The other girls say nothing. They know their role here is not to make conversation. I make my way around the table and take my seat. Brody Conway's arm snakes around my waist. With his other hand, he pushes my hair back and places a single kiss at the nape of my neck.

The hand that was around my waist slides back out then slips between my legs, at the apex of my thighs. His little finger teases the lace material of my panties, and I tense.

Kale makes eyes at me. I already know he's lowkey angry with me. To appease him, I lean into Brody Conway's body, drape my arms about his shoulders and give him a sweet smile.

I haven't let myself think about it, but when the men settle back into their poker game, my mind wanders back to my kiss with Jake. Little pleasure bolts go through me. I feel guilty for running, for leaving abruptly in the way that I did.

In my dreams, I get to date Jake Walsh. I get to have him. I get to kiss him again.

But my reality is something very different.

I can't give in to what he craves. But lord knows, I want to.

Chapter Twelve

Jake

'Push it, Walsh, come on. Punch it, let's go.'

Saturday, at the training center, after practice without pads, we're supposed to be doing gentle workouts on arms, chest, back and shoulders ahead of Monday night's opener. Lying on my back with my knees bent, my biceps tremble as I lift the barbell bar. Ordinarily, three fifty pounds would not be an issue for me, but today I'm fighting it.

Maybe it's lack of sleep. Who the hell could sleep after a kiss like that?

Fuck.

Rodrigo, one of the Mutineers' training staff, supports me at the last second, helping me lift the bar onto the stand either side of my head. I pull myself up.

'I need a minute.' I wince, exhaling, out of breath.

'S'up with you today?'

I massage my right shoulder. 'Not feelin' it.'

'Sore?'

'Naw. Just. Can't focus.'

'Take a moment.'

I get to my feet, sling my towel round my neck. Sweat drips from my chin. All around me in the gym, my teammates are concentrating on their final preparations before tomorrow's rest day. Because the season is about to start proper, and their sole focus is on that. The game. The win.

That's where my focus should be. But it's not. I'm focused on Serenity Harper. Anything else in my brain gets pushed out by her. Her smell. The taste of her. The way she moaned against my mouth when I kissed her.

I know I should say it was just a kiss. That I need to conquer this. But that kiss rocked my world. That kiss was sent from heaven. I've never had a kiss that blew my mind before. That I was so into. That left me wanting so much more.

She says she doesn't want me. Or that she can't have me. Or that I can't have her. But if that's true, how come she kissed me back like that?

I can't not have her. I can't just leave it. I need to see her again.

Yet, like Cinderella, she went racing out into the night. And it took every fiber in my body to let her go.

I can't let her go again.

'Walsh!'

My eyes snap up. Coach Holland is glaring at me. 'Fuck you doing just standing there?'

'Just need a minute, Coach.'

'You've had a minute! Get back to the workout!'

'Uh... sure, Coach.'

As the training session comes to an end, I hang back, putting in some extra minutes, hoping that the more I work out, the less I'll think about her. I'm last to hit the showers in the locker room, wet towels everywhere, most of the guys heading off for some family time, steam swirling about the place. My teammates bid me goodbye as they leave. I take a seat on the bench by my locker, a towel around my waist and stare at the floor.

'S'up, rookie?' I hear a gruff voice say, and Hud Briar is standing there, naked as the day he was born, his rock-hard body and bulging quads on show, all his tattoos and his impressive dick just hanging out for all to see. I don't know how long I've been sitting here, staring at nothing, trying to figure out my next move.

'Looks like you got somethin' on your mind,' he says as he turns. I note he's got a mirror hanging in his locker. He's grown a beard these last few weeks and is really into his personal grooming.

'Somethin' botherin' you?' he asks.

If anyone knows how I might feel right now, it's him.

I watch the last of my teammates depart, bidding us farewell. We'll see one another again tomorrow night at the hotel venue in time for curfew. It's just the two of us left. 'Let's say I met a woman...' I begin, and in his mirror, I think I see him smirk.

He shakes his head. 'I knew it. Guy only looks that miserable when there's a woman involved. What's the issue? It's not Lemon Conway, is it?'

'No, it's not Lemon. Though I do have to take her out tonight, by order of her mother.'

He sucks his teeth. 'Good luck with that. Back to the other lady. What's the deal?'

'She's not... technically, she's not available.'

His expression grows more serious. 'She's not a cheerleader, is she? Don't go there, man. That way misery lies, my friend. Believe me, I speak from experience.'

I try not to react. I'm not planning on sharing that information with anyone, even River. 'What happened with Harmony after the wedding? Anything?'

He pulls on a pair of underwear and adjusts himself. 'She reminded me why I should be out there tryna bag me a hottie and wife her up.'

I look at him. He hangs his head.

'Have you guys ever... gotten physical?'

'This ain't the tenth grade, Walsh. You can ask if I ever had sex with her.'

'Have you?'

He looks to the side. I see a muscle flinch in his jaw. He puts his hands on his hips. 'I fucking wish,' he sighs. 'Can't get past second base, despite my best efforts. This is the longest dry spell of my entire life. My dick thinks my hand is a pussy. And, like a fuckin' idiot… I can't move on.'

'Why not?'

He pinches his nose, shakes his head. 'You know, that fucking Erasmus dude was right. Can't live with women. Can't live without 'em.'

'I don't know how you do it.'

'Shit, I don't either. I don't know when Harmony Reese set up camp in my brain. Somewhere along the line, she claimed permanent residency. But she's also a loyal slave to the CMC and Kathleen Motherfucking Lafferty and her motherfucking rules.' His voice goes quiet and he turns back to his locker. 'And now I'm a motherfucking slave to her,' he mutters. 'Look, whoever she is, man, I recommend you extricate yourself now, before it's too late. Before you'd do anything for her, just to have her smile at you.'

I'm pretty sure I'm past that point already.

'You think I should cut ties?' I ask.

'Find somebody available. No controversy. Hey, maybe Lemon'll turn out to be a real nice girl.'

Why do people keep on saying that?

'If there's another guy involved, try and talk her into breakin' up with him. Don't be a cheat, man, that's not the answer either. If you're the one for her, she'll choose you. But women, they like to be pursued, you know? They like to feel like you're working for their attention. That they're desired.'

I raise my brow. I've been in what I thought were two serious relationships and nothing like that ever occurred to me. 'You think that's true?'

Hud is almost dressed. I'm still in my towel. 'Hell, yeah, it's true,' he says, pocketing his key chain. 'I saw the number of hoops my brother had to jump through just to get on a date with his wife, Ally. You put in the effort, she'll follow through, alright. If she's into you.'

'So… you think I shouldn't let it go?'

Hudson closes his locker with a bang. 'Okay, this conversation just got way too cryptic for me. I say if you like her, go get her.' He picks up his bag, holds up one finger. 'Except if she's CMC. Those girls, I recommend you stay well clear. Unless you wanna torture yourself for the next five years or whatever. I gotta go. Later, bruh.'

He puts on a pair of Ray-Bans and I bid Hudson farewell. Takes me a moment to realize that he gave completely conflicting advice. The locker room falls silent, save for the sound of water dripping from the showers.

I get dressed, but in my mind, I already know my answer.

CMC or not, there's no way I'm letting Serenity go.

—

On my route home, I drive out my way to The Bounty and pull up in the parking lot. I sit for a minute and watch through the windows. I can't see her. I leave the pickup and head for a copy shop on the other side of the road to purchase a pen, some paper and a bunch of envelopes. If she's not gonna give me her phone number, then I gotta go old school. Once I've got everything, I go back to my vehicle, get on my phone and spend an hour doing some research. When I'm happy everything's set up, I reach for the pen and scribble out my note. Takes me a few attempts until I'm happy.

The interior of the diner is quiet when I finally make it inside. I take a seat and watch as an older waitress brings me a menu.

'I'll just get a soda,' I say.

'That's all?' she asks.

'That's all.'

'Sure,' she says, keeping a hold on the menu as I order a Diet Coke with ice.

'Is Serenity here today?' I ask.

She shakes her head. 'She was here earlier. She left already.'

'Will you see her soon? You think you could give her something for me?'

She frowns. 'Uh. Sure, I guess?'

I pull out a sealed envelope with Serenity's name written on it and pass it to her. I think I see her lips twitch into a smile. I wait for my soda, and I can't stop my knee from skipping up and down. In the parking lot, my expensive pickup stands out.

I can't get away with coming here much longer.

—

When I get home, River's in the den watching TV with her feet up.

'You wanna go catch a movie or something?' she asks once we've exchanged hellos.

'Can't. Gotta take Lemon Conway out to dinner. I gotta go in a half hour.'

She throws her head back and covers her eyes. 'I forgot. You're so darn *nice*. And not even a little bit *dumb* for agreeing to this. Why you going so early anyway?'

'Told her I need my beauty sleep. Tomorrow night's curfew at a hotel before Monday night's opener.'

'I guess no nightcap for Lemon then.'

I pull a face. 'Like that was ever gonna happen.'

'So why are you even taking her out then?'

I give a pronounced shrug. 'When Samantha Conway asks you to do something... I guess you gotta go do it.'

River snorts. 'That's ridiculous. You know, she and Mom are like kindred spirits. Both tryna set you up on dates with girls you don't wanna go out with.'

I rub my eyes. I see Serenity's face staring back at me and hope she gets my note.

'How about you call somebody and get them to go see a movie with you?'

It's her turn to shrug. 'Maybe I'll ask Dad.'

'I was thinking somebody your own age.'

She goes quiet and pulls a thread on her jersey.

'There ain't a girl from school you could go hang out with?'

'Sure. Maybe.'

'Did you make a friend yet?'

'Mostly I just talk to the girls back in Philly.'

'I meant an in-person friend. Like IRL.'

'Don't you have to get dressed? You're gonna be late for Lemon.'

I look at my watch. 'Shit, I am.'

'Go, go, your majestic greatness,' she says and shoos me away. Her attention goes back to the TV.

-

I take the white Tesla to the Country Club, not the pickup. Technically, it's my Dad's Tesla, but I bought it. On arrival, the car is taken away by a valet.

I straighten out my shirt and jacket, blow my cheeks out. Last time I was stood in this spot, I was talking to Serenity. Now I'm here about to go on a date with a different woman altogether, and I can't get Serenity to go out with me.

I feel like all the staff's attention is on me when I say who I'm here to see. Maybe they feel sorry for me. I'm led through to a lounge area that I didn't see at the wedding. It looks a little tropical, the chairs surrounded by cheese plants. Lemon sits on a bar stool with her back to me. Her white dress is cut low in a V-shape all the way down her back. It occurs to me that if it was Serenity wearing that dress, I wouldn't be able to keep my hands off her. Yet, this is Lemon, and if I'm honest, it's a little dressy for a first date.

'Hey, handsome,' she says to me with a big grin on her face when she sees me, the same smile that bares all her teeth. 'You look *gorgeous*.'

I look down. I'm wearing a pretty standard shirt and tie matched with a pair of chinos. 'Thanks, Lemon. You look nice.'

I think I see a flash of disappointment in her eyes when I don't compliment her further. Yet I don't want to give her the wrong idea. This is a one-time only deal and I feel shitty enough about it already.

'Shall we have a drink at the bar before we go into dinner?'

She has this habit of looking deep into my eyes for longer than is necessary.

'Uh, sure. I can't really drink, what with Monday night's game being the season opener. I'll just have a soda.'

More soda. Lemon glowers at me playfully. 'My, my, aren't we a good boy?' she breathes, and just as I suspected, it feels like she's flirting with me off the bat. I don't understand why someone with her confidence couldn't ask me out on a date herself. She's a grown woman. Why her mother has to do the work for her, I'll never understand.

Lemon orders me a non-alcoholic cocktail and I ask her if she wants to move to seats by the window, shielded behind some more plant life and away from prying eyes.

'Are you interested much? In football?' I ask, once we've sat down.

'Oh, you know,' she says with a wink. 'I can't *not* be interested. My grandpappy force-fed me football my entire life. Can I try your drink?'

'Uhh, sure,' I say as I pass over the glass. She holds onto it and drinks from the straw, then puckers her lips. 'Ooh, I like that one,' she says. 'That's tasty.'

I look down at the drink. I need to get to the bottom of whether Lemon was the whole reason I was drafted by the Mutineers.

'So do you give your grandpappy your picks for the draft?'

She bats my question away with a wave of her hand. 'Oh, I mean, for sure, but he ain't ever gonna listen to the likes of little ol' me.'

A bubble of relief floats up in my chest.

'I mean most of the time...' she continues, and the bubble bursts. 'You wanna know the truth? I don't think he was one hundred per cent gonna pick you in the build-up to draft day. There were a *lotta* meetings.' She rolls her eyes as she says it. 'You know how it is. Everybody's got their own opinion. The coaching staff for sure wanted you, but my grandpappy needed a little... you know. A little push in the right direction. He took me out for lunch one day and said "*Lemon, gimme my answer*". So, in a way... I guess you could say that this year I had final say over who got picked.'

I sit with my back straight while she drinks. She seems like your average southern belle, yet there's something odd about her, like she's just saying all this to get attention. Maybe she's invented the whole thing. There's a sad look in her eye that I can't figure out.

'You're a franchise man,' she continues. 'You're gonna have a *looong* career with the Mutineers, I can tell.'

She averts her gaze as she drinks, almost like she doesn't wish to make eye contact with me. 'What's your role in the organization, Lemon?' I ask. 'I mean... what is it that you do?'

'Oh, I do plenty. I mean, my brother Brody, he got the brains. He's the future of the Mutineers brand, for sure. I work for my Momma. I do all kinds of things. I go where I'm needed. I know all the staff at the Danube on a first name basis.'

I nod my head. Seems like a pretty good way of saying she does nothing at all. 'Right. I guess, I mean, is that what you see yourself doing in life?'

'I wanted a career in fashion. But Momma says... it's better I stay in the family business. My grandpappy only has two grandchildren. Brody and me.'

'How old is your brother?'

'Twenty-seven. I'm twenty-three.'

'What about your father?'

She stiffens, then glowers at me. 'We do not talk about that man. He left. Then Momma cut him out of her life when he started seeing somebody else. He got remarried.'

Lemon's attention seems to waver. I look around the bar and it's quiet. My heart sinks because I want to be on a date with

Serenity, getting to know her better. No offense to Lemon, but I don't wanna be sat here. It's not like I'm ever gonna be her boyfriend.

I think about the note I left for Serenity at the diner. When she'll get it. If she'll read it. If she'll respond to my request.

Lemon's talking again. I know I should be listening.

I just want this so-called date to be over.

Chapter Thirteen

Serenity

Kathleen's command echoes across the locker room. 'Ladies! Get your poms and line up! Final checks!'

I'm all ready to go. In a quiet corner, poms at my feet, my back to the wall, I'm looking down at the small slip of paper concealed in my hand with Jake's neat handwriting on it. Staring at it makes my heart flutter, but the moment I hear Kathleen's voice, I refold the note, retrieve my poms and walk over to my locker. I secure it back inside my duffel bag and check that no one has seen me.

It's Monday night. First game of the official season. The Danube Stadium is packed to the rafters. There's a commotion as my squad mates have thrown down their makeup bags and hairbrushes, picked up their poms and lined up, side by side in one long line, which I join.

Kathleen raises her chin. We all follow her lead. As is customary, we stand with one leg out in front of the other, with our knees slightly bent.

She starts walking, hands behind her back. For a moment, I forget to breathe.

Further down the line, Kathleen stops. 'Persia, I thought I told you to do away with the caterpillar eyes?'

'The extra liner compliments my eye shape.'

'It's not regulation, sweetheart, go redo it, please. It makes your eyes look too dark.'

'But, Kathleen—'

'Better make it quick, Persia.'

Persia lets out a heavy sigh and stomps over to a mirror. I keep my smile fixed.

'Shawny, that hair makes you look like somethin' outta *Back to the Future*, sweetie, you're gonna have to tie it back. Maybe rethink your choice of shampoo.'

'Yes, Kathleen.'

Shawny moves.

'Angel, you got lipstick on your teeth.'

'Yes, Kathleen.'

'Leona, there're scuff marks on those boots. Either clean 'em off or get a new pair.'

'Yes, Kathleen.'

Leona dives in front of me. 'Okay, next. Serenity?'

'Yes, Kathleen,' I say, and my voice comes out shrill.

She looks me over. 'Very nice, good effort.'

'Thank you, Kathleen.'

She moves on and Jewel elbows me in my side, offering me an encouraging grin.

I swallow. We were at rehearsal all of Sunday afternoon, practicing our routines on the field. This morning, I headed to the diner for my usual early morning shift, only to be handed a sealed envelope with my name on it.

I sat down at a table just to open it, my fingers trembling, because I knew who it had to be from. Inside was Jake's note.

> *If I died tomorrow, I'd die happy, because you let me kiss you.*
>
> *You're on my mind, all the time.*
>
> *I can't let this go, but I respect that you might have to.*
>
> *But if there's still a chance, meet me on Friday at 5 p.m. at:*
>
> *Saltwood*
> *10309 Parkland View*

Canyon Rock

> *It's a cabin. The picture online shows it has a red mailbox. There's no driveway but it's down a slope, behind a line of pine trees.*
>
> *I'll be waiting. Hope to see you. Jake x*

Somewhere on the other side of this stadium, he's getting ready in the players' locker room. I haven't seen him since I ran away from his pickup.

And now he says he wants to see me again.

A half hour later, we're in the tunnel, in formation in two parallel lines, ready to make our entrance onto the field. Mutineers' staffers surround us with walkie-talkies. We're delayed, due to some kind of security issue; some wayward fan running onto the field. All around I can hear the noise of the crowd echoing above us. Kathleen is not happy, because our second number will overlap with the team's entrance.

Maybe it's because we're running late, but when I hear a commotion behind us – a clacking sound against the smooth concrete at my feet – I realize the players are lining up behind us in the rear of the tunnel. Their cleats hammer against the floor, each player holding onto his helmet, eye black on his face like war paint.

I glance back, my gaze searching. I crane my neck a little. I just want one glimpse of him.

Then he's there, partway back, his smooth navy-and-white number fourteen jersey clinging to his broad chest, made bigger by the shoulder pads. And for a second, our eyes meet. I lean out of line to my right to get a better look before—

WHAM.

The Mutineers' team mascot – a guy dressed from head to foot in this giant, ridiculous pirate-like outfit with stripes on the pants and a triangle hat – slams into the back of me and sends me sprawling to the floor.

The first thing I hear is dramatic gasps from all the girls. Ashlyn, a fifth-year veteran with long, wavy blonde hair with a pink hue, offers me her arm and tugs me back up.

'Sorry!' a voice shouts from inside the costume, as the mascot continues out of the tunnel onto the field.

'Conor McGrath, you're an asshole!' Shawny hollers after him and both Harmony and Kathleen's eyes flash in her direction.

'You okay?' Jewel asks me in a whisper.

I nod, dust myself off then glance back again for barely a second. Jake Walsh has a face like thunder, all his ire directed toward the opening of the tunnel, where Conor McGrath's waving mascot is being met by cheers from the crowd.

It's at that moment, I don't know if I can hold out. I don't know if I can continue to resist him.

Kathleen is given the green light. That's our cue. The sound from the crowd raises up a notch. The atmosphere thrums under the floodlights as we emerge into a packed stadium, to begin our opening number.

Monday Night Football. It feels like the whole of America is watching.

I want to look back at Jake. But I resist.

Girls Girls Girls begins over the sound system. My heart beats fast. The Danube has a natural grass pitch, rather than artificial turf. We use the full-length of the field for our routine, forming one line by linking arms over our shoulders so that the duration of the chorus is made up of synchronized high kicks. We bend and wind for the remainder, shaking our poms, so that the crowd is well and truly entertained.

I see Kathleen to one side of the field, wearing a mic. She indicates to Harmony that we're going straight into our second number, Guns N' Roses *Welcome to the Jungle*, and we're still dancing to the track when the players are announced over the sound system.

I'm facing the direction of the tunnel. I get a good view of Jake, emerging through dry ice, his image beamed onto the jumbotron above his head. He doesn't look at me, not for one second. He pulls on his helmet and runs right past me, his eyes steely, focused solely on the game.

It stays that way, for the duration.

And when it's over, the team walks away with the win.

Watching him, mud-splattered yet victorious, I know I can't hold out anymore.

—

Friday night, it's almost dark. In the car, I lean forward, one hand on my steering wheel, the other holding onto my phone and Jake's note. The way through Canyon Rock is winding, narrow and treacherous. Tall trees rise up on both sides.

Am I taking the right road?

The week has dragged. Every shift at The Bounty. Every dance on stage at Surly's, since Monday night. All building up to this moment. My request for a night off from the club was turned down by Kale.

I'm late. Jake's note said 5 p.m. but it's almost six now. I definitely took a wrong turn back there somewhere when I lost navigation, due to no signal.

I slow down when I see a crooked green-and-white sign pointing to the left. It reads 'Parkland View'. I hold my breath and switch on my indicators. This is the one.

There are no streetlamps out here. I slow right down and squint through the windshield because the trees cover the sky. The ground is uneven, making my C-Max rock from side to side.

Then I see light up ahead.

A cabin.

Just as he described.

There's no driveway, just a clearing, a steep incline beside a red mailbox. The cabin has a porch, and I recognize his pickup parked up outside the garage.

We're thirty miles north of central Canyon. Nobody is gonna see us out here.

I kill the engine and wait in the driver's seat. I exhale. There's no going back now.

I swallow when I see the front door open and Jake Walsh comes out onto the porch. He's wearing a fitted pale green T-shirt and grey flannel shorts and there's a smile of surprise on his face. He's had a haircut since Monday night's win.

My heart flutters. I shouldn't be here. I can't even stay that long.

I open my car door. I changed at the diner into jeans, boots and a red top. The top is like a corset, except a little more demure than something I would wear for a shift at Surly's. From the way his eyes roam over my body, I can tell that he likes it. I'm nervous, so I clasp my fingers together.

'Hey,' he says softly.

'Hey,' I say back, glancing around to double check that we're alone. There's more light further up the road, perhaps more cabins nestled in amongst the trees.

He walks down the porch steps, hands inside his pockets. 'I was beginning to think you weren't gonna show.'

I force my fingers apart and point behind me. 'Sorry. I got lost somewhere back there. Took a wrong turn.'

'So... you got my note?'

I nod my head once. I'm not sure I should confess how many times I've read it. 'I got it.'

He looks more nervous than I do. 'Would you like to come inside?'

'Sure.'

My phone is switched off, hidden away in the glove. I close and lock my car door and my lips twitch when I try not to smile.

'After you,' he says, holding out one hand.

I go ahead and climb the porch steps, walk through the open door. Inside, the cabin has wood floor, walls and beams. The décor is pretty, yet sparse, a set of deer horns mounted above a fireplace. There's a large brown couch with pillows.

'How did you find this place?' I ask.

'Oh. Uh. It's a rental. I paid up front. Got the keys for a couple' months.'

I can't conceal my surprise, because that says to me that he plans on making this a regular interlude. Unless he plans on inviting anybody else up here.

'Uh, are you hungry?' Jake asks. He clears his throat as he closes the front door behind us. 'I brought Chinese food. Do you like Chinese food?'

'Sure,' I say lightly, though if I'm honest I barely ever order takeout because it's too expensive. 'What did you order?'

One hand goes to the back of his neck. 'I got, uh... I didn't know what you'd like so I just ordered a variety of stuff. Kung Pao chicken, spring rolls, chilli wontons, firecracker spicy beef... that sorta thing. You're not a vegetarian, are you?'

'No, I'm not.'

'No nut allergies?'

'No, I'm good.'

'Can I get you a drink? A beer? A soda?'

'Soda's fine. Thanks.'

'Do you like Dr Pepper?'

'Sure.'

'Have a seat, I'll be right out.'

I pull off my jacket. He takes it and hangs it beside the door. I notice the beads of sweat at his temple. It's not warm in here, so my guess is he's nervous.

I sit down and wait. He comes back with my drink, then disappears again. I check my watch. I probably have about ninety minutes before I'm gonna need to head back into the city, and the thought leaves me a little miserable inside.

I can hear him heating food in the microwave. We don't really talk as Jake brings all the dishes out onto the table. I like that he's made so much effort.

'Thank you for this,' I say as he pulls me out a chair.

There it is: the hint of a smile. 'Guess I'm always tryna get you to eat.'

He takes a seat on the opposite side of the table, and I help myself to a small plate of food. He waits for me before serving himself.

'So, did you take Lemon out?' I ask as we start to eat.

'I did.'

'How was it?'

He gives an exaggerated nod. 'Uh… as I thought. She's… definitely not my type.'

I giggle. His gaze flits to mine. 'What did y'all talk about? Was she the reason you got drafted?'

'Honestly? Hard to tell.'

'Does it matter? I mean, you could take it as a compliment. You could say she's got a nose for talent.'

Finally, his shoulders relax. 'You think so?'

'If Monday night was anything to go by, you're the Mutineers' best hope of reaching the Super Bowl.'

'Is that what your friend Jewel says?'

I'm laughing again. 'Not just her. I heard them talking about you on Canyon radio. I pay attention. I may still not understand what's happening on that field but… I know if you're the one making the touchdowns, then there's a reason you were a first-round pick in the draft. And if Lemon told her granddaddy to go after you… I'm just saying. Maybe Lemon is smarter than everybody makes her out to be.'

'I think you're right. She is smart. Smart but lonely. I get the impression her family don't think so highly of her.'

I've heard the way her brother talks about his sister, so I know that's true.

'Do you like the food?' he asks.

'Delicious,' I say.

'You really have no idea what's going on on that field?'

I put down my fork. 'I mean... I'm learning. Jewel knows *a lot*. She comes from a family of football players. But at the end of the day, if the music starts playing, and my squad leader tells me to dance, then I just do as I'm told.'

He's watching me with a gentle expression. It was the same expression he had on his face the night he asked to kiss me, and it makes my belly flutter. 'Okay, one day I'm gonna teach you the rules of football,' he says.

'I'd like that,' I say, and I note that his gaze hasn't left mine.

And then the moment's gone. 'I couldn't believe that idiot Conor McGrath barging into you like that,' he scoffs. 'Wearing that dumbass costume.'

'I looked back, 'cause I was tryna look for you.'

'Really?'

'Did you not see me look back?'

'I thought it was a more general... you know, sweeping look, like a... take in the scene kind of a glance back.'

'Not really. I wanted to see you.'

We've stopped eating. I'm aware that we haven't talked about it. Our kiss a week ago.

He swallows. 'I bought us phones.'

'Phones?'

'Like cell phones. So we can message one another.'

'You mean like burner phones? Like in the movies?'

'Exactly. Dedicated phones so we can communicate. To get round the cheerleaders-can't-date-players problem. Then you don't ever have to give me your real phone number.'

My eyes go wide. He gets up and goes to a backpack that's over on a bench. He reaches inside for two cell phones. I abandon my food at the table and move closer to him, taking a seat on the couch.

'I hope you don't mind,' he says. 'I bought 'em from this store downtown. Set 'em both up. Put a secure PIN on 'em too. This one is zero, one, two, eight. January twenty-eight. It's my birthday. I didn't know your birthday.'

He hands me a phone and I punch in the number. 'July sixteen,' I tell him.

'I'll make that my code.'

I open up the phone. It's nicer than my ordinary handset. 'You bought these just for us?'

'Is that alright?'

I nod lightly. 'I guess.'

He's back to looking nervous. 'I mean... I didn't want you to risk anything. By talking to me. I figure I can't get away with coming to the diner too many more times either. And if you decide you don't wanna see me, then... well, I guess you got yourself a free phone.'

The words are out my mouth before I can stop them. 'You've really thought this through, huh?'

His smile is awkward, kinda crooked on his face. 'I've thought about it a lot. How we could do this... given our situation.' He pauses, his hands going into his pockets. 'I've thought about you a lot too.'

It's at that moment I'm done with conversation. I put down the phone and get to my feet. I sense this ain't a guy with a whole lotta experience in making the first move.

'See, here's the thing, Jake,' I murmur. 'I wanna do more than just talk to you.'

I wait. Watch as my words sink in. Something stirs between my thighs. I need to be kissed by him again.

I step closer. He abandons his phone, but his Adam's apple bobs up and down.

When I put my palms flat against his T-shirt, I feel a solid wall of muscle, on a level that's almost ridiculous. When I raise my chin, he dips his head. The initial moment our lips touch reminds me of a first kiss: a light, innocent brush, tentative, like nobody is quite brave enough to really go for it.

He takes my hand and leads me to the bedroom.

Standing opposite him, next to the massive bed with pristine white linen, I tug at his T-shirt. I want him to go for it already, the memory of our last kiss making my intimate muscles pull taut in need. When his lips meet mine proper, I forget all about the rules I'm supposed to follow, about the fact that I can't stay here tonight. While it feels like he's trying to be a gentleman at first, within a few seconds, it's like we're picking up where we left off inside his truck, pawing at one another, only this time it's with an acceptance that we're gonna take things further than that. My tongue tastes his and it sets off a chain reaction in me, the whimper that escapes my lips like a sound I don't even recognize. My head sags back as his lips go to my neck, but I'm greedy now and want more of him. My body's screaming for it.

I lift his T-shirt, running my fingers down the hard, muscular savannah that is his chest. He lets out a shaky breath. He tentatively fingers the hem of my top, and I help him lift it over my head. I'm wearing a pretty, strapless lace bra, baby pink and cut low, and I can tell by the way he looks at me that the swell of my breasts ignites something inside him. I reach around the back and unclip it, the bra falling away. I step closer, my nipples grazing his chest, sending pleasure shock waves through my abdomen.

'I wanna see you,' he whispers. 'It's hell not being able to talk to you.'

I press myself even closer to him, and he captures my lips with a rough moan. I arch my back a little and his hands palm the globes of my ass through the denim.

'Should I take these off?' I whisper against his mouth.

'Yes, yes, take 'em off,' is his eager response.

I unbutton my jeans, shimmy them over my hips until they drop to the floor. He helps me out of them, so that I'm down to my panties. Without warning, he swings me into his powerful arms and lowers me to the bed.

He crawls up my body and his kisses are deeper now. He's slowed things down, perhaps on purpose. We're not pawing at one another, but the atmosphere feels hot and heavy. He moves his mouth to my breasts, his tongue darting out as he licks and sucks at my nipples, taking his time to devour each one, and I run my fingers through the crisp hair at the nape of his neck.

His right hand drifts down my body. He shifts off me, encouraging me to open my thighs for him. He's gentle in his movements, a little innocent in a way, teasing yet unsure.

His fingers slip further downwards and graze the material of my panties. 'Wow, you're... they're... your panties, they're drenched,' he says, almost in surprise.

Then his fingers slip inside the material to touch me. I close my eyes. It's been so long since any man did this. My hips buck and I cry out at the sensations. He rubs my folds, and I slow my hips for him, encouraging his movements, willing him to find my clit and send me spiralling over the edge.

But instead, Jake returns to kissing me. 'I'm sorry it has to hurt the first time,' he whispers against my mouth and, less than a second later, my eyes fly open.

Chapter Fourteen

Jake

In my arms, Serenity goes rigid. I raise my head to look down at her and remove my fingers from between her thighs, which she then immediately clamps together. Her pretty green eyes are ablaze, blonde hair splayed out over the pillow.

'Y-you thought I was a virgin?' she questions, and that's when I know I've messed up.

I pull back a little and search her face. 'I... I figured you were, yes.'

She looks straight up horrified. Then she wriggles out from beside me and gets to her feet, covering her naked breasts with one arm, picking up her panties with her free hand.

'Why would you think that?' she blurts when I'm still on the bed. 'Why would you think I'm a virgin?'

I shift my body so I'm on my knees. My heart begins to hammer. 'I... it was just... at the lake, I said about my body count, and you didn't say anything, so I figured... I just thought—'

Her panties back on, she's picked up her bra. She turns her back and fastens it. 'I didn't say my body count because it was higher than yours, and I didn't wanna embarrass you!'

My stomach turns over. *Fuck*. 'Oh,' is all I can say.

She bends back down, grabs her jeans and tugs them over her hips.

'I need to go,' she mumbles.

'Wait, what?' I say and shoot to my feet. 'What do you mean, you need to go? We can talk about this. I'm sorry I thought you were a virgin.'

'I told you I had a boyfriend in high school!'

'So? That doesn't matter. Plenty of girls have a high school boyfriend and they don't sleep with them. Some girls wanna wait for the right guy to come along…'

In my mind, I'm tryna say something helpful but it doesn't seem to work because she's even more spun out. 'Jake, I don't know where you went to school, but in my high school, if you went with a guy, you *went* with a guy, if you know what I mean.' She violently shakes her head. 'I don't know why I came here,' she mutters. 'We don't know each other… at all.' She picks up her red top and pulls it over her head.

'Okay, I got it wrong, I'm an idiot. I'm sorry. We can talk about this.'

'I'm sorry,' she whispers, and there are tears in her eyes. 'I gotta go. I gotta be somewhere.'

I can't lose her, not for another week. 'Serenity, please. Don't leave. So, you've been with a couple of guys, it's all good, I'm totally cool with that.'

She puts one hand to her forehead, like she can't believe me. 'Eight. That's my body count, alright? If you really need to know it. Eight guys.'

Okay, I was not expecting her to say that. But it's too late because she's seen my reaction. I swallow.

'I lost my virginity at sixteen,' she says, maybe in her own defense. 'So, technically, that's one guy per year. So please don't get all judgy on me.'

'I'm not judging you, I swear it. I would never do that.'

'You already did! Look, I didn't grow up in this perfect little neighborhood like you! Where I come from, there were certain expectations placed on girls my age. Please. Let me go.'

I step out her way and she walks right by me, back into the cabin's living area, wiping her eyes. I struggle to pull on my shirt and go after her. 'Serenity, please, I just wanna talk. That's all.'

She grabs her things. I hover around her like a fly in the Texan heat.

She stops. When she speaks, her voice wavers. 'Jake, you're a really nice guy. Like… too nice. And I never meant to lead you on. But I shouldn't have come here tonight. I… I'm sorry.'

Then she looks to the floor.

'Serenity… look, I don't… I don't expect anything from you. All I wanna do is get to know you. Spend time with you. We don't have to do anything, just… hang out. Please. I can't stop thinking about you.'

Her eyes fill up again. She blinks back the tears.

'At least take the cell phone,' I say. I get it from the table and press the unit into her hand. I don't tell her that I can't handle another week without another word being exchanged between us. Before I let go, I relish the feeling of her fingers against mine.

She keeps her eyes on the floor, but nods her head.

'Stay with me,' I say.

'I'm sorry,' she says, before she turns and walks out the door.

When it slams behind her, I stop and stare. I could bet my heartrate's above 180 right now, the amount of adrenaline that's coursing through my body.

I've fucked up. Badly.

I hear her car engine, and for a moment, her headlights dance across the room as she pulls away, the sound of her tires crunching across the track.

Then she's gone.

I lower my body to the couch and cradle my head in my hands.

I groan, because I'm the biggest fucking idiot that ever lived.

How could I have got it so wrong? How could I have mistaken her for a virgin?

I raise my head. Because she's sweet, and I couldn't imagine any guy being good enough to get close enough to her. I was a long shot at best. Usually, my instincts are good, and I'm not gonna start doubting my judgement now. She passes the fucking Mom test. Hell, she's practically aced it already. And not that it matters what my mother thinks, but I know for a fact that Mom would love Serenity. And she's right, there are expectations on girls that I'll never be able to understand in the same way. There's more pressure on them. It's the same reason I worry about River and teenage guys who are total horndogs.

She felt so good in my arms. Better than good. Incredible. Everything about her. Her scent, her soft moans, the way she reacted to my hands. How wet she'd gotten for me. My whole life, I've never been so revved up for a girl before.

Eight guys. Shit. Four times my own number. And probability states that at least some of those were good lovers. Irrational insecurity has taken hold of me, more than I'd like to admit.

Man, I'm such a fuck-up. I grab the new phone. I consider all the stuff I wanna say to her, but then I pause, knowing that I need to think about this before I just type in the first thing that jumps into my head. This requires a considered response.

First and foremost… an apology.

—

A short time after, I'm behind the wheel in the pickup, heading back into Canyon, a heavy sensation in my gut, weighing me down. The cabin is all locked up. I take it at an easy pace. The last thing I want is for Ren to think I'm stalking her on the roads, if I were to catch up with her. I only wish she'd stayed so that I could have asked for her forgiveness.

The lights are all on when I roll into my driveway. I frown at the sight of a shiny, black Buick SUV out on the road in front of the house, a driver waiting in the front with the window rolled down. I look back to the house. Something is off.

When I walk through the door, I freeze. My parents are sitting side by side in the den. Opposite them is Sam Conway. Dad's back is straight, which it literally never is.

'Jake!' Mom squeals and jumps to her feet. 'Sweetie, where were you? We tried calling.'

To my left, Sam Conway also gets out of her chair, real slow. She's wearing a navy pant suit.

'Uhh, I'm sorry... I was hanging out with some of the guys,' I say.

'Ms Conway paid us the honor of an unexpected visit,' Mom says, the light in her eyes dancing.

'Hello, Jake,' Sam Conway says, her voice kinda breathy. 'Please forgive me for dropping in like this.'

'Not at all,' I say, but my top lip twitches involuntarily as she shakes me by the hand. 'I was hoping for a quiet word,' she says, and my heart sinks, because I know what this is gonna be about.

'We were all talkin' about how well you're doing on the field,' Mom pitches in.

'Absolutely,' Ms Conway says. 'My father is thrilled. We all are.'

'All the way to the playoffs,' Dad says out of support. 'Then maybe all the way to the Super Bowl.'

'Let's not get ahead of ourselves,' I say as I clear my throat. I need to get this conversation over with. 'Did you show Ms Conway the back yard?'

'No,' Mom says, looking to our guest. 'Would you like some more lemonade?'

Ms Conway's lips are pursed together. I'm guessing she didn't much appreciate the first round.

'I'm fine, really, you're too kind,' she says to my mother, but the smile doesn't reach her eyes. 'Why don't you let Jake show me the yard?'

My parents exchange looks as we turn our backs. They're not dumb. They know how much power Samantha Conway holds in NFL circles, and how much sway she has over the man who got me drafted.

'How good of you to bring your family with you to Canyon,' Sam Conway says to me as we step outside onto the veranda that overlooks the pool.

The air is warm. There are lanterns hanging from the fence that River bought, and the pool lights are on. I swallow. Tonight is not going as planned.

'They wanted to come,' I say.

'They're incredibly proud of you. And so they should be.'

'Ms Conway, I don't mean to sound rude, but I did what you asked. I took Lemon out. Is that why you're here?'

She inhales, the smile on her face still fixed. 'You did. And I am most grateful to you.'

I find myself trying to pick out all the parts of her face that have undergone some kind of surgery. It's hard to place her biological age. I'm guessing she wouldn't own up to it.

'Lemon tells me you had a very lovely time. She said you were the perfect gentleman. A man like that is hard to find these days.'

'I'm sure Lemon will meet a very fine young man one of these days, ma'am. Someone who'll take good care of her.'

The smile twitches. Her eyes crease a fraction. 'You'd be surprised… in a place like Canyon. Jake, I'm not going to waste your time, or mine. I'd like you to take Lemon out on another date. I'm reliably informed that there is no other female in your life, and that you haven't been seen out dating anybody. You should have no trouble taking my Lemon out on a few more dates. Show my darling girl a good time.'

I knew it. I knew this was coming.

'Ms Conway,' I begin, but I'm literally lost for words right now. 'Look. Lemon is… Lemon is a nice girl. But I don't… I don't feel… I don't have those kinda feelings toward your daughter, ma'am.'

'Did I say I required you to have feelings for my daughter?'

'No, ma'am, but—'

'Then do as I ask. Take my daughter out. Take the time to get to know her.'

I'm grappling with what to say to her. 'For what purpose, ma'am?' I question, as my frustration boils over. 'I don't understand. I didn't get the sense that Lemon wanted to spend any time with me.'

'Oh, she does. She just takes time to... warm up to people. My Lemon can be a shy girl.'

I can't not say it. 'And if I say no?'

Her amber eyes flash. She was not expecting those words to come out of my mouth. Any kind of defiance. She lowers her voice. 'You do know Coach Holland and I are *very* close, Mr Walsh?'

My breath hitches. What. The. Fuck.

'Are you... are you threatening me, ma'am?'

'I believe I am, yes.'

I stand there, my heart slamming in my chest. All I can hear is the lapping of the pool and the breeze going through the palm leaves above the back fence. Her eyes don't leave mine.

'Thank you, Jake,' she says with the same thin-lipped smile. 'I very much appreciate you keeping my daughter happy. You have a lovely back yard, by the way. Great pool.'

—

When she's gone, I avoid my mother practically falling over herself with questions about why Samantha Conway would want to pay me a visit, and head upstairs to my room.

'Jake?' a voice says behind me when my hand goes to the door handle.

I pause. 'Not now, River,' I respond to my sister, without turning to face her. I feel bad, but right now, I just wanna be by myself.

I close the door behind me and lean the back of my head up against it. Blow out my cheeks. How the hell did I get into this goddamned mess?

The girl I like ran out on me because I thought she was a virgin.

The girl I don't like – and for reasons I can't fathom – has her mother hunting me down like a crazy fucking coyote.

I am screwed.

I go to the bed, take out the phone that I planned to use for Serenity. I switch it back on, a little flame of hope in my chest that she's sent me a message.

Only there's nothing.

I sit down. My fingers hover over the keys.

I type out a message.

> I'm so sorry.
> I messed up.
> Please forgive me.

After the message has been sent, I'm tempted to write more. To start begging, I guess. I toss the handset because I know it's not a good look.

For a minute, I hold my head in my hands.

I think of the look on Serenity's face. It's replaced with Lemon and her puckered lips, then finally merges into Sam Conway telling me how close she is to Coach Holland.

Shit.

When I first came to Canyon, I did not think that life would turn out to be this complicated.

Chapter Fifteen

Serenity

On the road back into Canyon, on the dash, the fuel light switches on. When I pull into the nearest gas station, I kill the engine. In the driver's seat, I let out a shaky breath, because it feels like I've been holding it since I left the cabin.

I close my eyes.

He thought I was a virgin.

My bottom lip quivers. It won't stop. I bite down on it, sucking on my own flesh. It felt good to kiss him again. Too darn good.

The worst thing? He's the kind of guy who makes me wish I could be a virgin again. Because all those other guys I've been with, they pale pretty far in comparison. And I wish I could cancel them all out.

I never went with a sweet guy before. A guy who truly cares.

I didn't go to the cabin with the intention of sleeping with Jake Walsh. I didn't think we'd go that far. I guess I hoped I'd get to kiss him again, but his kisses got me so worked up.

At Surly's, when I'm half naked and dancing for a bunch of total strangers, I don't see it as a sexual thing. Sure, they do, but for me it's a way to make money and pay off my father's debt. That's all it's ever been for me. A means to an end.

I've not been with a man for two years. I wouldn't say I've been starved, but when Jake's hands were on my body, it was like he flipped a switch. Half-dressed, with his eyes on my body, it felt like I was on fire. His mouth was so warm, so welcoming.

When his fingers slipped inside my panties, need blossomed in my belly, and everywhere else. I was ready to give myself to him.

He thought you were a virgin, Ren.

God, did it disappoint him that I wasn't?

Does it even matter? Because there's no universe in which he can be mine.

—

At the back of Surly's, at the door, Jaxon is waiting on me.

'Go get changed,' he instructs me. 'You and I are goin' on a trip.'

I slow my steps. 'What do you mean?'

'I mean, boss wants me to take you somewhere. So go get changed. You're not needed here tonight.'

I raise my chin. 'Where you takin' me?'

Jax rolls his eyes, all impatient. 'Ren. Come on. We gotta go. Go put your outfit on.'

'You expect me to just walk outta here in my boots, my panties and a corset?'

'I got you a coat.'

Twenty minutes later, I've reapplied my makeup in a hurry and I'm wearing an emerald and black lace corset with matching panties, my hair tucked underneath a long, lilac-colored wig. Jax wraps a long coat around me and I fasten the buttons before we head on out to the parking lot.

'You gonna tell me what's goin' on?' I ask, once I'm inside the car.

'You're on a job for a private client tonight.'

My stomach rolls over as we pull out of the lot. Shit. I'd bet a million bucks the client is that asshole Brody Conway. I shake my head in disgust. 'Is it who I think it is?'

'All I got was the address. We're heading to the waterfront.'

We stop at some lights. 'Does he pay me the money?'

'Client already paid up front.'

'How much?'

'Can't say.'

I let out a gruff sigh because, once again, I won't see a dime of that money.

'You'll add it to my ledger—'

'Already did.'

'Thanks, Jax. And the expectation is that I... what?'

'Client already knows the rules. He can't touch you. Same as if you were dancing at the club.'

'And is it...'

'Yeah,' he mumbles, and I know he's referring to *Surly's Rules*. He swallows like he doesn't like it.

'And where will you be?'

'Right outside.'

'And if he violates the rules?'

'Client knows who you belong to. But if you need me, you holler at the top of your lungs, and I'll break down the goddamned door.'

'Thanks, Jax.'

I lapse into silence and watch the light from the streetlamps skim through the interior of the vehicle. I think about running out again on Jake. Wonder where he is now. If he stayed at the cabin.

I should have stayed. Should have listened. I feel guilty seeing Brody Conway again knowing what Jake and I did – or didn't do – tonight.

When we make it to the waterfront, my body goes tense with dread. Jax drives into an underground lot. Checking his phone, we take an elevator to the fifteenth floor, my body still wrapped up in a long coat. I stand behind him, like he's my protector. My bodyguard. Except I know all too well that he doesn't hold a whole lot more power than I do in this situation.

Inside a windowless corridor, outside the condo, Jax rings the doorbell, then stands well back. Moments later, the door opens ajar, but I can't see who is behind it. I look at Jax who gives me an affirmative nod, and I slip inside.

Brody Conway closes the door behind me. I stand and wait as he comes back round to face me.

'Good evening, Serenity,' he says, all calm and casual. He's wearing grey flannel pants and a fitted black polo. 'How very nice to see you again. Thank you for coming to my side of town.' He holds out his arm. 'Can I take your coat?'

For a moment, I don't move. I resent being here. I resent Kale McCoy for sending me to this slimeball. The way he smirks at me makes my skin crawl.

I untie the belt on the coat, then unfasten the buttons. Pushing it back over my shoulders, Brody steps forward to take it from me, his gaze purposefully travelling the length of my body.

'That's much better. Come on in, can I offer you a drink?'

'No, thank you,' is my response. 'You have thirty minutes.'

He tilts his head to one side, making like he's disappointed. 'My, my, we're very down to business this evening.'

I hug my waist. 'You're not paying for my courtesy.'

'Let me show you the apartment. The view is incredible.'

He leads me through into a substantial living area, then through some sliding glass doors, to a sizeable balcony. I've never seen Canyon from this high up before.

I remain standing while Brody sits down on the outdoor love seat, placing both hands behind his head.

'I wanna see the breeze in your hair,' he says. 'Lose the wig, Serenity.'

Changing my hair has always made me feel like a different person. Like, when I take it off, I'm not a private dancer anymore. I don't work in a strip club. I hate that Brody Conway blurs those lines. Slowly, I reach up and slide the lilac wig from my head. I take out the bobby pins and let my real hair fall about my shoulders.

'*Much* better,' he says, then pats the seat next to him. 'Come,' he adds. 'Siddown by me.'

I do as I'm told. I wonder if his new wife knows about this apartment. If it even belongs to him, with its fancy Asian artwork and expensive furniture. I can feel Brody's eyes on me. He pushes my hair to one side and brings his nose close to my skin.

'You smell so good,' he whispers.

His fingers are on my thigh, stroking my skin, edging close to the hemline of my panties.

'You are exquisite, Serenity. I can't wait for you to undress for me.'

I push away his fingers. 'Then come to the club. I don't do private home visits.'

'Oh, I think you do. Your boss says you do. I bought you something special to wear just for me. So that I can watch you take it all off.'

'Does your wife know I'm here?'

Before I know it, his hand has grabbed my chin, those creepy long fingers digging into my jaw, turning my head. 'Don't you fucking bring my wife's name into this.'

Every muscle in my body has gone taut. His grip doesn't loosen, but his voice goes back to being smooth like silk. 'Now be a good girl and go get changed for me. You'll find your outfit in the bedroom.'

I pull away from him, get to my feet and rub my jaw, my galloping heart slamming into my ribcage. I need to be careful here.

I walk back through the apartment to the bedrooms. My body is tense. I'd rather dance naked in front of strangers than satisfy Brody Conway's needs for another moment. On one of the beds, laid out flat, is a set of red lingerie, sheer lace stockings and a suspender belt, red pumps and a choker chain. My jaw goes slack. I check the label. It's a high-end brand of underwear.

When I'm dressed, I look at my reflection in the wall-length mirror. Presumably he accessed my staff record to get my measurements – in the same way he'd gotten my phone number – and everything fits like a glove. I think of Jake, how he'd react to seeing me dressed like this, and I feel shame in my actions. A girl like me doesn't deserve a guy like him.

I make my way back through the apartment. In the living area, Brody is relaxed on the couch. The drapes are now closed.

'Wait, wait,' he says as I approach. 'Walk slow.'

I adjust my pace, my heels hitting the marble floor. I feel Brody's eyes roaming over my body. He exhales, long and slow. 'What did I say? Exquisite.'

My expression reveals my true feelings.

'Come on now, Serenity. You can't raise a little smile for me?'

'You're running out of time,' I warn him.

He's drinking whiskey on the rocks. The glass is balanced on his knee and he's manspreading. The lights are turned down and he's put out a simple wooden chair in the center of the room, which I presume is my stage.

'Kale tells me this is your specialty,' he comments.

'Are you gonna give me some music?'

'Give me a twirl first,' he says, and I note that he sucks his breath when I show him my almost bare ass.

'You know,' he muses. 'If you didn't belong to Kale, I'd make you mine, princess.'

'I'm not your princess. And I'd rather we get this over with.'

His eyes flash at me givin' him lip. 'My little cheerleader then.'

I finish my turn and face him. He's fired a warning shot.

'Now let's not be unpleasant,' he warns me. 'I paid for a good ol' fashioned strip tease. So... let's take it all off, shall we?'

No sooner does he switch on some upbeat music, my eyes glaze over. I remind myself that he's just another redneck who takes pleasure from watching a pretty girl remove her clothes. I can dance for the man, keep him happy. I can show him my body, and he can look all he likes.

But he can't touch me. He doesn't get to have me. And I'll never give myself to him.

This is just another job. A little titillation. It's the tease he loves.

I straddle the chair. I make eye contact with a married Brody Conway. I roll my hips and work my body in time with the beat. As the outward layers come off, on the inside I steel myself. I think of Jake, and how I wish I'd given myself to him this evening. How I wish I hadn't paused when he called me a virgin. Hell, maybe I should have pretended I was, but there's so much he doesn't know already that I don't want to add that to the list.

The truth is I'm scared to be honest with Jake, because as soon as he knows the truth about me, I know he'll walk away.

There are so many decent girls out there he could talk to, and he thinks I'm one of them.

I want to dance for him like this, then have him sweep me into his arms and take me to bed.

But the truth is I'm dancing for a client. This is my job. I do it for the money.

When the song is almost over, I ease the lace thong from my hips, and it drops to the floor. And, once more, I'm fully naked in Brody Conway's presence.

When the music comes to an end, he leans forward and gives a slow clap. I stand there in silence.

Brody licks his lips. 'Do one thing for me?'

I frown. 'What?'

'Sit down on the chair for me.'

I turn and go to plant my ass on the chair, but he stops me.

'No, no, like you did at the beginning. Straddle it.'

I pause, because I know what he wants. The chair has an open back, and he wants me to spread my legs for him.

My jaw clenches. I remind myself that it's all just for show, though the idea makes my stomach churn. I do as he asks, and his eyes come alive at the sight of my pussy, splayed open for him.

'So, so perfect,' he says in a low growl.

'Time's up,' I say, and get to my feet. Keeping my thighs together, I crouch rather than bend to collect the lingerie and the shoes from the floor then march on back to the bedroom.

I don't even bid him goodbye. Once I'm dressed and my coat is back on, I walk out the door, where Jax is waiting for me.

It's gone two a.m. by the time I make it home. I gotta get to the diner by eight.

A part of me knows I can't go on like this. There's tension in my lower back. My ankles are sore. There's an ache deep in my glutes and in my hamstrings. I feel like I have old lady knees. My body aches from this constant, punishing schedule.

In front of the mirror, I peel off my false lashes, but I hardly have enough energy to remove my makeup. I force myself into cleaning it all off, before I give a big yawn. I throw on an oversized T-shirt and cotton panties then crawl under the covers.

In the darkness, in the comfort of my bed – the same one I've been sleeping in since I was a girl – my mind goes back to Jake. I think about the cell phone he gave me.

I switch the light back on and go to my bag. I turn on the handset, then enter in the security code – Jake's birthday – just as he told me.

I'm thinking about what to say to him when some messages pop up:

> I'm so sorry.
> I messed up.
> Please forgive me.

My heart beats faster. I climb back into the bed and snuggle under the covers, like a teenage girl with a crush. Because that's what this feels like.

The next message reads:

> I'd never try to pressure you. I hope you know that. I'll understand if you decide you can't see me because it's too risky for you. For the record, I think it's a dumb rule, but it's not my decision.

His final words read:

> But, also for the record, I'm completely crazy about you.

I bite my lip, trying to stop my smile from spreading. It doesn't work. Underneath the covers, I type:

> I'm sorry I ran out on you. Again.

When I hit the send key, a moment later, three dots appear to show that Jake is typing:

> Are you still awake?

I pause. I don't wanna have to explain that I just got home from working two out of my three jobs, plus a drive out to pay him a visit at the cabin, and that I'm beat.

The dots appear again and another message pops up:

> Don't suppose we could talk? Can I call?

I push back the covers and sit up. I don't wanna wake my dad, but equally, I need to apologize. Again. Always again.

Sure, I type and hit the send key.

Within seconds, the cell starts to vibrate. It's a voice call.

'Hi,' I say in a whisper as I answer.

'Hey,' he responds, and it sounds a little strangled.

'I gotta keep the noise down. My dad's sleeping.'

'That's cool. You're up late.'

'I couldn't sleep.' Not that I've even tried.

'Me either. I just… I needed to say I'm sorry again. About earlier. I totally assumed something about you, and it was wrong of me to do so.'

I feel like he's rehearsed that sentence a few times. Not that it sounds disingenuous, just that I detect that same trepidation in his tone.

'I'm sorry I walked out. I shouldn't have done that either. I guess I kinda panicked that you didn't really know me. That we didn't really know each other and already we were… you know.'

'I agree with you one hundred per cent.'

I believe him. I feel like he's being honest with me. And, though I can't be fully honest with him, I need to get to the bottom of something.

'Can I ask you something?' I say.

'Anything.'

I dip my head and pull my hair over one shoulder. 'Do I make you, like… nervous?'

He makes an *uhhh* sound before I hear his awkward laugh. 'Honestly? I thought I'd cracked the whole talking-to-girls thing in high school. I never met a woman who turned me into a complete mess before.'

There he goes, being all cute again. 'Do I take that as a compliment?'

I hear him exhale. 'Yes. That's definitely a compliment. You are… seriously, you're the most beautiful woman I ever laid eyes upon. And the sweetest. And I don't say those things lightly. All I wanna do is get to know you. Spend some time with you. And we don't have to… you know… worry about anything else.'

Most guys I've been with, they're not shy to talk about sex. Who'd have thought a rugged football player of all people can't even say the word? 'Okay. I think I can handle that,' I tell him.

He sounds excited. 'Seriously? Are you free tomorrow night?'

My heart plummets in my chest. Saturday, I work a day shift at the diner, followed by another long shift at Surly's. There's no way Kale will let me have the night off on a Saturday.

'How about Sunday?'

He sounds unsure. 'I have curfew Sunday night, before Monday's game. My mom likes me to accompany her to church in the morning. I could get to the cabin, but we wouldn't have long.'

'It's just that… tomorrow is… it's gonna be difficult for me.'

'I can be at the cabin two o'clock Sunday?'

'I have practice at the Danube Sunday morning. What time is team curfew?'

'We gotta be at the hotel by eight-thirty.'

'Then we'll have a few hours, right?'

I can tell he's masking a degree of disappointment in his tone. 'Right. Okay.'

'So…' I hum, 'I'll see you Sunday. Two o'clock. And don't be nervous.'

He laughs at that. 'I'll try not to be. See you then. Get some sleep.'

'Night, Jake.'

I hang up and fall back against my pillows. The phones were a good idea.

But meeting up with him again at the cabin on Sunday? Maybe not so much.

Because I can feel it in the butterflies in my stomach.

The ones that tell me I'm falling.

Chapter Sixteen

Jake

Sunday morning, the pastor is halfway through delivering his sermon, but all I can think about is sex.

Or sex with Serenity, to be more specific.

I can't get my mind out the gutter.

I stood under the shower this morning, getting myself off to thoughts of her. How she might taste. What it might feel like to—

I feel River's fingers poke into my side and I flinch. 'He's talking 'bout you, idiot,' she hisses from the side of her mouth.

'What?' I whisper back.

'Just smile and wave, moron,' she adds.

I force a smile. Raise my hand in a little wave. I have zero idea what the pastor just said about me. I only know that the last few weeks, he keeps mentioning my name like I'm some kind of minor celebrity in these parts. I glance back and now the entire congregation is looking my way.

When the service is over, we go to lunch at an Italian joint with chequered tablecloths across the road from the church. The pastor is there, accompanied by his wife and their daughter, who I'd guess is older than River but younger than I am.

I'm sat next to River, my fingers playing absent-mindedly with my fork, thinking about sex with Serenity again when my mother's voice cuts through my daydream.

'Yes, well Jake is in high demand these days. Friday, Samantha Conway herself stopped by our place. Jake's taking her daughter Lemon out. Do you know Lemon Conway?'

The pastor's wife looks a little embarrassed, but it's nothing compared to the level I'm feeling. The base of my neck is burning up.

'Why you keep checking your watch?' River whispers beside me.

'I'm not,' I say.

'Sure, you are,' she says, eyeing my smartwatch, 'like every five seconds, you switch it on.'

'I got curfew tonight, that's all. I'm just thinking 'bout that.'

'You got somewhere you gotta be in between?'

'No.'

'So do you… wanna hang out later?'

I look her in the eye. It's weird seeing her in a pretty dress. And if there's one person I hate lying to, it's River. My mother's still yabberin' when I run my fingers through my hair and lower my voice. 'Alright, there's somewhere I gotta be later. Before curfew.'

'Oh. Where you goin'?'

I wince. 'Kinda can't say.'

'Why not?'

I can't make eye contact with her. 'It's complicated.'

'Why's it complicated?'

'I can't say that either.'

She gives a shrug, twirling a little saltshaker between her fingers. 'Whatever,' she mutters. 'I never see you anymore anyways. Wish we'd never come to this stupid-ass city.'

'You made some more friends at school yet?'

'Not really. I met this one guy in my history class. He got in a car accident last year. He's in a wheelchair. Missed ninety per cent of his senior year, so he's repeating it. He was nice to me. Shame his brother's such an asshole.'

'Who's his brother?'

'That guy, Scottie Lincoln. The one who was at the wedding? People say he's only mean because of his brother's accident.'

'That's no excuse. What about other girls?'

'Too many cliques, you know? So far, I don't seem to fit in with any of them. And with the winter formal coming up...'

Her voice trails off. 'What about the winter formal?' I ask.

River mumbles something in return but Mom is talking over her.

'Jake, sweetie, did you know that Mary Ellen here graduated from UCLA?'

I force another smile. Across from me, the pastor's daughter turns a shade of bright red. Seems Mom forgot about Lemon Conway real quick.

—

I'm not the first to arrive at the cabin. Serenity sits on the front porch steps, a silver dish in her lap.

When I pull into the driveway in my pickup, she gets to her feet, the tightest pair of bootcut jeans hugging her hips and thighs, and the sight of her gets my heart pounding. I take in the curve of both her breasts, just peeking out over the scooped neck of her tight, white tee. She's wearing a black-and-white chequered shirt over the top, knotted at the waist, her hair hanging loose.

As I have continually reminded myself since church this morning... I am not here to have sex with Serenity Harper. No, sir. No matter how much I want to. I respect her too much. I just wanna get to know her.

Except, when I get out the pickup, she beams at me. I swear, this girl is gonna melt my heart.

'Are you hungry?' she asks, holding up the dish. 'I made cherry pie.'

I put one hand on my swollen stomach. 'I just came straight from lunch. But, hey, if you made it, I'm eating it.'

I climb the steps. She's on the porch.

'Hey,' I say.

'Hey, back,' she says with a smile.

'Thanks for coming out here.'

She gives a tight shrug. 'Figured I'd try not to run away this time. Should give you my car keys or somethin''.'

I laugh. 'We should get inside.'

She's left a small bag by the door. There's a canister of whipped cream at the top. I pick the bag up for her and she follows me. Inside, there's an odd aroma of Chinese food left over from Friday night, and I realize I failed to take out the trash.

'Sorry about the stink,' I say.

She walks into the kitchen, puts down the cherry pie and pulls herself up onto the countertop, allowing her legs to swing below her. She looks back at me in a way that makes me wanna march right over, push myself between those thighs and make her forget every single one of those eight guys she's been with.

I quickly load the leftovers into a trash bag and put it in the garbage can at the back of the house.

When I get back, Serenity has a knife and is cutting two slices of the pie onto plates.

'You want cream?' she asks, and I nod in confirmation.

'You really made this?' I ask as she squirts a big circle of cream onto my plate, then holds it out to me.

'Practice finished a little early and I had a couple of hours to kill. I made two, one for my dad too. He likes it.'

'He's lucky to have you. How's he doing?'

She seems awkward. 'I think he's lonely. My neighbor, Mrs Oakley, looks in on him from time to time. He watches baseball most days. On TV.'

'Not football?'

'He doesn't really get the ruckus around football.'

'Maybe I'll need to convince him.'

I dig into my cherry pie.

'Do you like it?' she asks.

A smile dances across my mouth. 'This is the best cherry pie I've ever eaten,' I say with my mouth full.

'Well, there's more where that came from. If you stick around long enough, you can eat another slice.' She pauses before she adds, 'What time you gotta leave?'

Disappointment floods my veins. I hate the curfew. Players aren't allowed to be accompanied, not even the ones with wives and kids. The rules for the Mutineers state that lights out is at ten-thirty, and all cell phones are banned. 'I can prolly push it 'til eight, then run all the red lights on the way back into the city. Get to the hotel with like a minute to spare.'

She beams again, and licks her fingers, and my gaze lingers on her lips for a moment too long. 'We've got time then,' she says. 'Time to get to know each other.'

My thoughts have turned dirty again. I snap out of it and finish my pie. We move to the couch, a wide gulf between us.

'Tell me something about you,' she says. 'What got you into football?'

I cock my head to one side. 'My grandfather played football, my uncle and my dad. Kind of runs in the family. My grandfather was quarterback for the Steelers. My dad played center for the Atlanta Falcons.'

'So... you're like NFL royalty?'

'You sound like my sister.'

'I do? River, is that her name?'

'Yeah. Riv. River. She hates me right now.'

'Why?'

''Cause she had to move out here and start a new school. Claims everybody hates her and it's all my fault.'

'She's what, sixteen?'

'Seventeen.'

Her lips twist. 'Ouch.'

'Why, ouch?'

'Seventeen is a tough age for a girl. I should know. Of course she's gonna hate you. Does she have a boyfriend?'

I scoff. 'Definitely not.'

She grins mischievously. 'That you know of...'

'I think I would know if River had a boyfriend. I'm not even sure she's been kissed yet.'

'Maybe that's not the sort of information she's gonna share with her big brother. More like her girlfriends.'

'We're close. Me and River. I feel like she'd tell me, but, hey, maybe you're right. Had you been kissed when you were sixteen?'

The words are out my mouth before I realize my mistake. She bites her lip. I wince and squeeze my eyes shut.

'Shit,' I say and look to the floor. 'Sorry. I didn't mean anything by it.'

'It's okay,' she says with a smile. 'I mean, sixteen is young. Sure it is. But the guy was my steady boyfriend at least. Same couldn't be said for some of the other girls in my class.'

He slides one hand around the back of his neck. 'I was nineteen. When I… you know. I had a girlfriend in high school, but she was part of this group of girls who were like this… purity gang. Saving themselves for their husbands or something. So that wasn't happening. We kissed a few times but that was it.'

'So, who was the girl when you were nineteen? College girlfriend?'

'Yeah. We were both… we both had our V cards. I did the whole candles, soft-lighting, Taylor Swift soundtrack, pillows on the floor, all that stuff.'

She looks surprised.

'What?' I ask.

Surprise turns into what seems like embarrassment. 'Nothing, I, just… that was nothing like my experience.'

I wait for her to continue. She doesn't look me in the eye when she talks. 'The night I lost my virginity, my boyfriend didn't even ask how I felt after. I remember he went to dispose of the condom, then picked up the TV remote and watched an entire NBA game before saying another word to me… There was definitely no soft lighting or Taylor Swift keeping it all romantic.'

I watch her. God, she's beautiful. I feel angry at her high school boyfriend, even though I can't even picture his face. 'Well, that guy's a fucking idiot.'

'He didn't last very long. Both on the night in question, or after. Couple' weeks later, he slept with a friend of mine.'

'Wow.'

'So I slept with *his* friend, shortly after that. As like a revenge thing, I guess.'

I laugh. 'Holy shit. Still no Taylor Swift soundtrack?'

'Definitely not. Ugh. It was at a house party. God, we were in somebody else's bedroom with the door locked. I'm not proud of it. That one wasn't romantic.'

'Has there ever been a… you know… a romantic one?'

'Once. I'd just turned eighteen. He worked in a paint factory. He was my boyfriend for a while. He was the most… considerate.'

'Why'd you break up?'

'We drifted.' She sighs, the sigh morphing into a snicker. 'Plus, he always smelled like turps.'

We both laugh. I'll put him in the 'fucking idiot' category along with the rest of them.

'What about you?' she continues. 'What happened to the college girlfriend? Taylor Swift soundtrack.'

'Well…' I feel myself blush. 'She was the captain of the cheer squad.'

'No!' Serenity shrieks.

'She cheated on me with my teammate.'

Her face falls. 'Oh.'

'I won't lie. It kinda sucked.'

'I'm so sorry.'

'Didn't you just tell me your boyfriend did the same thing?'

She gives a shrug. 'I mean, sure, but we weren't in love or anything, we were just dumb teenagers. So… what happened after that?'

'Uh. I jumped from one serious relationship into another. Gracie Olavsen. Social sciences major. Kind of a brainiac. She dumped me. Said she didn't wanna be a token NFL bride or have her career defined by any success I had as an NFL player. And that was *after* the draft.'

Serenity's raised her brow. She blinks.

'So, you see, I didn't exactly sow any wild oats in college,' I add. 'I mean, that's my body count, right there.'

'But you were a loyal boyfriend,' she says, and I sense she's trying to make me feel better. 'Which is a hundred per cent better than most guys I know.'

I can feel myself blushing again. *Calm it down, Walsh.* I know I shouldn't say what I'm about to say, but I guess I'm gonna do it anyway. 'I'm just not exactly Mr Experience.'

She watches me, a cute little smile on her face. 'Didn't anybody ever tell you it's quality over quantity?'

All this sex talk is putting me at half-mast. I shift position on the couch. Damn if I don't wanna be her number nine and blow all those other guys out the water. I know I can't ask for a breakdown, but the athlete in me needs to find out the competition.

'So… Mr Turpentine. Was he your only boyfriend other than high school jackass?'

She smiles shyly at my question and plays with her shirt sleeve. 'My last boyfriend had his own bar. Turned out that wasn't all he had. There was a wife and two kids at home I didn't know about the whole time I was dating him.'

'Jesus. How long were you dating him?'

'A few months. She tracked me down and confronted me at The Bounty one afternoon. It was humiliating. The worst thing was, she didn't believe me when I said I didn't know about her existence. About the kids' existence. She was ten years older than me. I felt like such a cliché. Put me off meeting a guy online ever again.'

She inhales. 'Anyway. That was more than two years ago, and I've not been on a date since. Until you. So, I might be a little more experienced, but I'm very out of practice in that department.'

We both stare at one another for a moment, then look away. When I look back at her, she's blushing as hard as I am. We both descend into laughter.

'So, we're Mr Inexperienced versus Miss Out-of-Practice,' I say.

It feels like we're on a level. Or maybe something changed in the atmosphere, I don't know. But I feel like I can be wholly honest with her right at this moment.

'Gracie Olavsen. The brainiac? She might have been my girlfriend, but we only had full sex once.'

Serenity frowns. 'Only once? How come?'

'She said… she said I was too big for her, and it was uncomfortable.'

Serenity snickers again. 'Is that you trying to show off?'

'I'm serious. She didn't like… you know… she liked other stuff. She liked me to go down on her, that was it.'

'But what about you?'

I blow out my cheeks, but I feel comfortable telling her this, and I never told anyone else. 'Usually, I'd just jack off in the bathroom once she'd fallen asleep. Man, have I just crossed a line?'

She's laughing and it seems like we're okay.

'You're a Mutineers running back. You should have women lining up to sleep with you, you know that, right?'

I can tell I'm blushing again. 'Yeah, they all DM me to tell me that, but… I don't know.'

We're quiet for a moment. Serenity runs her tongue along her bottom lip, then bites it with her teeth. Something crackles in the atmosphere.

'What kinds of things do *you* like?' Serenity asks.

I feel a surging sensation in my balls. Oh fuck. The sex talk just tipped over into something else. *Fuck, Walsh, quit blushing.* 'I like you,' I say.

Before I know it, she's gotten to her feet. She rids herself of shoes. She then takes two steps, lowers herself back down, straddling my thighs. I go from half to full mast inside of a second.

'I like you too,' she whispers.

I shift a little under her and look up. Those eyes. Sparkling with a special brand of sweetness. Innocent almost, like those eight other guys were really a myth. Like they didn't even really touch her. Leaning my head forward, we pause for a moment, just watching each other.

'I want you,' I whisper on an exhale.

'I want you too,' she says.

In that same moment, it's like each of us is nervous about making the first move. Our lips brush together once, twice, then on the third brush we hold, our lips finally locked. Desire for her explodes in my gut. I wonder if she realizes how hard she makes me, how much power she has over me right now. My hands go to her waist, shifting her so that my dick is pressing up between her legs through her jeans. I want her to know what she does to me.

She pulls away, breathless. 'Do you have...?' she asks, gazing down at me and her hair frames her face.

'Yes,' I say and capture her lips again as our tongues get reacquainted. I think I bought condoms out of desperation and hope, not expecting to have to use them this soon. Now I'm glad I had the presence of mind to go buy protection. I'm not the kind of guy to convince a girl that I don't need to suit up. And, hell, I'm nervous because it's been a while since sex involved being inside a girl, but when Serenity whimpers against my mouth, I know she wants this as much as I do. Blood rushes south and I swear if that was the last sound I ever heard, I'd die happy.

She backs up to a standing position. I watch her slowly untie the knot in her shirt. The material drops from her shoulders to the floor. Underneath, her tee clings to every curve. She watches me as she peels it off, lifting it over her head, and it follows the shirt. She's wearing the prettiest white lace bra adorned with tiny flowers and the sight of her breasts swelling above the lace drives me wild. My body is on fire for her.

Next her fingers drift down to the waistband of her jeans. Serenity unfastens the button with one hand and shimmies the zipper down, giving a peek of the white lace trim of her panties. She works the denim over her hips, sashaying a little left to right, leaning forward to give me a delectable view of her breasts bobbing up and down as she moves. My breath is shaky. She steps outta the jeans and lets them go, pushing them aside with her foot, with one hand bringing her hair over her shoulder.

As she straightens, I swallow. My gaze roves hungrily over her body. The white underwear is stark against her glowing skin. But the way that she's standing there in just her lingerie, it's like she's offering herself to me, and an invisible force clamps around my heart. I gotta have this girl. I want the world to know she's all mine.

When she turns and walks to the door to the bedroom, glancing seductively over her shoulder, my eyes drift lower. She pauses, runs her fingers down the wood frame. She's wearing a thong, a narrow triangle of fabric skimming across her hips, the smooth skin of her ass bared for me. Desire roars in my veins. I get to my feet, go to my bag to get the box of condoms, kick off my shoes and follow.

Serenity backs onto the bed. The linens haven't been straightened out since we were here a couple' days ago. She gets on the sheets and kneels for me, her thighs spread apart, waiting as I get undressed to my boxer briefs. My knees sink into the mattress as I come to face her. Her hair is still pushed over one shoulder, so I tilt my head, my lips making contact with one side of her neck. She moves her head too, allowing me increased access.

'No hickies, okay?' she whispers, and I detect a giggle. 'Kathleen would hang me out to dry.'

I cease sucking on her soft skin, my lips puckering instead to gentle kisses. My left hand is at the small of her back. I take a sharp intake of breath as her fingers cup my balls, sliding all the way up the length of my rigid shaft, over the black cotton of my underwear. I can't help myself. I let out a growl as I pull her to me, capturing her mouth again, the heat between us undeniable. I want to take my time with her, yet at the same time, I want to claim her, make her mine, give in to my basest physical needs.

'Serenity,' I whisper between kisses.

In a second, she unclips her bra and it falls away. The feel of her peaked nipples against my chest is incredible. My dick twitches in anticipation. I pray I can hold out. My hands move to cup her breasts, my thumbs massaging the taut buds. I lower my head and take one in my mouth at a time, sucking and licking the perfect little pink pebbles, which flourish the more attention I give them. Her hand goes to the back of my head, and she groans with need.

Fuck. That noise. I may not hold out.

I go back to kissing her with the same level of passion and intensity inside the pickup after we'd been to the lake, breathless and eager. She responds, pressing into me, our hands roaming over one another's bodies. Wordlessly, I urge her to shift, so that she's no longer kneeling, but lying down for me. She does so, a multitude of pillows meaning she's propped up, hair now splayed out, meaning she can watch as I hook my fingers into the lace of her thong and ease it down her thighs. She lifts her ass a fraction to help, so that I can peel the material away, her knees slightly bent, her legs slightly open. When she's fully naked, I can see the folds of her pussy, slick and wet and swollen for me, and that's when I know I'm not gonna go the distance.

She puts one arm above her head. I love her confidence as her eyes go to my underwear, as if to say 'your turn'. Straightening again, I take them down, careful not to catch my dick, swollen and rock hard. I get to my feet to retrieve a condom, but when I lower myself back to my knees, she's there to assist, opening the packet and taking the latex in one hand and my shaft in the other. She takes care to roll it all the way down and secure it in place at the base. Then she goes to lie back down. I watch her arch her back a little, open her thighs a fraction wider, taking both my hands in hers and encouraging me to move forward.

'Can I touch you first?' I ask, because the memory of her wet pussy against my fingers has not left me in the thirty hours since I last touched her.

Serenity gives me a sweet smile and nods her head, even takes my hand and guides my fingers to the places they wanna go. Her back arches further as I move against her inner thigh, before encountering her warmth, my fingers tracing the line of her pussy before sliding against her clit. She lets out a tremored sigh, a sign that permits me to go further, do more. Little lightning bolts explode in my balls and up my shaft, my dick flexing, telling my fingers to hurry things along because he's dying for entry.

I tell my dick to hurry up and wait.

Her eyes are half-lidded as I massage her clit. I find her entrance and slip one finger fully inside before adding another. She's tight and so fucking wet. Her head tilts back as the pad of my thumb brushes up against her clit. Her breaths are erratic. She moves lower, getting herself comfortable. My mind starts to race as my dick gets more impatient. I shift my body, so that I'm above her and I can gaze down at her face, my fingers still lodged inside her.

'Jake,' she whispers, and I'm undone. I've hit my limit. The sound of my name on her lips almost sends me over the edge.

My body's between her open thighs. Most guys I know don't like missionary position because of the upper body strength required for prolonged thrusting. Us pro-athletes, we've got no problem with it, because compared to some of the workouts we're expected to do, sex in the missionary position feels like a walk in the park.

'Serenity,' I say, and her eyes float open. We watch each other for a moment, searching one another's expressions. She gives me a small nod, as though giving her consent.

Reaching down, I grasp my shaft, edging forward, seeking entrance.

'Look at me,' she murmurs, and I lift my eyes. She places one hand against my cheek just as the tip of my dick finds where it needs to be. She opens her legs even wider, tilts her hips as I push, and with complete eye contact between us, I feed myself inside her, as deep as I can manage as her eyes roll back in her head. I immerse myself in the feeling. To be joined with her like this, with her… it's fucking heaven.

A wince flickers across her features.

'Does it hurt?' I ask.

'No, no,' is her reply. 'It feels really good.'

I try to say something, but it comes out as a grunt as instinct takes over, and my hips begin to move of their own accord. I feel Serenity's thighs shift, and realize she's wrapped her legs around my waist, and is grinding with me.

We fall into a steady rhythm, not too fast, not too slow, my hips working, hers rocking in sync with each drive.

'Yes,' I moan, and she whimpers in response. She pulls me closer, our kisses wild, breathless and messy. After a minute or so, I feel a burn in my upper arms. She's rasping now, and I pray I can bring her to a release before I lose control and come inside her. I want so badly to leave her satisfied. I move my hand to her hip, lift her knee higher, which shifts the angle of my thrusts so I can drive deeper. Her eyes fly open. I watch as her mouth opens, as though she's trying to vocalize something, but our movements have robbed her of the ability to think straight.

'Right there,' she manages, 'oh god, Jake, don't stop, don't s—'

Her breasts bounce with my every thrust. On her face is a look of tormented ecstasy that I will never forget so long as I can draw breath. She's sensational. She's *mmm-ing* and *aah-ing* like she's edging closer until out of nowhere, she gasps. There's a split-second moment where she's still, before her head goes back. She pushes her chest out and that's when I feel it. The walls of her pussy gripping me, in spasm. Unbridled, blissful cries fill the room as her body shudders, and I feel her come around me.

I slow my speed, but pride pounds in my veins. That was me. I made her feel that good.

Her eyes flutter open and her hand goes to my cheek.

My breath is uneven, like I just fought my way through an offensive tackle. 'You're beautiful,' I splutter.

She breaks out into a huge smile, verging on a laugh, like she can't quite believe what just happened. My balls tighten at the sight of her all sated, sweaty and post-orgasm.

'Do you mind if I...?' I ask, because every cell in my body is screaming out with desire for her.

She nods enthusiastically. I pick up speed again. I can't hold out much longer, but the concern I felt at leaving her unsatisfied is gone. I stroke into her, over and over, and her nails claw my back.

'That's it,' she murmurs, and I feel my climax start to build, the explosion beginning deep within my balls. My hips grind erratically, before my dick twitches and pure, unfiltered pleasure pulses through my bones. The noises that emerge from my lips are almost savage, but damn if Serenity ain't smiling up at me as I fill the condom, our gazes locked, driving into her until I'm spent.

My body goes limp. I sink down, careful not to crush her, sliding out of her and using my elbow to lower myself down by her side.

We lie there for a moment, bodies in disarray, naked and breathless.

'Are you alright?' I breathe.

'I'm good,' she hums in return.

I sit up to deal with the condom. I get up and walk butt naked to the bathroom to dispose of it. When I come back,

Serenity's snuggled under the covers. The apples of her cheeks are tinged a rose pink, her skin dewy with afterglow, her hair splayed out over the pillows. I climb inside with her, and she tangles her legs up with mine, leaning her head against my chest. For a few moments, neither of us talks.

'Can I make an observation?' she says eventually.

I clear my throat. 'Sure.'

'What was the name of the second girlfriend? The brainiac?'

'Gracie Olavsen.'

'Oh. Okay, well… It's just that I think Gracie Olavsen might have been missing out.'

My laughter comes from deep within my chest. I sink lower and stroke her hair, kissing Serenity's lips.

'I never had good sex like that before,' I whisper against her mouth.

'Me either,' she says back and then we're doing the eye contact thing again. The mood between us is so intense that I almost look away.

'I need to tell you something,' I say.

'What is it?'

'Sam Conway paid me a visit. After I left here, Friday night. Wants me to take her daughter out on another date. Practically threatened me when I refused.'

Her eyebrows creep up. 'Another date with Lemon?'

I shake my head. 'I swear, there's nothing to it. She thinks I'm single, which I'm clearly not, but I can't tell anybody else that yet.'

'You're not single?' she asks with a smile.

I flash her a grin. 'No, and I'm hoping neither are you.'

I lean forward, kiss her mouth, use my tongue. I linger, because I want her to know that I'm being serious. 'I'm crazy about you, Serenity. I know the rules. I know what you're risking for me. But you're my girl, okay? I mean, if you… if you wanted to be.'

'I want to be your girl,' she says. 'I guess I'm just scared of what happens if we get found out.'

I lean up on my elbow, support my head on one hand. 'Then we just keep things between us, like we have been, just us two. Nobody else needs to know. We meet here. 'Til we can figure all this out.'

She reaches up and strokes my face. I think I might be obsessed with her. Or maybe I'm falling in love.

She's everything I want.

'What do you say?' I ask, and I can't shake the trepidation in my voice. Not for the first time today, I'm nervous.

She sucks on her bottom lip, as if she's thinking on it.

When she nods her head, it's slow, as though maybe she's unsure, because she's the one taking all the chances.

I'll take it. I know I can protect her from anything. So long as she's mine, we'll be unstoppable.

When I lean down and kiss Serenity Harper's lips again, I know that nothing can stand in our way.

Contract or no contract.

Chapter Seventeen

Serenity

Monday Night Football. A half hour before we're due on the field to begin our routine and we're two cheerleaders down: Mona and Persia. I'm in my uniform and my hair and makeup are done. In the locker room, everyone is mostly ready. While the mood not so long ago was upbeat, Harmony's been summoned upstairs, along with Ashlyn, her deputy. I've heard whispers, but I'm keeping my head down.

'She's toast,' Shawny comments as she tugs on her boots. 'There's no way they'll let her stay.'

She's talking about Persia. Next to me, Jewel looks surprised. 'You really think that's true?'

'In that hoochie outfit, in a club, at three in the morning, drunk and still downing liquor? There's no chance they'll let her keep her place on the squad.'

Jewel lowers her tone. 'You don't think they'll just give her a slap on the wrist and let bygones be bygones?'

Angel takes a seat next to Shawny. She's crossed her arms over her chest. 'She might have gotten away with it had she not been photographed.'

A cry goes up from Imara, a fourth-year veteran with the second longest legs you ever saw, after Angel's. 'Don't forget putting it out on her 'gram!'

Jewel leans over in my direction and lowers her voice. 'Some of the girls are saying Persia wanted out of her contract, like she was tryna get fired. That's why she decided to party hard on Saturday. Like she's had enough.'

My stomach is churning. 'Why would you actively go do that though? After everything it took to get on the squad? Why throw it away like that? All careless?'

I realize I could be talking about my own situation. Yesterday, Jake and I had sex one more time at the cabin before he had to leave. He keeps telling me how crazy he is about me, which makes me feel warm inside. And I can't wait to get a glimpse of him on the field tonight. Careless is one thing Jake and I can't afford to be.

There's a commotion when Harmony enters the locker room, flanked by Ashlyn. Harmony hasn't changed yet, and wears skinny jeans, a dark green T-shirt and a leather jacket. Ashlyn is in her uniform already.

Harmony addresses us all, concern etched into her features. 'Alright, CMC, gather round, listen up.'

We all gather. There are worried faces.

'Okay, I'll start with Mona,' Harmony says with a sigh. 'Kathleen and Ms Conway have put her on temporary suspension. If she can lose the weight she's gained and fast, then they'll allow her back on the squad.'

'Oh, come on,' Angel blurts. 'Her fiancé ran off with her sister. If that happened to me, I wouldn't just console myself gorging on a box of Snickers ice cream.'

'I'd eat the whole goddamned Snickers ice cream bar factory,' Shawny chips in.

I don't know Mona. We've maybe exchanged a few words, tops. All I know is that she's a second-year veteran who has copper-colored hair, a straight nose and grey eyes. She's the smallest of all of us, and the rumour going round is her CMC uniform shorts have gotten a little too snug due to a recent revelation about her fiancé hooking up with her younger sibling.

'She knew the rules,' Ashlyn states from behind Harmony. 'She signed the contract, just like everybody else.'

'We all know what we signed,' Imara says, sounding tetchy. 'But ain't nobody able to predict what's gonna happen in your personal life. They should cut Mona some slack.'

'I get that some of you are gonna be bothered by this,' Harmony says. 'But Ashlyn is right; Mona signed the contract. The rules are in place for a reason. We protect the Mutineers brand, at all times. People are scrutinizing us every second of every day. Mona will claw her place back on the squad. Lacey's gonna visit her after tonight's game, aren't you?'

All eyes go to Lacey, another flame-haired second-year veteran who nods her head, but my mind is reeling. I shift my position. I wipe my upper lip, which is now dappled in sweat. I'm already breaking two rules in my own contract. I waver a little and take a step back. From behind me, Jewel grabs my shoulders and gives them a squeeze.

'All okay?' she asks, and I force my best smile.

'What about Persia?' Angel asks.

Harmony looks to her fingers. 'I tried, but... I'm sorry. Persia's not gonna be coming back.'

There are gasps from everyone in the circle. Jewel's hands cover her mouth.

Ashlyn shushes everyone. 'Let her speak!' she raises her voice, referring to Harmony.

'I spoke to Persia this morning,' Harmony continues. 'Asked her to justify her behavior, and the photographs from Saturday night, if she wanted out or if she'd rather stay. She wanted to stay. Kathleen wanted to sanction her, but... Ms Conway wanted her gone. I'm sorry.'

Everyone talks at once. 'Rules are rules!' Ashlyn shouts over the commotion, exchanging glances with Harmony.

A moment later, the door to the locker room opens. Samantha Conway enters, wearing a face like thunder. She's followed closely by Kathleen.

Sam Conway rarely comes to the CMC locker room, unless it's to double-check on our appearance. Except now, everybody freezes at the sight of her, unsure what to do with themselves.

'Harmony, please go get changed,' she says smoothly to our captain. Harmony nods, moving to her locker. She looks to the rest of us. 'Everybody else, please take a seat.'

Instantly, I back up to my changing station – with my own life-size photograph in my Mutineers uniform as the backdrop – and sit my butt down. Everybody else does the same, in double quick time.

I remember the day they took my photograph in my uniform. I was so full of hope, that becoming part of the CMC would change my life for the better. That I was going to *be* better. That I deserved to be here.

Now all that's been brought into question.

I watch Sam Conway for a moment. She's dressed in a suit that's as sharp as her cheekbones. She's wearing bright red lipstick, and her face contains barely any fine lines for her age. The worst thing is that her son looks just like her. I think of the look on his face when I was naked for him, and it makes me shudder.

'Now,' Sam Conway begins, looking to her perfectly manicured nails. There's malice in her tone. 'To be down one cheerleader is unfortunate. To be down *two*? Well, that's practically unheard of.'

She attempts a smile. It kind of looks how the devil might react to receiving a bumper crop of sinners, standing guilt-stricken at the gates of hell.

She paces up and down. I dare not breathe.

'Miss Takeda's behavior this weekend was unacceptable. *Unacceptable.*'

That last word comes out as a hiss and the air in the locker room turns thick. Nobody wants to put a foot out of line. My stomach is clenched.

'May I remind you all,' Sam Conway continues, 'that you are here to represent a *brand*. You tarnish that brand, there will be *consequences*. If any of you need reminding of the terms of your contract, then that can be arranged. If you cannot abide by those rules, then Kathleen will show you the door, and I will be damned sure to *lock* it behind you.'

She pauses to let that sink in. A part of me wants to blurt out what I've been doing these past few weeks. I look at Harmony, who is now dressed. Could I have held out like she is doing… could I have tried harder to resist Jake Walsh's advances… those are the things that bother me the most. I thought – hoped – that if I told Kale McCoy I had secured a place on the CMC squad, he might let me have a break as a dancer at Surly's. That I could somehow hit the pause button on my other, less official, 'agreement'. But he didn't relent, and here I am, signed up to a contract whose terms I'd already broken before I even put pen to paper.

When Ms Conway is gone, I use the bathroom. Standing at the mirror, I grip the sides of the washbasin and lean forward. I want to splash cold water on my face, but I can't risk the damage to my makeup. I wouldn't want anyone to believe that I was anything less than perfect. Because, if I believe Ms Conway, that's what I'm here to represent. Perfection.

The first time I put it on, I'd never been prouder to wear the CMC uniform. Yet now, I've sullied it.

I'm startled when behind me, a stall opens. Harmony emerges to wash her hands.

'Ren?' she says. 'Everything alright?'

I force a smile, switching off the faucet. 'I'm fine.'

'I'm sorry about Persia. I feel guilty I couldn't persuade them to let her stay. I hate to say she brought it on herself, but… some girls, they don't like being told what they can and can't do.'

'It's not your fault,' I say, and I watch her wipe a little tear, before checking her eyelashes in the mirror. 'Same for Mona.'

Harmony sighs. 'Sometimes I think… in the twenty-first century, how can they still hold us to these standards? We talk about equality, but where's it gone? A girl can be a brain surgeon, a scientist, she can fight in the military, but heaven forbid a cheerleader should gain a few pounds.'

'Maybe the question we should be asking is why we still have cheerleaders,' I say, because she's right.

'Because we bring the family-friendly pep, remember? We bring the wholesome, we make it all shiny, before the men come along and cover everything in mud and grit and sweat.'

We laugh together. I like Harmony. A little like me, I wonder if she's hiding things.

Behind us, I hear a flush. From the furthest stall emerges an elegant, pale-skinned woman, with cropped, jet-black hair and a pair of headphones hanging around her neck. I've never seen her before. She comes and stands next to me, switching on the faucet.

'You're athletes, ladies,' she states as she washes her hands, looking in the mirror. 'Just like the players. Hell, they couldn't do what you do.' When she's done, she shakes her hands dry, walking backward toward the exit and giving us a wink as she goes.

'Who was that?' I ask, because clearly, she was listening in on our conversation.

'Carlie Kessler,' Harmony says with a smirk. 'DJ Stash. Responsible for the entire sound system in the Danube. The one who plays all our music?'

'Oh. Right,' I say.

'Come on, let's go,' Harmony says. 'We're gonna be late.'

—

Armed with our poms, on the walk from the locker room to the tunnel, we're escorted by security. Tonight, I'm consumed with self-doubt, as though somebody's gonna recognize me as a dancer at Surly's. Is it inevitable? That one day they'll all know. I have visions of myself in Sam Conway's office as she fires me when she finds out the truth. Like Persia, I wouldn't be allowed back. I look at the faces of my fellow cheerleaders. Seems like there are less smiles than on a usual game night. Like we all know one wrong move could spell the end of our time as CMC.

And that applies to me more than any of them.

The smiles are soon back on our faces though as we begin our set. Kathleen says that a smile puts the 'cheer' in 'cheerleader', and that a cheerleader without a smile is like a Christmas tree with no lights, or a cake without icing. I don't see it that way. I love how being a cheerleader brings joy to others. With our smiles, we give others hope, and for just a few minutes, their problems melt away. We make it okay to believe in something better... to believe in dreams.

When I dance at Surly's, I take zero satisfaction from it.

But this. Being in front of an entire stadium of people and lifting them up is a buzz like no other. It's my dream. And it's bigger than just me. I feel a part of something.

On the field, we dance and flip and high-kick our way through *Girls Girls Girls*, until the players are welcomed onto the field and we break off into our smaller groups.

I can't help but look Jake's way, and every time I do there's a serious scowl on his face, whether he's on the bench or making a play.

Tonight, as it turns out, there isn't much to cheer about. Game two of the season and the Mutineers are losing. At the final whistle, the score is seventeen to six to the opposition. I watch him shake hands with members of the other team, before most of the Mutineers players disappear back down through the tunnel toward the locker room.

'Well, that sucked,' Jewel mutters to me as we leave the field, smiling and waving to the thinning crowds as per our contracts. 'Now we're stuck with community outreach.'

'What do you mean?' I ask.

'Come on now, Ren, don't you keep up with the emails? You mean you didn't sign up to anything?'

'I've been busy, I guess.'

'The next two games are away games,' Jewel explains. 'Meaning, the Mutineers team travels, and we got nobody to cheer for. So, we, you know... head out into the community.'

'What was I supposed to sign up for?'

'Visits to old folks nursing homes, being present at opening ceremonies, meeting kids in schools. The sign-up sheet went out a couple' days ago.'

'I must have missed that.'

Back in the tunnel, Jewel hooks her arm through mine. 'Something on your mind?'

'I've been busy is all.'

'Sign up to the same things as me. Then we can hang out. Us rookies need to stick together. Besides, I wanna know you better, Ren. We can talk about why it is we're both still single and which boys we like.'

She's giving me a huge grin. I adore Jewel. We went through all the auditions together. But she's another person that I can't give away my secrets to, and it hurts like hell that I have to lie to her.

'Shame the one I like is off limits,' she says with a dramatic sigh.

A memory of Jake and I naked and in bed together filters through my mind and I feel the base of my neck warming.

'God, the sight of his ass in those white pants,' she giggles. 'Jake Walsh deserves a medal for that alone. The view from the twenty-five-yard line is pretty sweet on the offensive, lemme tell you.'

I'm grateful for the noise and the hubbub as other CMC members pile into the locker room after the end of the game and Jewel changes the subject.

I want to go home. A little voice tells me to quit, that I can't keep this up.

That I don't deserve to be here.

That I'm a liar.

But I look around me. Despite the low pay and all the petty little rules that we're meant to follow, I love this job. I love how it makes me feel, compared to working at Surly's and waiting tables at The Bounty. I feel *honored* to be here. And I earned my spot.

Yet now I'm forced to question which I love more: my membership of the CMC, or being with Jake.

Because whichever way I look at it... I can't have both.

And I fear time may be running out for me.

—

'Hey. How was the game?'

Dad is still up when I get home. He's got a blanket over his knees.

'They lost,' I tell him, and close the front door behind me.

'Oh. I'm sure you're very disappointed, sweetie.'

I laugh gently, walk over and run the back of my hand over his forehead, just to check he's not running a fever. He has a permanent wheeze these days, and quite often, his lips turn blue. 'Don't try to convince me you care about football, Daddy.'

'Give me the World Series over the Super Bowl, any day of the week.'

I tuck his blanket around him, then put my hands on my hips. 'Did you eat yet?'

'Patty Mays brought me some leftover lasagna. I left you some in the fridge.'

I think about Mona. I can't help it. 'Honestly, I'm not real hungry, Daddy.'

'You should eat something. You're working too hard. All for us. It's my fault. You should be out, having fun, meeting guys... Are you... seeing anyone?'

I feel myself blush. 'I, uh... it's nothing. It's not serious.'

My father's expression brightens. 'So, there is somebody.'

'We're tryna keep it on the down low, Daddy. It's not a thing.'

'What does he do?'

I mean, I can't say professional football player. 'He, uh, works at the stadium.'

'Well, that's nice. I hope you'll bring him home one day.'

I adore my Dad, but sometimes he forgets the things I have to do to pay off his debt. It's not a selfish thing – he's wrapped up in his own illness and I think he's blocked it out of his mind. Or maybe it's that he's unwilling to accept the truth of my situation. On Sundays, when I'm around, I batch cook food for him to last the entire week, to ensure he never goes hungry. But the reality is, I'm not here enough for him.

Once I've helped him into bed, I head to my room. Exhaustion washes over me. I've removed my makeup and I'm wearing my pyjamas, and I'm about to switch out the light when my phone vibrates on the nightstand.

I pause. My gaze flits to the light on the screen. I note, with a touch of disappointment, that it's not a message on the Jake phone.

I pick up the handset and unlock it, then navigate to my messages.

> I'm impatient to see you, Brandy Velvet. You looked so hot in your Mutineers uniform tonight. I'm excited for our next encounter.

Disgusted, I delete the message and toss the phone.

A moment later, the Jake phone vibrates. A message pops up.

> Hey there beautiful girl. I have a whole free day tomorrow. I'd love to spend it with you xx

In contrast, Jake's message makes me smile. But the smile is soon wiped from my face when I think about Persia's fate, and Sam Conway's warning earlier this evening. I start typing, a guilty knot in my stomach.

> I can't. I have to work.

Moments after I send the message, he calls me.

'You work too hard,' he says, no sooner have I answered. 'You could take a vacation day?'

'All my vacation days are booked in advance, and they're all taken up with CMC activities.'

'Then how about you call in sick to work? Think of all the fun things we could do at the cabin together.'

'I... Jake, I can't. They're stretched as it is.'

His voice loses its confident, persuasive tone. Instead, it softens. 'I've got two away games coming up. I won't get to see you. Not as much.'

As much as it pains me to admit it, his absence might make things a little easier on me. I keep coming back to my exit route for this situation. The only way seems to be to break his heart. To pretend that I've lost interest, even when I haven't.

Why can't I have both?

'Serenity?' he says when I say nothing.

A thick layer of anguish lines my stomach. 'They fired a cheerleader today,' I tell him.

'They did?'

'Persia Takeda.'

'What they fire her for?'

'She broke the terms of her contract. She brought the Mutineers brand into disrepute by having her picture taken in a club and drinking alcohol. That's all she had to do, don't you see? Jake. I'm having sex. With a Mutineers running back. In secret.'

'I know,' is his agonized response. 'I know you're the one carrying all the risk here, I know that.' Except he doesn't know. He doesn't know the half of it. How I spend the rest of my time.

Tears come spilling out. Maybe it's the stress of the past few weeks but I can't stop the tide.

'I wanna be with you,' Jake says. 'In fact, I can't stand being away from you. And it's not just that I'm crazy about you, I'm falling for you, Serenity. But the last thing I wanna do is pressure you into anything.'

I hug my knees and try to get my emotions under control.

'Forget tomorrow,' he says. 'I can be free any night this week. We can talk this through.'

'I can't,' I say, and I get choked up on the lies I keep telling him. 'I gotta take care of my dad.'

'Then I can help. Introduce me to your father.'

I want to tell him that I'm not who he thinks I am. Or who he wants me to be. 'Jake, no. I can't.'

'One hour. You can't spare one hour just to talk to me?'

'Maybe it's for the best,' I choke out.

His voice grows hoarse. 'Please. Don't do this.'

'I've done too much already. I'm sorry. I have to go.'

I hang up the phone. There's a tightness in my chest that makes it harder to breathe. I let the sobs overcome me, and I bury my head in my pillow to muffle the sounds.

Chapter Eighteen

Jake

Friday morning, I lie in bed and stare at the ceiling. I wonder if I'd been more of a bro, a big dumbass fuckboy, going out every night to strip clubs and having random hook-ups with women I met on Instagram, whether I would have gotten laid a shit ton more in my life by now and Serenity would still be talking to me, because, hey, I'd be fucking irresistible to women.

Except I'm not irresistible to women. At least, not to the one that I want.

I haven't spoken to Serenity since Monday night when she hung up on me.

I'm trying not to be a selfish asshole here. And yet, I can't shake the feeling that there's something more to her keeping her distance from me.

My whole life, I've toed the line. High school star athlete. The steady, reliable, nice guy who never drank too much, never slept around, ignored all the girls who slid into my DMs. I don't even know why anymore.

Serenity. There's another story. She's beautiful, and I'm not the only guy who knows it. And I know she's not a rulebreaker, but it's like, even if there was no contract, she doesn't seem to have time for me.

It makes my heart ache that maybe there's something in her life I don't know about.

Or maybe some*one*.

My phone lights up on the nightstand. I reach for it, and squint at the screen.

'S'up, Cap?' I answer to Dalt Briar.

'Hey, man. Just checking in. Checking you're cool with… you know… the news this morning.'

I sit up in bed. 'What news?'

'Oh, crap. You ain't seen it. Ally did say to me that I should ask you that first. I figured you would have already.'

'I don't get what you're talking about,' I say.

'Pictures of you and Lemon Conway are all over the local news. It's just… you know… stupid paparazzi shit.'

My eyes close. 'Fuck,' I grind out.

'You took her out again?'

'Yesterday, for lunch. It was warm, we sat outside.'

'Yeah, well, there must have been a photographer pitched up. The pictures are pretty clear.'

'Goddamn it,' I snap, and push the sheets back. I go to my desk and open my laptop. This week cannot get any worse.

'Look, if you want, I can ask the guys to go easy on you. Tell 'em you didn't have a choice.'

'I didn't.'

'That sucks, man. You shouldn't have to put up with that.'

I wince, because it feels like he might be referring to Lemon, rather than Sam Conway. I'm sure he can take a guess at the latter's behavior. But Lemon's got a good nature, despite me having zero attraction toward her.

I rub my eyes. 'I can handle myself. With the guys. There's no need to say anything. I'm more pissed at the photographer.'

'Okay, so long as you're sure. See you at practice.'

I bid Dalton goodbye, hang up and go online.

NFL RUNNING BACK JAKE WALSH SPARKS ROMANCE RUMOURS WITH MUTINEERS' OWNER HANK CONWAY'S GRANDDAUGHTER

I sigh when I see the photo, because of course it looks like I'm completely smitten with Lemon. Her head is thrown back, laughing at something I've just said. To the outside world, it looks like we're into one another.

I rest my elbows on my knees, bury my face in my palms. What with losing Monday night's game, getting knocked back by Serenity and having my picture taken with Lemon for the local gossip pages, it's not been the best week of my life.

I call Lemon.

'I'm so happy I wore a pretty dress!' is her reaction when I tell her.

'I'm serious, Lemon, people are gonna ask you if we're together. I need to know what you plan on telling them. This whole dating thing… it was never meant to be public knowledge.'

Plus, Lemon doesn't know about Serenity.

'Nobody's asked me anything,' Lemon says.

I can't help but roll my eyes. She's a sweet enough girl but not always the sharpest tool in the shed. She seems to have no inclination that her mother might have had a photographer waiting near the venue of our date on purpose, so she could hold me hostage, knowing it would be harder for me to wriggle out of taking her daughter out again if people were talking about us like we're a couple in real life. I bite my lip, infuriated. 'But they will, Lemon. We need to get our story straight.'

The 'date' itself was fine, I guess. I was honest with her, stopping short of speaking about Serenity. I told her that I was interested in someone else. And while I used to think Lemon had a crush on me, something about her behavior around me no longer fits that theory. While at her brother's wedding, she was making it obvious that she was staring at me, yet I can't help but wonder whether those initial flirtatious glances were the result of her mother pressuring her into showing an interest. But since we've had a few dates, Lemon seems uninterested in me as a potential partner. I'll be the first to admit it's confusing.

It all boils down to this being part of her mother's masterplan. The woman who right now already has my *cajónes* in a vice. My golden boy reputation doesn't exactly help. So, while I can't deny anything, I don't want to confirm anything either.

'I'll call the Mutineers' publicity team,' I tell her. 'If any journalist asks for a statement, we can just say we're friends and we're having fun and exploring whether there might be more there. How does that sound?'

Lemon giggles. 'That sounds fine to me.'

'Uhhh, Lemon?'

'Yes?' she says.

'Just so we're clear. We're not interested in one another, are we? We're doing this for your mother's sake, yes? So she gets off your back about finding a serious relationship and I get to keep my spot on the Mutineers. Smoke and mirrors.'

We talked about this. On our so-called date. I don't know why, but – a little like Serenity – I always get the feeling there's something Lemon ain't telling me. 'Yes, yes, of course,' she says. 'Smoke and mirrors.'

'I'll call the publicity team now, right?'

'Right. Right.'

'Stick to that line, okay?'

'I sure will.'

When I hang up, I toss my phone and place two hands behind the back of my head.

I'm beginning to really dislike Samantha Conway. There's no way in any possible universe she didn't set this up.

It makes me wonder what else is going on that I don't know about.

I want to talk to someone about the situation I've found myself in. I could talk to my teammates but they'll just give me shit.

I look at the other phone. The Serenity phone. It remains charging and unused on my desk. I haven't switched it off since Serenity blew me off on Monday. She's the only other person who I can talk to about this freaking weird Lemon situation. I wonder if she's seen the news, and what she makes of it. I pick up the phone and unlock it, thinking about sending a message. I blow out my cheeks and think the better of it.

If she wanted to change her mind, she could contact me.

And she hasn't.

—

Dalton Briar must have said something to my teammates, because at our non-contact training session for team drills, nobody even whispered a word about Lemon. Not even Hud Briar, and that's saying something about Hudson.

When I get home around three, I'm hunting round in the fridge when I hear the front door slam. The next thing I know, River is racing up the stairs in what sounds like floods of tears. I inhale a hastily made sandwich before heading up to her room.

When I bang on the door, she shrieks at me, 'Go away!'

I hover outside in the corridor. A weird sensation washes over me. River never really had too many hormones flying around as a fourteen- or fifteen-year-old and I wonder if they're just hitting now. I've never really seen her cry before. At least, not like this.

'Come on, Riv…' I say softly, knocking on the door again.

'Go away! I fucking hate you!'

'Woah, what did I do?'

Her voice comes back through the door. 'You brought me to this damn place! You're the reason I have zero friends and nobody wants to go near me! You're never even here anyway, you're always busy doin' somethin' else! Why couldn't you have signed with the Eagles? Then I could have stayed with my real friends!'

I'm through with being yelled at, so I barge into her room. She's on the bed with her shoes off, the quilt all crumpled, her eyes puffy and black makeup staining her tear-streaked cheeks.

'What's goin' on?'

Big soft plushies come flying at my face. 'Get out!' she hollers again. 'Get out, get out, get out!'

'Not until you tell me what the hell is up.'

She breaks down then and buries her face in her hands. I sit down on her bed and rub her back. Girls like that when they're crying. Gracie Olavsen was a crier, especially when she was on her period. I got pretty good at soothing her.

I snort. This is why women don't find me sexy. Because I'm soft. I'm too fucking nice.

'Don't laugh at me,' River snaps through her tears.

'I wasn't.'

'Then what was that noise you just made?'

'Nothing, I just… I was thinking about something else, sorry. You gonna tell me what's with the ugly crying?'

Another plushie hits me square in the face.

River takes some breaths. 'Something happened at school today.'

'I take it, it wasn't good?'

River wipes her tears, tries to compose herself. She gives a big sigh. 'You remember I told you about the winter formal?' she asks.

'Winter formal? Sure, yeah. What about it?'

'You remember when we went to that wedding, and I told you there was a waiter there who I recognized from school?'

'Uh. Sure.'

'Scottie Lincoln. Today I found out that he told every guy at school not to invite me to the winter formal.'

I blink at her. 'Wait, what?'

'You heard me. And the worst thing about it? I found out in the bathroom, while I was inside a stall when some girls came in and started talking about how nobody was gonna invite me because Scottie told them not to. And they were *laughing* about it.'

More tears spill over onto her cheeks and her face crumples. Anger balloons in my chest.

'Why would a guy do that? Because he wanted to ask you?'

'No, he already has a date!'

She's sobbing again. I get up and pace next to her bed. 'So lemme get this straight. This asshole already asks a girl to the winter formal, but he goes around telling every other guy in your class not to invite you? Why the fuck would he do that?'

'I don't know. I think because I told him I couldn't get free tickets to any of your games.'

'So fucking what? Even I don't get free tickets to the game!'

'He's a jock. Everybody worships the ground he walks on.'

'He plays sports?'

'He's on the soccer team.'

I stiffen. 'They play after school's out?'

Her eyes flit to mine, like she can read my mind. 'Yes. Maybe. I don't know. Jake, just leave it okay, I can handle it.'

Rage in my stomach threatens to boil over. Nobody treats my sister that way. I hold out my hand to her. 'Put your shoes on. You're coming with me.'

She's still wiping tears. 'No. Just leave it.'

'Riv,' I say, my tone forceful. 'Some guys might be happy to sit back and watch their baby sister take shit like that from some ugly high school douchebag. But not me.'

—

Thirty minutes later we've pulled up in my pickup beside the chain link fence that surrounds the playing fields at River's high school.

River didn't say a word the entire journey here. Just leaned her arm against the doorframe and rested her chin on her hand. She's wiped her face clean of tears and makeup but there's no mistaking she's been crying. Now she's staring from the window in the opposite direction from the soccer game that's playing on the other side of the fence.

The ball of rage in my stomach has ruptured. I'm haemorrhaging anger and frustration, and maybe it's not only because of River's situation. I'm angry that I haven't been there for my sister. I'm pissed at Sam Conway too, for making me take her daughter out on dates, like it's an unwritten rule in my NFL contract that my pro-career depends on making her family look good. I'm frustrated at the hold Serenity has over me, and I have this creeping suspicion that there's something she's not telling me, like maybe she's fooling around with me but I'm not the only guy in her life. I know her father's sick. But there must be another reason for her never being around or always needing to leave. And I think that reason has been staring me in the face all this time.

'Which one is he?' I ask in the driver's seat with the window down.

River glances over at the game for a brief second. Their uniforms are black with yellow numbers.

'The number ten,' she says.

'That's Scottie Lincoln?'

'That's him. Can I go now? I don't wanna be here if you're gonna talk to him.'

'Where you gonna go?'

'Meet me at the mall? You can buy me a McFlurry.'

'Fine.'

She opens the car door. 'Look, just don't hit anybody, okay? He's not worth it.'

'Don't sweat it, Riv. I know what I'm doing.'

When River's crossed the road, I take the pickup round to the school's front entrance. I park across the road from the main lot and I wait.

I don't have to wait long before the game is over and the kids with cars are filtering out into the lot. I get out of the pickup and cross the road. I keep my sunglasses on. I'm wearing my varsity jacket from Penn State.

I watch Scottie Lincoln bid farewell to his buddies and approach his car – a black sedan – carrying a black sports bag over his shoulder. He's searching around for his keys when I approach him from behind.

'Are you Scottie Lincoln?' I ask calmly.

He turns his head and recognition flashes across his features. 'Woah, you're—'

He doesn't even get to finish his sentence before I've body slammed him into his car door. His eyes go wide with fear.

'That's right, I'm Jake Walsh, asshole, and my sister goes to this school. You know who my sister is, you piece of shit?'

'River,' he sputters. I'm leaning so close to him I can see the sweat break out on his upper lip.

'Did you tell all the other guys in this school not to ask my sister to the winter formal?'

'I can explain, man,' he says.

'Did you do it?' I demand.

'Yeah, I did it,' he manages, 'but, hey, you gotta understand—'

'If I didn't play for the NFL,' I interrupt him, 'and I didn't value my career as highly as I do, then you should know, right about now I'd have separated your nut sack from your body. You come within ten feet of my sister again, you'll be hearing from me, you sorry-ass motherfucker. And next time I won't be so fucking soft on you.'

I shrug him off. The guy looks speechless.

'Hey, man—' he calls out in a strangled tone, but I walk away. I cross the road, and head back to my pickup.

—

I buy River dinner at the mall, though we keep getting interrupted by Mutineers fans wanting autographs. One woman even asks me about my relationship with Lemon. River finds it hilarious and it's good to see her smiling again at my expense.

We don't say another word about the winter formal or Scottie Lincoln. Inside, I'm still simmering.

When we reach home around five, I know I need to pack for my trip tomorrow for the away game. But something's bothering me.

I check the Serenity phone. I know there'll be no messages or missed calls, even though a part of me wants her to have contacted me, telling me she's changed her mind.

But doubts linger in my mind about why she was always making excuses, and I want the truth.

Right now, early Friday evening, this was our time. Only a week ago, I was kissing her, and I thought she might have been a virgin.

I realize now that I was totally naïve.

Because I think I know now what's really been going on.

I pick up the phone from my desk. My fingers hover over the screen. She'll have finished her shift at The Bounty by now.

She answers on the first ring, her voice a little breathy and unsure. 'Jake?' she says.

I hate how my heart swells at the sound of her voice, how it grounds me, puts me back on her leash.

I close my eyes and rub my forehead. 'Hey. I, uh, wanted to meet you. At the cabin. Tonight.'

'Tonight?' she asks.

'Just to talk. There're some things I'd like to say to you. How about eight o'clock?'

Her voice tremors. 'Eight is difficult for me.'

I roll my eyes. There she goes again. This is why I don't feel I can entirely trust her. 'I travel tomorrow. Eight is the only time I can do. You don't have to stay long. Maybe a half hour.'

She goes quiet. I taste bile at the back of my throat because she's no doubt thinking what excuse she can make up to not come see me.

'Alright. I'll be there at eight,' she says softly.

—

I get to the cabin early. My mood hasn't improved. If anything, it's worse. I walk into the bedroom to witness the bed linen still tied up in knots and I'm reminded of everything that happened

Sunday afternoon, and what a goddamned idiot I've been. I find myself pacing, waiting for her to show.

At just after eight, I hear tires crunching on the track. I stiffen. I hear her car door open and close, the sound of her boots against the porch steps. Usually, the sight of her makes me weak.

Not today.

When she knocks on the door, I open it. I swallow when I see her face. This is gonna be harder than I thought.

'Hi,' she says.

I open the door wider. 'Come on in,' I say, trying to keep my voice free of any emotion.

She steps inside. She carries a bag slung over her shoulder. The sleeves of her sweater are too long for her arms, and she tugs nervously at the material.

I close the door behind her.

'How are you?' she asks.

I'm not doing this. Getting into banal conversation. I didn't come here for that.

'Thanks for coming,' I tell her in a tone that's even more detached than the one I was going for.

Her eyes flit to the bedroom door and I see her swallow. Like she's remembering how good it was between us.

'Look, I know you're busy with something so… I came here to say… I think I figured it out.'

Her eyes search mine. I remind myself that resistance is the only way I'll overcome this.

When she speaks, her voice sounds a little stifled. 'Figured what out?'

'It's another guy, isn't it? I'm just your side piece. You're either in a relationship or there's some other guy you're hooking up with. I figure there has to be a reason you're never available.'

She looks at me for a moment, then turns her head to the side, biting down on her bottom lip. Her chin trembles and her eyes turn glassy.

She takes a moment to compose herself. Her voice quivers when she speaks. 'Because that's the first conclusion you'd draw, ain't it? Forget about the rules of my contract, forget that my father is sick, I can't spend time with you so that automatically means I'm cheating on you with another guy—'

'Are you?'

She glares at me. I'm a little taken aback to see the level of rage that flashes in her eyes.

'Everybody wants something!' she explodes. 'You want my time, the Mutineers want my time, my father needs me, everybody needs *something*!'

'You're doing it again,' I say to her, and I keep my voice steady.

'Doing what?' she yells.

'You didn't answer my question. About whether there's another guy in your life.'

'Would you like that?'

I grit my teeth. The thought of it is torture. 'Of course not. I just wanna know what's going on with you. I need to know the truth. Is there somebody else?'

'NO!' she practically screams at me, and at the same time, her cell phone starts ringing in her bag.

She covers her face with her hands, maybe in reaction to her phone, I'm not sure.

I don't know what else I can ask. The ball is in her court.

The phone rings out. Moments later, it's ringing again.

'Goddamn it!' she curses.

She looks stressed as she pulls her cell from her bag. She walks past me in the direction of the bedroom and lowers her voice.

'What the hell, Jax?' she hisses and my whole chest tightens up, because maybe Jax is *the* guy.

I hear the muffled voice of the person at the other end of the phone.

'I know, I know,' Serenity says. 'I left a message with Mila, did she not tell you?'

The voice says something else.

'I'm a half hour away,' Serenity says, flustered, before she adds, 'No, don't send anybody. I'll be there, okay? I'll be there... Can you stall for me?'

The voice is talking again. I move closer to her.

'It wasn't my intention to make him mad, Jax. Just... I'll leave now, alright? I'll be there soon.'

She hangs up the phone.

For a long moment, there's quiet in the room. I'm prepared to let her explain, so I stay silent.

She exhales. 'I work in a club,' she states quietly. 'It's on the west side of Canyon.'

'What... like, you t-tend bar or something?'

She looks at me, and tears fill her eyes when she says, 'I'm a dancer. A private dancer. I take off my clothes on stage each night, for cash tips. I'm a stripper, Jake. That's what I do. It's my other job.'

I take a step back, reeling. Her admission is... so far from what I imagined.

'I don't—' I say, stunned. 'Is that supposed to be a joke? You... yanking my chain for some dumb reason?'

'What, you don't believe me?'

My mouth opens to say something. In this moment, I don't know what to believe.

'I have to go,' Serenity stutters, an edge to her voice. 'I have a shift. If you want proof, then follow me. Get in your car and follow me back to Canyon. You'll see for yourself... you'll see the truth about me.'

She drops the phone back into her bag and stalks over to the main door of the cabin. With one hand on the door handle, she looks at me, tearful eyes questioning. 'Are you coming?'

I look her up and down, confused as hell. Then I swallow my doubts.

'Yes,' I say.

—

It's dark on the ride back into Canyon. I sit in the cab of my pickup, my grip on the wheel unusually tight, my headlights illuminating Serenity's license plate on the back of her car.

The radio's on low. Questions go in circles round my head.

Serenity claims to be a stripper. My Serenity. *Can it be true? But why? And for how long?*

Back in Canyon, the rain's coming down. Nearer the center of town, the traffic grows heavier. I stick close on her tail. She knows I'm here. We head west before taking a left into a parking lot.

I follow. I don't park up, but she does, and then I watch as she hightails it inside the back of a building.

I peer through my rain-soaked driver's side window into the darkness.

Then it hits me. I see the red neon sign and I realize I've been here before, the night I celebrated with my fellow teammates when us rookies officially joined the Mutineers' roster.

To Surly's Tavern.

Chapter Nineteen

Serenity

Kaycee — aka *Heaven Scent* — is the only one in the communal dressing room when I burst in from outside, my hair damp from the rain.

I drop my bag, double over and grasp my knees. I let go with one hand and cover my mouth. The noise that emerges is a muffled, strangled sob.

'Hey, Ren,' Kaycee says until she hears my cry, before she adds, 'Oh, honey, what's wrong?' and gets to her feet.

I straighten and bury my face in my palms. I'm late and I know I should be getting ready, but the entire journey here I was being followed by Jake. I saw him pull up in the parking lot.

I pace back and forth. I want to know if he's coming into the club, or if seeing me run inside was enough.

'Sweetie, you need to calm down,' Kaycee says. 'You want some water? Shot o' bourbon? What the hell happened?'

I wipe my eyes. I steady my breathing, tuck my hair behind my ears. 'This guy I've been seeing… he's just found out why I'm not free most nights.'

She winces. 'Oh, lord, honey, I'm so sorry. He didn't suspect a thing?'

'He thought I was seeing another guy.'

'That's sweet. Did you tell him you're seeing *lots* of other guys?'

There's a wry smile on her face like it's meant as a joke, only I don't find it funny. 'He followed me here. In his pickup.'

'He comin' inside to watch the show?'

I feel like crying again. 'I have no idea.'

She grips both my shoulders in her hands. 'For your sake, I hope he doesn't. They're clamorin' out there tonight, sugar. Takes a guy mighty sure o' hisself to handle seeing his girl up on stage like that.'

My voice tremors. 'That's what I'm afraid of.'

-

I hear Jax's voice over the mic. 'Give it up for our own… Baby Bullets!'

I've been lingering backstage, trying to take in the faces of the majority-male Friday night crowd. My heart is racing. I lean back, a gap in the curtain allowing me to glimpse the main door and those still coming in from the rain to pay the entry fee. Yet, I can't see Jake anywhere.

I wonder if he pulled up in the parking lot, took one look at this joint then decided to leave.

He's not like the average Surly's patron, that's for sure. Would I want him to see me dressed like this? I look down. I'm wearing a pair of frayed Daisy Dukes, bleached and cut extra low, a chunky belt, a blue denim studded bra with a matching denim jacket over the top, white cowgirl boots and a white, vintage cattle rancher cowboy hat. My wig is long and straight, a shade of light, chestnut brown.

The answer to '*do I want Jake Walsh to see me dressed like this?*' is 'no'. Yet a small part of me wants to say 'yes'.

Talia's coming off stage. She plays to the minority emo crowd, her outfit all gothic black and intricate lace. She comes down the stairs and starts pulling dollar bills from the tops of her boots and hemline of her panties, her surgically enhanced breasts still on show.

'Hey, Ren, you alright?'

I look beyond her shoulder, my eyes still searching for him. 'Hey,' I mumble.

She grins and flashes a hundred-dollar bill in front of my eyes, pleased with herself. 'Got some high rollers in town tonight. Go get 'em out there.'

'You fellas ready for more?' Jax's voice goes out over the mic, and there is whooping and cheering in response.

The stage-lights alter to blues and greens.

'Back by popular demand,' Jax says. 'You folks can't get enough. Our favorite red dirt country gal… Texas' finest, give it up for *Braaaaandy Velvet*!'

There's more cheering. I'm thankful for the low light tonight. *Cowgirls* by Morgan Wallen comes over the sound system. It's a slower tempo than my usual routines. I know the moves by heart because I've danced them a hundred times before. Within the first minute, I'm writhing on my hands and knees on stage. Soon, I toss my jacket and hat. So far, so normal. Except my heart is beating so fast I can't think straight, and for every guy who whistles at me, I have to search his face to check if he's Jake. As I make my way to the pole at the end of the stage, my eyes flit out to the crowd, my hips gyrating, sliding my palms down my thighs to more whistles. I go down to a squat position, hands on my knees spread wide, and once more, and my eyes sweep further back in the shadows, checking the tables, trying to glimpse the faces.

I perform on the pole, sliding it between my legs, hooking the back of my leg around it and leaning back until I'm as far back as I can go. Already there're guys waving dollar bills in my direction. I grab the buckle and remove my belt, but I take every opportunity I can to scour the spectators, even upside down.

The moment I slither out of my denim bra and let it drop to the stage floor is when I see him. Holed up and alone in a corner beside a table, cap pulled low on his forehead. I recognize the logo, and he's wearing the same pair of beige-colored pants he was wearing at the cabin.

I feel like I wanna puke. Yet the dancer inside me has this weird notion that I want to impress him, and that, hell, if Jake Walsh knows I'm a stripper, he might as well know I'm not half bad at it.

I continue to dance. The volume of the catcalls raises a notch. With my arms behind my head, I grab the pole, pressing my butt into it as I slide all the way down, my breasts thrust forward and fully on display. It's a move that the regulars all love, and how I make the best tips.

It's also a move that has Jake Walsh getting to his feet and heading for the door.

As I watch him go, my body instinctively grinds to a halt. The music keeps playing. After a beat, when I let go of the pole, watching the door, the catcalls are replaced by jeers. The protests grow in volume as I lean down and grab my top, then turn and run from the stage.

Without looking back, I burst out the back door into the parking lot. I glance left and right and see the back of him heading for his pickup. I'm holding my bra top to my breasts but the back ain't yet fastened.

'Jake, wait!' I call out, running toward him. The rain's coming down now. 'Jake, please, wait up!'

He turns and I almost crash into his chest.

I look up at him, eyes pleading but I realize he won't return my gaze. Under the streetlights, I can see that his jaw is set in a fixed line. The cap is pulled down so low that I can't properly see his face.

'I'm sorry,' I say, and my voice breaks. 'You wanted to know. Now you know.'

I see his Adam's apple bob up and down just once. His hands go into his pockets.

Behind me, I hear the shriek of the door hinges. Talia comes racing outside. The rain drips down my face as I wait for Jake to respond. When Talia reaches me, she throws a coat around my shoulders.

'Ren! Are you crazy? What the hell you doin' out here? You can't race from the stage like that in the middle of your routine!'

She wraps me in the coat, and I pull it round me, still pressing my top to my chest. My eyes don't leave Jake's face.

'I need a minute,' I tell her.

'Sweetie, you don't got a minute. Jax is gonna be out here any second. You need to get back inside.'

'Please, say something,' I say to him.

The door sounds again. Jax comes out, flanked by Hurley.

'Serenity, what the fuck?!' he hollers angrily at me at the top of his voice.

Jake looks up at him, takes a step back. I'm crying now, my tears mixing with the rainwater. I want him to say something. Anything. But his expression remains impassive.

'Serenity Harper, get the fuck back inside, *now*,' Jax says when he reaches me.

'Please, just one minute!' I beg.

'Move. Now,' he warns me. 'Hurley, get this motherfucker out of here.'

Hurley steps forward. Jake reacts fast. He throws up his hands and backs away. I feel Jax's hands grip my shoulders, turning me back round to walk back toward the club.

When I glance over my shoulder, Jake is walking toward his pickup.

—

'Boss'll see you now,' Jax says soberly to me on his way out at the end of the night. 'Night, Ren.'

'Goodnight, Jax.'

It's past three a.m. The club is closed. I feel numb. Everybody else changed clothes and went home already. Somebody told Kale what happened earlier, and he's decided to keep me behind. I feel like a naughty schoolkid sent to the principal's office.

I yawn. Wearily, I get to my feet. I've been back on stage for three separate routines and completed four private lap dances. I haven't seen a dime of my earnings, other than to pull the dollar bills from the pockets of my Daisy Dukes.

I keep my head down. I don't need to look up to feel Kale McCoy's presence. He's imposing enough to make himself known.

The office is dark. He sits with his feet on the desk, the light from his laptop screen illuminating his whole face, his shirt collar wide open.

'You wanted to see me?' I say quietly.

He fixes me with his stare. 'Come where I can see you, sweetheart.'

I grip my left thumb inside the fingers of my right hand and approach with caution. Kale is prone to outbursts and, on occasion, throwing things.

'Heard there was an incident tonight,' he says.

I'm guessing Jax was the one to tell him. Kale raises one hand and with one finger beckons me over to his side of the desk. Nervously, I walk round.

On the laptop screen is the grainy image from the club's CCTV that faces the parking lot. He hits the play button and I watch myself race out after Jake, the picture obscured a little by the rain. But you can tell that it's me, and Talia when she follows with the coat. There's no sound.

Kale hits the pause button and presses the tip of his finger to the screen.

'Who is this, and what's he to you?' he asks.

I look to the floor. 'He's nobody. He's just a guy.'

'He your boyfriend?'

'No. I mean—'

' 'Cause you better have a damn good reason why you'd abandon that stage mid-performance, Serenity.'

My shoulders slump.

'I ain't hearin' my reason, baby girl.'

I let out a shaky breath. 'It won't happen again, I promise.'

He leans back in his chair and his eyes wander down the length of my body. 'I won't hold it against you. Kaycee saved your bacon out there. You know you're still my prettiest girl, Serenity, but I swear, you pull a stunt like that again and I will hang you out to dry. Tonight's earnings won't be going in the ledger. Call it payback for you messin' up the show.'

I open my mouth to object. It means everything I've done tonight has earned me a big fat zero. 'That don't seem fair to me,' I whisper.

'Fair? Fair is you not running off that stage mid-performance and making this establishment look bad! I want every man who comes in here to believe he could get with you. But if you're running off after some fight with your Ivy League boyfriend... kind of ruins the illusion, don't it?'

No matter what I think, I nod my head in agreement.

'May I go home now?' I ask.

He flicks his wrist dismissively. 'Go. Get outta here.'

I turn and walk to the door.

'Oh, and Serenity?' he says from behind me. 'Tomorrow night. Brody Conway wants to spend a little more time with you.'

I swallow hard. I know I'm pushing it when I say, 'You can't send somebody else?'

I can see his expression darken, even in this light. 'Seems he's quite taken with just you.'

'He makes me feel uncomfortable.'

'That's too bad. He pays me a lotta clams. So, mind you do as he asks.'

Tears prick my eyes. The last thing I want is to spend my Saturday night with Brody Conway. But I don't have anything left in me to argue.

'Goodnight, Serenity,' Kale says as I walk out the door.

Crawling into bed, it's nearly four a.m. Thankfully, other than squad practice, I don't gotta work tomorrow.

My body aches. Memories of the look on Jake's face when he left the club linger in my mind. I reach for the phone he gave me.

There are no messages. Nothing.

I type out what I want to say, then wonder if I should send it.

> If you'll let me, I can explain.

I hit send, and I'm asleep before my head hits the pillow.

In the morning, there's no reply.

Chapter Twenty

Serenity

'Wait… you're not coming with me?'

Saturday night, there's a black limousine in the Surly's parking lot. Jax looks at me and winces. 'He sent a car,' he mutters.

'But a *limo*?' I ask, because nothing could be less indiscreet.

'Best go get yourself changed,' Jax says.

My heart's in my throat. 'And what if he breaks the rules?'

'Then tell us after. The driver will be sure to return you to us later on this evening, Ren.'

My bottom lip trembles.

'I'm sorry,' Jaxon adds.

After a limo ride to the same oceanfront condo, the driver escorts me up to the apartment. As before, Brody Conway opens the door for me, and I slip inside.

'Serenity,' he says, taking a step back. 'Let me take your coat.'

I slip out of the overcoat and hand it to him.

'Very nice,' he says as his eyes rake over me. He's wearing a white shirt with the collar open, and a pair of black suit pants with nothing on his feet. 'But I think I can go one better. Your outfit for tonight is in the bedroom. Can I get you something to drink first?'

'I had a drink of water in the limo, thank you.'

'You didn't open the champagne?'

'I had nothing to celebrate. And for the record, I was kind of grossed out by your collection of dirty magazines.'

'Funny, I thought they might help get you in the mood.'

'In the mood for what?'

'Why don't you go and look in the bedroom?'

I lose patience and march past him, knocking into him on purpose as I go. I walk to the same bedroom that I changed in before. Yet the moment I see what's on the pristine bed, I come to a halt.

Laid out flat is some bondage-style underwear. Black leather strips punctuated with silver, metal-edged holes.

Next to it: a CMC uniform.

He wants me to dress as a cheerleader, then take it all off for him.

I turn on my heel, and march back out to Brody, who has hung up my coat somewhere and is now waiting for me in the living area, a drink in his hand.

'No,' I say with force. 'I'm not doing it.'

Then he does something I don't expect. He starts laughing. 'Do you know what the best thing about it is? It's not even fake! That there is a genuine, bona fide CMC uniform. You know who it belonged to? That bitch who put pictures of her booty on the internet.'

'Persia Takeda,' I whisper in surprise.

'That's her. And now, they're all scrambling around, thinking she stole it from the Mutineers family. No, I knew I had to have it. She got smaller tits than you but... no matter. I like a tight fit. You know, I urged my mother to fire her? For the sake of the brand. That's what I love about you, Serenity, you're so good at keeping all this so... private.'

'You have no morals,' I hiss.

'Says the girl who takes her clothes off for a living. Go on, now... run along and get dressed. You know what happens if you don't.'

I stand my ground, my chest rising and falling. I have the urge to flee the apartment, but the driver clearly works for Brody, and I can't leave dressed the way that I am now without my coat.

'And if I still refuse?'

The humor from a moment ago drains from his face. He takes a step closer and places one long finger against my chin, pressing upwards so that my face is tilted toward his. His eyes meet mine. 'Then let me just check I've got Kathleen Lafferty's number in my cell.'

We remain like that for a few seconds. He wants me to know he's not bluffing, so he casually reaches for his phone in his pocket. He looks down and begins scrolling through his contacts.

I push his finger away and look down. When his thumb hovers over Kathleen's name, I relent. Reluctantly, I walk back to the bedroom.

It takes me a good ten minutes to get dressed.

When he sees me in the CMC uniform, complete with the boots, his expression turns lustful. 'There she is,' he breathes.

He's sat on the couch, one ankle resting on the opposite bent knee. His gaze roves over my body hungrily. 'It's a good fit on you,' he then says. He lifts his hips a fraction and leans further back into the couch.

I stand there and feel like a fraud. I'm bringing shame onto the CMC. Persia's shorts are snug on my hips, and Brody was right about the top with the big 'M' emblazoned across it, which is too tight, making it sit higher up my midriff. The bondage-style underwear has no coverage; it's all straps, so the curves of my breasts peek out from underneath.

'I should have brought you a pair of poms,' Brody muses.

'I'll need some music,' I say flatly, keen to get this over with.

'Don't worry, sweetie,' he says, swiping something on his phone before I hear the opening bars of *Girls Girls Girls* fill the apartment.

I cock my head to one side, give him a look that says *you cannot be serious*.

His lips twist into a sardonic smile. 'I want high kicks,' he breathes.

I loathe everything about him. He twirls his finger midair as if to say *get moving*.

For a brief moment, I close my eyes. Steel myself. It has to be a dance that incorporates both cheerleader and private dancer. I have to conjure up the essence of both somehow. 'Could you start it again, please?' I ask.

Brody Conway sips his drink. 'Focus, Serenity,' he responds in an impatient tone, as he restarts the track.

As I dance for Brody, I think about Jake. It's the only way I can get through this. To imagine I'm dancing for him and that he's the one admiring my body. His game is tomorrow night. I wonder what he's doing right at this moment.

I work my hips. My hands go into my hair. I block out my surroundings, and Brody's shameless admiration of my moves. I flick my hair, pretending there are poms in both my hands. He cocks his head for the high kicks, because he wants the view between my thighs.

Halfway through the track, when I'm still fully dressed, Brody raises his voice. 'Come on now, Serenity. Don't be shy.'

I hate him. My top is first to be cast off, the 'M' of Persia's top still visible when it lands on the marble floor. The leather straps of the underwear trace the shape of my breasts but do nothing to cover them. I keep dancing to the music, and Brody licks his lips the moment I lower my fly. Soon, I'm dancing in nothing but the underwear and Persia's standard-issue CMC boots.

When the track comes to an end, Brody beckons me over. I haven't removed the underwear. Quite frankly, it makes no difference to my modesty if I remove it or not.

'Come,' Brody says. 'Dance in my lap.'

I hesitate. I have no idea how much Brody has paid Kale for tonight. I feel thrown to the wolves. Even Jaxon has abandoned me. What I wouldn't give for Jake to come here and throw a punch at Brody's self-satisfied-looking face. Because, even after the events of last night, he hasn't yelled at me or rejected me.

Not yet anyway. There's still a tiny flicker of hope inside me that Jake can forgive the choices I've made.

'Sit on your hands,' I command.

Brody pauses, then does as he's told.

'No touching,' I remind him. 'At all. Not during, not after.'

'Yes, ma'am,' he says, before removing one hand to grab his phone and start the music, then replaces his hand under his thigh.

I don't recognize the track. The tempo is slow, but not too slow. I exhale, and lower myself down on him, facing him. I can feel his arousal swelling up through the taut material of his suit pants.

Inside me, I pull the invisible rip cord. The rip cord to my emotions. The one that allows me to do this night after night with men who have wives and girlfriends and children.

The only thing I think about is Jake. What I can say to him to earn back his trust.

I almost make it to the end, too. Until the track begins to fade and Brody frees his hands from underneath his thighs. His hands go to my waist, pulling me hard against him.

'God, you're so beautiful,' he rasps, and I squeal, writhing to extricate myself from his firm grasp. 'Spend the night with me.'

'Get off me!' I shriek, my arms flailing. 'No!'

One hand goes to the back of my head, and I feel the pressure of his long fingers that pen me in, even as I struggle. 'Yes, Serenity,' he breathes. 'I want all of you. This isn't enough.'

'Get off me! Get off! Let me go!'

I twist in his lap and fall to the floor. I scramble, working my arms to crawl across the smooth marble, but he grabs one of my ankles and yanks me back. The dancer in me rotates my hips sharply and I'm able to flip onto my back, supported by my elbows, at the same time kicking out with my legs.

'You asshole!' I holler. I fight hard as I back up, scrambling away from him. He gets to his feet and looms over me.

'I'm serious, Serenity,' he says. 'Kale told me about the deal he made with you. What you're doing for your father. I swear to you, spend one night with me and I can make it all go away.'

I lose balance. In shock, I fall flat on my back, the air pushed from my lungs. I gasp for breath. For a moment, I can't move.

Above me, Brody Conway offers me one hand. I don't take it. Instead, I get to my feet unaided. My emotions running high, I suddenly feel very naked in his presence. I shake my head, the words taking some time to form in my mind. How dare Kale share with Brody Conway the details of our arrangement?

'That's not what I do,' I stutter. 'I'm not that kind of girl. I'm sure you can find somebody else who does that kind of thing to satisfy you.'

'That's just it. Nobody satisfies me like you do, Serenity.'

'It's all just an act! Do you think this is all real? You think I want to be here? Well, I don't!'

'You're so desirable when you're all riled up.'

'Kale had no business telling you about my father's debt.'

Heat rises to my cheeks. I turn to walk back to the bedroom to get changed. I feel his fingers grab mine and he's yanking me back.

'One night,' he whispers. He pulls me close, so that my back is pressed into his chest. I feel his hot breath against my ear, and I can smell liquor there. 'Imagine. You'd never have to work in that redneck titty bar ever again. Just think about it. All I'd ask in return is you submit to me. Let me live out my fantasy with you. Satisfy my need for you fully. I'd satisfy your needs too. And in the morning, your father's debt would be paid. You'd be free.'

I've been dancing at Surly's for so long, I've forgotten what freedom is.

'What's stopping you?' he continues. 'Your CMC teammates would never have to know. We'd use protection. You'd have my undivided attention… all night long. Think about it… it could be a pleasurable experience for you. What better sacrifice to help your father? To lie back and let me pleasure you.'

Bile rises in my throat. It takes everything in me not to pull away from him. My eyes close. It would be another deal with yet another devil, yet this is one contract I never plan on agreeing to.

'You're a married man,' I say.

He nips the curve of my ear between his teeth. 'This has nothing to do with my wife,' he says in a low tone.

'I'm sure she'd disagree.'

He presses his long fingers into the small of my back. 'What have I told you, Serenity? Leave my wife out of this. This is about you and me. I don't desire her the same way I desire you. The more I see of you, the more of you I crave.'

The same hand slides from my back to around my waist, pinning me to him. He presses kisses to my neck, and I flinch.

'I could make it so good for us,' he breathes.

The arm that is pinning me to him loosens, and his fingers drift lower, skimming briefly between my legs.

I stiffen. 'Can I go now?' I ask.

'Promise me you'll take some time to think about it,' Brody says. 'I think you'll find we would both benefit.'

'I promise I'll consider your offer,' I say, if only to appease him, and to allow myself to wrench free of his grasp.

I return to the bedroom. I close the door and lean my back against the frame. I'm trembling with fury, yet once more, tears sting the corners of my eyes. I wipe them away and begin wriggling out of the bondage-style underwear.

I need to get out of here. I never want to return to this apartment again.

When I'm dressed, I walk back out. Brody waits for me with my coat. He helps me into it, like a gentleman would do, except he's no gentleman.

'I left a little sweetener in the pocket,' he says. 'Mind you don't tell Kale. Think of it as a sign of things to come. I look forward to seeing you again. Think hard on that decision. Think about how grateful your daddy would be.'

He pinches my chin between his thumb and forefinger. I leave without another word.

Downstairs, in the back of the limo, when the driver has closed the door, I check the pockets of my coat and pull out a pile of bills.

My tip for tonight – my sweetener from Brody Conway – is a cool one thousand dollars.

—

Back at Surly's, I head straight to the office.

'Everything alright?' Jaxon says as he opens the door.

Behind me, I can hear the noise from the bar. I glance back. Must be a full house. Mila looks to be on stage as *Candy Chains*.

'Can I come in?'

'Sure,' Jax says as he opens the door wider.

Inside, Kale has his feet up on the desk.

'Fella keep his hands to himself?' Jax asks.

Kale lifts his chin at the question, as though paying attention.

'Absolutely,' I lie. 'It was all fine. He gave me a tip.'

'How much?' Kale asks.

'Thousand dollars,' I say and hold out the cash.

Kale moves lightning fast.

I pull back. 'I want it in the ledger.'

He glares at me. 'Jaxon, get Serenity's ledger.'

Jax goes to the safe and does as he's told. He flips the notebook open to the latest page, then reaches for a pen and writes the amount down.

He comes over to show it to me and I hand the cash to Kale.

'That should make it two hundred and eight to go,' I say, because I stay on top of this stuff.

'Two hundred and eight thousand, that's correct,' Jaxon confirms, and I keep my gaze level with Kale's.

'Is that everything?' Kale asks.

I smile politely. 'No. I'm not feeling so good. Wondered if you'd mind if I head home early tonight?'

I keep looking directly at Kale.

He crosses his arms over his chest. 'What's wrong with you?'

I put one hand on my stomach. 'Got real bad cramps tonight. Due my period any day now.'

If there's one thing Kale hates, it's one of his girls talking about girl problems. Misty once taught me that it was the easiest way out of a shift, but you had to pick and choose carefully when to pull a code red.

Kale dismisses me with a flick of his fingers. 'Fine. Head on home. Jax, tell Kaycee and Talia that Serenity had to go. I'll need them up on stage for another round tonight.'

'Thank you,' I say.

'Need you back here tomorrow night though. Swallow a bottle of Tylenol, I don't care. Want you back on that stage, collecting those tips.'

A soft smile touches my mouth once more, because I used to be afraid of him. And now I see him for what he really is.

'Of course, Mr McCoy,' I say obediently. 'I'll be here, no question.'

In the car, on my route home, a message pings on the CMC group, from Harmony.

> No practice tomorrow because of away game.
> Meet at my apartment for team bonding. 10 a.m.
> Apartment F, 3580 Century Drive, Boulder Creek.
> See y'all there.

While I'm thankful that I don't have to drive all the way across to the Danube Stadium, equally, I'm nervous about what 'team bonding' entails outside of official training.

When I get home, I check on Dad. Lately, he's been sleeping with a portable oxygen concentrator for his emphysema, so I check the tube is all hooked up properly. Satisfied, I head for the kitchen and eat a handful of walnuts before I go upstairs to my room.

I'm taking off my makeup when the tears come. A moment later and I can't wipe them away fast enough, the events of the past few days overpowering me. When the floodgates open, my body is wracked with uncontrollable sobs, so all-consuming that I have to cover my mouth to stop the sound from waking my father.

All I want is to speak to Jake. I check the phone and there's nothing. He'll be on curfew tonight at some hotel or other in Cleveland. I take my chances and dial him, not expecting him to pick up. So, when I hear his voice at the other end of the line, I'm unprepared.

'Serenity?' His voice sounds deep and masculine.

'Hi,' I say softly. 'I didn't know if you'd answer. Or if you'd take the phone with you.'

'I can't really talk,' he says. 'I'm on curfew.'

'I know. I just wanted to say that I'm sorry.'

He's quiet for a long moment. 'I'm sorry I didn't call. I needed a little time to... process.'

'I get it. I know it wasn't what you expected. When do you fly back?'

'Monday.'

'I'm free Monday... I'd really like the chance to explain some things.'

'You don't have to work?'

He puts the emphasis on the 'work' so that I know he's referring to my *other* job. 'Club's closed Mondays. That's why Monday Night Football... well, it ain't a problem for me.'

'Oh,' he says, and his tone is flat. 'Listen, I gotta go.'

'Good luck at the game,' I say, sounding hopeful.

'Thanks,' he says, and hangs up.

I place the phone on the nightstand, then exhale. I feel another hot sting of tears. Then my personal phone vibrates.

I read a string of funny messages from the girls about what we should do for team bonding.

When a separate message comes through to my phone, I read the words and stiffen. The fury that I felt in the limo ride back to Surly's returns to my chest.

I'd sink my face in your pussy and make you feel so good, Brody's message reads. *Think about it…*

I should block him; I know that I should. But right now, he has me in a stranglehold. And while he's presenting his proposal as a choice, I know it's not a choice I'm gonna be free to make. Brody Conway has already made up his mind that he wants me in his bed. If I refuse to comply, he'll expose me.

It's not something I want to do, but I can see only one way out of this. And it's the only way that Jake and I might still have a shot.

I need to quit the CMC.

Chapter Twenty-One

Serenity

Boulder Creek is a suburb due south of Danube Stadium, on the east side of Canyon. I've heard some of the players live on modern, gated properties here. I'm sure to park my Ford C-Max a decent distance from Harmony's apartment block. I've known these girls a while now, and I'm grateful that none of them is yet to see the car I drive.

When I arrive, most of the other girls are pulling up in their own vehicles, or getting dropped off. When Jewel sees me, I give her a wave and she comes racing over, her curls bouncing with every step.

'Hey, Ren!' she beams.

'Hey,' I smile and give her a hug on the street. I woke up finding my resolve to quit had softened after sleep, though I still don't see any way out of my situation without me being exposed as a liar.

'You nervous?' she asks.

'Nervous? About what?'

'You know. Our first team bonding session.'

I frown. 'Should we be?'

Jewel's eyes go wide. She lowers her voice. 'I hear Angel and Shawny said they're gonna spice things up a little.'

Upstairs, Harmony welcomes everyone to her apartment. 'Phones at the door!' is the instruction given to everyone and so, laughing, I surrender my cell. Stepping forward, I take in my surroundings. Her place is light and airy, with artwork on the walls and pictures of her extended family in frames. It tasteful. Demure. It's the kind of place I can only imagine leasing. In the kitchen, there are fresh pastries, fruit and coffee and everybody helps themselves.

'When you're ready, take a seat!' Harmony trills over excited voices.

She's brought out extra chairs. It takes a few moments for everybody to settle. Next to Jewel, I sit on the carpet and hug my knees.

'Welcome everybody,' Harmony says as the room quietens. 'Welcome to our first team bonding of the season.'

There is applause. Jewel elbows me in my side and I smile. Harmony makes it sound like a ritual, which it is.

'Admin points first,' our captain continues. 'Everybody signed up for their community outreach choices, yes?'

There is a 'yes' in unison. In the end, I signed up to the same projects as Jewel.

'Okay great,' Harmony says. She sobers. 'Second point, Mona opted out of today.'

There are some sighs of disappointment. 'I invited her but… says she's not coming back until the weight is off.'

I see some of the girls roll their eyes, keeping their views to themselves.

'Come on, ladies, it's what we signed up for,' Ashlyn reminds everyone, twisting her pink-blonde braid between her fingers.

Harmony waits for the room to settle again. 'Third point. I know there's some gossip and rumours flying around already…'

'Persia Takeda…' Angel says in the same voice as a movie trailer, 'and the case of the missing uniform.'

On the floor, I feel my muscles tense.

'For those of you who haven't heard,' Harmony continues, 'Persia Takeda's CMC uniform has gone missing. I want y'all to know that Persia's been questioned and she denies any theft has taken place,' Harmony states, raising her eyebrows a little disapprovingly at Angel.

'How the hell would she have even gotten into the stadium anyways?' Shawny interrupts from behind me.

'Exactly,' Angel echoes. 'They took her security badge the same moment they fired her ass. There's just no way.'

'I say they're tryna make out like one rotten apple can taint the whole barrel,' Imara argues with her mouth full of crescent roll. 'Like, they wanted to endorse their own decision to have her fired, like, *oh, in case there was any doubt, she stole her own uniform, looks like we were right about her all along.* You know what? I think they knew Persia was badass and they decided she didn't fit the mould.'

'Like, we all make mistakes,' Shawny adds.

My stomach churns. I keep my gaze fixed on the carpet. To think that I know precisely who took Persia's CMC uniform and that last night I wore it myself.

What would they all think of me if they knew the truth?

'Look, let's not speculate,' I hear Harmony say, but it's hard to hear over the voices that are screaming at me in my head. 'There'll be an investigation. Hopefully Persia will be exonerated.'

'I can already guess the outcome of *that* investigation,' Angel grumbles from behind me under her breath.

Solana, a Hispanic third-year veteran, speaks up. There's an excitable glint in her eye. 'Speaking of speculation, what's the order of play for today?'

There is movement as the attention of the room shifts to Angel and Shawny on the couch, wearing smiles that say butter wouldn't melt in their mouths.

'We don't have the green light yet,' Angel says, looking across at Harmony and Ashlyn.

Harmony holds up her palms, as though in defeat. 'What happens in this room stays in this room, alright?'

Jewel and I exchange nervous glances.

'What's it to be girls?' Ashlyn asks.

Angel takes in the expectant faces all around her. 'We thought about *Never Have I Ever*. But in the end, we went with good ol' *Truth or Dare*!'

There's whooping and applause. My stomach churns. Jewel squeezes my bicep.

'And we've got *questions*!' Shawny sings, pulling out two hats containing slips of paper that she's seemingly been hiding all this time. I feel a sense of impending dread.

'Can I please confirm that everybody left their cell phone at the door?' Harmony asks, a little nervously.

'First of all,' Angel says to the group, 'who wants cocktails?!'

'It's ten-thirty in the morning!' Ashlyn objects.

There are cries of 'I'll have one!'

'Ren, you want a cocktail?' Jewel asks me.

'Sure, why not?' I say nervously.

I stay seated while Jewel returns from the kitchen with some bright pink fluid in a glass, the ice cubes clinking.

'What is it?'

'Think it's supposed to be like an island punch or some kind of Sex on the Beach,' she replies. 'Try some.'

I do, and I can already taste a hint of vodka. A few minutes later and Angel is organizing everybody to sit in a circle.

'We go round that way, but youngest cheerleader goes first,' Shawny announces. 'Tori, that's you! Truth or dare, honey?'

'Hold up, are there dirty truth or dares in here?' Harmony asks.

'What would be the fun in clean truth or dares?' Angel asks.

Harmony pulls a face. I look across at Tori, a nineteen-year-old fellow rookie whose blonde hair is a similar shade to mine. Her cheeks have flared a shade of crimson. 'Uh... truth, I guess?' she squeaks.

Angel's hand dives into her hat containing folded slips of paper. 'I should warn y'all, there's only three questions in here.'

'Go easy on her, please,' Ashlyn says in a warning tone.

Angel pulls a slip of paper, reads the question, then thinks the better of it. She chooses another. 'What is your bedroom kink?' she reads out.

Tori blushes for a second time, placing both hands on her cheeks. 'My what? My bedroom kink? What even is that?'

'It means how do you like it nasty in the bedroom?' Solana says.

'Uhm. I don't know! My, uh, boyfriend licked Ben & Jerry's out of my belly button once, does that count?' Tori giggles, and the room descends into laughter.

'Oh, honey, it counts!' Angel cries as she moves to the next girl, who also picks truth.

After that, Harmony is next in the circle. 'Truth,' she says. 'But I literally reserve the right to lie.'

'NO lies!' Shawny counters.

Angel pulls out a question, a wry smile creeping onto her features. 'Given the choice, which Mutineer team player would you invite into your bed and why?'

There is a chorus of 'Ooooh' as Harmony rolls her eyes. 'I think we all know the answer to that one, Angel, thank you.'

'It has to be a team member who hasn't been there before!' Solana hollers.

'He's never,' Harmony says with a degree of sincerity and some of the girls look surprised. 'I don't know why y'all think that.'

'So...' Angel begins.

Harmony goes on the defensive, crossing her arms over her chest. 'Hudson Briar has never been here. And I've never been to his place either. Even if it is about six times the size of my apartment.'

'So, are we allowed to know how far you *have* gone?' Shawny asks.

Harmony looks coy. Resistance is not something I've ever really showed Jake, whereas Harmony's obeyed the rules from day one.

'I answered the question,' Harmony says sweetly. 'I don't have to say nothin' else.'

The room erupts as everyone wants to know the details, me included.

'Alright, alright, we may have had a moment. At Brody Conway's wedding. In the men's bathroom. I may have gotten a little carried away.'

Shawny leans forward. 'Carried away *how*?'

Harmony blushes. 'He may have… Oh my lord, I am not getting into this. Next person!'

Angel and Shawny move around the circle. After Leona, Ashlyn and Imara take their turns, then it's Jewel's time to choose.

'Truth,' she grins.

Angel picks up a piece of paper. 'Same question,' she says. 'Which current, serving Mutineer would you have your wicked way with?'

'Jake Walsh,' Shawny coughs out, muffling the sound with her fist, and everybody laughs. Everybody except me, because on the inside, I'm in a panic.

'Not gonna lie,' Jewel hums and I can't look her in the eye. 'Jake Walsh is some serious hot property. I'd ride him like a regular rodeo.'

There are literal squeals. 'Yee-haw!' Angel hoots and Harmony holds her face in her hands, like this wasn't quite the team bonding she'd hoped for.

'He is my official NFL crush, and I am crushing *hard* on that boy,' Jewel admits, and her words are pin pricks against my skin. I picture the last time Jake saw me in the Surly's parking lot. His look of blank indifference. Like in that moment, seeing me up on stage, he'd made up his mind that he no longer wanted anything more to do with me.

He'd be better off with a kind-hearted girl like Jewel.

'Ren, you're up,' Angel says, and I snap back to the game. There's no way I want to be asked that same question.

'Um. Everybody else said truth,' I say, 'so I guess I'll go dare.'

'Finally!' Shawny exclaims, dipping into her hat and selecting a slip of paper.

'We dare you to...' Her eyes skim the words. 'Read out in front of the group the last message on your phone from a guy.'

I raise my brows in my best poker face. 'Oh,' I say.

'Girlie, go get your phone!' Angel hollers at me.

I get to my feet. I can feel the muscles in my legs tremble, because I know exactly who the last message in my phone was from and what it said.

'She can't do it, somebody else has to read it!' Leona argues.

'I'll go!' Jewel volunteers.

I walk out into the corridor. I glance back at Jewel and panic. All our phones are lined up beside the front door. I swiftly locate mine, wondering if I have time to delete Brody's message to me last night. Except Jewel bounds up behind me and grabs my cell.

'Unlock it, unlock it!' she commands.

'Come on, this is dumb...' I murmur.

Jewel holds out her hand. 'Unlock it and hand it over.'

My mind goes into a spin. What if she reads Brody's message out loud in front of everybody? And how in hell do I explain it? I think about pleading with Jewel then and there.

Limply, I unlock it, and hand it over.

Back in the living area, Solana is saying, 'Ren seems like too sweet a girl to have any skeletons in her closet, you know.'

I look at Jewel, who is navigating to my messages. My heart goes into overdrive, yet I manage to maintain my fixed smile. All of my squad mates' attention goes to my fellow rookie.

I look at her face. It's hard to decipher what she's reading. I'm too scared to say a word.

'Come on, Jewel,' Shawny chastises her. 'Read it out loud.'

Jewel laughs, but it comes off as awkward. 'It's from her dad, I think, it says *hey honey, can you pick up some of that microwave popcorn I like on your way home?*'

My lips twist. I exhale, but it's shaky.

'See?' Solana hollers. 'I told you. Too much of a cutie. And I applaud you, Ren, for taking such good care of your daddy.'

There are murmurings of approval.

'But what we *really* want is to read Hud's messages to Harmony,' Angel pipes up, winking in the direction of our captain. 'Now those DMs gon be *filthy*.'

'Number one, he doesn't have my number,' Harmony clips, 'and number two, since when do I have to do a dare? I had my turn already.'

'Just messin' with you, Cap,' Angel says with a wink.

'Here's your phone,' Jewel says to me so no one else can hear. I raise my eyes to hers and suddenly it feels as though the air has shifted. I know by the look on her face that she's read at least part, or the entirety of, Brody's message to me last night. I look away quickly, and turning on my heel, go to put my phone back, unlocking it in the corridor. Sure enough, Dad's message from yesterday about the popcorn is there, staring back at me on the screen.

I clutch my cell to my chest. Tears sting the corners of my eyes. Do I pretend like everything is normal? Like nothing untoward just took place.

I hear arguments next door about whether, as ringmasters, Angel or Shawny will be doing their own truth or dare.

I place my phone back beside the door with all the others. When I re-enter the room, Jewel is back on the carpet, hugging her knees.

'I think what we *all* wanna know is...' Solana says as she looks playfully between Angel and Shawny, 'if you two have ever...'

I witness Shawny's blush of embarrassment. Angel, on the other hand, is unflustered. 'That question is *so* last season,' she sighs. 'Can we just move on? Who's next?'

I reclaim my seat on the floor. I try to catch Jewel's attention. It's quickly clear to me that she doesn't plan on looking my way.

When *Truth or Dare* comes to an end, conversations flow more freely, and the atmosphere relaxes a little. I keep one eye on Jewel, because she hasn't said a word to me since she looked at my phone. I'd almost prefer not to speak to her, because talking only leads to me telling a bunch more lies.

In the end, I catch her alone in the kitchen. When I go stand next to her, neither of us speaks, until we both speak at the same time.

'You first,' she says.

I take a breath. 'I know you saw something... on my phone,' I say.

She looks down, to a plate on the counter piled high with potato chips that have remained untouched. 'I didn't wanna embarrass you,' she responds after a moment.

'I appreciate that.'

'Was it from a guy you're seeing, or something?'

She wouldn't have known it was from Brody because I never added him as a contact in my phone, yet it forces another lie out of my mouth.

I shake my head. 'It's some weird Mutineers fan, I think, who got hold of my number from somewhere and he's harassing me.'

'Ren! Why didn't you block him?'

It's a valid question. 'I did. The first time.' I shrug. 'Then he just changed numbers.'

'You need to tell Kathleen about that shit. Immediately. We don't have nearly as much security as the players. Imagine that douchebag decides to follow you, what then?'

I tear up, mostly because I hate lying to her every time I open my mouth, and I'm fit to burst. 'Jewel, I'm in some real hot water. I may have to quit the squad.'

My voice breaks as I say it. Her eyes go wide. 'No!' she blurts at full volume, and both of us look to the door. The other girls are all still in the living area. She grabs on to both my hands and squeezes my fingers. 'No,' she whispers again. 'What do you mean, quit the squad?'

'I wish I could tell you everything, but I can't. Not right now.'

'I wouldn't tell a soul.'

'Jewel, I… I can't.'

She looks at me for a moment, as though thinking about something. 'It's okay.' She puts her arms around me. 'Whatever it is, you cannot quit. Do you remember how hard you worked just to get here? How brilliant everyone thinks you are?'

I pull back and wipe my face. 'I don't wanna quit. But I may not have a choice.'

'Does Harmony know? That you're even thinking about it?'

'Nobody knows. Except you now.'

Her gaze turns steely. She squeezes my biceps with her hands. 'As your fellow rookie, I won't let you quit. Everybody loves you, Ren. If you're in a jam, then people will understand. Is it really so bad?'

I want to tell her that the guy she likes is the guy I like too, only I don't think he likes me anymore. I want to tell her that most days when I get home, I shed tears because it feels like I'm falling apart at the seams, and I don't have anyone else I can talk to about it. I want to tell her that most days I skip lunch because I don't feel like eating, but now it's become a thing. I want to tell her that I don't feel worthy of this cheer squad, because I'm a liar, and one day everything is gonna come crashing down around my ears.

Except I force a bright smile. 'I'll be alright,' I say, because I don't even know where to start.

'Atta girl,' Jewel says with a grin as she wraps me in a bear hug, practically lifting me off the ground. 'Now quit talking about quitting and tell Kathleen some creep is messaging you.'

Chapter Twenty-Two

Jake

I've often thought my dad might be my biggest fan. Which would make me the most ungrateful sonofabitch on the planet right about now. He's making me a late lunch, consisting of my favorite breakfast foods: bacon, eggs and hash browns with a stack of fluffy buttermilk pancakes after my three-hour flight back from Cleveland. He hasn't quit talking about Sunday night's game.

'You keep putting up that many yards, you'll get to the hall of fame in no time,' he's saying at the stove. He fills up the plate and slides it onto the table in front of me, the delicious aroma filling my nose. I help myself to ketchup then dig in immediately.

'You know, on the radio this morning, they said the same thing I said to your mom, last night in front of the TV. I ain't never seen a player hurdle his opponent twice in the same game. But you went ahead and did it, Jake. Spectacular.'

'Mmm,' I respond with my cheeks full.

'No matter what that defensive line threw at you, you kept on finding the pocket. Dang near Speedy Gonzales.' He moves his hand in all directions, making *pitchow* sounds.

'Mmm,' I say again.

'And that catch in the third quarter!' He slaps his knee. 'You could see Dent had gone down, and you went for it.'

'Mmm,' I comment for a third time.

He frowns at me. The room goes silent, except for the sound of my knife and fork hitting the plate. 'But you don't look happy,' he says.

'I am happy,' I say. 'I'm happy for my team. We got the win.'

My dad shakes his head at me. 'Son, when are you gonna start giving yourself some credit? You were dynamite out there! You wanna know what your granddaddy said?'

He's referring to my maternal grandfather, Art Mackabee, career quarterback for the Pittsburgh Steelers way back when.

I wipe my mouth with one of my mother's floral napkins. 'What'd he say?'

Dad's waving his phone at me. 'He said "kid plays better than I did!" Do you know what that means, coming from your grandfather?'

I laugh but it fades. I can't talk about the real issue I'm having.

Yes, I played a great game. And I'm thrilled about that. I am. We carry on like this, the Mutineers will make the playoffs, no sweat.

That's not what's on my mind.

All I can think about is Friday night.

Serenity.

Serenity.

Serenity.

She's invaded my brain. Waltzed on in and taken charge. Though *waltzed* is the wrong word.

I can't stop thinking about her up on that stage at Surly's. The way she moved. The way she danced. It was mesmerizing. And to watch and listen to those guys whistling for her... I'd never experienced jealousy like it until that night. Watching them watching her, half-naked, I wanted to take out every motherfucker in that room. Beat his ass to a pulp.

Am I still mad at her for not telling me? Yes.

Does it mean I feel any differently about her? I keep telling myself that it should.

But she's all I've thought about since the moment I left her in that parking lot.

When I'm finished, I push my plate away. Wipe my mouth on the napkin one final time. I hear the front door slam and

River enters the kitchen, tossing her book bag and kicking off her shoes.

'Hail to the king,' she mutters in an understated kind of way. 'How long you been back?'

'Not that long. How was school?'

She gives a nonchalant shrug. 'School was school.'

'That kid give you any beef? What was his name again?'

'Scottie Lincoln. No, I don't think he was there today.'

'Good.'

'Congrats on your win.'

'Thanks. You watch the whole thing?'

'Of course. That was a sweet catch in the third quarter. Was Cleveland nice?'

'I don't know. All I saw was a stadium and the inside of a hotel room.'

We hear an engine out front. I crane my neck. It's followed by a car door slam, and it sounds like it's close by. I get to my feet and take my empty plate to the sink.

'You expecting visitors?' I ask River.

'No. Are you?'

'Nope.'

I go past River and walk to the front door, stepping out onto the front porch. A car has pulled up outside close to the kerb, its trunk wide open. On the near side, the passenger door is open. I frown as I witness Scottie Lincoln helping a second young guy from the passenger seat into a wheelchair. The other guy is taller than Scottie, broader too, and is wearing a high school varsity jacket and blue jeans.

'Uh, hey.' Scottie Lincoln raises his voice when he sees me. 'Give us a minute.'

I watch as the second guy takes control of the chair and wheels himself onto the sidewalk.

I frown. 'You fellas want something?' I ask.

Scottie Lincoln looks awkward. 'This here is my older brother, Wylder.'

'Hey,' Wylder says, keeping hold of the rims on the wheels. 'Nice to meet you. We wondered if River is home.'

My frown has morphed into more of a menacing stare. 'How do you know River lives here?'

Just at that moment, River comes barging out of the door onto the porch. She looks at me and the two men. 'What's going on?'

I lean my head toward them. 'Scottie brought along his brother. Wylder.'

River turns to look at the guy in the wheelchair. He has wide shoulders, and I can't help but wonder if he's an athlete or football player. 'Hey,' she says, and it seems like he's familiar to her. 'You disappeared. I've not seen you in a while.'

He manoeuvres himself forward a fraction, so that the wheels are touching the grass on the front lawn. Scottie closes the car door and remains where he is.

'I was up in Austin,' he replies. 'Some specialist physical therapists are tryna help me walk again. When Scottie told me what happened with your brother... I just needed to explain a few things. Look, Scottie did go around messaging all the guys at school not to invite you to the winter formal. But... he did it because I asked him to. I didn't want anyone else asking you when I couldn't, because I was upstate. I asked around for your phone number so I could ask you, but nobody I knew seemed to have it.'

I look at River. Her cheeks are bright red. Then she walks down the steps toward him. 'You were gonna ask me?' she questions.

He nods his head. 'So... what do you say? Would you maybe let me take you to the winter formal?'

'You guys should have been up front with me,' River says, and I'm proud of her for standing up for herself. 'Both of you. Wylder, you should have got Scottie to ask for my number. Scottie, you made a fool outta me, in front of the entire senior class.'

This time it's Wylder turning a shade of red. Scottie stares at his fingers.

'But thank you,' she then adds softly. 'I'd love to go with you.'

I see Wylder's broadening grin. 'That's awesome. I'll make it up to you, I swear. But I should tell you, I can't do much dancing.'

River shrugs. 'We'll figure it out.'

They're cute, I'll give 'em that.

'You guys wanna come in for a soda, or something to eat?' River asks them both.

'Sure,' Wylder says, brightening. 'If it's okay with your brother?'

River snorts. 'Oh. Don't worry about him.'

Wylder manoeuvres himself toward the front path. He looks back at Scottie. 'A little help?' he says.

The younger brother jumps to attention and rushes to his brother's aid.

'Here, allow me,' I say, walking down the steps, and together, Scottie and I lift Wylder's chair up to the porch with him in it. River gets the front door as Wylder wheels toward it.

'Thanks, man,' Scottie says to me, looking awkward.

I run one hand around the back of my neck. 'I'm sorry about Friday. You should have said.'

'What, when you were about to punch me in the stones?'

I hold out my hand to him. 'I should have heard you out. I apologize.'

'It's alright, man,' he says, and we shake hands. 'Things aren't always black and white, I guess.'

His words hit me, and I know in that moment that I need to call Serenity.

Upstairs in my room, I pace up and down. I wait until four o'clock. I figure she'll still be at the diner for her shift. Just after four, I call her dedicated cell.

'Hey,' she says as she picks up. Her tone is soft and subdued.

'Hey,' I say back, and I wonder if I should have driven to the diner to do this in person. 'You at the diner?'

'Yeah. I just finished my shift. You back in Canyon?'

'Yeah.'

'Heard you had a good game.'

I would have thought she'd try and watch it, but then I remember: she was working. 'We got the win.'

'That's awesome. I'm real pleased for you.'

'Thanks.'

We lapse into silence. I know I was the one to call her. I spent the entire weekend thinking about her. Yet I still don't know how to unpack this whole thing.

'Jake?'

'Yeah.'

'I was hoping that you would let me explain some things to you. I'm not… at the club tonight. Can I meet you somewhere? I could drive up to the cabin. I just need to look in on my dad.'

I associate the cabin with the Serenity from before. Right now, I don't want to meet her there. Yet we don't have anywhere else.

'Does your dad know about me?' I ask.

She pauses. When she speaks, her voice sounds thicker. 'No.'

'I'd like to see where you live.'

'Jake… we can't. What if we're seen?'

'Give me the address. I'll head out just before it gets dark. You can let me in real quick.'

She goes quiet. 'You're mad at me. That's why you want this, isn't it?'

'I wanna know the real you, Serenity. Not some version of you. I want the truth. Just tell your dad I'm a friend. Does he know—'

'—that I work at Surly's?' she finishes for me. 'He knows.'

'Alright then. Message me the address. I'll be there tonight.'

She doesn't respond for some time, like maybe she's wrestling with something. 'Okay,' she then says. I hear her exhale. 'I'll see you there.'

We hang up. I wait for an address. Eventually, it comes through.

> 2932 Spring Chase, Temptation Heights

When I moved to Canyon, there were two places folks told me not to go: Temptation Heights, and the township of Rapture, in the northeast.

I check where to find it exactly. Temptation Heights is on the southwest side of Canyon, due farther southwest than Surly's Tavern. It's not somewhere I've ever visited. I've never had a reason to.

Until now.

At some point on my way to Temptation Heights in my pickup after dark, the landscape changes and the traffic thins out. Tall buildings give way to low-rise houses made from wooden slats painted white and surrounded by chain link fences. Some windows are boarded up and covered in graffiti. The streetlamps don't work so well out here. Where there is grass, it's patchy and dry.

It's not the Canyon I was sold when I signed my NFL contract. Far from it.

In front of me, a racoon crosses the road, the headlights bouncing off its feral eyes. I jam on the brakes and my tires screech to a halt. I peer out. The road surface is littered with potholes and fractured concrete.

I take a left into Spring Chase and slow my speed. The houses here are small and close together. I lower my window, and I can hear a dog barking in the night air over the sound of the cicadas.

Outside number 2932 – the number painted on the side of the white mailbox – I pull up onto the curb behind Serenity's parked car. I raise my window, kill the engine then crane my neck. I can see through the window that the lights are on. There's a small wooden porch and a screen door.

I look down at the flowers I brought with me. Suddenly, it feels like they're too much, but I pick them up by the stems anyway and open the door.

On the street, the dog barking grows louder. I glance around me, but there's no one else around. As I enter the gate, the screen door opens. Serenity comes out onto the porch. In the shadows, I can see she's wearing jeans and a fitted white tee, her hair tied back in a high ponytail.

'Hey,' I say, and even after the events of Friday night, it's like I'm looking at her in a whole new light. I don't think I ever gave her enough credit.

'Hey,' she responds. Her tone is light. She seems nervous.

'I, uh, I brought you these,' I say, holding out the flowers. 'By way of an apology.'

She walks down the steps. 'They're beautiful. Thank you.'

I hand them over and she searches my face. 'I think I'm supposed to be the one apologizing to you.'

I hold her gaze. If we were in the cabin, I'd ask to kiss her. I've missed her, even since Friday. I think I'd forgive her anything, and hope that she can forgive me for walking away from her like I did in the parking lot at Surly's. 'You've got nothing to be sorry for,' I tell her, and she looks like she might cry. 'I mean, don't get me wrong,' I add. 'I was a little surprised.'

She bites her lip. 'So… you're not mad?'

'Not mad, no. Not anymore. Just a little curious maybe.'

We stand there, in her front yard, face to face. I feel an urge to ask her if she knows what kind of hold she has over me.

That I'd do anything she asked if it meant even the tiniest shot at making her happy. Stripper, or no stripper, I don't care. I just know I've never met a woman like her before and all I wanna do is cherish her. Make her mine.

'You wanna come inside?' she asks. 'I can introduce you to my dad.'

The porch steps creak as I walk up. The dog has quit barking though now I can hear a man hollering at the TV in the house across the street. The screen door grates and I notice it's coming off its rusty hinges.

'How long you lived in this house?' I ask.

She turns to face me. 'I've lived here my whole life.'

'It's… it's cosy.'

She tilts her head and glances up at the ceiling, which, when I follow her gaze, I realize is a spiderweb of cracks and lines. 'It's not, it's crumbling,' she says miserably. 'But it's home, and we don't have the money to fix it. Come meet my dad.'

She first puts the flowers in the kitchen and then I follow her into a living area. There's an old TV showing a Dodgers game. Serenity's father has his feet up on the worn-out couch, the insides spewing outta one end where it's come apart at the seams. He's wearing a mask hooked up to some kind of oxygen tank, attached to a metal cart on wheels. He looks frail and a little emaciated.

'Daddy,' Serenity says. 'This is Jake, who I was telling you about. Jake, this is my father, Glenn Harper.'

He looks up from the couch. Serenity inherited his eyes. His are bright, despite his obvious illness.

'It's nice to meet you, sir,' I say.

He goes to stand, albeit a little slowly and removes his mask.

'No, no, please don't get up,' I add.

'It's fine, son,' he says, then shakes my hand with more force than I would have expected. 'Always nice to meet a friend of Serenity's. You're a football player?'

'Yes, sir.'

'More of a baseball fan myself.'

'So I heard. I hope you're not disappointed.'

'You kidding? Serenity never brought a young man home before. I've been waiting all this time… figured she's too busy. Working too hard.'

'She does work too hard,' I say, but I can't say anything else because Glenn Harper is coughing.

'Daddy, put your mask back on,' Serenity chastises him. 'Sit your butt down, come on.'

'Yes, ma'am,' he responds to her commands, and I smile at her strength. I'll add 'caring' to the list of things about her that appeal to me. Glenn returns to his original position as instructed, replacing the mask over his nose and mouth.

'Jake and I are gonna have a beer on the back porch,' she tells him, and to me, she lifts her chin, tilting it toward the back of the house.

Outside, I take a seat on a ramshackle chair; some of the slats are missing. Serenity returns with a couple of bottles.

'Are you allowed to drink during the week?' she asks, hovering above me.

I resist the urge to reach out and trace my fingers around the back of her thigh, right at the crease of her knee, over her jeans. 'I can have one.'

She nods her head. I pull the other chair a little closer toward mine and she lowers herself into it, passing me an open bottle.

I swallow a mouthful of beer. For a moment, I just watch her. Our knees are touching, and she plays nervously with the end of her ponytail.

'Dad has oxygen therapy, though it's not regular,' she says. 'They show up with the tank out of the blue and then some other guys come and take it away again. Ideally, he needs the treatment twice a day, but we don't get that.'

'Do you have insurance?'

'We have a managed care program. We get tax credits. It's not perfect but we get by.'

'And you work three jobs.'

She raises her eyes to me and her voice trembles. 'I only get paid for two of 'em. It's not enough.'

My frown is deep. 'I don't understand. I thought you'd... I would have thought it's good money... you know. Taking your clothes off.'

This time she looks away. Presses her lips together. I reach for her hand and squeeze her fingers. 'I just want us to be honest with each other,' I tell her.

Her eyes come back to mine.

'Can we do that?' I ask. 'Be honest? No matter how bad you think it is.'

It takes a moment, but she nods her head, then takes a breath.

'When I was growing up,' she begins, 'my dad wasn't around all that much. He worked various jobs; I never quite knew what he did day to day. One minute he was laying carpet, the next he was fixing somebody's refrigerator. Some nights he spent in a bar someplace, and he'd roll on home after I'd gone to bed. But there were some nights when we were a family. My mom worked as a nurse, then she quit that, and she worked in a hardware store for a while. By the time I turned seventeen, she'd had enough. Said she wanted to leave and that I should go with her. But by then I knew my dad was sick and had landed in some hot water.'

'What kind of hot water?'

'He'd been gambling and got into some serious debt that year.'

'How serious?'

She doesn't answer immediately. 'A little less than a half million dollars all in.'

'Holy shit.'

She lets out another heavy sigh. 'The debt was with a man named Kale McCoy. He owned a casino, and also a titty bar in Canyon... Surly's Tavern.'

I grip my bottle of beer a little tighter and shake my head, hardly able to believe what I know she's about to tell me.

'Soon after my mom left, Kale paid us a visit. The moment he saw me... I guess he saw potential. He asked how old I was, and we made a deal. The day I turned eighteen, he had me at the club, learning the ropes—'

I shoot to my feet, the chair scraping back against the rustic wood. I pace up and down for a moment as she watches me.

'How could your own father let you do that?' I say, keeping my voice low.

She gives a shrug. 'He was scared. He didn't want me to do it, of course, but you don't mess with these guys. I knew what would have happened if I'd have said no.'

Questions rip through my mind. So, she's not doing this by choice, but to save her father's life?

'Do you get paid anything at all?'

'No. I keep a ledger. Every shift I work goes toward paying off the debt. So does every tip I make. Every lap dance. I don't get to see a dime of that money, though I do well for tips. And I keep track. I keep a copy here in my room.'

'How much is left to pay?'

Her throat works. She puts down her beer which she's barely touched. 'Two hundred thousand dollars. Give or take.'

On the inside, I reel. 'And you can't quit?'

She glances back toward the house. 'For a while, my daddy kept on telling me he'd win the money back. But then his health took a turn for the worse. And I didn't have a choice.'

'You're being exploited. It's forced labor.'

'What would you have me do? Bake cookies and sell them by the side of the road? I don't have that kind of money, Jake. If I do this, I keep my father alive. And one day, the debt will be paid.'

'You've been doing it for, what, five years now? You'll practically be thirty.'

'You think I haven't worked that out? Plus, every day, I wait for the moment where somebody recognizes me as a member of the CMC. Every. Single. Day. And every day I'm breaking the rules of my contract. And that doesn't even include my relationship with you.'

I take a step back, tryna take this all in. There's anger in her tone. She works in a strip club to repay her father's substantial debt. She works as a waitress to earn a basic wage. She lives out her dream as a cheerleader for the Mutineers. I knew what she was risking when she agreed to date me, but I didn't know the magnitude of it. What she risks every time she leaves the house. It makes me admire her resilience. It makes me love her more, and I think I've known for some time that I do love her. It makes me want to fight for her.

'As a cheerleader, I make less than half what an NFL waterboy makes, per year,' she states. 'Did you know that? What is your contract worth?'

I quit pacing and swallow the thick lump in my throat. 'I get it,' I mumble, because I feel ashamed to say the figures out loud, despite it being comparable to what my contemporaries make or reflecting what I put my body through.

Serenity presses her fingers to her forehead. 'No offense, Jake, but you'll never get it.'

'I'll give you the money,' I say. 'I'd give you the money in a second.'

She looks up at me. Her eyes are filling up. 'I know you would,' she whispers. 'But I can't take it. I can't be indebted to you like that. I couldn't live with myself.'

'Why the hell not? You'd never have to dance like that again. You could pay me back instead, not that I'd ever ask you to.'

'No,' she says again, her voice raw with emotion, and I know it's out of pride.

'You've done everything you can do,' I argue, careful that her dad doesn't hear me. 'You've done more than enough for your father. Let me take that burden.'

'Jake. I don't need a hero. And we're still getting to know one another.'

'I don't care.'

'And what happens when you're no longer crazy about me? And you're down two hundred thousand dollars?'

'I'm already on track to hit a thousand rushing yards for the season. I'll get a general performance bonus. Serenity, I don't care about the money. And for the record, I'm gonna be crazy about you 'til they put me in the ground, seventy, eighty years from now.'

'You don't know that. You didn't know the truth about me until a few days ago.'

'You could drive a garbage truck for all I care, or clean goddamned restrooms! I'm not gonna feel any different about you, whether you're taking your clothes off for guys, or not.'

I've raised my voice. We both look back at the house, and we're probably both thinking the same thing, worrying if Glenn Harper overheard me or not.

Serenity bows her head. 'I'm not a damsel who needs saving. I've taken care of my own shit since I was seventeen.'

I don't answer for a moment. 'What are you saying?'

Once more, her voice shakes. 'I'm saying I can't carry on like this. I told Jewel yesterday that I need to quit the CMC. But if I quit, and we come out as a couple, I'm pretty sure people will quickly figure out who I am and what I do. And I couldn't do that to you. The golden boy of the Mutineers can't be seen going out with a stripper.'

Her words have got my heart slamming against my ribs, worse than if it's a free-for-all on the field. The adrenaline is pumping. If I don't act now, I could lose her. And I can't lose her. I abandon my bottle of beer to the wooden railing and go to her.

I grab her hands and pull her to standing. Her thighs touch mine as I hold her close.

'I'll go,' I say. 'If you can tell me you don't care for me, then I'll go.'

In the darkness and shadows, our faces are almost touching.

'But, know this,' I continue. 'Every cell in my body belongs to you. I don't care what anyone else thinks; I'm not giving up on us without a fight. I'll admit I had you all wrong, but it doesn't change how beautiful you are in my eyes, or how sweet or good-natured or how kind. And seeing those guys cheering for you when you undress for them is like somebody ripped open my chest, tore out my heart and served it back to me on a platter all chopped up into tiny pieces. But you have good reasons for doing what you do, and I'll honor those reasons. But, if you want to, go ahead and tell me you don't care about me, and I'll walk away. Right now.'

On the porch, she clings to me. I feel her chest rise and fall with uneven breaths. When she says nothing, I'm fearful of the rejection yet unwilling to let go. That is, unless she has the courage to tell me that she doesn't want me, in which case, I'll be forced to accept defeat.

Fuck, I love this girl. I don't ever want to admit defeat.

She pulls back. 'Close your eyes,' she whispers.

I search her face then reluctantly do as I'm told.

The next thing I feel is her lips as they brush against mine. Soft and warm and inviting. Relief floods my veins. I kiss her back, yank her hard against my body, deepening our kiss. My heart is pounding so fucking hard now that I'm breathless, and when I pull back, she is too. Yet I'm smiling at her.

Until the moment she says, 'Jake, there's something else.'

Chapter Twenty-Three

Serenity

Kissing Jake Walsh is everything. The way he pulls me to him so that I can feel every rock-hard muscle underneath his clothes. The way his powerful arms go around me, making me feel like he could protect me from anything or anybody. And his lips, the way they move against mine? It makes my mind go hazy with desire and my legs tremble. There's no way in hell I'm letting him walk away.

But, on the porch, as much as I want to lose myself in him, a little voice in my head reminds me that I haven't told him everything. That there's one more topic I've yet to raise.

I try to ignore it, but the voice grows louder with every touch of his lips.

I pull back. He's as breathless as I am.

'Jake, there's something else,' I say.

He searches my face. 'What is it?' he asks, and his hands go into my hair. 'Tell me.'

I breathe out. 'Almost two months ago, I had to perform a lap dance at the club. Kale told me I had to do it…'

'Go on,' he says, after a moment, urging me to continue. 'It's alright.'

'The dance was *Surly's Rules*. Which means the girl, she has to take everything off. I danced for the client naked. I couldn't see his face; he wore a hat the whole time. He wasn't allowed to touch me, but he seemed… I don't know. Interested in me. It wasn't until we went to his wedding that I realized that the client was Brody Conway.'

In the shadows it's hard to decipher his reaction. 'Brody Conway?'

'He knew me by my stage name, Brandy Velvet. Then he cornered me at his wedding. Wanted to know who I really was. He'd put two and two together, that I was CMC but also an employee of Kale's. I was Kale's bachelor party gift to Brody, only since that day—'

My voice trails off. I hate that I have to confess this to Jake, of all people. Except he takes my hands in his and gives them a squeeze in reassurance.

'I'm not gonna judge you,' he says. 'You can be honest.'

I take a breath. 'Since that day he's become more insistent. I've been taken to his apartment twice, both times to dance for him. To strip naked for him, while he watches. He even had me wear a CMC uniform. The last time I was there, he told me that he wanted to sleep with me. I refused, of course. But if I don't do what he wants, he'll expose me, and I'll lose my position on the squad.'

Jake looks at me. I bite down on my bottom lip. I know he said he won't judge me, but I'm terrified of how he might react. He takes a single step back, the soles of his shoes scuffing against the porch's wooden slats.

'Wait,' he says in an even tone. 'Brody Conway. As in Lemon's brother? As in that creepy, no-good-fucking-waste-of-space who sits up on high waiting for his granddaddy to bite the dust? You're telling me that Brody Conway is blackmailing you?'

'Yes,' I manage, and my voice breaks. 'I don't know what to do. It's why I need to quit the CMC. It's the only way.'

'Don't you fucking dare,' Jake growls and there's a different tone in his voice. One I don't recognize. I've never heard him mad before. I didn't think he could get mad, but his voice quivers with genuine rage when he says, 'Don't you dare give up on your dreams because of that piece of shit. I'll rip out his throat.'

'Jake, we can't do anything. Brody's untouchable. Look at who his mom is. He's heir to the whole damn Mutineers empire. Plus, he knows about my deal with Kale, because Kale must have blabbed about it. He knows everything. You talk to him, and he could derail your entire career.'

Jake goes back to pacing. His hands go to the back of his head, and he exhales shakily. 'Does he know about us?'

'Nobody knows about us.'

'Not Kale McCoy?'

'I mean, he saw you at the club, Friday. He asked who you were to me, but I didn't tell him.'

'Does Kale know about Brody's request?'

I swallow. 'No. At the club, we have a strict no-touching policy. But Kale is the one who sent me to his apartment. Kale seems to let Brody have whatever he wants, so I don't know what kind of hold Brody has over him.'

'When?' Jake asks. 'Did Brody give some kind of a time limit on his sick offer?'

'He keeps sending me messages. *Think about it*, he says, but it's clear he wants it to happen. Eventually, I'm gonna run out of time.'

In the dim light, I can see a muscle pulsate in Jake's jaw.

'Jake, if I quit the CMC, then the only thing for him to expose is my job at the club. Sure, it might damage the reputation of the Mutineers, temporarily, but I'll already be gone. They couldn't fire me. And you and I—'

I don't get to finish my sentence. Jake comes back over to me. His mouth crashes into mine and he kisses me with an intensity I've never experienced before. His hands slide roughly into my hair as he pulls me back to him.

'I need you to promise me one thing,' he grinds out as he pulls away, our foreheads touching as we lean into one another. 'I need you to promise me you won't ever quit the CMC.'

'But I have to—'

'No. You don't. Brody Conway doesn't get to win. Over my dead body. Right now, the only clause you've broken in your contract is getting involved with me. Only nobody knows that, and we'll keep it that way for the time being. Until we can fix all of this.'

'But how do I fix this? How do I fix any of it?'

'With my help. You're not alone. I'm gonna be with you. I swear, Serenity, we're gonna figure all this out.'

I wrap my arms around him and hold on tight.

—

Dad has fallen asleep on the couch. I switch off the TV and holding Jake's hand, I lead him up the stairs. My belly's fluttering by the time I open the door to my room.

I let him go in first. There's only one light on, a cylindrical ceramic table lamp with little cutout stars, bathing the interior in a celestial glow. It's a small room, with only a single bed, a rundown wooden closet, a green velvet covered armchair, and a low dressing table backed by a long, horizontal mirror. The Venetian blinds are closed. I had little notice Jake was coming here, so I didn't have time to clean up, and there are piles of clothes strewn about the place.

'This is me,' I say nervously, because it's hardly the palatial suite.

He goes over to the wall, where there are framed photographs of me in my younger years, some with my mom, or my dad, and some taken with old friends.

'That's me in high school,' I tell him.

He turns around and smirks, pointing at the photo. 'You were a high school cheerleader?'

'Yup. It was the only thing I was ever any good at.'

'I know that's not true,' he says. 'Do you keep in touch with your high school friends?'

I look to the floor. 'Not really. I never had any time to hang out with them. I never told them about my job at Surly's. Some went to college. Eventually, they all just drifted away.'

Jake comes back over to me. He lifts my chin with his fingers. 'None of this is your fault. You know that, right? All you ever tried to do was to help your dad.'

He rests his hands on my hips. In response, I snake my arms around his shoulders, my skin already craving his touch. An ache blossoms between my thighs. He lowers his head a little, and I don't hesitate. Jake Walsh, standing in my bedroom, is not something I expected to happen any time soon. I've never had a guy in here, at least not in that way.

Our kiss is slow at first. A tingling sensation fizzes up my spine and I savour it. Jake's hands go to my waist, lifting the hem of my tee and he slides his fingers underneath. I help him out by removing my tee altogether, so that he can openly admire the shape of my breasts swelling out over the top of my cami. He does more than that by lowering his lips to each one in turn, trailing kisses across the curves of my skin.

'Won't your dad hear us?' he whispers into my neck.

I smile. 'Not if we're quiet.'

'Deal,' he says, and he's still smiling when his lips collide with mine.

All that honesty on the porch is like a drug, a banned substance that just got legalized and I want more of it. Like, in time, I'll need another hit. Despite everything, it feels good to unburden myself to someone who has offered me nothing but support. Jake could have walked away when he saw me on stage at Surly's, but he hasn't. He's listened and showed empathy and maturity, and I'm grateful. He's even offering to bail me out. And maybe I should let him, but in my mind, it would taint what we have.

We alternate between kissing and removing one another's clothes, until we face each other, naked, standing on the wooden floorboards.

'I have a condom in my wallet,' he says with a swallow, indicating his Levi's, which are now in a heap on the floor. 'I know that makes me sound like a seventeen-year-old horndog.'

I reach out and cup his balls, which feel heavy and full, then slide my fingers along the length of his shaft and give it a firm stroke. 'So long as it hasn't been there since you were seventeen,' I say lightly.

His eyes are half-lidded as I continue in my movements, visceral desire trouncing any humor he might have found in my comment. 'Nah-uh,' he manages.

'Then that's okay,' I say.

'You keep on doing that, I am not going to be able to concentrate,' he replies shakily.

I don't stop. 'When we had sex at the cabin,' I say, 'I feel like you were with a version of me, not the real me.'

His eyes are fully closed now as I stroke him. I'm so turned on that I feel wetness leak out of me, a throbbing sensation low down and close to my opening.

'Say that first bit again,' he whispers.

I slow my stroke. My lips twitch. I love watching what this is doing to him. 'What? When you and I had sex at the cabin?'

'I like hearing you talk about it.'

The fingers on his right hand trace the line of my belly, close to where I'm stroking him. They sink further and I spread my feet apart, bending my left knee a little and raising my heel to allow him access, all the time keeping to my steady rhythm. A low groan sounds at the back of my throat as his fingers dip between my wet lips and he begins a slow exploration, finding the spot that makes me shudder. With my free hand I grip his shoulder for balance.

'I liked it when you were inside me,' I say.

He lets out a low groan. 'Like this?' he asks, as he shifts his position a fraction and two of his fingers slide up inside me.

I gasp, and let go of him, pleasure taking over, my head falling back. 'Like that. Yes. Yes.'

I grip both his shoulders as he fucks me with his fingers, drawing me closer, so his arousal is pressing up into my abdomen.

'I like the real you,' he breathes, and he crooks his fingers, rubbing my G-spot. 'Tell me what else you liked.'

'I liked watching you come,' I breathe, and at my words he removes his fingers from inside me, gathering me up in his arms and kissing me with the same intensity as on the porch, only this time, our kisses are messy, needy and heated.

And then he's gone again, bending down and retrieving the discarded pile of denim from the floor to locate the branded square foil condom packet from his wallet. He dumps the jeans, and using his teeth, carefully splits the packet down the middle, sliding out the O-shaped rubber and rolling it straight down his shaft.

Taking my wrists, he guides me down to my single bed and soon after I feel the weight of his body against me.

'Oh,' I hear him say in a low, breathy tone and I lift my head.

He's looking to his left, at the full length of our bodies reflected in the long mirror of my dressing table in the celestial light. I see a duskiness in his expression at the realization that he'll be able to watch us for the duration of our lovemaking.

'I've never done that before,' he whispers before I can say anything.

'Watched yourself?'

'Or watched somebody else.'

'Then I have an idea,' I whisper.

'What is it?'

I lean up and kiss him, gently guiding him off me. Then, shifting my butt, I turn my back to him, so that my ass is pressing against his groin and I'm full-frontal in the mirror. Jake watches my reflection closely. Then, lifting my left leg, I hook my toes up behind his left knee, allowing his dick full access to my wet pussy.

Jake groans, his eyes never leaving mine in the mirror. Moving his body a fraction further down, he allows me to reach behind, grasping him, before feeding his shaft into my opening. I'm fully splayed out for him, and when he pushes, he fills me almost completely.

'I can see *everything*,' he mumbles, heat filling his gaze as it lands in the mirror at the place where right now, we're so intimately joined. I feel a fresh rush of moisture at what feels like an erotically charged moment, and Jake bottoms out. He groans again. 'I'm so deep.'

I watch in the reflection as he lifts his knee a fraction, pressing up inside me. I moan as he begins his rhythmic thrusts, our eyes meeting in the mirror.

'Fuck, Serenity,' he mutters as his hip movements swiftly turn erratic. 'You feel so good.'

I can't drag my eyes away. I feel so full of him, blissful sensations shooting up from my toes all the way up my spine. He's watching to gauge my reaction, but he's taking so much from this too. Reaching up, I take his hand, guiding his fingers to my clit, and showing him exactly where I need to be touched. It only adds to the heat of the scene being played out by both our reflections.

'Touch me here,' I say.

And he does. Jake moves inside me, and when his fingertips brush against my clit I let out a high-pitched moan, not so loud that anyone outside of this room might be able to hear, but loud enough to let him know that he's in the right place. Circling my bundle of nerve-endings with the flat of his fingertip, my hips move with his, almost of their own accord.

'Yes,' I whimper. 'That's it. That's it.'

The scene being played out in my mirror is almost primal. Jake thrusting into me from behind, my body open for him, his fingertips massaging my clit as we move, bringing me closer and closer to my release. Pressure builds low down, a deep ache, like a coil tightening inside me, the delicious friction caused by his fingertips cloaking me in insane amounts of pleasure.

As I peak, my body starts to tremble. My eyes drift shut, my head falling back as my orgasm sweeps me up in its powerful wake, pleasure pulsing through me, the walls of my pussy spasming around Jake's erection as still he thrusts inside me, his fingers working their sexual magic. I make no sound as I climax, merely open my mouth and let the waves crash over me, though when I open my eyes, I realize Jake's lustful gaze hasn't left mine. His fingers drift from my clit back to my hip as his movements turn jerky. He looks at me in the mirror as his orgasm hits a few moments later, keeping his eyes open for as long as he can before the sensations get too strong and the pressure of remaining silent means he must look away from our reflection and finish out his climax by growling into the curve of my neck. Then his body goes limp and I feel him slip out of me.

We lie there for a moment, breathless, with a sheen of sweat covering our bodies, my butt still pressed into his groin where I've lowered my leg. His arm goes over me, caressing my breasts.

'That's the hottest thing I've ever done,' he whispers and the way he sounds so surprised makes me giggle. 'If you and I ever buy a house together, we are getting a mirror exactly like that one.'

Chapter Twenty-Four

Jake

Driving back into the city in my pickup, I switch my phone back on. A few moments later it's ringing, as Lemon's name appears on screen. I don't answer.

After five back-to-back missed calls, I pull over on the side of the road and call her back.

'Lemon, I'm behind the wheel,' I say, with her on speaker. 'What's the emergency?'

'I need you to break up with me!' she wails at the other end of the line.

The way she says it, it's like we're involved in a passionate relationship, when in reality, all I did was take her out to lunch.

'Lemon, we're not together. I thought we both knew that.'

'I know!' she howls back, and her quivering cries fill the cab. 'But the whole of Canyon thinks you and I are dating!'

Okay, so that's true, but that's exactly how Sam Conway wanted it.

'Look, I'm more than happy to break things off. But you gotta talk to your mom. Tell her you're not into me.'

'She won't s-stand for it,' Lemon sobs. 'But my real girlfriend just d-dumped me! I don't know what else to do!'

I stare through the windshield at the traffic racing by on the highway. 'Did you just say *girlfriend*?'

'Yes!' Lemon exclaims. 'Except since you and I got into the news, she's been avoiding me. And now she says she can't see me anymore!'

I swear this is the most fucked-up situation I have ever been in.

'Lemon, why didn't you tell me you were gay?'

'Because nobody knows that yet!' she wails again.

'You did tell her, right? That it was your mom who ordered me to take you out? That there's literally nothing between us?'

'I told her, but she says a guy like you must have a ton of girls, except she's never seen you with anyone else, so either you're gay and you haven't come out yet, or you're fucking my brains out in secret!'

Her words are followed by yet more howling. How is it she and Samantha Conway are related?

I blink. 'Hold up a sec,' I say. 'Who's your girlfriend?'

'Well, it *was* Carlie Kessler, until she broke up with me!'

'DJ Stash?'

'Yes!' she yowls. 'But Momma doesn't know that yet!'

'Oh, Jesus,' I say, more to myself, rubbing my eyes. I have bigger things to worry about right now than Lemon's dating dramas or her interfering mother.

'Can you please call her?' Lemon asks in a shrill tone.

'Who? Carlie? What? No. Lemon. I can't get involved. This is between you and your mom. And Carlie. I can't help it if your mom doesn't know you're into same sex relationships.'

'Momma thinks that I need to be with a *guy*... like you. You know... handsome, successful... athletic... a golden boy. Me bein' gay is not exactly in her playbook.'

I growl at the use of her term 'golden boy'. I'm done with it. Her voice is getting higher and higher, and I'm exasperated.

'Lemon. Pull it together. You like this girl, you gotta tell her. You gotta come out to your mom and tell her to back off.'

'But how do I convince Carlie there's nothing between you and I?'

I let out a heavy sigh. Shake my head. 'Send me her number.'

I hear Lemon trying to calm herself. 'Thank you,' she murmurs through her sniffles. We say our goodbyes and I hang up.

It doesn't get weirder than this, and my guess is I'll soon be paid another visit by Samantha Conway.

If only I could tell her what her son's been up to.

—

'Hey, honey, how was the gym?'

Mom's at the sink with the faucet running when the front door slams behind me. Okay, so I've had a workout, just not the kind she's imagining. I toss my car keys onto the side and wander through to the kitchen.

'Good. Uh. Yeah,' I say. 'It was fine. River's friends go home?'

'Oh, they stayed for dinner,' Mom says. 'What delightful boys. So tragic how Wylder was hit in his car like that. He's determined to walk again. Such a brave soul.'

'Did River tell you he invited her to the winter formal?'

'She did! Honestly, I'm so pleased for her. Now I just need to find you a nice girl. How's Lemon? Are you taking her out again anytime soon?'

'Uh,' I begin, unsure what I should even tell her anymore. 'Yeah. I will. Where's Dad?'

'Watching the game. River's upstairs.'

'I'm, uh, gonna get a shower.'

Upstairs, in my ensuite, I stand under the shower and relive the time I spent with Serenity at her house. I fantasize that she's here with me, naked with the hot spray running down her skin, between her breasts and over her nipples, and in a second I'm rock hard again, remembering the look on her face as she rode out her orgasm, shortly before I joined her there. One hand flat against the tiles, I fist my dick, bringing myself to a climax in under a minute, thinking of how good she looked in her bedroom mirror. After I've lathered myself up, my head goes back, and I curse because I hate that I still have to keep our relationship a secret.

In my bedroom, I'm almost dressed and pulling on a shirt when there's a knock at my door.

'Come in,' I say, and River opens the door. I rub the damp towel over my hair.

She looks at me through slanted eyes. 'Gym, huh? Wouldn't you have showered there? Before you came back?'

'Showers were out of order. Problem with the, uh, water pressure, I think.'

She stares at me. Her lips twitch. 'The water pressure, right.'

'What?' I question.

She glances back at my door, which is still open, and lowers her voice. 'Mom and Dad might be convinced by your *I-went-to-the-gym-for-a-workout-with-the-guys* act, but you're not fooling me. Something is up with you.'

I snort. 'Nothing is up with me. Are you happy that Wylder asked you to the formal?'

'Don't change the subject. And for the record, yes, I am. Are you gonna tell me or not?'

'I don't know what you're talking about.'

'Is it a girl?'

'What girl?'

River takes a step forward. 'It's a girl, isn't it? You've fallen for somebody, but for some reason that I cannot fathom, you don't want to tell anyone about it. Am I right? This has been going on for weeks. You, disappearing all the time.'

This is why I don't love living with my family.

'You're crazy. That's wacked out.'

'Oh, is it? When Wylder and Scottie were leaving, I noticed your gym sneakers by the front porch. Did you run on the treadmill barefoot or something?'

'I took a different pair of sneakers.'

'Oh yeah, which ones?'

'They're at the gym.'

'Which gym were you at? The one at the training ground? When everybody else in the squad had the night off?'

I don't answer. Instead, I let out a sigh. 'Riv, can you just quit it with the questions?'

She gives a shrug like she doesn't care. 'Fine. But I got your number, dude.'

She then turns on her heel and goes to leave.

A lot of things go through my mind at once. 'Riv, wait. Wait.'

She turns around, brows raised. She crosses her arms over her chest. She's my baby sister and I don't enjoy lying to her.

'Close the door,' I say.

She does as she's asked, though she still doesn't look impressed.

I wait until she turns around. 'It's a girl, alright. I'm seeing somebody, but right now it's a big secret and it needs to stay that way.'

River practically jumps on the bed, sits herself down, crosslegged. She's gone from sceptical to thrilled inside of a minute. 'Spill,' she says. 'And don't skimp on the details.'

I massage my eyes with the palm of my hand. 'Her name's Serenity.'

'Cute name.'

'She's CMC. A Mutineers cheerleader.'

She stares at me for a moment. 'Oh... shit? Doesn't that mean—'

'Yup. They spell it out in her contract. She can't even talk to me, let alone date me. And that's not all. She works at a strip club on the west side of Canyon.'

River wrinkles her nose. 'When you say she works in a strip club... she works... behind the bar?'

We clearly think in the same way. 'Not exactly,' I murmur.

River raises her brow. 'So... she's a cheerleader *and* a, a what, a... *stripper*?'

'She prefers "private dancer". But the bosses at the stadium don't know and you cannot say a word. She's got her reasons.'

'Which are?'

'Riv, whatever I say to you right now stays between these four walls, yes?'

She nods once. 'Understood.'

'You cannot tell any of your friends.'

'Not a problem; I don't have many.'

I roll my eyes. 'Not even the ones back in Philly.'

She seals her lips with an invisible zipper.

'And not even your new boyfriend.'

'It's a little soon to be labelling him that, don'tcha think?'

'Whatever. This stays between you and me. *Capiche?*'

'*Capiche.*'

One hand goes to the back of my neck. 'Serenity's got a debt to pay. Her father's gambling debt. She dances to pay back the debt to the club's boss. She's been doing it for the last four and a half years.'

'Woah, that must be quite a debt.'

'It's a lot.'

'If you like her that much, you should offer to pay it for her.'

'I already did. She won't have it. Says she doesn't need a hero.'

River leans her head to one side and smiles. 'I like her already.'

I pace up and down, hands going into my hair. 'She's like a slave there. Every tip she makes goes to her boss.'

'I mean, okay, so she doesn't want a hero, but sounds like she needs somebody like Gramps.'

It takes a moment for her words to sink in. I stare at her. 'Wait, what?'

'Like, didn't he study employment law after he left the NFL?' River carries on.

Every muscle in my body tenses because River just came up with the solution to this problem. 'Riv, you're a genius,' I breathe.

She gives me a knowing smile. 'Well, I mean, I'm not *royalty* like you, but I have my uses.'

I bound over to her and wrap her in a hug. 'You're a queen. I hadn't even thought of Gramps.'

'Does that mean we can invite him to Texas?'

'I'm gonna call him first thing tomorrow.'

'You can let go of me now. I wanna google your girlfriend. What's her last name?'

I let her go. 'Harper.'

'How old is she?'

'Twenty-two.'

'You gonna tell Mom and Dad?'

'Nope.'

'Sensible. Bein' a stripper an' all... she might not pass the Mom test.'

I wince. 'I've never cared less about the fucking Mom test.'

River softens. 'Do you love her? Is she the one?'

I don't have to consider my answer for very long before slowly, I nod my head. River crumples, bites her lip. 'Can I meet her?'

'One day. I promise you.'

'What if the Conways find out? Would they fire you for being in a relationship?'

I've thought about it. 'I doubt that. I might get a fine for misconduct. But Serenity?'

I wince, because it's inequality at its worst. Though she represents the Mutineers brand, she doesn't win points and can't get us to the playoffs or Super Bowl. She's both expendable and replaceable, at virtually no cost to the management.

I imagine some might argue that I am not.

'They'd fire her in a nanosecond,' I say.

Chapter Twenty-Five

Serenity

'Hey! What are you guys doing here?'

Tuesday morning, at The Bounty, I have visitors. Three members of the CMC – Jewel, Leona and Shawny – have all come for a late breakfast, unannounced.

'You look cute in that apron,' Shawny says as I embrace her. Her white-blonde hair smells freshly shampooed. 'We always said we'd crash one of your shifts for breakfast.'

'Can you go on a break and sit with us?' Jewel asks, squeezing my hand.

'Let me take your order first,' I say. I've only been here an hour.

'Do you have any kombucha?' Leona asks as she slides into the booth.

I giggle at my fellow rookie's request, because The Bounty doesn't exactly offer the world's healthiest set of breakfast options. 'I can get you a black tea?'

Shawny swipes up the menu. 'Are you kidding me?' she says. 'I want calories. Fried steak and eggs. With a chocolate shake on the side.'

'Coming right up,' I say emphatically.

'Seriously?' Jewel questions, looking Shawny up and down. 'How come you literally don't gain a single pound after inhaling that?'

'It's literally all I'll eat for the rest of the day.'

'How about you, Jewel?' I ask.

'Can you do a whites-only omelette?'

Shawny gives a derisive snort at Jewel's selection. I give her a wink. 'For sure.'

'I'll have the same,' Leona says sweetly and hands me the menu. 'With the tea. Will you eat with us, Ren?'

I look around. The diner is quiet. 'I'll see if I can get away with it.'

When their food is ready, I take a seat at the table. My back is to the door but there's another waitress on duty. I've made myself a latte at the machine and I rip open a sugar sachet, pouring it into the cup. Kathleen never has to know.

'Can you *please* give us the update now?' Jewel says in Shawny's direction.

Shawny's brow gives a devil-may-care double bounce. She lowers her voice. 'So, I heard this from Angel, who heard it from Reeta, one of the ground staff, who heard it from one of the security guys at the Danube.'

She sucks her chocolate milkshake through a paper straw. 'Yesterday, big face off takes place between Lemon Conway and her momma, right in Momma Conway's office. Jake Walsh? Turns out, not having a thing with Lemon, at least not anymore. Lemon's *not* found herself a new fuckboy, but a fuck*girl*. Started as friends with bens but now very much a *thang*. Turns out Lemon is gay. And Momma Conway is so *not* pleased.'

'Oh my lord, who?' Jewel asks, her eyes sparkling and hungry for gossip.

'Only Carlie Kessler.'

All our eyes go wide. 'The DJ?' I ask.

'Get outta here!' Jewel blurts simultaneously.

'Get this. Lemon's screaming at her mother that they're in love, that she and Carlie wanna be together, that it's been going on for a while, etcetera, but Samantha Conway is like, *no, no way, the brand cannot handle you bein' a lesbian, she's so disappointed*, yada yada...'

'That's so mean,' I comment, though a part of me is relieved. 'Poor Lemon.'

'Hold up, isn't Lemon, like, twenty-three?' Jewel asks. 'Surely, you'd tell your mom where to get off?'

'Not if your mom is Sam Conway, and you're one of the heirs to the holy Mutineers empire,' Shawny says, crossing herself. 'I mean, it's fine for your daughter to be fucking your star player, but another *girl*?'

'She is a snob and a half,' Jewel says.

'Good news for you, though, right?' Leona comments toward Jewel. 'Means Jake Walsh is now a free agent.'

'So long, CMC,' Jewel laughs with a little wave of her fingers, and I laugh along with her, because I have no idea what else I can do, the same knot in my stomach forming whenever his name comes up.

'You know, I can picture Lemon and Carlie Kessler together,' Jewel then says. 'I think they make a cute couple.'

'Not as cute as you and Jake Walsh,' Leona adds.

'Duh,' Jewel says but she finishes it with another laugh.

'Sam Conway must be pretty pissed though,' Shawny says. 'Turns out her daughter ain't so keen on her team's star running back.'

'Don't you mean Jewel's future husband?' Leona laughs.

'Jake 'n' Jewel has a certain ring to it, don't you think?' Jewel giggles.

I keep a smile on my face, but inside it's starting to hurt. Not just because I want to be open about Jake and me, but because I hate lying to my friends about the first serious relationship I've had in years.

On the other side of the table, I see Jewel's eyes go wide. She lowers her voice. 'Oh my god, what is *he* doing here?'

A tingle goes down my spine. I turn my head toward the door. My world narrows as Brody Conway saunters into the diner wearing a suit.

'No fucking way,' Shawny whispers. 'What are the chances?'

'Why would he even come to a place like this?' Leona questions.

I look over. The other waitress is busy. I swallow. 'I should go.'

'Ugh. Tell us what he says,' Jewel hisses as I get to my feet.

As I turn and approach him, I feel Brody's gaze burn a trail down my body, dressed in my Bounty uniform.

'Good morning, sir,' I say tightly when I reach him, sweat breaking out on my upper lip. 'Have a seat, I'll fetch you a menu.'

I don't allow him time to respond as I head straight to the bar for the menu and my notepad. All three girls are brazenly looking his way.

When I return, he's sitting down, his back to Jewel, Shawny and Leona. My gaze flits to them and they're still gawking. I pass him a menu, and I feel self-conscious that there are stains on it. He's not dressed like our usual clientele. I've never mentioned my regular job to him, so in order to find out where to find me, I suspect, once again he's gotten the information from my CMC employee record.

'What can I get you?' I ask.

'Honestly?' he drawls as he peruses the contents. 'A reply would be nice, Serenity.'

Over the last four nights he's sent more sexually charged messages to my phone. I've not replied to a single one.

'I've been busy,' I say stoically.

'With what?' he asks, and he makes eye contact with me for the first time, my stomach rolling over with dread.

'You should know there are three CMC members sat over there. They're all wondering what you're doing here.'

He turns around on purpose and looks pointedly at them. Shawny and Jewel produce charming smiles. Leona looks away.

'How did you know I worked here?' I ask.

'Oh, I've known for a while. I like how that skirt is so short it only just covers your ass. Reminds me of your cheerleader uniform.'

'Not here,' I swallow. 'Please.'

'You seem to be ignoring me, Serenity. Is the idea of clearing your father's debt not attractive to you?'

I'm conscious I'm being watched. 'Would you like to order breakfast?' I ask, my pen still poised.

'What would you recommend?'

'The American classic is always good.'

'I'll take an espresso and a date for our night together.'

I feel my cheeks burn. 'This is my place of work,' I whisper. 'This is so totally inappropriate.'

'Well, you seem to be running me around in circles, like the tease that you are. You know what I want, so just give in to me. I've told you; I'll make it good for you.'

'Like I said, this is my place of work. I can't discuss this in here.'

His gaze darkens and he lowers his tone. 'I don't get an answer now, then your life will implode, Serenity. I'll make sure your father's debt to Kale is *doubled*. And perhaps I'll go see your friends over there. Talk to them about what you do after the sun goes down.'

It's everything I can do to hold it together. 'Please. Just, please. Take your coffee and leave.'

He gets back to his feet. I glance at the girls to my left. In the booth, they are finishing their meals and appear to have lost interest in what I'm doing. 'Friday night,' Brody says with a gruesome smirk, as he leans closer to my face. 'I want you naked in my bed, primed and wet for me, and you'd better come there willingly. You're not there, I'll spill all your dirty little secrets to the goddamned world. I'll take that espresso to go.'

I try to stop my fingers from trembling as I prepare his coffee and ring it through the cash register. Brody pays and walks out of the diner without so much as a backward look. I watch him walk back over to his expensive car, and I swear I don't breathe for a whole minute. When he's gone, I glance back over to Jewel. The girls have finished eating and are talking amongst themselves. I shrink away from the register, bypass the kitchen, and go to the cramped, windowless staff room where Bounty employees take their breaks.

Alone, I pace, and cover my mouth with my hands. I can't stop shaking. I go to my locker and the tears are already falling. I can't stop the tide. I open the padlock and pull out my bag, my fingers still trembling as I pull out the phone I use with Jake and switch it on.

'Hey,' he answers. He's in his pickup, his tone upbeat. He sent me a message late last night asking if I would permit him to help me if it didn't involve money.

'Everything alright?' he asks.

I try to pull myself together. 'I'm at The Bounty. You won't believe this. Brody Conway just paid me a visit.'

'Sonofabitch!' I hear Jake curse, and it's followed by a thud, like he's punching the steering wheel several times. 'What did he say?'

I check the door and lower my voice. There's no use trying to pretend like I'm not in tears. 'He wants me at his apartment, Friday night, or he goes public with everything he knows. He gave me that ultimatum then walked out.'

'Shit,' Jake mutters, then he goes quiet for a moment. 'I'm on my way to the training facility. When I'm done, I'm heading straight to the airport. There's somebody I gotta pick up. Can you meet me at the cabin after your shift? I need you to bring that ledger you told me about. Your copy of it.'

I wipe my face, trying to compose myself. 'Okay. I can do that.'

'Does Brody expect to see you before Friday?'

'I... I don't know. I don't think so.'

'Then we've bought ourselves some time. I promise you, I'm gonna help you every step of the way. Do you trust me on that?'

I'm squeezing my phone so tightly. 'Yes,' I say. 'Yes, I trust you.'

'Then meet me at the cabin. After your shift. Bring the ledger. Don't forget it. And Serenity?'

'Yes?'

I wait for his response, but nothing comes, just the sound of his truck whirring in the background. There's a long pause before he says, 'I'll catch you later.'

'See you later.'

I hang up the phone and replace it back in my bag in my locker. Going to the rusty mirror, I wipe away some of the eye makeup that's running down my cheeks and make myself presentable.

'There you are,' Jewel says on my return. I straighten my apron. 'What did Brody Conway have to say?'

'Oh, not a lot, said he was just passing through,' I say, and I can't look her in the eye when I say it. 'Something about a business meeting on this side of town.'

'Did he order something?'

I shrug. 'He asked me to talk him through the menu, but in the end all he wanted was an espresso to go.'

'Did he recognize you?' Shawny asks.

I force a smile. 'I think so. I mean, he didn't say as much outright.'

'I find him kinda creepy,' Leona says. 'Anyone else think that?'

'One hundred million per cent,' Shawny confirms. 'No man has any business having fingers that long and slender.'

Jewel makes noises like she's gonna blow chunks.

'Ren, can we get the check?' Shawny asks. 'Much as we love your company, sugar, it's getting late, and we'd best get out your hair.'

On the road up to the cabin, in the fading light, there's torrential rain. It's a great time for one of my windshield wipers to snap clean in half. I cling to the steering wheel and slow my speed, praying I can make it to the cabin without having a collision.

By the time I reach the cabin, through the downpour, I spy Jake's pickup already parked up. I squeal as the water hits me and I slam my car door shut, racing up the steps to the porch.

The door opens and almost immediately I run inside. Jake closes it behind me, and I practically launch myself into his arms. His arms go around me, and we cling to one another, water dripping from my hair and clothes.

'Hi,' he whispers.

'Hi,' I say back.

I love his smell. I love the way he feels. I love everything about him. And I've tried hard these past few weeks not to admit that to myself.

'I've brought somebody to meet you.'

I pull back. 'Oh?'

Smiling, he looks to his right. I follow his gaze. 'Oh!' I say in surprise, because there's a tall, older man with a kind face and grey hair standing in the middle of the living room.

'Serenity,' Jake says. 'I'd like you to meet my maternal grandfather, Art Mackabee.'

'Hello, Serenity,' the man says, and holds out his hand.

I go to him and shake it. 'It's a pleasure to meet you, Mr Mackabee.'

'Please, call me Mac. Jake's told me a lot about you.'

I grit my teeth. 'Not all of it good, I'm sure.'

'On the contrary, he told me about your predicament.'

I sober. It used to be the only people who knew about my arrangement with Kale, were Kale, myself and my father. I used to be so ashamed of it. Jake made me see that none of this has ever been within my control.

I nod my head. 'I'm kind of in a tight spot,' I say, as my throat constricts.

He has kind eyes. 'Serenity, I'm a lawyer. I specialise in defending those who have been dealt… shall we say a lousy hand by their employers. Did you bring the ledger you talked to Jake about?'

'Yes,' I say. 'Oh, but I left it in the car.'

'Could we get it?'

Jake holds out his hand. 'D'you have your keys?'

I fish around in my pocket. 'It's on the front seat,' I tell him as I hand him the key.

Jake goes back out into the rain. Mac indicates that I should have a seat. 'If you'll excuse me for getting straight down to business. Perhaps you could start with how your father first came to know Kale McCoy? And then perhaps tell me as much as you know about Mr McCoy himself.'

I nod my head.

'How long do you have?' Mac asks.

I offer him a smile. There's something reassuring about his character. 'My shift begins at eight. I'll need to be gone from here by seven.'

He checks his watch. 'Then we have two hours. Jake brought us takeout.'

'He's thoughtful like that.'

'He certainly is.'

'Were you a football player?' I ask.

His eyes crease at the sides. 'I was. Though we didn't earn as much money back in those days. Your boyfriend is much more talented than I ever was.'

I giggle. 'Nobody's ever called him my boyfriend before. Not to my face.'

Having him called that gives me a warm sensation in my stomach. At that moment, the door to the cabin opens again and Jake dashes back inside, water from the rain cascading off his jacket. He takes out my ledger, which is pressed inside to keep it dry.

'Do you think he is?' Mac asks me.

We're both looking Jake's way. His brow is furrowed. 'What?' he questions.

'Yes,' I say to Mac, and he reaches for a notebook. 'He very much is.'

Chapter Twenty-Six

Jake

At eight-twenty, Serenity sends me a text. *He's here*, she says.

At the house, we've already had dinner. Though I wasn't hungry, my stomach tied up in knots. The TV is on. Gramps and I are both wearing suits. He thought we'd be taken more seriously that way. Sat on the couch opposite me, I give him a nod and slide my phone back into my inside pocket.

'So, remind me where it is you're going tonight?' Mom asks innocently, without taking her eyes off her property show.

'Uh, it's a hotel bar over on Main,' I tell her. 'I forget what it's called exactly.'

'And your father is not invited, why? He was an NFL player too.'

She already doesn't like that I surprised her with a visit from Gramps yesterday, or that he's not wanted to spend every second of his day with her today. 'Figured I don't wanna be seen like I'm bragging, you know?' I tell her. 'Besides, the guys just wanna shake hands with the legend that is Art Mackabee. They can meet Dad anytime. Some of them have already.'

On the other couch, River puts her arms around my dad's shoulders. 'You're still a legend to me, Daddy,' she murmurs. 'Even if you were never a quarterback.'

'Everybody just *loves* a quarterback,' Dad replies with a sigh of acceptance.

'You snapped that ball with the best of 'em,' River says, by way of consolation, rubbing his head. 'It's a shame nobody was paying attention.'

Dad rolls his eyes playfully at her.

River knows everything. She was desperate to accompany us, just so she could see the inside of a strip club. I managed to talk her down. She knows why we're going, and why she can't come along.

'Shall we go then?' Gramps says, getting to his feet, and I do the same. He then picks up a black zip-up binder – the contents of which I hope will be Serenity's salvation and her ticket out of working for Kale McCoy.

'Have fun you guys,' River says, and checking Mom and Dad aren't looking my way, holds up two crossed fingers toward me.

I offer her a nervous smile in return.

'Yes, go enjoy yourselves,' Mom says. 'Daddy, don't you be getting carried away now. I know what happens when younger players start offering to buy you a beer.'

'I'll be on my best behavior,' Gramps mumbles as we head for the door.

—

At Surly's, the music is loud and the lights are low. I follow Gramps inside the entrance, the both of us bathed in a glow the shade of neon pink.

'You ever been to a strip club before?' I ask him over the noise.

'A few, back in the day,' he responds to my surprise. 'They just weren't dressed up quite as nice as this one.'

We pay the entry fee. I've kept my cap on, as I know from Serenity that the CCTV is extensive. A waitress shows us to a table near the stage and she gives Gramps an odd look, as though he's a senior citizen and looks a little too respectable for a joint such as this.

'I'm here to speak to Jaxon,' I tell her, and she gives me a nod. We order a couple of beers. The girl on stage is not Serenity. She's raven-haired and dancing wearing only a thong and a pink feather boa. She seems popular with the guys surrounding the stage.

Gramps watches her.

'You think we can do this?' I ask him.

He drags his eyes from the stage and fixes my stare. 'Depends on whether our friend Mr McCoy is prepared to play hardball.'

It's a while before Jaxon makes his appearance. He wears jeans and a jacket, a logo on his T-shirt that's snug around his belly.

'You're Jake, right?'

I stand and we shake hands. 'Yes. This is Art Mackabee,' I say, introducing my grandfather.

Jaxon seems a little nervous. 'Mr McCoy's in the office. I'm gonna tell him you're here like we discussed. Wait here. Like I said to Serenity, I can't promise nothing, okay?'

'I appreciate you trying,' I tell him.

From what Serenity has told me, Jaxon's always had her back, and he knows her situation.

He disappears. It's some minutes before he returns, and this time, there's a guy with him, the size of a house.

'Mr McCoy will see you,' Jaxon says. 'This is Hurley. You'll be frisked. That's standard. You got a problem with that, you can head on home.'

I nod in agreement. Gramps gets to his feet, holding his leather binder.

As we're directed backstage, I glance left and right, searching for Serenity. I glimpse her for the briefest of moments, and she grants me a hopeful smile, and I'm glad she knows that we're here. Seeing her makes my chest ache, and I know how much I want this meeting to succeed. The pair of us don't have time to exchange words as a split second later, the guy called Hurley is roughly frisking me, checking my pockets, then doing the same to Gramps.

When Jaxon opens the door to the office, my heart starts to thud.

I go in first. Gramps thought it would be best if I made the introductions, to lull Kale McCoy into thinking that my grandfather's just a useless old man.

I remove my cap. I note that Jaxon doesn't remain in the room.

'Mr McCoy,' I say, keeping things polite. Southerners like their hospitality. 'Thank you for agreeing to speak to us. My name is Jake Walsh and this is Art Mackabee.'

We shake hands. Kale McCoy's got a firm grip. He eyeballs me but pays little attention to Gramps. He then indicates that we should sit down, where two seats have been placed facing the desk. The guard, Hurley, remains with his back to the door.

'What can I do for you, gentlemen?' McCoy ventures.

I hold my ground. 'We're here to talk to you about Serenity Harper.'

At my words, his eyes slant just a fraction, as though that's not what he was expecting me to say. 'Serenity?'

He leans back in his chair. Goes back to eyeballing me. 'That's right,' he says eventually. 'I know you. You're that guy. You were here. You're the pro football player.'

'Yes, sir, I am.'

He looks to my grandfather for an extended moment. 'So, he's here to beg me to let Serenity go. What does that make you?'

'His lawyer,' Gramps says. 'I'm here to ensure nobody fucks around.'

McCoy leans his elbows on the surface of his desk. 'Then this is gonna be a very short meeting, old man. Let me make this clear to you, gentlemen. Serenity belongs to me. I don't care who her *boyfriend* is, so long as she shows up and keeps those dollar bills rolling in. So, I suggest you get the fuck out of my club.'

He says the word 'boyfriend' looking right at me. Neither me nor Gramps moves a muscle. So far, exactly as expected. 'This is a very nice venue you have here, sir,' I say. 'But with no disrespect to you, you keeping Serenity here like a slave… it's not gonna fly. Not anymore.'

McCoy lets out a derisive snort. 'Slave. She's hardly chained up in the basement.'

Gramps clears his throat. It's overexaggerated. McCoy glares at him like the old man might have a heart attack right here on the floor of his office.

This time, Gramps is the one eyeballing McCoy. 'Have you ever heard of debt bondage, Mr McCoy?'

'Debt bondage?'

'It's a form of modern slavery. Compulsory labor. Indentured servitude. It is banned in international law, in most domestic jurisdictions and in all fifty of our great United States. People in debt bondage very often work for wages below that of the federally mandated minimum, often based on a verbal 'at-will' contract, with none of the required employment conditions, such as family leave, sick leave or mandatory breaks. The agreement that was entered into by yourself and Ms Harper was consistently anchored in your favor. You waited until she was of legal age before you took advantage of her and employed her on the basis that she would work for you to pay off her father's financial debt. US federal law considers the use of debt, or the threat of financial hostage-taking, as a form of coercion for forced labor. You, sir, are therefore breaking the law.'

Watching my Gramps tear shreds off this motherfucker, I've never been happier. I can see a muscle flexing in McCoy's jaw, his face like thunder. When Gramps stops speaking, McCoy sits back in his chair, as though he's just survived an onslaught.

In football, we call it a dog pile.

'Furthermore,' Gramps continues, and McCoy's brow creeps up his forehead, 'you and Ms Harper have both kept a ledger for the duration of her time in servitude. Not only did you withhold all her tips, you failed to adequately recompense her for her time served as a dancer at this establishment, and you refused her a salary to allow her to increase the amount of debt she was able to repay during every shift she worked. As her employer, you were legally obliged to pay her the federally mandated minimum wage, which you denied. Again, sir, you broke the law, on top of the several laws you had already broken.'

It's hard to tell in this light, but McCoy looks like he's turned a shade of beetroot.

Nothing's holding Gramps back. 'And so, to conclude. I have studied Ms Harper's ledger in detail. As she helpfully documented all the hours she worked in your establishment, since the day she turned eighteen, including most federal holidays, by my calculations, at the Texan minimum wage rate, she has fully repaid the debt owed to you by her father, minus thirty dollars and eighty-six cents. You should consider that a good deal, because I know you pay your other girls a lot more.'

McCoy brings both his clenched fists down hard on the surface of the desk. 'Enough! Get the hell out of here, both of you! Hurley, escort these two out. Bar them for life.'

I glance back. The man mountain that is Hurley approaches. I look at Gramps and we both get to our feet. McCoy can't even look us in the eye.

I hold out my hand. 'Thank you for your time, sir.'

He slaps it away. 'Fuck you! Get out!'

I straighten my suit jacket and allow Gramps to walk out in front of me. Hurley opens the door and neither one of us looks back.

At the entrance, Hurley crosses his arms and puffs out his chest, glaring at us down his nose. The size of him, he'd make a half decent tight end. 'Gentlemen, you are barred from entering these premises *forthwith.*'

He looks to Gramps when he says 'forthwith', as though he's trying to prove he was paying attention back there in the office, but perhaps to say he was impressed by my grandfather's legal jargon.

Outside, I look at Gramps nervously in the parking lot, heading for the pickup. 'What now?'

'We wait,' he responds. 'Let that sink in.'

'Why didn't you open your binder?'

'There's nothing in it,' Gramps says. 'Just a few sheets of blank paper. I carry it around to make me feel like I can still pass as an attorney.'

'Believe me,' I smile. 'You still do.'

—

At one a.m., when Serenity calls me, I'm lying in bed, wide awake.

'I'm parked on Oak Trail. Is that near your place?' she says.

I bolt upright. 'I'm on Rockwell Drive. I can get in the car. Don't go anywhere.'

'I'm outside number 408. Near the corner of Boston Avenue.'

The house is quiet when I slip out the front door. The pickup is in the driveway. It takes me less than five minutes to drive to her location. Serenity's opening the car door before I've even parked up.

When I get out, I slow my pace. In the shadows of the trees, it's hard to see her face. My breath hitches when I finally see her, black eye makeup smudged down her face where she's been crying so much.

'Oh Jesus, what happened?' I growl. 'Did he hurt you?'

More tears leak down her face. 'No.'

I take her hands in my mine. 'Then what happened?'

She breaks out into a broken grin. 'He let me go.'

My heart is thrumming hard in my chest. 'What?'

She nods her head. 'He said I wouldn't go back if I knew what was good for me. I managed to say goodbye to the other girls... then I left.'

I'm speechless. I grab her in a bear hug and squeeze her to me, burying my face in her hair. Then I lift her off the ground and she squeals in genuine delight. 'Are you serious?' I ask, when I put her down again and cradle her face in my palms.

She's trembling. The tears are still streaked down her face and she's as breathless as I am. 'Jake. My father's debt is fully paid. Kale said I don't have to work there anymore. I'm free.'

At the realization, I pull her back to me, crushing my mouth to hers, the moan coming out of my mouth one of intense relief, not for me, but for her, that she doesn't have to take her clothes off for anybody else but me, and she didn't have to pay a dime to Kale McCoy to say *sayonara* to that whole goddamned outfit.

I love kissing her. I would die kissing her if I could. When she breaks our kiss, she wipes continuous tears, shaking her head in disbelief and pacing on the sidewalk in the dark. I want to reach for her, but she needs this. I know she needs to process. And we're the only ones out here. No one is gonna see us together tonight.

'You don't understand,' she says, her voice quivering, more emotional than I've ever seen her. She pulls her sleeves up over her hands, wiping her cheeks. 'My whole life, no one has ever done anything like this for me. I never thought this would happen. I never *believed*… And I don't know what you said to him… and I know I said I didn't need a hero… but you… you came along and crashed into my world. You did this for me, Jake. You *and* Mac. You're both my heroes.'

I smirk. 'I'd settle for being your boyfriend.'

'Shut up!' she teases me, and within seconds she's back in my arms, just where I want her. 'You are my boyfriend.'

We kiss for some time. 'I wanna take you home,' I whisper against her mouth. 'You can leave your car here. Spend the night with me.'

'I want to,' she whispers between kisses, my fingers sliding into the waistband of her jeans. 'But I need to check on my dad and tell him the good news. But soon, I promise you.'

'The whole night,' I say, resting my forehead against hers. 'So that I can wake up with you in my arms.'

'I want that,' she says, but then her mood shifts, and she looks down to where our fingers are entwined.

'What is it?' I ask.

'One problem down,' she says with a heavy sigh. 'Two to go.'

'You mean Brody Conway,' I grit out.

She raises her eyes to me. She's not crying anymore, but her eyes are glassy.

'You could just tell him you don't work for Surly's anymore,' I say. 'So the deal is void. Or... you could send me to tell him. In my mind, I've been cooking up ways to remove his face from the planet.'

My words make her smile, and I can't help but kiss her again.

'I never told Kale about Brody's ultimatum,' she says.

'Why not?'

She gives a shrug. 'I think I thought I could handle it. That I could handle *him*. But if I don't show up to his apartment Friday night, he's gonna tell people what I do... what I *did* anyway.'

I search her face. It seems that unless she complies with Brody's demand, she's screwed no matter what she does.

'Then we stay one step ahead,' I say.

'By doing what?'

I move my hands to her waist. 'It would mean telling a few people about you and I.'

Her shoulders droop. 'That was problem number three.'

I stroke her hair. 'You and me. This is not a problem. It's the terms of your contract that's the problem.'

'Who would we need to tell?' she asks.

'People that we trust,' I emphasize. 'Plus, I told River already. She kinda guessed something was up.'

'What did she say?'

'Well, she's desperate to meet you.'

Serenity smiles. 'Likewise.'

'Will you let me set something up?'

She nods her head. 'But that still doesn't solve the Brody problem.'

'Trust me. I have an idea how we deal with that piece of shit. Come here.'

I wrap my arms around her, and she presses her cheek into my chest. It makes my heart do crazy things. Like I wanna say those words to her again, like when I was in my truck on the phone to her, but I was too damn scared to say them out loud.

'Serenity,' I whisper.

'I love you,' she says back, pressing into me, holding me tighter, and every muscle in my body tenses up, like I'm about to explode. 'I know it's only been a short time. I know we've only slept together twice. I know it's probably too soon, but I do,' she murmurs. 'I love you, Jake.'

I pull back and search her face. If I could bottle how she looks at this moment, I would. Dewy-eyed and beautiful in the moonlight. She bites down on her bottom lip and looks like she might start crying again, or like she might have said something wrong.

'I love you *so* much,' I say roughly, because the words are raw at the back of my throat, and because I've never felt this way before her. I didn't know a person could feel that strongly for another human being until she was standing there in that grocery store that day, and those feelings have only gotten stronger every second I've spent in her presence. 'I would do anything for you.'

Her face lights up. In my heart, I know she feels the same way. 'You already did,' she says.

My heart swells. That we've exchanged those three little words only strengthens my resolve. And I know exactly who I need to call.

Chapter Twenty-Seven

Serenity

My phone flashes up another message from Brody.

> Can't wait to bury myself in that sweet wet pussy of yours tomorrow night.

At the wheel of my C-Max, my skin crawls. On any other night, I'd be driving, on my way to Surly's. Thursday nights are always busy at the club. So, it feels surreal that instead, I don't have to dance for tips and I'm driving around the wide streets of Boulder Creek after dark, trying to locate an address that Jake has instructed me to go to. I think about parking in some shady spot and walking the rest of the way. Except that I know I need to start being honest with people: I used to be a stripper, and I drive a shitty car. A shitty car that's making weird noises as I crawl along the curb.

Brody's message aside, my stomach is tied up in knots. I know who we're seeing tonight, and what we're gonna say. I know Jake is right, that it's time we fessed up. It doesn't make me any less nervous.

Jake requested the meeting. Asked specific individuals to show, because he had something confidential to tell them. But, to ensure they would all agree, he hasn't mentioned my name. And they don't know it's me who is gonna show up at the door.

When I reach the house, it's stunning, just as I knew it would be. A gated property, with a white front, lit up from the outside, and a substantial, paved driveway with several cars parked up, including Jake's pickup. This is what years of being an NFL quarterback gets you. I park my car and push down the nerves threatening to spill over.

I brought flowers. Seemed like the sort of thing you do if you live in this neighborhood.

Before I ring the doorbell, I gulp a breath. There's no going back now.

A pretty, petite blonde woman opens the door. 'Hi!' she beams at me. 'Come on in!'

I step inside, taking in the impressive hallway, like something you see on all those home shows for the rich and famous.

'I'm Ally,' she says, holding out her hand. 'Ally Briar.'

'I'm Serenity.'

'You're CMC, right?' she asks, and there's a glint in her eye when she says it. I can't work out if she's surprised or excited.

I smile back at her. 'Right. It's my rookie year.'

'Well, come on in.'

'These are for you,' I say, and hand her the flowers.

She blushes. 'You're too sweet. They're beautiful, thank you. Come on through.'

I swallow. I follow her into a living room with sliding glass doors and a high, vaulted ceiling. It's like something you'd see in a magazine.

Dalton Briar and Hudson Briar get to their feet. Dalton's looking at me with a raised brow. I've never spoken to him before, but he knows I'm CMC, and everybody knows who he is. Hudson Briar stands there with his legs wide apart, his thumbs pressed together, stoic. Up close, he's even bigger than he looks on the field.

I glance to my right and find myself looking at Harmony, who is already standing. She looks both surprised and distinctly uncomfortable, and has purposefully distanced herself from the men in the room, her back pressed into one corner.

And then there's Jake. My Jake. He's standing with his back to the fireplace, but he's looking at me.

'Hey,' he says softly.

An awkward silence descends over the room.

'So... can I get anybody another drink?' Ally asks. 'Serenity?'

Harmony looks to me, then to Jake and back again. Just as we planned, she was not expecting to see me walk through the door. 'W-What is this?' she murmurs.

Jake reaches for my hand. I don't stop him. His fingers feel warm as they interlace with mine.

'So,' Jake says as he addresses the others, 'we came here to tell you that... Serenity and I... we're in love. We're a couple.'

I swallow. Jake squeezes my hand in reassurance, yet suddenly it feels like it's too hot in here.

The moment the news has sunk in, Hudson Briar inhales sharply. A muscle flexes in his jaw. His chin juts out as his gaze turns on Harmony. Her eyes meet his and, in the corner, she blanches. I see the quiet devastation on her face as she watches him stalk from the room. A moment later we hear the front door violently slam, and Harmony flinches at the sound.

Dalton shakes his head.

'I'll go,' says Ally awkwardly, and goes after Hudson.

'I don't understand,' Harmony says moments later. 'How did this happen? Y'all never should have even exchanged more than a couple of words. Y'all shouldn't have even been in the same space. We shouldn't even be in this room together.'

She indicates to the pair of us. I look at Jake. 'We met in a grocery store,' I say, trying to keep the guilt out of my voice but it creeps in. 'By accident. Before the first game of the pre-season. I didn't know who Jake was and he didn't know I was CMC.'

'We didn't mean to break any rules,' Jake adds. 'If anything, it was my fault. Serenity tried to get rid of me. But I didn't let her tell me no for an answer.'

Harmony buries her face in her palms. Dalton rolls his eyes. 'Is it really that big of a deal?' he says, pointedly in her direction, because she's still backed into a corner.

'It's clause five of the contract!' she snarks back at him.

'So you've been telling my brother the last five years! Yet it seems like these two managed it.'

He's indicating toward Jake and me. Harmony is visibly conflicted.

'This is bad,' she mumbles.

'Bad for who?' Dalton asks in disgust.

'It's against the rules!' Harmony exclaims.

'Oh, the rules, the rules, always the goddamned *rules*,' Dalton sighs.

'It's alright for you, there's nothing in your contract about not bagging yourself a member of the CMC!'

'And if there was, I would have had it removed! Not that it makes a difference to me, I'm married.'

'But that is exactly why you guys get to do whatever you want, and as cheerleaders, we are held to a completely different standard!' She waggles her finger between us. 'Nobody can find out about this. This cannot come out.'

'There's more,' Jake says, and my stomach rolls over. 'You might wanna be sitting down for this.'

'What do you mean, *more*?' Harmony questions. 'Oh god, you're pregnant.'

'I'm not pregnant,' I reassure her.

I can see her chest rising and falling, the distress etched into her features.

Behind me, I hear the front door open. Moments later, Hudson reappears in the threshold. Sheepishly, he clears his throat as he re-enters the room, pushing his fingers through his beard and ignoring Harmony completely. I see the hurt in her eyes as she tracks him coming back across the room.

'What'd I miss?' he mumbles.

'Nothing,' Dalton states. 'Same old shit about not breaking any precious rules.'

'Wouldn't wanna upset Kathleen Lafferty now, would we?' Hudson says.

'Oh, come on, you both know as well as I do that it's not Kathleen who sets out the terms of the CMC contract,' Harmony states, and it seems even she's realized that it's a little silly now, her keeping her distance.

'Can you all please sit down?' Jake raises his voice, exasperated. 'We're not done yet.'

Two of them do as they're told. Then Harmony takes a step forward, pulls herself up a chair. Jakes squeezes my hand again. 'You okay to do this?' he whispers to me.

I'm as ready as I'll ever be. This is the moment I get to lay everything out.

The room goes quiet. All eyes are on me. I snatch another quick breath, then look at Harmony first. 'When I first applied to join the CMC, I wasn't entirely honest about what I did for a living. I wrote down that I was a waitress at The Bounty diner... which is true, that's my day job. But I didn't write down that... until very recently I was a private dancer at Surly's Tavern on the west side.'

The room is silent. Harmony is stunned. 'A... I'm sorry, a p-private dancer?'

'A stripper,' I clarify in a whisper, and it makes my chest ache to say the words out loud to my squad captain. 'I worked at Surly's for five years. Until last night, in fact.'

I can tell by the looks on their faces that the captain and quarterback and the Mutineers' wide receiver were not anticipating those words to come out my mouth, but it's also clear that they know exactly what and where Surly's is. Harmony too, because her eyes drift shut.

'Wait,' Jake says, pleading with them. 'Hear her out.'

I swallow the lump that's lodged in my throat. I realize that Ally has come back into the room and is lingering in the doorway. She's heard everything I've said.

I tell them everything: the gambling, the debt, and how I've been juggling three jobs these last few months. How Jake and his grandfather helped set me free.

I look at Jake when I finish talking, and I'm on the verge of tears again. That's when I notice the other three are staring at me.

'You're like a superwoman,' Ally says behind me.

'And she takes care of her father, who's sick,' Jake says, and there's a note of pride in his voice.

'How have you even had time for each other?' Harmony asks.

I laugh and look at Jake. 'We haven't had all that much. Jake only found out that I was dancing in Surly's last Friday night.'

Hudson Briar is glaring at me. 'Hold on just one sec,' he says, and gets to his feet. 'You mean to tell me that for the past two months, you've been dancing as a Canyon Mutineers Cheerleader, in front of a crowd eighty-thousand strong, and not one of those people recognized you as a stripper from Surly's Tavern?'

'Private dancer,' Harmony corrects him, but his expression sours at her addressing him directly. He averts his eyes, and the reaction is not lost on Harmony, who suddenly looks miserable.

'It's pretty much a miracle, I know,' I say to Hudson. 'I wear wigs at the club, but we get football fans in all the time.'

'That's wild,' he mutters.

'But it's another rule broken,' I say. 'Technically, I've brought the Mutineers into disrepute.'

'No, you haven't,' Harmony argues. 'Nobody knew. And you don't work there anymore.'

I take another deep breath. 'What if the wrong person knew though? And they found out retrospectively?'

'What do you mean?' Harmony asks. 'Which wrong person knows about it?'

I look at Jake. He gives me a small nod of encouragement.

'I'm being blackmailed,' I admit.

'By who?' Dalton demands, and there's fury in his tone.

I look at my fingers, entwined with Jake's. It's like I can feel his strength seeping through into my bones, but I still hate that I have to confess.

I lift my head and look Dalton in the eye. 'Brody Conway,' I say.

The room goes silent again. Very slowly, Dalton leans back in his chair. I can see a muscle flexing in his clenched jaw. Hudson looks at his brother, who in turn raises his eyes to his wife. I glance behind me. Ally Briar has locked eyes with her husband.

'I told you, didn't I?' she murmurs softly.

'I don't understand,' Harmony blurts before I can say another word.

Hudson shakes his head. 'That no good motherfucker,' he whispers.

Dalton lowers his head, running his fingers through his closely cropped hair.

'Wait, what are you all talking about?' Jake asks.

'I can't fucking believe it,' Dalton says.

'I can,' his brother responds.

'You mind if I tell them?' Dalton says to his wife.

Ally consents. 'Go ahead.'

'About four years ago,' Dalton says, addressing me in particular, 'Ally starts getting these explicit messages sent to her phone. Sexual stuff, fantasies, that kinda thing. We didn't know who from. She blocked the number, but each time, more would show up. Then one day, at an event at the Danube, she gets talking to Brody Conway. He follows her to the bathroom, grabs her, presses her up against the wall and starts telling her what he wants to do to her.'

I look at Ally in surprise.

'He used the same language as the phone messages. We took it to the police, but nothing was captured on CCTV, there were no witnesses, and they couldn't trace the phone numbers back to him. He denied it; cops said there was nothing more they could do. I almost resigned my position, especially when it seemed like Samantha Conway was working double time to have the whole thing hushed up.'

'I didn't know that,' Harmony says to Ally. 'I mean… there have always been rumours but I'm so sorry.'

'It's okay,' Ally responds. 'Thank you. I didn't sleep for weeks after that.'

'And there's been nothing since?' Harmony asks.

Ally comes further into the room. 'Nothing. Thank god. Everything stopped after he cornered me. But I've avoided him and the next time I saw him was at his wedding.'

'Which we didn't wanna go to,' Dalton adds.

I can feel the tension in Jake's fingers. 'What rumours?' he asks.

'That Brody Conway has always been creepy as fuck,' Hudson growls.

'When I was a rookie,' Harmony interjects. 'We had a cheerleader leave the squad. No notice, no reason, nothing. One day she was there, next she wasn't. We heard rumours later that she left because Brody was obsessed with her. Wouldn't leave her alone.'

Dalton levels his eyes on me. 'I need to know everything.'

All attention returns to me. Heat flushes the base of my neck. 'He came to the club once, about two months back. I had to give him a lap dance. By order of the boss, it had to be… without any clothes at all. We call it *Surly's rules*. I didn't know it was Brody at the time, then when we went to the wedding, I knew.' I look at Dalton and Ally. 'After that, the messages started coming. He had me to go a waterfront apartment at the bay. I had to dance for him then. Then the time after that—' I look at Harmony and I feel the sharp sting of tears. 'He had Persia's CMC uniform waiting for me on the bed, so that I could take it off in his presence.'

Harmony explodes. 'He had what?!'

'He bragged about taking it from her locker.'

She shakes her head. 'That asshole!'

'I'm sorry that I did it,' I tell her.

'Don't be. By the sounds of it, you didn't have a choice.'

I feel a heavy weight on my shoulders as I exhale. 'Now he's threatening to tell everyone that I'm a stripper if I don't spend the night with him.'

'You are kidding me,' Ally blurts in disgust.

'He's expecting me tomorrow night,' I confess. I reach for my phone and bring up tonight's message and hand over the handset to Jake. 'This is the message he sent me twenty minutes ago, on my way over here.'

I watch Jake read the message. A moment later, he's on his feet, his fingers ripped from mine. He paces the room, looking at Dalton, shaking my phone in the direction of his captain. 'I wanna thrash this worthless prick,' he seethes. 'No mercy.'

'That shitbag is a total momma's boy,' Hudson reminds us all with a gruff sigh. 'Got full protection from his mother. He's untouchable.'

'What are you gonna do?' Ally asks me.

'I have an idea. If it doesn't work, then I don't know what I'm gonna do. But I know I'm sure as hell not gonna sleep with him.'

'Does he know you've quit working at Surly's?' Harmony asks.

'No. Not yet.'

She shrugs. 'So, can't you simply tell him you don't work there anymore? That the deal is off?'

'I don't think he cares. He requested that I come to his apartment to get me away from Surly's. He did it on purpose, I see that now. It won't matter to his mother either when it comes out. And if I don't do as he asks, it's only a matter of time before it will come out. She'll fire me from the squad quicker than she did Persia Takeda.'

'I won't let that happen,' Jake interjects.

'Nor I,' Dalton echoes.

'Me either,' Harmony says, getting to her feet. 'And it's another reason why you two… your relationship can't come out. At least not yet. It'll only give them more ammo.'

I'm touched by their coming to my defense, but I hear Hudson Briar snort.

Harmony turns on him. 'And you! You are keeping this a secret too. Keep them talking about us instead.'

His tone is lazy. 'What? How you've resisted me all these years?'

'If that's what it takes, then yes.'

'Your wish is my command, princess,' Hudson fires back with a roll of his eyes, before he gets to his feet. 'You know what? I'm getting out of here. Serenity, it's been a pleasure meeting you.' He holds his hand out to Jake. 'Walsh, whatever happens, I got your back. Should you need any assistance with Brody Conway, I'll gladly punch his lights out.'

I watch his sister-in-law square up to him. 'And just where do you think you're going?'

Hudson crosses his arms over his chest at Ally standing in his way. 'You don't need me here. And I can't sit in a room with *her* any longer.'

Behind him, Harmony is visibly crestfallen.

Hudson looks back at his brother. 'Can you please call off your attack dog?'

Dalton's lips twitch. 'Naw, I'm just gonna let her bite.'

'Quit it!' Ally blurts. 'Hudson, no matter what you might think, tonight is not about you, or your long-running, *will-they-or-won't-they* relationship with Harmony. Tonight is about Jake and Serenity, who, in case you didn't figure it out yet, need our help. So, sit your butt back down in the chair, get on your phone and order us some Doordash, *pronto*.'

'I love my attack dog,' Dalton drawls with a grin, putting both his hands behind his head.

I press my lips together. They're all so nice.

'What am I ordering?' Hudson bites out.

Ally cocks her head to one side and grants him her best smile. 'Why don't you ask Harmony what she'd like to eat?'

I notice Dalton chuckling to himself. Unimpressed, Hudson pushes one hand into his pants pocket.

'I wouldn't say no to some Chinese food,' Harmony says.

Hudson doesn't even look at her, just reaches for his phone and wanders over to the window next to Jake. I watch Harmony closely. I know yearning when I see it. When her eyes flit back to mine, I mouth *I'm sorry* at her.

Don't be, she mouths back with a shake of her head.

'Nobody goes anywhere,' Ally announces, and takes a seat next to her husband. 'Not until we figure out what to do about Brody Conway.'

Chapter Twenty-Eight

Serenity

Friday morning, my car won't start.

'Want me to come pick you up?' Jake asks when I call him.

Last night felt liberating. Confessing all my secrets to people who weren't there to judge me, who all had my back. And telling people that Jake is my boyfriend? Magical.

From Dalton and Ally's house, he walked me back to my car. Knowing now I was barely gonna make it back to Temptation Heights in one piece, I wish I'd taken him up on his offer of sneaking me into his bedroom to spend the night at his place.

'As much as I wanna say *yes*, it would take you forty-five minutes to get over here in morning traffic, plus another half hour to drive me to The Bounty.'

'Yeah, but that'd be a whole half hour I got to spend in your company.'

I find myself grinning in my front yard. 'You'd be late for training.'

'I'd think up some excuse.'

'In case you forgot, we still have to be careful, you know.'

I hear him laugh at the other end of the phone. 'I know, I know. I just... I wish it could all be out in the open. I want everyone to know you're my girl. No more sneaking around.'

'One day,' I sigh, because after last night, it feels like we've had a taste of freedom, and now we both want more.

'So, what about later?' Jake asks. 'How are you gonna do the thing if you don't have wheels? You won't let me drive you to work, at least let me pick you up after your shift.'

I'm nervous about later. The possibility of seeing Brody Conway again.

'Alright, I'll let you do that part. Pick me up at my place. Tonight. Around seven fifteen?'

'Already counting down the hours, baby.'

'See you tonight.'

'I love you,' he says, and I swear I'll never get over it.

'I love you too,' I tell him, and I mean it with my whole heart.

-

I'm finishing giving Dad his dinner when Jake's pickup rolls into the driveway after dark.

'You seem to have a visitor,' Dad mumbles. 'That the same boy as before?'

'Daddy, I'm not seventeen,' I remind him. 'Jake's more of a man than a boy.'

Dad snorts. 'He's a football player is what he is. He your boyfriend now?'

'He is,' I say dreamily. 'But I'm in trouble if anybody finds out about that. So don't go telling the neighbors. He can't stay.'

'Won't say a word, sugar. So long as he treats you right.'

I could tell him a thing or two, about men not treating me right, but instead I stay silent. 'You got everything you need? I won't be late back.'

His eyes are already trained on the baseball game on TV. It's a rerun of last year's World Series.

'Say howdy to Jake.'

'I will. Call Mrs Oakley if you need anything. I'll see you later.'

I kiss him on the cheek, grab my bag and leather jacket and head out the door. When I made it home, I changed into a floral skirt, a lightweight tee and a pair of brown and black cowgirl boots.

Inside the cab, Jake smells freshly showered, his hair still damp after his training session. He leans over and I kiss him enthusiastically on the lips.

'How you feelin'?' he asks, when I pull back, not wishing to get carried away, though it's hard when he smells this good.

I bite my lip. 'Honestly? I'm a little nervous.'

'Dalton will be with you the whole time. And I'll be close by. I won't let anything happen to you, I swear it.'

I smile at him. 'Do you know where we're going?'

He looks at the sat nav screen. 'Already put in the address. Dalton sent me a map pin that's one block away.'

I nod. 'Then let's do this.'

He starts the engine. In the shadows, he smirks at me. 'Hey, guess what? Hudson was an hour late for training today. Coach tore strips off o' him but he still had a huge grin on his face.'

My eyes widen. When Hudson left his brother's house last night, he definitely wasn't smiling.

'You think…? Did you ask?'

Jake pulls away from my house. 'I asked. He definitely wasn't talking. But he looked pretty darned pleased with himself.'

'Oh my god. Do you think they…?'

'He looked pretty pissed at her when we left. I don't know what went down after that but today he looked like he'd literally had no sleep. Like he was drunk on something.'

I sink my teeth into my bottom lip, reach across and take his hand, which is resting on the wheel. 'Maybe if it comes out that we're not the only ones…' I say hopefully, and he squeezes my fingers tight, 'they might drop the clause from our contract?'

He presses his lips to the back of my hand while keeping his eyes on the road. 'We can't hide it forever. Besides, I wanna take you out. Have the whole world see that Lemon Conway and I are most *definitely* not an item. And that I'm in love with the most beautiful girl in the whole of Canyon.'

The curve of my ear touches the headrest. 'Shut up, I am not,' I argue softly.

'That's a matter of opinion, and respectfully, I disagree.'

I watch the road for a second, the familiar streets of Temptation Heights passing us by. I want what he wants. I want to be out in the open, not sneaking around after dark. And I find myself wondering if maybe I'm willing to give up the thing that I thought I wanted most in the world, just to say that I'm his. Because there's an indescribable force that pulls me to him, and there has been for weeks now.

'I need to tell Jewel before anybody else finds out,' I tell him. 'I owe her that.'

He nods. 'I get it. Look, I know I said we can't hide it forever. But it's complicated. So, for now, like I said the other night, we keep it on the DL, until we work all this out.'

I study his face. 'You're gonna hate me for saying this, but you really are the fabled golden boy, you know that? You have the biggest heart of any guy I ever met.'

He looks pleased with himself. 'We're all like this where I come from.'

'Well, even so, your momma raised you right.'

'Speaking of my momma. I'd like to introduce you one day.'

I nod my head. 'I'd like that.'

'I should warn you, she can be a little… like, she has a very specific type of girl in mind for me.'

I raise my brow. 'Lemme guess, if I switched out taking off my clothes for a college education, she might give me the time of day?'

I see him wince. He indicates, turning at the next set of lights. 'She's gonna love you, I promise. Especially when I tell her you're the angel I'm gonna marry someday.'

—

About a half hour later, Jake's pickup pulls up on a side street near the oceanfront behind a white sports SUV. I know it's Dalton and Ally's vehicle because she sent me their license plate.

Jake kills the engine, then in the silence, he exhales. He slides one hand around the rim of the steering wheel. Throughout the journey, he'd grown quieter the closer we got to our destination. 'Are you alright?' he asks.

I nod my head. 'I won't be alone, remember.'

He lets go of the steering wheel and massages the knuckles on his left hand. 'I wish I could go up there with you. Show that clown what I think of him.'

'I know. I know you wanna protect me. But he can't know about us. That would make things even worse. He'd have more hold over me than ever.'

He shifts in his seat. His fingers cup my cheek.

'I know you'd be there in a second if you could,' I add for good measure, because I can tell by the look on his face that he doesn't wanna let me go.

'I'll be there, waiting for you when you get out. I talked to Dalt. He won't let Brody anywhere near you. He's the cap, I trust him.'

The truth is, I can't get enough of Jake Walsh. In his presence, my insides turn to goop. And now we're edging closer, caught up in a moment. The second our lips touch, I almost jump out of my skin when behind me somebody knocks the window of the pickup. My head whips round and I see Ally Briar's face in the darkness, staring at us both, her blonde hair pulled into a high ponytail.

'Hey there, lovebirds,' she hums as I open the door.

'Sorry,' I mumble as I get out. 'Are we walking over?'

'Dalt thinks you should walk,' Ally says. 'Hey, Mr MVP, you know where we're going?'

'Yup. Follow behind me.'

'Are you alright?' Ally asks me.

I give her a nod and she squeezes my hand. Nerves tangle in my stomach.

I give Jake a small wave.

Either tonight is gonna fix things, or my CMC career is well and truly over.

'Are you alright?' Dalton Briar asks as we walk side by side toward the oceanfront condo at the bay where Brody Conway is expecting me.

My forced smile belies my true feelings. 'Everybody keeps asking me that.'

'I get it,' Dalton says, pushing his hands down further into his pants pockets. 'You shouldn't even be having to do this in the first place. I feel like a part of this is my fault.'

For a brief second, I stop in my tracks. 'How is any of this your fault?'

'When Ally told me what Brody had done, I was advised by those around me not to approach him and to avoid confrontation. I still had significant time left on my pro contract. I knew at the time that if I did what I wanted to do, I would have landed myself with an assault charge. But if I'd known then what I do now… that he was gonna go after other women? Let's just say I regret my actions from four years ago. That asshole needed to be taught a lesson. But I'm not an idiot. Jake's in the same situation I was. He just got drafted. He's at the beginning of his career. Brody's not worth throwing away that level of talent on.'

'Brody Conway is your typical trust-fund kid,' he continues as we cross a road, 'who was never told, *no you cannot do that*, or, *that's not how you behave*. He's always gotten away with doing whatever he wants with impunity. He stands to inherit his grandfather's fortune, and he's never done a proper day's work his entire life.'

When we reach the condo, we walk through double glass doors into a lobby. We cross direct to the elevators.

'Can I be honest with you?' Dalton asks me as we wait for an elevator to arrive.

'Of course,' I say, looking up at him.

He swallows. 'I spoke to Jake last night. Before you left. He reminds me a little of me at that age. The day I met Ally at college, I knew I was never gonna want anyone else. But I'm not lying when I say you are holding that guy's heart in your hands. He's willing to throw it all away for you. That's how much power you have over him right now. He's so in love with you, he's quit caring about his career, or how much talent he has on the field.'

I hear a *ding* sound, signalling that the elevator has arrived. Except I can't move. I stare at Dalton Briar in the lobby of the condo, unable to respond to what he's just told me.

He cocks his head toward the open elevator, indicating that I should go in first. When I walk inside, my legs feel like lead. This whole time, I'd been so scared of falling for Jake. Of giving my heart to him and risking everything. I was so worried, I hadn't even noticed he'd given his heart to me about three times over. It might not say so in his contract, but he's also taken a risk by falling for me.

'This probably comes from a place of selfishness,' Dalton continues as I hit the correct floor button and the doors close in front of us, 'but Jake's the Mutineers' MVP right now. Without him, we'd have lost every single one of our opening games. He's the reason we're on top, and we can't lose him.'

'Are you asking me if I'm in love with Jake?'

Dalton shrugs. 'I guess that's what I'm asking. And if you're not... just to let him down easy.'

I break out into a smile. I can't help it, even though we're climbing closer toward the wolf's lair. 'If I'm holding Jake's heart in my hands, then I promise not to drop it. I promise to take very good care of it, for a very long time.'

Dalton smiles at me. 'Okay, that's a relief.'

'And for the record? After tonight, if I'm fired from the CMC, then so be it.'

Dalton sobers, like he's just remembered why we're really here. 'Let's hope that's not gonna happen.'

We grind to a halt. The elevator doors open and Dalton follows me out. Wordlessly, I point to the door and I know we need to move fast.

'Just liked we talked about, remember?' Dalton whispers and moves ahead of me.

I note that he's light on his feet. He takes up position, flattening himself against the wall to the left side of the door, arms by his sides, head turned toward the door. I take a gulp of breath and gather my strength. I have no idea how this is gonna go. I don't want to be the person responsible for the legendary Dalton Briar having his contract cancelled.

Reaching up, I press one finger on the doorbell.

I can hear music playing inside. I know he'll check the spy hole. There's movement at floor level before the door opens.

Brody Conway stands there in grey suit pants and a white shirt with the collar open, dark hair falling into his eyes. He's holding a drink and it's clear that he's pleased to see me.

'Hello, Serenity,' he says in a husky tone.

One second later, I take a small step back.

Everything happens quickly. I see Dalton move right on cue, lightning fast over the threshold. I can only see his broad back, but I see the glass drop from Brody's hands and hit the marble floor, shattering on impact.

I follow inside and close the door behind us, stepping over the pieces of glass.

Dalton hasn't touched Brody, who's backed away fast, hands in the air like this is a stick up. But he's backed himself all the way into a wall, Dalton bearing down on him.

'Not quite who you were expecting, huh, Brody?' Dalton grinds out, their faces close.

I didn't know if Brody would be frightened of the Mutineers' captain, but the color has drained from his face, and his suave demeanor has evaporated.

'Did you think we wouldn't find out about you?' Dalton continues, and even in the low light, I can see the fury in his eyes. 'That you thought you could get away with it this time? I got news for you. You fucked with the wrong people.'

My heart beats faster at Brody's level of fear. 'Please... I meant nothing by it. Please don't tell my mom about this.'

Dalton takes a step closer. Brody lets out a terrified whine. 'Worried about your inheritance, you low-life piece of shit? Mommy won't be impressed, huh? Seems you care more about that than your brand-new wife finding out what kind of excuse for a man you are.'

Brody's broken out in a sweat and Dalton hasn't even laid a hand on him. His eyes flit to me. 'I'll not say another word to Serenity, I swear it. I'll never contact you again.'

'Where's Persia's uniform?' I demand.

He swallows. 'In the bedroom. Can you both just please leave?'

'Do you need it?' Dalton questions me.

'I'd like to get it back.'

'Go, quickly,' Dalton orders. 'Gives me a chance to talk to Brody about what he did to my wife.'

'Oh god,' Brody snivels. 'I'm sorry. I'm sorry. I'm so sorry.'

I race to the bedroom. Brody's lit candles around the bed. There's a pack of condoms lying atop the sheets. Next to it is Persia's CMC uniform and a set of red lingerie, all laid out for me. He was going to have me wear all of it. Without contemplating what might have happened, I scoop up Persia's uniform and go to leave the room. After a moment of consideration, I turn back and grab the box of condoms too and push everything into my bag.

When I go back out into the main living area, Dalton hovers over Brody. Neither man says a word.

'You done?' Dalton asks me.

'I'm done.'

Dalton backs away from Brody. 'Just like I said,' he says to him, before he takes me by the elbow and ushers me out the door. I don't look back.

The same elevator is ready and waiting to take us back down.

Dalton checks his phone. 'They're downstairs in the lot,' he says, punching the button for the basement.

'You didn't lay a finger on him,' I say once the doors have closed.

Dalton takes a moment to respond. 'Didn't need to,' he sniffs. 'I break a finger... that's my season over. Plus, he ain't worth the punch.'

I press my lips together. 'What did you say to him? When I went to the bedroom?'

'I told him to watch his back. Because the moment my NFL career is over, his ass is grass.'

'I'm sure he'll sleep well tonight.'

'You get any more messages from him...'

'You and Jake will be the first to know. I promise.'

Dalton shifts his stance. 'Okay, maybe don't tell Jake. I'm not sure I'll be able to hold him back for a second time.'

When the doors to the elevator open, we're in the basement parking lot. I recognize it from before. When we emerge, I see Jake in the distance, waiting for me by the pickup, a hopeful smile appearing on his face when he sees me.

I walk quickly toward him and before I know it, he's swept me into his arms. The relief is almost overwhelming. His lips are soft and warm and welcoming – everything I want and need – and I cling to him.

He pulls back and searches my face. 'Everything alright?' he asks. 'How did it go? You were quicker than I expected.'

While he's still talking, I nod my head furiously. 'Dalton didn't even need to touch him. He was terrified.'

Jake's attention flits to Dalton, who has moved up behind me. 'Good. Can't thank you enough, Cap.'

Ally has come over too and tucked herself into Dalton's side. He gives a shrug. 'Yeah, well, didn't wanna break a nail,' he says. 'Now get outta here, both of yous.'

We say our goodbyes and head for the pickup.

On the route home, I tell Jake everything that took place, except for the part about Dalton telling me I had his running back's heart in my hands.

Nearing Temptation Heights, he goes quiet.

'Maybe drop me a couple of blocks from my place?' I suggest quietly.

He blows out his cheeks, and I know he doesn't like it.

'Guess we can't have people keep seeing this truck in my driveway,' I add solemnly.

'I know,' he responds.

I know Temptation like the back of my hand. I grew up in this dog-eared neighborhood. Rode my bike around these tired roads.

'Take the next left,' I say to Jake.

He frowns.

'I'm taking us a different route.'

He does as he's told. Soon, the place I'm looking for comes into view. Not that it's really visible from the road.

'There's another left coming up.'

'I can't see a damn thing,' he says.

I point. 'There. See it? Turn in here.'

We're in a disused lot where weeds grow out between the paving slabs, lined by some tall trees. There's only one streetlamp, and most of the time it flickers, a little broken, like everything else in Temptation Heights.

Jake kills the engine. He peers out the windshield. 'What is this place?'

I unbuckle myself and lift my hips, wriggling out my panties and sliding them over the rim of my boots. In the dim light, I hold him up my lacy underwear.

'I think we need a celebration,' I say with a smile. 'You ever had sex in a truck, Jake Walsh?'

Chapter Twenty-Nine

Jake

The moment Serenity slides into my lap and straddles me without any panties on, my dick roars to life. Every sensible thought leaves my mind, leaving me with a feral need to fuck her, right here, just like this, her back pressed up against my steering wheel. And not exactly being Mr Experience, I've never had a girl ride me before.

'Holy shit,' I breathe. 'No, I've not. Have you?'

'It'll be a first for me,' she says, still smiling down at me, and my chest expands with the thrill of it. Finally, I can be her first at something.

'Hold up, I don't have any protection,' I say.

Serenity leans back over to the footwell on the passenger side of the cab. For a second, she rummages around, then she's squarely in my lap again, dangling a box of condoms in front of my face.

'Courtesy of Brody Conway,' she says.

His name on her lips does something to me. Rage rises in my throat at the thought of her having to be with him tonight, but instantly, she sees my reaction and quells it, kissing my lips, cradling my cheeks.

'No, no, baby, don't think about him,' she says between gentle kisses, shushing me. 'It didn't happen. It's you I want. You're the one I want inside me. It's all over now.'

I pull her down to me and capture her lips. My hands slide underneath the floaty material of her skirt as I cup the globes of her naked ass, pushing her down harder onto my swollen dick. She whimpers, and when our tongues tangle, my balls tighten, and my need for her skyrockets.

'Brody Conway can go fuck himself,' I growl against her mouth.

She hums a little laugh. 'Meanwhile, we'll take his condoms, so you can fuck me.'

'Damn right.'

I reach down and pull the lever under the seat. The base springs backward, giving us more room. My hand slides around to the side and pulls a second lever, and the seat back reclines to an angle.

'Better,' Serenity says, and, tossing the box of condoms behind her on the dash, reaches for my belt buckle. 'Let's get this off, shall we?'

Moments later, I lift my hips a fraction so she can pull the strip of leather through the loops in my jeans. She tosses that too, then goes to work on my button fly. I love watching her.

'Lift your hips again,' she orders me and lays one hand flat against the window to raise herself up a fraction, giving me room to shove my jeans and my underwear down to my knees. My dick springs free, engorged and thick, my balls aching with a need to fill her up. Lowering herself back down, her right-hand wraps around my length and gives me a firm tug. It almost sends me over the edge.

She reaches round behind her, back to the dash, and brings back the box.

'Let's get one of these babies on,' she says.

While she's tearing at the cellophane covering, I reach down and slide my fingers up her inner thigh, then to her pussy. She has to quit what she's doing when my fingers find her center, and I rub circles on her clit.

'Jake,' she whimpers. 'Oh, god.'

'You're so wet.'

'That feels so, so good.'

I slide two fingers inside her. She's completely drenched for me. 'Fuck, Serenity,' I breathe and inside the cab, where the tiniest sound is magnified, I can hear my fingers making wet sounds as I pump in and out.

Mewling with pleasure, she tosses the cellophane. Within a second the box is open and she's pulled out a single foil pouch. Everything else gets tossed too and she tears at the packet with her teeth, throwing the foil pouch over her shoulder.

I let her take control. Watching like this, sexy and panting and needy, I know I'll never love anyone else. She's ruined all other women for me.

She grips my base and slides the condom down my full length. I remove my fingers and slide her arousal over her skin before adjusting the fit a little, fisting my dick just once, anticipation hanging in the air.

Serenity removes her jacket. It too gets discarded. I do the same. In the cramped space, all I can hear is our heavy breaths, desire making the air inside the cab turn thick.

She raises herself up again, getting into position and my hands hold her waist. She moves closer. She reaches down, gripping me, shoving the hem of her skirt out the way and nudging me closer to her entrance, sliding my tip against her clit, her eyes partially closed.

And then I'm there, nudging into her, sinking slowly, steadily, mindlessly into her warmth.

I reach up and tilt her head toward me. 'I love you, Serenity,' I whisper, as our mouths meet in a searing kiss, at the same moment she sinks fully down onto me, and I'm buried all the way to the hilt.

I moan deep and low into her mouth. She feels incredible. Better than incredible. Like I'm making love to an angel.

I break the kiss and for a moment, we're lost in one another. Serenity rests her forehead on mine. Our hot breaths mingle. When her eyes flutter back open, she's staring down at me in the shadows. There's lust there, for sure, but something else too. I recognize it, because I feel the same.

'I love you, Jake Walsh,' she says. 'So much.'

I kiss her again, stroking my tongue into her. I'm yet to use my mouth on her gorgeous pussy, but I'm patient, because I'm not going anywhere and I'm not gonna try it in my truck. A second surge of desire hits my balls.

'You're gonna make me come too soon,' I say.

The little laugh that escapes her mouth is infectious. 'I haven't even moved yet.'

'Take it slow, okay? It's so deep this way and you're so fucking tight.'

'You're so deep inside me.'

'Does it feel good?'

She starts rolling her hips then. I see her body physically tremble as she whimpers. Her movements are slow and gentle, and they send lightning bolts up my spine. 'So good. So goddamn nice.'

In the darkness, I gather up the material of her skirt. I wanna see the point where we're joined, and I want to play with her clit some more.

'Baby, I know we're in my truck, but…'

She stops moving. 'What is it?'

I glance out the driver's side window, already steaming up. I swallow.

'Don't be shy,' she smiles.

'I think I want you naked.'

And just like that, she's grinning down at me, biting her lip. 'I want that too.'

With a few seconds she's removed her tee and unclipped her bra. There's no grace to it. She's not trying to tease. Her skirt has an elasticated waist, and she lifts it all the way over her head. When her clothes are gone, I marvel at her perfect tits.

'Better?' she asks.

'Fuck, yes,' I say, but I shudder, because I'm too close. I caress her breasts and circle her nipples with my thumbs. 'This is exactly what I wanted. You in just your boots.'

I see her smirk, and she starts rolling her hips again. We both groan.

Serenity arches her back against the steering wheel. It drives me even deeper inside her, which I didn't think was possible. But it grants me access to her clit and reaching down, I press my thumb against it, rubbing her again in soft, slick circles.

'Mmm, oh yeah,' Serenity says, her head going back.

Slowly, she builds her speed. I watch her tits bounce up and down as she rides me with abandon. My hips push upwards with an uncontrollable need to thrust into her. My balls are ready to explode and I can feel my finish bearing down on me, tingling at the base of my spine.

I increase my speed against her clit in a rhythm that is gentle yet punishing, telling myself that I can't come first, yet the way she's riding me, I almost can't take it.

'Jake, it's there, right there,' she whimpers, 'don't stop, don't stop.'

I keep rubbing her, keep to the rhythm. When I look up at her, her eyes are closed, and she's basking in the sensations my dick and fingers are giving her.

'Reach for it, baby,' I growl, my chest swelling with pride. 'Take it.'

Her hips are moving erratically now as she chases after her release. I'm thrusting upwards into her, rubbing her clit and the entire cab is shaking under our movements.

'I love you,' Serenity moans again. 'I love you, I... it's building, I lo... Oh god, I'm gonna c—'

She comes with a cry on her lips, her entire body writhing and pulsing as she rides out her orgasm, her hands pressed up against the roof of the cab. Moments later, while she's still climaxing, the sensations of her pussy clamping around my dick push me too far over the edge. There's an explosion of pleasure in my balls as I peak, spilling every drop of my release into the condom. For what seems like an eternity, both our moans fill the cab.

I remove my fingers and Serenity collapses against my chest. I wrap my arms around her, and for a moment, we lie against the seat together, catching our breath. I lean over and grab my jacket, covering her.

She nuzzles my neck. 'Thank you,' she whispers. 'But my knees hurt, I gotta move.'

Our kiss is lingering. I stroke her thighs still straddling me. After a moment, Serenity lifts herself up and I slide out of her. Carefully removing the condom, I tie it off, while in the passenger seat, Serenity pulls on her tee and skirt, rooting around in the footwell for the panties she tossed away.

I lift my hips and pull my underwear and jeans back up. The windows are fully steamed, and inside the cab smells of sex. In my head, I vow that this isn't the only time we're gonna do this.

'In case you were wondering,' she drawls, but then a giggle escapes her lips as she retrieves her panties from the footwell then wriggles back into them, 'that's my favorite position.'

'Mine too,' I laugh. 'At least it is now.'

I'm glad it's dark in here because heat rushes to my cheeks.

'Wait—' she says after a silence.

Now I just want the ground to swallow me up. I wipe my hand through my hair. 'You remember I told you about Gracie Olavsen? The science major?'

'The brainiac?'

'You remember I told you we only had full sex once?'

'I remember.'

'So that was…' I clear my throat. *Jesus, Walsh.* 'Well, I never had a girl go on top before.'

She cocks her head to one side, a sweet smile on her face. 'So… two firsts for you tonight.'

'Yeah, I guess.'

She holds my gaze for a moment. So fucking sexy. I can't get enough of her. Then she reaches across and her right-hand dips into the open fly of my jeans. She strokes her palm down the column of my shaft over my underwear. In a second, I'm half-mast.

'What time's your flight tomorrow?' she asks.

When she moves her hand up and down, I can barely think straight. 'I gotta car coming to my house, eight a.m.'

'Then we've got time,' she says as she increases the pressure of her movements. When her hand sinks further down into my fly and she cups my balls, I'm fully charged and ready to go again.

Her tone is playful. 'How about two for two?'

-

By the time I walk through the door to my house, I'm missing her already. There's an ache in my chest that exists only for her. I don't even wanna get on that plane tomorrow for our next away game.

Dad, Gramps and River are watching TV. Mom's in the kitchen, cleaning up after family dinner, another dinner I missed.

'Hey, sweetie!' she hollers. 'How was training?'

'Good,' I mutter. She doesn't mention that fact that training finished hours ago.

'You eat, already?'

My stomach rumbles. I'd just been ignoring it up to now, but now I think about it, I'm famished. 'Got any leftovers?'

She goes to the oven and grabs a mitt, pulls out a steaming hot plate of food. 'Way ahead of you there.'

I toss my sports bag and go to the table, taking a seat.

'I was at the tennis club again today,' Mom says, still moving around. I pick up my fork. 'Saw Olivia Francis again. You remember? The weather girl on WKRZ. Still single, honey. Still pretty.'

I drop my fork and it clatters. Mom's head whips around.

'Eat your food, honey, before it gets cold,' she says.

I grit my teeth. I'm done pretending. I just drove halfway across Canyon, back from making love to my girl twice in the cab of my pickup, once again, sneaking around. Not that it wasn't hot as hell, but not being able to tell people that Serenity is my girlfriend is making me hell to live with.

'Ma,' I say, then swallow the lump in my throat. 'I have a girlfriend.'

She blinks at me. 'I'm sorry, what?'

Before I know it, River's stuck her head around the door. I hadn't noticed, but the TV is no longer audible.

'I'm sorry I didn't tell you. Her name is Serenity. She's a CMC squad member.'

Mom straightens. 'She's a cheerleader?'

'Which is why I'm not allowed to date her. So, we've not been able to tell many people.'

River has a wide smile on her face. 'I don't understand,' Mom says cautiously.

'It's part of her contract. She's not allowed to talk to anyone on the pro team. But we didn't know… at least not initially. But I'm crazy in love with her. And I'm not just saying that because of some dumb crush. She's it. She's the one for me. For life. And, look… just so you know, she's a waitress. A local Canyon girl. She didn't go to college. She's not majored in meteorology or anything like that…'

Her lips are pinched together. She looks over to the window. 'How long have you been… dating?'

I note that River's smile has wavered. I swallow. 'I first met her back in August.'

Mom's brows crawl up her forehead. 'And you're only just telling me this now?'

'I'm sorry, Mom. Like I said, we couldn't tell anyone.'

'You couldn't even trust your own mother? When we moved out here… for you?'

'Mom, if you think she's not good enough—'

'Don't be ridiculous, honey.'

I get to my feet. 'You're always tryna sell these college girls to me!'

'I'm not trying to *sell* anybody to you. All I meant was that a man in your position, you need to be careful of other people's ulterior motives.'

'Serenity doesn't have any motive! She just wants to be with me! I told you, I'd find my own girlfriend.'

We stare at one another for a moment in the kitchen, as though this is a face off.

'It's true, Ma,' River pipes up. 'He's really happy. And I, for one, cannot wait to meet her.'

Mom hasn't moved. She looks down at her fingers. 'And what about me... and your father. Are we worthy enough for an introduction?'

She emphasizes that last sentence, not meeting my eyes, as though questioning whether they would be.

I grin at her. 'Of course you are, Mom. I can't wait for you to meet her.'

I abandon my untouched food and wrap my arms around my mother, the woman who raised me. The woman who got me where I am today.

'I got a lotta stuff I need to tell you, Ma,' I say as she holds me tight.

That's the moment I know that I need to take this to the higher ups. On Monday, when I get back from the game, I'm going straight to Hank Conway. Make things official with Serenity, whether the owner of the Mutineers likes it or not.

I refuse to keep our relationship a secret anymore.

Chapter Thirty

Serenity

Saturday morning, walking through the Danube Stadium parking lot in advance of practice, I see Jewel up ahead. 'Jewel!' I call out. 'Wait up!'

'Hey, Ren,' she says when I reach her, though her tone is subdued, and she doesn't quite seem herself. 'Did you walk here?'

'I took the bus,' I say, out of breath. 'Car engine is busted. Can I talk to you for a minute? In private?'

Jewel frowns. 'I mean, I guess? I've barely seen you lately.'

'That's kinda what I wanted to talk to you abou—'

I squeal when one arm goes around my middle and Harmony's chin comes to rest on my shoulder. 'Hey, girls. Jewel, can I borrow Serenity for a sec?'

Harmony doesn't wait for an answer, just twirls me around and links her arm in mine. I glance back and Jewel's got irritation written all over her face. I give her an apologetic look, yet I don't want to wait too much longer before telling her about Jake.

'You and I need to have a talk,' Harmony says, as we head for the staff entrance, keeping her voice low but tense with excitement. 'Ally said it went well last night.'

'I mean... he got the message. Plus, I got Persia's uniform back. It's in my bag. Just need to figure out how to return it so nothing looks amiss.'

'Don't worry, we'll figure it out.'

It's only then that I notice something different about her. She doesn't look as turned out as she normally does. Her hair is tousled, and there's a mischievous glint in her eye and it makes me smile.

'So, you and I might be in the same boat,' she says, leaning over and whispering in my ear.

We both giggle. 'I figured you might be. What happened?'

Before we enter the CMC locker room, Harmony checks who is following, then pulls me to one side.

'Thursday night, Hudson was so mad.'

'I remember.'

'And driving home, I couldn't stop thinking about you and Jake. How you'd put each other before any stupid rules or contract. So, I turned my car around and drove right on over there to his place.'

I grin. '*And?*'

'Hammered on his door until he answered. Asked him straight up if he was in love with me and when he said 'yes', practically threw myself into his arms. Not that he complained after that moment.'

'Jake said he looked pretty happy at yesterday's training session.'

'I had to go to work! Don't think I've ever been that sore.'

I lower my voice again. I can see Jewel approaching. 'Was it worth it?'

Harmony bites her lip. 'Every. Orgasmic. Second.'

We collapse into more giggles. It feels good to be able to share this with her. Except the look that Jewel throws me the minute she enters the CMC locker room tells me that my fellow rookie doesn't like being left out of the conversation.

'Can we talk more about it later?' Harmony says with a grin. 'I can't wait 'til they're back Monday.'

I think about how good sex with Jake was in his pickup. Twice. 'Me either.'

I follow her inside. Some of the girls are already dressed. I'm careful not to show anyone the contents of my bag when I put it inside my locker.

—

Practice over, we're back in the locker room.

'What was it you wanted to tell me?' Jewel asks when I'm still dressed in my CMC uniform and we're sharing a mirror, removing our makeup and eyelashes before a shower.

'Maybe we could go somewhere? Grab a coffee?' I suggest. 'I can't really say it in here.'

She looks at me, perhaps for longer than is necessary.

'What is it?' I ask.

'Nothing,' she says with a heavy sigh. 'Didn't have you down as the secretive type, is all, Ren.'

'I'm not being secretive, I promise,' I say.

She grants me another withering look in the reflection. 'I've come to realize there's a lot I don't know about you, Serenity,' she says.

I don't have time to respond, because the door to the locker room is thrust open and Kathleen Lafferty walks through it.

Every cheerleader looks her way.

Her gaze falls on me. She seems pale.

I've seen that look upon her face before. Because it's disappointment.

'Serenity,' she says. 'Ms Conway's office. Now.'

—

I follow Kathleen in silence. We ride the elevator up to the fourth floor where the offices are situated. Kathleen turns to me. She's about to speak when the elevator comes to a halt and another Mutineers' employee steps inside.

I look to the floor, keeping my gaze fixed on Kathleen's shoes. When we reach the fourth floor, my heart begins to thud hard in my chest.

I feel everyone's eyes on me. I'm in full uniform, almost full makeup. I'm not supposed to be here.

Nobody says a word to me, or Kathleen. We reach a door and Kathleen's hand goes to the handle. She turns my way, but she doesn't look me in the eye.

I see her swallow. 'I wish you'd come to me,' she whispers, then opens the door.

Light floods my face. Kathleen leads me inside an office with full windows overlooking Canyon's business district on the far side of the parking lot. There's a substantial conference table. Samantha Conway is waiting for me in a navy pant suit, killer heels and deep red lipstick.

'Close the door, Kathleen,' Ms Conway says. My bottom lip begins to tremble as Kathleen shuts the door.

In the silence that follows, I glance down and my body goes rigid. On the glass surface of the table, there's a printout of a photograph. It's a picture of Jake and I, arms around one another, kissing.

Tears sting the corners of my eyes.

I recognize the moment it was taken: in the basement parking lot of Brody Conway's apartment building, last night. The image is grainy, like it was pulled from CCTV, but there's no denying it's our faces that are locked together.

I forget how to breathe. The thing I've tried to cling onto, the one thing I'm not supposed to have... it's gone. Because it's out in the open.

I look at Ms Conway, to Kathleen and back again, then grasp my fingers together. I know that the expression on my face gives everything away.

'In the early hours of this morning, I received two anonymous emails,' Ms Conway begins in an icy tone. 'The first contained this image. The second contained an accusation so heinous, I can scarce believe it to be true. It stated that *you*, Miss Serenity Harper, an upstanding, valued, respected member of our CMC community, a *rookie*, have been moonlighting...'

She stops, as though in disbelief, and pinches the bridge of her nose, as though she's trying to compose herself. My stomach does a flip. 'Have been moonlighting as a *stripper* on the west side of Canyon. And not only that, but that you were employed at the establishment in question even before you were welcomed into our squad.'

She raises her chin. Looks down her nose at me with such disdain that I can't hold back the tears anymore. 'So, I sent somebody to look into it. And—'

'I can explain,' I whisper, looking to Kathleen, whose shoulders sag when she realizes the accusation is true. 'Please. I can explain everything.'

'I don't need to hear your explanations,' Ms Conway hisses, her tone now jagged. 'It's bad enough that you already broke the terms of your contract.' She swipes up the photograph and thrusts it in my direction. 'Do you deny it?'

'We didn't mean for it to happen,' I say, but I already know it's useless. I am done for.

'And yet you seemingly thought it prudent to continue – no, had the *audacity* to continue – despite knowing the rules, despite knowing how *I* feel about this sort of... frivolity. The CMC stands for everything that is good and pure. There is a reason fraternization is prohibited. It's not good for the players, it's not good for the brand. You *represent* the brand, Miss Harper, you do not sully it! The brand is bigger than you will ever be. The brand matters more than your very existence ever will. How dare you think you can come here and break the rules that *I* give you. You've disgraced yourself. You've let down your squad.'

'I'm so sorry,' I say weakly.

'You'll be more than sorry.'

'I didn't have a choice about working at Surly's. My father, he—'

'You had no business bringing your kind near this stadium. This is sacred ground. You weren't even worthy of an audition! You are not worthy of that uniform. Take it off.'

My mouth falls open. 'I'm sorry, wha—'

'You heard me, take it off. It would seem you would know what you're doing when it comes to taking off your clothes. Kathleen, get me her things from her locker. I'll have her escorted out. Call security on your way back up.'

Even Kathleen looks surprised. I offer her a pleading look as I watch her leave, because I don't want to be left alone in a room with only Samantha Conway for company.

'Take. It. Off. Now.'

I snap back to reality. I can barely swallow the lump in my throat. Hot tears run down my cheeks, my heart thumping so fast in my chest that I can't think straight. Fingers trembling, I unzip my boots and kick them off. I wipe more tears before shimmying out my shorts, then lift my CMC 'M' branded top over my head until I'm standing there in just my underwear. I pick up my uniform and fold it on the table.

I know I should fight back. Yet, equally, I know the power she has. Looking at her, I know I'll never dance with the CMC again.

We wait, for a long while, in awful silence. I hug my waist, feeling exposed and cold too, under the air con vent.

'I accept that I should never have gotten into a relationship with Jake Walsh,' I say in a small voice, in my own defense. 'I know I've broken the rules. I know I don't deserve to stay. But I want you to know... I danced at Surly's because I had to. I had to pay my father's debt. I did what I had to do. And maybe I should have spoken to you and Kathleen before I auditioned. I was scared. I never thought I'd make it as far as I did.'

'Stop talking,' she fires back at me while we wait for Kathleen's return. 'You will leave here today; you are not permitted to return. You are no longer a member of the CMC. You are fired, Serenity. Plain and simple.'

More tears follow. I can't stop them now.

'And don't even think about contacting Jake Walsh. The plane is on the way to Tennessee. I've instructed Coach Holland to remove all phones from the players as we speak. Nothing can distract from tomorrow night's game.'

'They're not children,' I manage.

Ms Conway opens her mouth to speak but she is interrupted by Kathleen re-entering the room, holding my bag and my clothes, her face like thunder.

She looks to me, in my underwear. She puts my bag on the table and slides the zipper open. Silently, she looks to Ms Conway. Then she lifts out Persia's uniform.

Fresh tears fall.

'Can you explain this too?' Kathleen asks me.

'What is that?' Ms Conway questions.

Kathleen pulls out the crumpled uniform in full and lays it out on the table. 'Why do you have this, Serenity?' she asks. 'Why do you have Persia Takeda's missing uniform in your bag?'

Ms Conway physically gasps.

'I—' I begin, but I don't know how to continue.

I straighten. Wipe my tears. Acceptance creeps in. Yes, it looks bad, but I remind myself that this isn't my fault. I only tried to get it back.

I raise my chin. I don't have anything left to lose.

'You might want to ask your son that question,' I say in Samantha Conway's direction.

Something flashes across her features. 'Kathleen, did you call security?'

'I did,' my squad leader says grimly.

Ms Conway's eyes come back to mine. 'Get dressed. Take your things and go. I don't ever want to see you near this stadium again.'

Samantha Conway stalks out. The door slams behind her. I step forward and grab my clothes. I dress quickly – aware that Kathleen is waiting on me – and when I'm done, I wipe tears from my face and collect my bag from the table. Kathleen opens the door and two burly men enter the room, dressed all in black.

'We'll need your door pass, ma'am,' the bigger of the two men says to me.

I root around in my bag and pass it to him.

Kathleen orders them, 'Escort her to her car.'

'I don't have a car,' I mumble, in what seems like a final humiliation. 'I came here on the bus.'

'Then escort her from the premises,' Kathleen corrects herself. She gathers up both sets of uniform. She doesn't even look me in the eye when she departs.

Moments after she's gone, I follow the two men out.

Chapter Thirty-One

Serenity

At the stadium perimeter, I exit onto the sidewalk, the two Danube security guards eyeballing me as I walk away. I hug my bag close to my chest. Within seconds, I reach for my phone and try Jake's number. There's no answer. He's in the air and if Samantha Conway is correct, his phones have been impounded. He's unreachable.

I tuck my hair behind my ears. My eyes are red and swollen; I can feel it. My entire face is puffy. On the inside, I feel numb.

I walk to the nearest bus stop. I try to hold everything in. Keep putting one foot in front of the other. Within moments of arrival, I hear a car approaching, its horn blaring out.

A large, white SUV shrieks to a halt. Harmony hollers at me from an open window, 'Get in!', and I look up in surprise. I spy Ashlyn in the back seat, her expression etched with both confusion and concern.

I do as I'm told and get in the car. Once the door is closed, Harmony swerves back into moving traffic, causing several cars behind to blast their horns at her.

'What the hell happened?' she demands as I buckle up.

My bottom lip quakes. 'They fired me.'

Harmony punches the wheel. 'Goddammit!'

I glance back at Ashlyn. 'Will somebody please tell me what the fuck is going on?' she says.

'What did Kathleen say?' I ask.

'She walked into the locker room and announced that you would be taking some time out.'

'Time out?' I question. 'Samatha Conway fired me. She said the words. I was escorted from the premises.'

'I've called an emergency meeting,' Harmony blurts from the driver's seat, as we lurch into another lane. 'We're assembling at my place. What did she have on you?'

'Everything. Said she'd received two anonymous emails, first thing this morning.'

'You mean *with best regards from your own son.*'

'They found Persia's uniform. In my bag.'

'Shit,' Harmony says. 'That asshole!'

'Can you slow down a little?!' Ashlyn squeals from the back seat when Harmony almost takes out a convertible. 'I'd like to make it to your apartment alive so I can make sense of what just went down back there.'

—

'Everybody, find a seat. Grab a space where you can. Get in here.'

The entire squad has gathered at Harmony's apartment. It's a crush. The girls squeeze in, perching on the arms of the couch and huddling on the floor. I look around at expectant faces. I can't believe they're all here. For me. I know some of them have jobs to go to. It seems Kathleen didn't provide an explanation for my being escorted from the stadium, and nobody wants to ask, but all eyes are on me all the same.

Shame still washes over me in waves when I think about my meeting with Samantha Conway. It doesn't matter to me that she knows. It was only a matter of time. But it matters to me that I've let all the girls in this room down. I draw my knees up to my chest and hug them.

Once everybody is settled, Harmony stands before us.

'I'm not gonna sugarcoat this, alright? Serenity's been fired. By Samantha Conway.'

There are gasps from every corner of the room. Whispers. Hands fly to mouths. I look at Jewel. She's the only one who doesn't look outraged. She just stares at me.

Slowly, I get to my feet.

'You're sure?' Harmony asks me.

I nod my head. My eyes are still swollen. I knot my fingers and take a breath.

And so, like two nights ago in front of the Briars and Harmony, I begin my tale again, about the double life I've been leading.

When I'm almost done, I look around the room. A silence has descended. A few mouths have fallen open. Jewel has crossed her arms over her chest and is looking at the floor. The sight makes my heart ache.

'Before anyone says anything...' I continue, and the feeling is akin to something heavy pressing hard against my chest, 'that's not all. I need to tell you that—' Tears well over. I swallow them down. 'I broke the terms of our contract. I know I did. And I didn't just do it once.'

I look at Harmony, perhaps because I need encouragement to say the words out loud. She looks sad, but she gives me a nod. I take another shaky breath and exhale.

'Samantha Conway also fired me because she found out about the relationship I was having. With Jake Walsh.'

I look at Jewel when I say the words, because I want her to know that I wish I'd taken the opportunity to tell her first. I'm expecting hostility. Instead, I get a hint of excitement.

'Hold up a sec,' Angel blurts, raising her hand. 'You were in a relationship with Jake Walsh?'

'Am,' I whisper. 'I am in a relationship with Jake Walsh.'

This time, there is a collective sucking in of breath. I look at Jewel, my face the picture of a thousand apologies. Her eyes widen to saucers, and she jumps out of her seat.

'Are you SERIOUS?' she shrieks. '*That's* what you've been hiding this whole time?'

'Uh-huh,' I nod. 'I'm so sorry.'

For a moment, she's speechless. '*Sorry?*' she repeats. 'What are you sorry for?'

'I know how much you like him.'

Jewel screws up her face. 'In a like… he's a stud, from far away, you know? I've barely said two words to him. I mean, he's cute, I'm jealous as hell, but… why didn't you tell me?'

'I didn't tell anyone 'til Thursday night.'

Jewel launches herself at me and gives me the biggest bear hug, practically lifting me off the ground. 'I'm so happy for you,' she whispers, and relief floods my veins.

'I was so scared to tell you. And, anyway, it's lost me my job.'

'Is that why Samantha Conway fired you?' Ashlyn asks.

I pull back from Jewel and nod again. 'For both those reasons.'

'Hold up,' Harmony says, getting to her feet. 'Serenity's not finished. Y'all need to hear everything.'

I offer her a pleading look.

Jewel is aghast. 'There's more?'

'Serenity was being blackmailed. By Brody Conway,' Harmony states.

It takes me a few more minutes to bring everybody up to speed, all the way up to Dalton Briar accompanying me to Brody's apartment last night. Jewel remains with me and holds my hand as she listens.

'That's how I got Persia's uniform back. He wanted me to wear it, but I took it, put it in my bag and brought it with me to the Danube this morning. It was still there when Kathleen brought it to the office when Ms Conway fired me. So, it now looks like I'm a thief too.'

'But you said Brody didn't know about you and Jake,' Tori says.

'He didn't. But I kissed him in the basement parking lot. The whole thing must have been captured on CCTV. Brody had all the evidence he needed.'

'And you think he's fed the whole thing to his mother *anonymously*?' Shawny comments. 'What a rotten creep.'

Jewel hugs me again.

'Does Jake know you've been fired?' Imara asks.

'Sam Conway ordered me not to contact him. Said she'd already told Coach Holland to take away all the players' phones before the game.'

'The game is tomorrow night!' Angel exclaims. 'What are they, twelve? That's ridiculous.'

'Surely we can get a message to somebody,' Lacey echoes.

The room erupts again. Harmony shushes everyone. 'I'll send a message to Ally Briar. She's gone to Tennessee. But, right now, there is nothing the men can do,' she says. 'This is up to *us*. When Persia got fired, I let it happen. I didn't push back. All she did was go to one party. Her actions didn't warrant her losing her job. The same for Mona. She was going through a rough time, and nobody had her back. I blame myself.'

Almost the entire room objects to her statement.

'Plus, I'm sure that Serenity is not the only one to have harboured a few secrets in this squad,' she says.

A second silence descends.

'I include myself in that group,' Harmony adds quietly.

'Please tell me you finally slept with Hud Briar,' Angel voices out loud.

There is laughter. 'I may have had some very good, very hot sex with Hud Briar, all night on Thursday and most of yesterday afternoon, yes.'

The room erupts once more and this time I giggle, because finally it's not me we're talking about.

'And do you regret not doing so earlier?' Ashlyn says with a salacious grin.

Harmony bites her lip. 'Let's just say it was worth the wait. And then some.'

Everybody squeals. A few of the girls punch the air. A weight lifts from my shoulders.

'Anybody else sleeping with a football player?' Jewel laughs. I give her a look of apology, but she squeezes my shoulders.

'I might have something,' Angel says. 'I mean, if we're sharing.'

The room quietens. All eyes go to Angel, mostly in surprise at where she might go with this, except she's glancing at Shawny. Shawny flushes an uncharacteristic shade of pink, and there's something in their shared look.

'By that I mean, *we*,' Angel adds.

Shawny smiles knowingly at Angel. Angel blows her a kiss and I gasp.

'I mean, the contract says we can't fraternize with the players, right?' Shawny says with a shrug. 'There's nothing about us not fooling around with each other.'

It's the first time I've seen her embarrassed about anything. Once the room has gotten over the latest revelation, Solana shrieks, 'Oh my god, are you guys actually a *couple*?'

Shawny rolls her eyes. 'I mean... we're practically living together.'

'You see, this is exactly what I mean,' Harmony says, before anyone else can ask questions, and she's back on her feet, next to me and Jewel. 'We are a sisterhood. We stand up for one another. We have one another's backs. And hey, some of us more than others. But we didn't stand up for Persia. Or Mona. And I'll be damned if we're gonna sit on our asses this time around and watch Serenity lose her place on this squad. I say we take a stand. We show Samantha Conway and Kathleen we mean business. That we don't get paid so little to get treated like infants or stand accused of things we categorically did not do.' She points to each face in turn, looking hopefully up at her. 'You come after one of us, you come after *all* of us. Now, who is with me?'

Almost every female in the room raises her hand. Everyone except Ashlyn.

Ashlyn says, 'Harm. I love you. You know I do. We joined as rookies together. But... and I know I keep saying this, but you know what we signed up for.'

'What do you stand for Ash?' Harmony fires back. 'Are we not in this together? Are we just window-dressing... here to make everybody else look good, for no money I might add, while our medial hamstrings are slowly shot to hell? What are we, if we're not a team? Are we just gonna stand here and watch our own backs?'

Ashlyn watches Harmony for a moment, as though digesting her words. She swallows. Slowly, she nods her head. 'Alright, I'm in. So... what is the plan exactly?'

'I got an idea,' Jewel says as her hand shoots into the air.

Chapter Thirty-Two

Jake

Samantha Conway is talking about something.

I'm not even listening. Monday afternoon, sitting on the opposite side of a conference table from her and I'm trying to curtail the rage that's swirling deep in my gut. Rage that's been there since Dalton pulled me over, still on the field in the final moments of the fourth quarter, the Titans defense weary from the pounding they just took, and told me that Serenity had been fired.

Brody Conway couldn't resist, and he threw her under a bus.

It had felt good there, for a brief second, still inside the stadium after the win, thinking Serenity and I might just have gotten away with it. But then there I was, on the sideline at forty yards, smashing my helmet to the ground, for which the NFL has slapped me with a violation for unsportsmanlike conduct.

The team flew back from Tennessee this morning. Now I'm in a conference room at the Danube, flanked by Dalton on my left, Harmony Rees to my right, and facing off with Samantha Conway, Kathleen Lafferty and Coach Holland.

'The matter will be handled internally,' Sam Conway is saying. She's trying her darndest to be civil, because she knows I'm the reason we beat the Titans by the margin that we did, and the Mutineers can't afford to have me giving anything less than my best right now if we wanna make the playoffs. 'Since you have not broken any terms of your contract, you will be given a small fine, and we will leave it at that. Miss Harper has resigned her position—'

'You fired her,' I interrupt in a low growl. 'You fired her personally and you had her remove her uniform in your presence. You demeaned her on purpose, and because you knew you could, and she was helpless to do anything about it.'

She levels her eyes on me. 'Mr Walsh. Would you speak to my father in that way?'

'I would if he'd had the balls to show up to this meeting, yes. As I would your son. But he seems to have been conveniently removed from this picture, when you know, whether you're prepared to admit it or not, that he was your so-called anonymous sender, and that he was the one continuously harassing Serenity these past few weeks. How hard did you have to beg the Jaguars to give him a job?'

She might not be squirming on the outside, but I can see it in her face. 'My son is going to Florida to gain valuable experience—'

I open my mouth to make a cutting remark, because I'm through with her grinding my gears, but Dalton interrupts me, loudly clearing his throat, to ensure that I don't. We agreed before this meeting took place that it wasn't a good idea for me personally to burn too many bridges, and not just because I'm signed with the team for the next four years.

'Ms Conway, perhaps we should address the elephant in the room,' Harmony says to my right. 'The matter of clause five in the CMC contract. We're all adults here. It shouldn't matter if a cheerleader and a football player fraternize with one another, or date, so long as both parties are consenting, and they behave in such a way that doesn't bring the Mutineers brand into disrepute. Jake and Serenity have done nothing wrong, surely, it doesn't—'

'She broke the rules, Ms Rees,' Sam Conway snaps. 'There are expectations. On all of the girls. Especially you.'

Harmony doesn't hesitate. 'How about we start by referring to them as *women*?'

Samantha grits out every syllable. 'The *girls* uphold and maintain a certain standard, which is in line with the Mutineers brand. There are expectations about how they carry themselves, and that does not, and will never include, cavorting with football players.' She looks to me and adds, 'No matter their worth.'

'What about your standards?' I query. 'Your chosen theme song for the CMC? The music video takes place in a strip club. And how about calling on the paparazzi when you're trying to force me to date your daughter? How about you try holding yourself to account?'

'Enough!' Samantha Conway hollers, hammering her balled fist down onto the glass surface of the table, in a way that reminds me of Kale McCoy. 'You may date Miss Harper, Mr Walsh, if you so wish, now that she is no longer a cheerleader, though given her history, I'm surprised that you would want to. She will not be getting her job back as a member of the cheerleading squad. There is no appeals process in such circumstances. She knew what she was doing. And you, Mr Walsh, are fined one thousand dollars for misconduct. You were aware of the terms of the CMC contract. You defied them anyway.'

'One thousand?' Dalton says and shakes his head. 'The NFL fined him more than five grand for tossing his helmet. Let's face it. You're afraid of pissing off your MVP. And clearly anyone here who's not a football player is expendable.'

'I agree,' Harmony echoes.

'Rules are rules, Mr Briar,' she says tersely. 'Like it or not.'

My rage hasn't abated. My gaze shifts to Coach Holland. He can't look me in the eye. This guy eats, lives and breathes football. He's coached here for more than ten years. He knows that Samantha Conway could fire him in a hot minute. He has a reputation for never getting involved in players' personal lives. Kathleen Lafferty, too, hasn't said a word, maybe for similar reasons. Fear of the Mutineers' matriarch.

I get to my feet and the chair legs scrape across the floor. Dalton and Harmony follow suit.

'Then we'll consider the matter closed?' Samantha says.

I fix her with my stare. I can't remain in her presence a moment longer, else I'm gonna lose it.

'Guess there's not a lot more I can do,' I say, and head for the door.

—

I head straight from the Danube to The Bounty parking lot. At just after four, I watch as Serenity walks out the door. I get out the pickup and she comes running straight into my arms. I capture her lips in mine, not caring who's watching. Her arms go around my shoulders. I'm starting to think I should have arranged for my own paparazzi, specifically for this moment, just so it's clear to the whole of Canyon who I'm interested in.

We talked last night on the phone, for the first time since she was fired, and again this morning.

'How did it go?' she says, breaking the kiss, glassy eyes searching mine.

My mouth set in a grim line, I shake my head.

Her shoulders slump. 'I appreciate you trying for me.'

'It's alright,' I say. 'I spoke with Cap and Harmony after. We're moving to plan B.'

She raises concerned eyebrows. 'You're sure about that?'

'With what the CMC has planned, it should send a clear message.'

She swallows hard. 'I don't want you to lose your job for me.'

I stroke her hair. 'You lost yours for me.'

'I'm not the one headed for the playoffs.'

'That's not the point.' I kiss her again. 'I do know where you are headed though.'

Her eyes widen again. 'We're going right now?'

I'm taking her to meet my parents and River. Gramps headed home already. Mom's cooking dinner, and I'll be damned if Serenity's not staying over. 'Are you cool with that?'

She smiles and nods her head, holding onto my waist. 'Is your Mom…?'

'She's excited to meet you.'

'Am I gonna pass the Mom test?'

'I told her I'm crazy in love with you, so I think you already did.'

She bites her lip. She's so cute when she's worried. 'Can I pick up some flowers on the way over? Just in case there's a chance she doesn't like what she sees.'

I open up the passenger side door. 'That's impossible. But okay, if you insist.'

—

'You think Serenity's passed the Mom test?'

I watch as River leans her head back, away from the sink, both her arms immersed almost elbow-deep in the suds. I follow her gaze. Dinner over, Serenity is still at the table, talking animatedly to Mom and Dad. Riv and I promised we would share the task of washing the used pans afterward.

River lowers her voice. 'I think she's surpassed any kind of yard stick that might have existed for the Mom test. In fact, I think she just obliterated the Mom test altogether. Look at her. She adores Serenity already.'

I pick up the pan that River just placed in the dish rack and dry it. I can't help but smile. 'You think I'm ever gonna get her back?'

'I hate to say it, but you might have a job on your hands. This might be the first of your girlfriends Mom's actually liked.'

I glance back. My heart swells just watching her, because I knew Mom and Dad would take to her immediately.

'Seriously,' River continues. 'She's really something. You guys make a very cute couple. I'm so happy for you.'

'Thank you.' I wrap my arm around her shoulders and plant a kiss against her hair. 'When you next seeing Wylder?'

'He's video calling me in, like, fifteen minutes.'

'So, you guys are serious now?'

River blushes. 'I like him. I like him a lot.'

I'm happy for her too. And that she's finally settled into school. 'Did I hear Dad say you're bringing him to the game Sunday?'

'Already organized the wheelchair access. Is there gonna be a game to watch?'

I raise my brow. 'I wouldn't wanna speculate.'

'You realize Sunday night your golden boy era comes to an end?'

I laugh. 'Thank god. 'Bout time I embraced my wild side.'

River sobers. 'For the record… I think that what you're doing for her… well, it's special. It takes balls. Standing up for somebody less powerful than you like that. And it's gotta be worth a try.'

'Even if they fire me?'

River punches me in the arm, sending soapy water everywhere. '*Especially* if they fire you.'

—

It's warm in my room. Even with the air con at full blast, Serenity lies naked with me atop the bed clothes, our limbs intwined, breathless post-climax, our bodies radiating heat in the darkness.

The fact that she just fell apart for me twice in quick succession – the first time the result of me just using my tongue – fills me with a deep satisfaction.

We lie there for a few minutes, coming down, cradling one another, our heart rates returning to normal.

'Jake?' Serenity says after a moment as she traces a line down my face with her finger.

'What is it?'

'I'm scared.'

I draw back and search her face in the shadows. 'What are you afraid of?'

'Everybody's sacrificing so much for me. I'm not sure I deserve it.'

I kiss her. 'I want you to know,' I tell her, 'that you come first. Above everything. I see you, and I see the rest of my life stretching out before us. And we're happy. Whether or not I remain in the NFL. I don't see it as a sacrifice; I see it as choosing to live my life the way that I want to. With you by my side. And you deserve *everything*. Your entire life, you've hustled. You've given and given. You don't have to do that anymore. It's just a simple fact that everyone else agrees with me.'

I feel drips of moisture on my fingers, and I realize Serenity is crying. She pulls me to her. 'Thank you,' she whispers against my mouth before she grants me the sweetest kiss. 'I know I said I didn't need a hero, but I'm glad that I have one all the same.'

I rub my thumb across her cheeks to dry her tears. 'I'm here. No matter what happens. I love you. You own my heart.'

'I love *you*,' she says with a gentle sniff, and I feel another surge of tears wet my fingertips. 'My heart belongs to you. I promise that it will, for always.'

That same heart that she's referring to, well it sings. I roll her onto her back, one hand pressing against her inner thigh, coaxing her to open her legs so that I can nestle between them. My dick swells instantly, pressed up against her pussy that's still warm and wet for me from before. I kiss her deeper this time, loving the way she moans and writhes against me, wrapping her legs around my waist. It's so easy to lose myself in her.

'I knew from the moment I saw you at that grocery store that I was never gonna want anybody else,' I whisper.

She strokes my face. 'I knew from the moment you came to my house that night and decided not to judge me. You've never judged me. You always accepted me for me.'

I don't wish to make light of the intense moment, but I can't help it. 'I mean,' I say with a smirk, 'I did think you were a virgin at one point.'

Sweet laughter escapes her lips. 'Other than that little blip. Nobody's perfect.'

I lean down and kiss her, slower this time. There's an electric current between us that has desire shooting up my spine. The little sounds that escape her lips only make me harder.

'Jake,' she murmurs, all needy, and once more I'm reaching for the box of condoms on the nightstand. When I slide inside her welcoming warmth for the second time tonight and our lovemaking begins again, I know that I'm home. Because home is where Serenity is. And I know nothing about that will ever change.

Chapter Thirty-Three

Serenity

Sunday night, I'm home with Dad. I've made us both an early dinner, which we eat in front of the TV. We've agreed that we'll watch the game. Kick-off is eight-twenty. It's the first home game of the season that I won't have been part of the CMC squad.

Just past seven, I hear a car outside. Opening the front door, I watch as an enormous black Escalade pulls up in our driveway. Jewel gets out, slams the door closed and practically swaggers up the steps.

'What are you doing here?' I manage in my surprise. 'Is that a new car?'

She glances over her shoulder, back at the vehicle. 'Belongs to Lemon Conway,' she says with a casual shrug.

I blink. 'Lemon Conway? The hell?'

'You know one thing that I've learned this week, Ren? That every single person who works at the Danube is afraid of Samantha Conway. No surprises there, I guess. They all despise her too. But, all the staffers, the grounds people, the security men and women, the coaches, the guys who make the coffee in the booths and the people who sell beer on game days, they all *love* Lemon. Yes, sir. They love Lemon because she's nothing like her mother. Lemon Conway has more power in her little finger than her mother and brother put together. And she's got business smarts that nobody ever gave her any credit for. Including all of us CMC.'

I stare at her, aghast. Jewel takes both my hands in hers and gives them a squeeze. 'We couldn't *not* have you be there tonight,' she says.

Dad gives me his blessing when I tell him I'm heading to the Danube for Sunday night football.

'How are you getting in if you don't have a ticket?'

'Apparently Lemon Conway's got it all figured out,' I murmur, in disbelief.

'Does that mean I can watch baseball now?'

I kiss his forehead. 'Yes, Daddy, it does.'

'Have fun, sweetheart,' he says.

It takes me a few minutes to change clothes, get organized and put on a little makeup. I grab my leather jacket on the way out. When I climb into the vehicle, there's a branded Mutineers cap on the seat. 'Put it on,' Jewel says as she grins at me. 'All part of Lemon's plan.'

'She can seriously get us in?'

'She came to us. Offered her help. At first, we didn't know what to believe, but Jake's straightened everything out. He came to see us all at practice. She's on our side. Or should I say yours and Jake's side.'

'I don't believe it.'

She reaches out and squeezes my hand. 'Believe it. Tonight, every single squad member has your back.'

I swallow down the lump in my throat. I'm nervous, but excited to see how tonight pans out. Jewel starts the engine and backs out of the driveway.

'And you promise you're cool with me seeing him?' I ask her.

'Honey, the way he talks about you... man, I just hope I get to meet a guy like that one day. And I am cool as a refrigerator about it.'

I grin at her.

'Will you stay with me?' I ask her.

'Don't worry. We called in some recruits. My job is to stay with you.'

I think I can guess what she might be referring to. My heart beats faster at the thought.

—

We cross town quickly, but traffic builds up outside the stadium. When we're close, Jewel makes a phone call, then slides into the VIP lane like it's nothing at all. When she pulls out outside the Danube south VIP entrance, a valet is already waiting to take the car. I get out, pull my cap down further around my ears and glance from left to right.

'Being here feels wrong,' I say under my breath to Jewel. 'Samantha Conway made it very clear I wouldn't be welcomed back here again.'

Jewel flashes me a grin before I hear a woman shriek, 'Well, there she is!'

I raise my eyes to find a bubbly-looking blonde standing in the doorway. She's wearing bright red lipstick that matches her shoes.

'I'm so excited to meet you properly, Serenity. I'm Lemon.'

'Hi, Lemon,' I say, as she gives me a firm handshake.

'We all good?' Jewel asks.

'Hold up just one second,' Lemon says, as a security guard hands her two lanyards with several passes hanging from them. She puts them over each of our heads, like a medal presentation. I glance down at the lettering that reads 'All Access', and I'm astounded.

'Okay, *now* we're good,' Lemon says. 'This here is Bobby. He's gonna take you to the sideline, near the tunnel, which should give you a great view of the field. My momma's upstairs still.'

'Everything still going to plan?' Jewel asks her.

Lemon looks thrilled. 'Carlie's got everything teed up. CMC is all set to shake the Danube to its very foundations.'

Jake told me that Lemon has resumed her relationship with Carlie Kessler, much to her mother's horror. 'Thank you,' I whisper to Lemon, before Jewel ushers me away.

In the next tunnel, following Bobby from security, I can hear the crowd above our heads.

'I need to know...' I say, with Jewel holding my hand. 'Am I gonna get everybody else fired?'

Jewel looks back at me, the same over-confident smile plastered on her lips. 'Safety in numbers, sweetie. Safety in numbers.'

'Are you sure about that?' I ask, the nerves creeping up the inside of my throat.

When we come out, we're pitch side, under the floodlights at the west end, facing the twenty-yard line. To our left is the entrance to the tunnel from which the CMC and all the players emerge. The Danube is packed to the rafters with fans and spectators.

Jewel and I take in the scene. 'Maybe keep the hat on,' she says, the smile on her face evaporating, having witnessed the size of the crowd, the TV cameras, and the fact that people's faces are being displayed on the jumbotrons at each end of the stadium.

I check the time. It's a little before eight. There's a smell of beer and popcorn in the air. It's about now that the CMC gets announced onto the field.

'Are y'alright?' Jewel asks me.

I don't know exactly what my squad mates are about to do. I know the gist, but I'm yet to see the routine that they've been secretly rehearsing all week.

'Is it very different?' I ask Jewel.

'A little different,' she says with a wink. 'I wouldn't call it family friendly either.'

As if right on cue, the announcer comes over the Danube's sound system. My whole body tenses, my hands going to a prayer position against my lips when the CMC are introduced.

The crowd cheers wildly and the lights flash for one of the highlights of the show.

They're wearing their uniform, as anticipated, as Harmony leads the squad onto the field to the sound of *Girls Girls Girls*. I do a quick headcount. In terms of numbers, they're four down. Jewel and I are missing, as are Persia and Mona. Other than that, everything is as it should be.

'How did you get outta performing?' I ask Jewel as we applaud their entry.

Jewel puts two fingers in her mouth and whistles. 'Called Kathleen this morning, told her I was puking my guts up.'

We both duck our heads as Kathleen emerges from the tunnel and stalks in a power walk parallel to the sideline just below us, miked up with her head piece and wearing a powder blue pant suit. It means Samantha Conway won't be far behind.

A few bars into *Girls Girls Girls* and, from the speakers around the stadium, there sounds out a scratch effect. The sound system falls silent. I see Kathleen's head snap up, and she's straight onto her mic with a furrowed brow. A ripple goes through the crowd.

Before I know it, a new tune starts up. And seemingly, the entire squad on the field knows exactly what to do. It's a moment before I recognize which song is playing.

'Jake asked if he could pick out the tune, all personal,' Jewel says to me with a grin. 'You're gonna have to tell us the meaning behind it.'

A smile dances across my lips. He's chosen Bonnie Tyler's *Holding Out for a Hero*, and it makes my heart sing. I hold my breath. On the field, I can see Harmony, Ashlyn, Angel, Shawny, Tori, Leona, Solana, Lacey, Imara… the entire squad. Armed with both their poms their movements are perfectly in sync, nothing less than I would expect. The navy and white 'M' symbols on their shirts pop under the floodlights.

The routine is upbeat and sassy. Jewel wiggles her hips in time with the beat. I glance further down the sideline at

Kathleen. There's a panicked look on her face. It's clear this is not the routine she was expecting.

After less than a minute, on the pitch, something shifts. All in unison, and in time with the chorus and the bang of the drums, each CMC squad member removes her shirt. My mouth falls open. Underneath, they're all in matching bikini tops, emblazoned with the same 'M' from our uniform, one on each breast.

I look at Jewel. 'What the hell?' I shriek.

'Customized bikinis, baby!' she squeals gleefully. 'Just wait,' she then says, raising her voice over the music.

I look back to Kathleen. She's furious, yelling at a security guard something crazy, jabbing her finger toward the field.

When the CMC hot pants come off, to reveal bikini bottoms underneath, I swear she blanches. The arches of the 'M' are literally emblazoned across their pert ass cheeks. In bikinis and boots, each girl is grinding her pussy into the ground. It's a classic Surly's move. And one that I didn't even teach them.

Halfway through the song, at the instrumental, a group of grounds people run onto the field, each of them holding what looks like a rustic, open back chair, which he or she plants directly in front of a CMC squad member. Two large black boxes are wheeled onto the field, which I've seen before when there are performances.

When the boxes are opened, two more women burst out in bikinis and join the routine.

'Oh my god!' I blurt. 'Persia and Mona? But how...?'

'What'd I tell you?' Jewel says. 'Lemon Conway has all the power around here. Just nobody knows it! And she was only too happy to oblige. She got all the grounds people on board too!'

I cradle my face. Each girl is straddling her own chair, just like my routine at Surly's, which, on the field, has turned a little X-rated.

Jewel leans closer to my ear, shouting over the din. 'So, a few of us girls may have visited Surly's Tuesday night. You know...

for inspiration. The ladies there were good enough to show us some of your signature moves. They really miss you there!'

I shake my head and grin, still in disbelief at what I'm seeing and hearing. I look around me. The crowd seems to be enjoying the show, although some of the mothers are covering the younger kids' eyes.

Kathleen is now apoplectic, still hollering at the buff security guard in black, who is doing precisely zip about the scene unfolding in front of the entire Danube crowd, his thick arms crossed over his chest. His colleagues aren't moving.

I'm dumbfounded. I can't believe my eyes. The routine that follows could make even the most skilled stripper blush.

That's when I see her, racing down the field toward the fifty-yard line. Her pink cheeks contrasting with bright red lips, uncharacteristic frown lines deep as a crevasse, and she's running as fast as her three-inch pencil heels will carry her.

Sam Conway.

'Here comes trouble,' Jewel says with a grin. 'You think Hank Conway couldn't be bothered to show tonight?'

'Hank Conway might be having a heart attack right about now,' I murmur, watching Ms Conway's arms flap in the air as she hollers at the top of her voice toward the security personnel, who are still outright refusing to do anything other than stand there.

When the CMC routine ends, there is applause from all sides. The crowd goes wild.

'They don't get that it's a protest,' Jewel raises her voice to me.

I look at Ms Conway. She's so angry she's practically baring her teeth. 'I'm not sure they need to,' I say.

I look at the tunnel to my left. The players should be making an entrance by now, but there's nothing. I know Jake is back there. And I know what he's about to do for me could cost him his entire career.

Chapter Thirty-Four

Jake

'Holy *shiiiit*,' Hud Briar says in a low tone. He's staring at the images from inside the stadium being shown live on a screen, as we all are.

To any onlooker, at the mouth of the tunnel, we look like any other NFL pro-team about to take to the field. Forty-six brawny athletes, eye-blacked up, padding on, the bottoms of our cleats clacking against flat concrete, helmets in our hands.

I smirk. Hud's referring to the sight of Harmony, of course, the woman we already knew he was in love with. Because right now the love of his life is dancing with pom poms in a goddamn barely-there outfit with the 'M' for Mutineers right across her bikini-covered ass, just like all the other members of the CMC. It's not exactly what you'd expect from women who are usually the essence of wholesome. They're bringing it.

I can see the faces of the crowd, the noise whooshing down the tunnel. I can see their shock and curiosity at this non-standard display. But they don't know the half of it.

I feel pride at what the CMC are doing for Serenity. I wonder if she made it into the Danube and if she's witnessing this.

Yet still, my focus is elsewhere.

Coach Holland claps his hands. He's wearing a hat and chewing gum. 'Alright, Mutineers! Let's go, let's go! Kick ass out there!'

A small silence descends. His white gloves on, Hud Briar slaps me hard on the back. It's a move that says *we're with you*.

I fill my lungs. Nobody moves.

'I said let's go!' Coach Holland says again.

And still, nobody moves.

Coach takes a moment to realize that something's up.

I clear my throat, raise my voice. 'Sorry, Coach. We're not going anywhere.'

Dalton Briar takes up position to my left, like we agreed. I'm flanked by forty-three of my teammates, all of them briefed, all of them supportive of the plan.

Coach Holland stops chewing his gum. 'The heck? You're shit-talking me.'

'Sorry, Coach,' I say again.

'Get the fuck out there!'

A ripple goes through the group. I glance back. Some of the guys shake their heads. I know these guys have my back, so it's not aimed at me, but my stomach ties itself in knots. 'Not moving, Coach,' I say.

Coach looks to Dalton, a pleading look on his face.

'Sorry, Coach,' Dalton says. 'He don't move, neither do we.'

Coach throws down his hat in frustration. 'Goddammit, you've all gone crazy!'

'I'll move when I've talked to Hank Conway,' I say.

'Hank Conway ain't even here tonight!' is Coach Holland's retort.

'His daughter, then.'

Somewhere, over a radio, a voice says. 'Coach, we're ready. Don't seem to have a team out here.'

Coach Holland punches the air furiously, then hollers at the top of his voice, 'Somebody git me Samantha Conway!'

Hud Briar nudges me. 'Here comes the cavalry.'

I glance up. Right on cue, Samantha Conway comes marching down the tunnel in her pant suit at triple speed, her face like thunder, the base of her neck bright red.

'What the hell is going on?' she hollers angrily. 'Why the hell aren't y'all on that field?'

She takes in the scene. Despite me wearing a whole lotta padding, I straighten my back and push out my chest.

'They're not moving,' Coach Holland confirms in defeat.

Samantha Conway explodes. 'What do you mean, not moving? The cameras are already rolling! The commentary is already gonna be questioning why there is only one team on the field.' She points a bony finger. 'Dalton Briar, you'd better get your team's asses out there, *right now*!'

Behind her, the CMC cheerleaders come down the tunnel, ushered by Kathleen Lafferty, also mad as hell. Some of them have already gotten dressed again.

I take a step forward toward her. 'I think you know what we want, ma'am.'

Sam Conway looks me over, her brows forming deep frown lines. 'You arrogant son of a bitch. You cannot hold me to ransom. How dare you?'

I push my tongue into my cheek. Every single cheerleader is looking my way, waiting. 'Seems the clock is ticking, ma'am.'

Sam Conway glances back at the group of women waiting on her response. 'No. I will not give Serenity her job back,' she clips.

'Then we're not moving. Until you do.'

I can almost feel the heat of her fury coming off her face. 'You're not thinking straight. You're thinking with what's in your pants. Not with your head.'

'Actually, it's neither of those things. I'm going with my heart.'

'You're insane.'

I glance back at my comrades. 'No ma'am. I'm a Mutineer. And this is a mutiny.'

Noises of approval ripple through my teammates.

'I'll fine you all,' Sam Conway breathes. 'I'll cancel all your contracts.'

'What are you gonna do without a single player on your roster?'

For the first time in her life, I think I might have rendered Samantha Conway speechless.

'Give Serenity her job back,' I continue. 'Give all the CMC a raise. Remove clause five from the CMC contract. Do those things, and we'll move.'

I watch her chest rise and fall. She glares at me, a crazed look in her eye. Like she's being squeezed on the inside. Two suited officials – maybe from the NFL – have come racing down here to find out what's causing the delay.

'Fine,' she finally snaps, through gritted teeth, poking another angry finger in my face. 'Serenity may rejoin the squad. I will give them all a reasonable raise. But, clause five stands. These girls are untouchable for a reason; I won't drop that rule. But if you marry Miss Harper, then I'll let it slide on this occasion.'

I feel my brow creep up my forehead. 'What?'

'You heard me. Marry her.'

'Sh-She's not here, I can't ask her.'

'Then somebody get a phone!' Samatha snaps back.

'She's *herrrrre!*' I hear a voice shriek from the back of the cheerleaders. I look up. Bodies move aside, the ladies all grinning in one direction.

Then I see her. My Serenity, walking through them toward me, ushered by her friend Jewel, the women of the CMC all offering her their support. She's been wearing a Mutineers hat, but she's taking it off.

'How the hell did you get in here?' Samantha Conway roars in her direction.

'I let her in, Mom,' another voice says, and everybody looks to the left, where Lemon steps forward. I smile at her, because none of this could have been done without my fake-date's unwavering support.

Samantha Conway glares at her daughter, incensed. 'You and I are gonna have words.'

Lemon crosses her arms over her chest. I sense that she's never felt more confident than she does today. 'Focus, Mom. Players out on the field, remember?'

'Well go on, then,' Sam Conway blurts at me, hands on her hips. 'Clock's ticking.'

'I haven't asked her father. And I don't have a ring.'

'I got one,' Harmony says to my right, and begins twisting a ring off her finger.

She hands it to me. I glance down at the delicate, slender, silver band in my palm.

I look back at Serenity, then to Samantha Conway.

'No,' I say, and there are horrified gasps among all the cheerleaders. I look at all of them, pleading. 'No, no, I don't mean, *no*,' I stutter, then fix my eyes on Samantha Conway's impatient face. 'What I mean is, I'm not asking Serenity to marry me because *you* want me to. I'm gonna ask her because I *want* to ask her.' Then I look back to Serenity, and there's still a smile dancing across her lips. 'Just so we're clear on that. Because I've never wanted anything more.'

Dalt Briar takes my helmet from me, and I drop to one knee. Behind Serenity, several of the cheerleaders let out a squeal. Even some of my teammates give a cheer.

'Alright, pipe down, all o' yous!' Hud Briar hollers, and other than the crowd in the stadium above our heads chanting for the Mutineers to make an appearance, there's silence. Harmony gives him a nod of approval, and he winks back.

I look up at Serenity. Her emerald eyes are sparkling with the tears I can tell she's holding back. I hold up the ring.

'Serenity Harper,' I address her. 'Light of my life. You've captured me, I'm yours forever, if you'll have me. Will you do me the honor of becoming my wife?'

In the moments after, she bites her lip. The tears spill over, and she gives a small but enthusiastic nod of her head. 'Yes,' she manages. 'It's a definite yes.'

I lose track of what happens next. I slide the ring onto her finger and everyone around us bursts into cheers and applause.

I suspect that for Samantha Conway it's more of a slow clap, but she's not the one I'm paying attention to. I get to my feet and wrap Serenity in my arms, and when my lips meet hers, she kisses me back with an eagerness that makes my heart swell. She's spent her whole young life looking after other people, and now I get to look after her, until the day I draw my last breath.

When we pull back, I rest my forehead against hers. The applause is still going, along with some high fives.

'Thank you,' she whispers. 'Thank you for everything.'

'You're worth it. I would have given all of this up for you.'

The look she gives me is full of love. I want to stay in this moment forever, but it's splintered by Coach Holland's voice, rising above all the others. 'Alright, that's enough romance for one day, now can we please get on the *fucking* field?'

There's laughter. Whooping. The sound of forty-six honed athletes, raring to play.

'Go get 'em,' Serenity says to me, and grants me one more kiss. 'I'll be here when you get back.'

Overtime

Serenity

'You know, one day, you're gonna have to quit looking at it.'

It's a Friday night. Above our heads are pretty fairy lights. I'm dressed in a long, silk slip dress. Jake is looking suave in a tux, his arm wrapped around my waist.

I lean into him. 'I am never gonna stop looking at it,' I sigh over the music, holding up my left hand as it cuts across a shaft of light from the dance floor.

'Purple looks good on you,' he says with a smile, stroking the fabric of my dress.

We're one of several couples chaperoning River's winter formal at her high school gym, and in accordance with River's strict instructions, we're keeping a low profile, tucked into the shadows behind the drinks table.

Jake's right about me being distracted; I keep catching myself getting lost in the ring he gave me, now settled on my finger. A stunning, soft square, double halo-mounted diamond, with larger, graduated stones on the band. Quite literally the most exquisite thing I'll ever own, I'm sure of it. His mother and River helped Jake pick it out, and he went to my father and asked for my hand, retrospectively, before asking me, properly, for a second time. Next to it, on my finger, is Harmony's slender, silver ring, which she let us keep, after Jake proposed at the Danube.

We spent bye week together. The one week in the NFL calendar where the Mutineers team had no game scheduled, allowing players a well-earned rest. Harmony quit the squad, the same day Jake and I got engaged. Everybody thinks she'll be expecting by Christmas, and by her own admission, she and Hudson want to start raising a family soon. Why wait any longer, she said; I know she waited long enough. Ashlyn has been appointed our new captain, and Samantha Conway reluctantly agreed that Persia and Mona could return to the CMC.

I heard Lemon's been given a promotion, and not a single individual got fired for allowing the CMC protest routine to continue on the field that day. Her mother's reportedly taking some time out 'for reflection'. She's given us a grace period, so that we can plan our dream wedding. My daddy wants to walk me down the aisle, and our list of guests includes each member of the Mutineers, the CMC, and some of the girls from Surly's Tavern too.

Both my squads.

'Oh, Jake, look.'

The crowds of high schoolers on the dance floor have parted, momentarily. We get a glimpse of River in her floor-length, silver satin gown. She's dancing up a storm with Wylder in his wheelchair. She's giving him her full attention, and he's performing spins in the chair, clearly trying to impress her.

I feel Jake move and realize that he's laughing.

'What is it?' I ask.

'Nothing. She's gone from thinking nobody liked her to being the center of attention.'

At the house, before we left, I witnessed both Jake and his dad get choked up, watching River walk down the stairs. I helped her with her makeup and her dress. In the few short weeks that we've know one another, we've gotten close. Bridget's helped me secure extra funding for my father, so that he has guaranteed oxygen when he needs it. She couldn't have been more helpful. Jake's talked about moving him out of Temptation Heights, once we're married. It's wonderful, having this whole new family. And I believe it now, when Jake tells me I have absolute power over him. But he doesn't know the power he has over me too. How deeply I've fallen for Jake Walsh. My hero. And how I can't wait to call myself his wife.

The music shifts. It's a slow dance. I turn into Jake, lifting his arms into position.

'I have a secret,' he whispers in my ear when he holds me.

'Oh yeah?' I ask. 'What is it?'

'I can't dance.'

I stifle a giggle. 'Then I'll teach you.'

'You will?'

I pull back. 'Sure,' I tell him, placing both my hands on his chest. 'We'll start with the basics. Then we'll graduate to the next level.'

He frowns, like he's unsure. 'What's the next level?'

I let go of him, wrap my arms around his neck and kiss his mouth. When I break the kiss, he looks at me like he wants nothing more than to get me home. My lips twitch. I emphasize my southern accent when I say, 'Cowboy, I was gonna offer to get you a pair of poms.'

And he's laughing again.

Acknowledgements

Thank you for reading *Off Limits*! I hope you enjoyed Serenity & Jake's love story as much as I enjoyed writing it.

I am about as British as they come (apart from the fact that I don't like drinking tea). When I realised that I would be writing about two quintessentially American roles – a cheerleader and an NFL pro-footballer – I knew I would need an American to look over the manuscript, to help remove any 'Britishness'. I therefore must thank Lila Whatley, for pointing out all my Britishisms and converting all the British spellings to American. I hope, as a result, the story has a distinctly American feel to it.

I must also send special thanks to Ed Parr for his knowledge of all things NFL, and his help in making it sound like I fully understand the rules of the game (I'm still learning). Writing the novel, I knew I didn't want Jake to be a quarterback, until Ed pointed out that running backs are not *that* tall...

Grateful thanks to my editor, Dan O'Brien. Working with you on our third book together has been an absolute joy. Your suggestions and insights always mean we end up with a better story (and soundtrack?) by the end of the process. I'm so grateful to Keshini Nadoo, Jennie Ayres and the teams at Hera and Canelo for working with me again on this sports romance, which I have so enjoyed writing.

A big thank you to Lindsey Harrad for her copyedit, to Vicki Vrint for proofreading the final copy and to Emily Courdelle for another incredible, eye-catching cover, which I absolutely love.

To my friends and family, both the writers, and the non-writers, you keep me motivated and you keep me sane. Everybody needs their own squad, and I am very lucky to have mine around me.

And finally, to the readers, reviewers and book bloggers. Thank you to those of you who have contacted me personally to say how much you have enjoyed my romance novels. It really means so much to authors to hear positive reviews, and it makes the hard work all worthwhile.

Follow me on Instagram @emmarae.author
emmarae.co.uk